NEW MOON
ON THE WATER

A Collection of Horror Tales

MORT CASTLE

DRP

Dark Regions Press
૭૭ 2012 ૭૭

FIRST TRADE PAPERBACK EDITION

TEXT © 2012 BY MORT CASTLE

INTRODUCTION © 2012 BY JAY BONANSINGA

COVER ART © 2012 BY VINCENT CHONG

EDITOR, JEFFREY THOMAS

PUBLISHER, JOE MOREY

ISBN: 978-1-937128-39-5

FRONT COVER DESIGN BY ANDREW SMITH

BACK COVER AND INTERIOR DESIGN BY
FIBITZ REALITY ADJUSTMENT
WWW.FIBITZ.COM

DARK REGIONS PRESS
300 E. HERSEY STREET, 10A
ASHLAND, OR 97520
WWW.DARKREGIONS.COM

ACKNOWLEDGMENTS

"Defining Horror: Nine Musings on The Nature of Horror" first appeared in somewhat different form in **THE BLACK SPIRAL: TWISTED TALES OF TERROR**, edited by Richard D. Weber, published by CyberPulp eBook Publishing, 2003

"If You Take My Hand, My Son," **MASQUES II**, edited by J.N. Williamson, Maclay and Associates, 1987

"Henderson's Place / The Girl with the Summer Eyes" first appeared as "Henderson's Place," in *New Infinity Review*, Vol. 4 No. 2, 1977

"A Circle of Magic" first appeared in the online publication *Storytellers Unplugged*, 2006

"The W.W. II Pistol," *One, the Writer's Magazine*, Vol. 1 No. 5, 1974

"Pop Is Real Smart," **MASQUES III**, edited by J.N. Williamson, St. Martin's Press, 1989

"Healers" first appeared as "Healers Trio," *2 AM*, Fall, 1988

"Buckeye Jim in Egypt" in slightly different form first appeared in **THE SECRET PROPHECIES OF NOSTRADAMUS**, edited by Cynthia Sternau and Martin H. Greenberg, Daw Books, 1995

"As Others See Us," *Blood Rose* (online), September 2005

"Father and Son," *Grue Magazine*, No. 7, 1988

"Bird's Dead," **MOON ON THE WATER**, A Collection by Mort Castle, Darktales Publications, 2000

"The Running Horse, The High, White Sound," *Dark Regions* #3, 1989

"Upstairs, Downstairs, And All About Vampires," **100 VICIOUS LITTLE VAMPIRE STORIES**, edited by Stefan Dziemianowicz, Robert Weinberg, and Martin H. Greenberg, Barnes & Noble Books, 1995

"A Someday Movie," *Cavalier,* 1974

"14 Short Horror Stories" in slightly different form first appeared in the Program Book of the 14th Annual World Horror Convention, 2004

"Party Time," **MASQUES I**, edited by J. N. Williamson, Maclay and Associates, 1984

"Love, Hate, and the Beautiful Junkyard Sea," **MASQUES IV**, edited by J. N. Williamson, Maclay and Associates, 1991

"I Am Your Need," **BRAINBOX II: SON OF BRAINBOX**, edited by Steve Eller, Irrational Press, 2001

"Moon on the Water," a considerably different version, under the title "Lady in the Lake," *Cavalier,* 1978

"Dreaming Robot Monster," **MIGHTY UNCLEAN**, edited by Bill Breedlove, Dark Arts Publications, 2009

"The Call," **VOICES FROM THE NIGHT: 27 STORIES OF HORROR AND SUSPENSE**, edited by John Maclay, Maclay and Associates, 1994

"Hansel, Gretel, the Witch: Notes to the Artist," *Dead of Night* #7, Spring/Summer 1993

"Bonds" first appeared in English in the online publication *Storytellers Unplugged,* 2008

"Other Advantages," *Cavalier,* 1975

"FYI," **MASQUES V**, edited by J.N. Williamson and Gary Braunbeck, Gauntlet Press, 2006

"In the Gypsy Camp," **A DARK AND DEADLY VALLEY**, edited by Mike Heffernan, Silverthought Press, 2007

"I'll Call You," **MASQUES V: FURTHER STORIES**, edited by J.N. Williamson, Gary Braunbeck, and Barry Hoffman, Gauntlet Press, 2006

"The Doctor, The Kid, and the Ghosts in the Lake" first appeared in slightly different form in *F Magazine* No. 9, 2010

"Dani's Story," *After Hours* No. 25, 1995

"Altenmoor, Where the Dogs Dance," *Twilight Zone*, 1982

"'I Don't Know,' Is What I Say" in somewhat different form first appeared in the online publication *Storytellers Unplugged*, 2008

Dedication

Jane, that says it all.

The Horror Tales

WHAT WE TALK ABOUT WHEN WE TALK ABOUT MORT: AN UTTERLY BIASED YET WELL-EARNED INTRODUCTION

by
Jay Bonansinga

Mort Castle commands a room like nobody I have ever known. Stocky, ruddy-complexioned, with a spume of sienna hair and whisk-broom mustache, he ambles into a college classroom or writer's workshop with the weary authority of One Who Has Been In Country ... One Who Has Fought the Good Fight. He is the perennial professor–tweedy, chalk-dusted, the wry observer–but the outer shell is deceptive. Mort Castle is also a rascal, an agent provocateur of the highest order, an innovator with a literary voice unlike any other writer in contemporary fiction—genre or otherwise. A former folkie musician, a lifelong busker with miles of banjo- and guitar-picking under his belt, he knows how to hold a reader like he knows how to hold a chord, letting the simplest riff ring and resonate long after the music fades.

I have had the pleasure of being an F-O-M (Friend-of-Mort) for more years than I would care to admit. I don't think I would be half the writer I am without Mort's influence and constant needling wit. But before I was the aforementioned F-O-M, I was an F-O-M of a different sort: I was a Fan-Of-Mort. I remember reading the kickoff story to Skipp and Specter's *Still Dead*, "The Old Man and the Dead," in the early 1990s. I marveled at the technique and power of this Hemingway tribute and I remember thinking, "This son-of-a-bitch who wrote this is as good as the guy to whom he's paying homage." That's right. I'll say it again. Mort's as good as Hemingway. Or take the novella—included here—"Buckeye Jim in Egypt." Everything you need to know about Mort Castle—as an artist, as a human being, as a banjo picker—is in there: the humanity, the sense of place, the magic, the history, the cosmic irony, the sorrow, the horror, and the humor.

I can hear the music of Bradbury in Mort's work. I can see traces of Robert Bloch. I can feel the crestfallen craftsmanship of Raymond Carver ... the stubborn brilliance of Harlan Ellison ... the surgical precision of James Ellroy ... and maybe, just maybe, echoes of Mark Twain ... like the faint call of a loon over the weeds along the Mississippi. That's the genius of Mort Castle. He's a miniaturist, conjuring dark wonders the same way Dorothea Lange, the great photographer of the Depression, captured an entire human era with the simple curve of an Okie mother's dishwater-scarred hand. A burnished acorn ... a gardenia in a woman's hair ... a beat-up Victrola ... a forgotten violin canted against the oven door of a Nazi death camp. These are the indelible souvenirs of Mort Castle's ever-widening story cycle. In these minimalist artifacts we walk away with something universal and timeless ... and also terrifying. Did I mention that Mort's stories are often as gut-wrenching as they are human and poignant? I would not call them horror. I would call them, if you'll pardon the impertinence, Mort-ifying.

There's an old *Saturday Night Live* sketch in which an orthodox Jewish *mohel* successfully performs a circumcision in a speeding luxury car, in order to prove the smoothness of the vehicle's state-of-the-art suspension. This is what Mort Castle does with story, with words, with images. While the trends and marketplace shift and bump and wax and wane around him, he ignores the noise and quietly goes about the business of cutting the finest diamonds. He crafts perfect little gems. But for me, friend and colleague and fan and adopted nephew of Mort, the most amazing phenomena at work here—as you, lucky reader, are about discover in these pages—bring us full circle.

This unassuming gentleman who holds creative writing classes and reading audiences and fan gatherings rapt is made of the same stuff as are his stories. He lives the same gestalt as that of his work. The warmth, the mordant humor, the surgeon's eye, the generous, open way about Mort is woven through every word of his prose. I will always think of Mort sitting across the booth from me at the 11 City Diner and Delicatessen in Chicago. "You need to eat more, *Bubie*," he says, noticing my sunken ribs. "Have another *latke* or I'm calling your mother." You see, Mort is the definition of *mensch*.

Just like his stories, he is wise, wonderful, and whimsical—and he packs a wallop.

Incidentally, I had the *latkes*.

You should, too.

—Jay Bonansinga
Evanston, Illinois

DEFINING HORROR:
Nine Musings on The Nature of Horror

1. You write horror? they (readers, students, writing colleagues, telephone solicitors, the FBI, etc.) ask me.

Do you buy horror? I ask them.

If they say "yes," I say, I write horror.

Stands to reason, then, that I'd have a handy-dandy, even a facile definition of horror.

I don't.

But I know it when I see it.

Just like Nixon's Supreme Court knew pornography.

2. Author, editor, attorney Doug Winter wrote in his 1982 anthology *Prime Evil,* a) "Horror is not a genre. It is not a kind of fiction, meant (for) a special shelf in libraries or bookstores." b) "Horror is an emotion."

This quotation is widely bandied about in horror circles.

To begin with b) why, yes, horror is an emotion. Got it. Had not thought it was one of the prime food groups or a means of vulcanizing rubber.

Joy, anger, melancholia, disgust, ennui are likewise emotions. Maybe even rapture, if we exclude pseudo-Christian overtones, and nausea, if we include Existentialists and French Symbolists.

But step into Barnes and Noble or Borders, visit the Info Desk and ask to be directed to the Disgusting Books section, uh-uh. Does not exist. *Nein.* No matter how detestable, with its bumper-sticker religion and 17th-century medical knowledge, Dr. Sagi Cobra's latest Oprah-endorsed tome, *Starvation for Spiritual Salvation,* is on the Self-Help shelf, not with other no-less-gaggifying books in the Disgusting Books section.

Ditto the other emotions.

But hot damn, a) horror is *too* a genre.

I can prove it.

Because it says so right on the spines of the books you'll find on the shelves underneath the *Horror* sign!

It was horror when for a dozen or so years it was disguised as Dark Fantasy or Supernatural Thriller or Crypto-Modern Gothic or Bleak and Baleful Suspense or what the hell.

But it's horror.

So there.

'cause Mort and Stone Cold say so.

3. So here comes Kurtz after peering right at/into the Heart of Darkness: "The horror. The horror." That's what he says.

Nobody thought to ask him what the hell he was talking about.

Someone did ask Joseph Conrad.

He answered in Polish.

4. "But I guess people read horror to release their deep-seated fear of death, provide a cathartic purging." That's a line from a note recently sent me by a young editor of a small-press anthology.

Logic would say that—facile logic: Freshman Psych class at a none-too-good community college

Maybe Logic would, and maybe an overpriced 13th-grade Psych text, but not this guy.

The stuff that haunts you, you never get rid of it.

Or ask any AA member when it is that the organization recommends you drop out. "You've got the alcohol thing taken care of. Good luck to you and so long!"

Just as there can be no purpose to the horror that bursts into your life, neither is there the possibility of ridding yourself of it.

Yeah, you can learn to deal with it.

The theatrical entertainer Prince Randian learned to deal with his horror. See, he was born without arms or legs, and so he became The Human Torso, and you can see him dealing in Tod Browning's legendary film *Freaks*.

5. Uh, are you thinking there's depth to this horror thing, not just reading for escape? That what you're thinking?

Pshaw, wouldn't want you to think that.

After all, this is *genre* fiction.

Pulp Pap for the Populist Populace.

Uh-huh.

P-tooey.

6. Horror is when I fall on the icy sidewalk and chip a bone in my ankle and the ankle will always hurt when it gets cold and I will always remember that there are icy sidewalks waiting, icy sidewalks and worse.

Of course, comedy is when *you* fall on the icy sidewalk.

Except when I am chock-full of Buddha compassion.

7. Alice Sebold's *The Lovely Bones* is masterfully written horror.

Joe Schlepper's *Humongous Groto-Ugly Face Eating, Snot Sucking Lumpy Puke Pus Monster* is also horror and it's every bit as well written as you might imagine.

To some readers, it might not matter.

(Now, is that horror, huh, huh, huh?!?)

8. Paul Bowles said, "The sky hides the night behind it, and shelters the people beneath from the horror that lies above."

Joseph Conrad said (this time in English), "My task which I am trying to achieve is, by the power of the written word, to make you hear, to make you feel—it is, above all, to make you see. That—and no more, and it is everything."

Mort Castle said, "Too damned many alleged horror writers can't see and they invite you to share their vision."

A true gentleman and a superb horror writer named Gary Braunbeck said, "Before there can be fear, before there can be terror there first must be a held breath of sadness and longing."

Sadness and longing.

Sadness and longing.

9. Here is the start of a story:

A five-year-old girl was abducted from outside her apartment house in California. She was molested and murdered.

That really happened. That really happens. It's terrible, and if you are one of the rare people who actually do cluck their tongues, then you might register this as a three-clucker. What a world!

But that is not horror. We did not get horrified at each new face on a milk carton. *The milk carton kids! Collect them all!*

Now, here's something else you need to know. And this, too, is true.

The little girl was carried off by a man who lured her with a request for help in finding his puppy dog.

That sort of cruelty, that calculated wickedness that understands childhood so well: A puppy is soft and funny and nice and kids love puppies.

And now we start to see it. He needed her assistance because he was kind of a heavy guy, couldn't bend down to look in all the places a puppy might hide. He told her, though she knew on her own, that the puppy would be lonely. The puppy wouldn't know where it was. The puppy would be frightened. The puppy would get hungry. The puppy would starve or eat something bad and maybe it would die and that was why she had to help him and when they found the puppy, he would give her a reward: five dollars.

Now, look at her face as she gets in the man's car.

You're starting to feel it, aren't you: This is the horror part, *amigo*.

It gets worse. I'm talking horror here. Look at his face. Look at his face. Look at his face.

Here is the horror.

Later, after he did what he did, after the child was dead, he had some good luck.

His missing puppy had found its way back home.

The dog, a terrier mix, one black ear and a droopy white ear, was waiting for him at the back door.

And the man was very glad that his puppy was home and safe.

Now, for me, that's horror.

And you?

IF YOU TAKE MY HAND, MY SON

—Johnny

He heard (thought he heard?) the voice, thought he knew it (The Old Man ... No, no way ...) and he slipped away once more and he was floating (though he lay in a bed in intensive care). He could see (though his eyes were shut, though he had slipped beneath the level of consciousness) a serene circle of colorless light beckoning him.

He knew it was Death.

And he was afraid.

Even if you don't believe or don't know if you believe, you grow up, you hear all kinds of things, heaven with the benevolent Boss Man always smiling at you while you're on eternal coffee break and hell with the Devil shish-kabobbing your soul at a constant one million degrees.... Or maybe nothing, just nothing at all, not even blackness, dust to dust ...

He feared death.

So his (silent) declaration was, *I am alive!* The spiking green EKG line proved he lived. He could watch it (see it in a way that was not exactly seeing but that was no less true than sight). The doctors (he'd heard them) said he had a chance, condition critical—but stable.

He drifted back toward life. Into the pain, the pain that was a ruined body with plastic tubes dripping fluids into him, sucking fluids from him, the (oh christ am I still screaming?) pain that told him straight flat-out for sure and for certain he was alive, pain that bloated him with a heavy hurting ballast.

The pain was an anchor to life.

But shit, not that much of a life, you stopped to think about it.

One fuck-up after another.

Guess you'd have to call this the Big One. The Ultimate Fuck-Up, rank it right alongside being born. A little self-pity there, Johnny? Sure. But if we can't feel sorry for ourselves, then ...

Well, let's not forget it was funny. Three Stooges. (*Nyuck-nyuck-nyuck.*)

1

Jerry Lewis. Pee-wee Herman. (Say, what are you trying to pull?!? Get it? Trying to ...) Must have looked like two different kinds of asshole. There I am ...

... telling the guy behind the counter at the 7-11, looked like a Pakistani, there's a gun in my pocket ...

... all I got is my finger for Chrissake. Who's got money for a gun?

... and he'd better come up with everything, every goddamn dime in the register there ... and Mr. Pissed-off Paki starts hollering, "I am a citizen! You are not stealing from the citizen. You get job, good-for-nothing shitheel!"

... Enter two cops, just going off-duty, and try this, one looks like Andy Griffith and the other like Don Knotts.... Maybe they want a cup of coffee, maybe donuts, maybe a pack of cigarettes ...

... so the Paki is hollering, "Here is now police protecting good honest citizen!"

... maybe Don Knotts's wife asked him to pick up a copy of the *National Enquirer* ...

... with the Paki hollering, "He is making here the robbery!"

... but whatever the cops come in for ...

... what they get is me, Johnny Forrester, Mr. Fuck-It-UP ...

And they're telling me, just like on TV, "Freeze!" and what happens is my hand freezes in my pocket, I mean, I cannot get my hand out of my pocket because my finger is stuck in the jacket lining, and they both have guns and they're shooting ...

... and what he keeps yelling is "Ow!"—when a bullet punched into his thigh—"Ow!"—one in the gut, in the old labonza there—"Ow!"

They shot him four times.

And he actually said, at least he thought he did (remembered trying to say), "Now will you just cut it out?"

Hey, that's memory, something that happened how long ago was it and I must have slipped back to it. Can't. Have to stay right here, right now, where I know I'm alive.

Alive. Not more dead than alive but (a balance) just as much alive as dead.

He moaned.

"Johnny..."

Knew this time there was a voice, not what (who!) he'd heard before, different ...

Her voice ...

"Johnny ... Don't you die." A whisper. "Oh, no Johnny, you die and it's over, there won't be any more us." A whisper. "I need you."

He opened his eyes.

Nancy, dark hair parted down the middle showing clean pink of scalp, eyes green and big (big like those pictures of kids you see in K-Mart) and her mouth all soft (little girl's mouth), face tear-washed, Nancy, looking so young (they went into a tavern for a few beers, and sure enough, they always carded her, really studying the driver's license that said she was 23), Nancy, maybe not all that pretty, not to most, I guess, but they didn't know how to look at her in the right way, and she loved hearing him tell her she was pretty and he loved telling her that because when he said it, she smiled in a way that made her just so goddamn pretty and she would be prettier still, you know, when they got the bucks together to have that one tooth of hers capped. Nancy (he'd drawn pictures of her in pencil, gave her one on Valentine's Day, that was a real nice day with Nancy), Nancy, standing at the side of the bed wearing a Disney World T-shirt (one of their dreams, a trip to Disney World) and those old blue jeans.

"Johnny ... Be all right. You'll see ..."

He wanted to tell her he loved her (only thing good and gentle and right in a fucked-up life) and his lips tried to say it, but what came out was a groan. "I hurt ..."

"I know, baby, I know. Johnny ..." She held a hand over him, as though afraid to touch him. "Johnny, I don't know what to do. I can't do anything ..."

The light. Brighter now. Making him squint.

There, in the comer of the room, where the wall met the ceiling

Shimmering glow

The light was Death

And there in the center

eyes

couldn't be The Old Man's eyes because The Old Man's eyes were as hard and bright as beer bottle glass

he saw The Old Man's eyes, so gentle

he saw The Old Man's face long and horsey and good-looking in a drawn Hank Williams country-boy kind of way

He saw his father

Who was dead

in the light

And his father said,

—*It will be*

all right, Johnny.

3

NEW MOON ON THE WATER

I'm with you now.

Johnny said, "You rotten old sonofabitch, when were you ever there for me!"

ℛ • ℛ

He eased away from pain and his father and dropped into remembering.

ℛ • ℛ

A Memory:

>His mother sat crying, night after night, and his father wasn't home, night after night, and now, his mother was drinking whiskey like his father drank whiskey. He kept asking (Yeah, even when we're little kids, we ask the questions we already know the answers to, there's something twisted in us that makes us grab onto the pain, like the way you keep poking your tongue at a bad tooth to get the hurt kicking up), "Where's Dad? When's he going to come home?" and after the answers his mother felt she had to give him, "He's got to be away for awhile, he's taking care of things, he's doing what he has to do," after all those sad lies, came the real answer:

>"He's out drinking in every gin mill and tavern and low-life roadhouse in Southern Illinois.... He is gone whoring with every low-life tramp who'll spread her legs and give him diseases."

>His father did come home. He was white-faced, shaky and sorrowful. "I'm sorry. I don't know what happens, like there's a nastiness in me, like there's a demon, just got to get out and do what it's got to do. But this time is the last time. You'll see. I'm going to change. Got it all out of me this time...."

>They believed him. This time. And for many years, damned near all the other times.

A Memory:

>It was one of his father's good spells. The Old Man was working regularly (heavy equipment operator, made damned good money when he worked, but you've got to be sober to work, always wanted The Old Man to put me up there alongside him on that big yellow Caterpillar), and in the evenings, nothing much, but they'd sit around and watch television, maybe some popcorn and cokes, and there was a feeling that they had a chance to ease into the familiar patterns of living that make everything all right.

4

So when The Old Man said, "Sure, I'll be there," for the Webelos ceremony, very big deal, advancing from Cub Scouts (just little kids) to that significant stage just beneath Boy Scouts, that time in your life when you thought you had a real chance to be something, well, he thought sure (this time) he could count on The Old Man.

But surprise, surprise! (Everything that happens is a surprise if you're a damned fool.) Was the Old Man there at the Webelos ceremony? Oh, Charley Hawser's father was there, and Mike Pettyfield's father, and Clint Hayworth's father, Clint Hayworth's father who was in a goddamned wheelchair, for chrissake, paralyzed from the goddamned neck down!

And Johnny Forrester's father? Forrester? That was him up to the Double Eagle Lounge, watching the Budweiser clock, listening to Patsy Cline on the jukebox, getting royally shit-faced.

So the new Webelos went home and cried and stayed up waiting and waiting and waiting. The Old Man came in, all loose smiles and Camel cigarettes and booze stinking.

"You lied to me! You told me you would be there. You lied."

The Old Man laughed, phlegm bubbling and cracking. "Guess I'm just a goddamn liar is what it is." Then he mussed up my hair. That's what he did, mussed my hair.

How could I ever forgive him for that?

"Good night, son," The Old Man said, and wobbled off to bed.

A Memory:

Maybe it really was a demon in The Old Man, one that grew bigger and stronger on liquor, because as the years went on, something turned The Old Man from a drunk to a mean drunk.

The Old Man started hitting. (—*Huh, you like that? That's what you're looking for? I got plenty of it and I'll give you all you need.*)

Like that call (I was nine, maybe ten) from the dime store (I got caught stealing). Here's The Old Man (—*A thief? I'll give it to you, give it to you so you remember!*) pounding away, and Mother has her hands over her face (*Stop it, you'll kill him, stop it!*), can't do a thing, and The Old Man's got a rhythm going, a whack, and a gulp of air, and a whack.

"Come on, you old bastard, hit me again! Come on!"

NEW MOON ON THE WATER

—Want more? Here's more for you, you little shit! I got plenty!
"Come on! You like it, don't you? It makes you feel good!"
—I like it fine, Johnny boy. See how you like it!

Memories:

(My) failures and fuck-ups. Kept back in seventh grade. "It was Johnny Forrester took my lunch money." Asked Darlene Woodman if she'd go to the eighth-grade graduation dance with me. Said she couldn't. Went over to her house and threw eggs and Mike and Dallas, her two older brothers, grab me and pound the living shit out of me. Next week I slashed the tires on Dallas's Ford.

Get to high school and right off I'm flunking classes. Like biology. Cut up a frog so you can see its guts. Me, I cut it up so all you get is this mushy mess. Like English, half the words in the things we're supposed to read, I have no idea what they mean. Like auto shop, and I mean even the shit-for-brains kids do all right in auto shop, but me, only reason I can tell an air-filter from my ass is my ass has two parts. Maybe it's because there's nobody to be proud of me if I ever manage to do something right or maybe it's because I was born to fuck up and that's it.

Except once I thought maybe, just maybe …

I was 16 and I sent off for this learn-art-by-mail course (working as a bag boy at the Certified so I would have had the money to pay for it). Always did like to draw, couldn't take art class in high school, not for "lower-track vocational ed students." But there I am at the kitchen table, working on lesson one, horizon lines and perspective, and then The Old Man comes up behind me.

—What is that shit?

So you ignore The Old Man

—I said what is that shit?

And then you can't ignore The Old Man anymore, so you tell him.

And he's laughing his ass off.

—You're going to be an artist like I'm going to be Emperor of fucking Ethiopia.

And that's when you tell him you hate him, you hate his fucking guts, and he's smiling, fists ready.

—Not any more than I hate you

so you slug him

6

but The Old Man is still tough, or maybe the booze has fixed him so he doesn't feel a thing, but he's got you by the throat, pressing you back onto the table, and filling up your face with his fist again and again and then you're on the floor on your knees and The Old Man is ripping up your drawing and your learn-art-at-home lesson book and laughing like crazy

—*Emperor of Ethiopia* ...

A Memory:

His mother died. Something went blooey in her brain and that was it. That left him and The Old Man.

A Memory:

... until he was seventeen, old enough to join the Army. The Old Man told him

—*Yeah, the soldier boy who'll keep the country safe* ...

He fucked up again, smoking dope one night and a fight with a black guy who said he talked like a goddamned redneck country-ass cracker. He punched the black guy in the mouth and the black guy broke his jaw so it had to be wired shut for ten weeks.

He got a general discharge, which meant the army didn't have to give him any benefits and proclaimed to the world, "Here is one certified asshole to be hired for any position in which fucking up is required." He moved to Chicago. He worked shit jobs when he could find shit jobs, got welfare and food stamps sometimes, and he was always close to broke or broke.

A Memory:

The Old Man died. Myocardial infarction. His heart shut down.

And of course the questions came, the "if only" and "I wish" and "what made" and "how did it happen" questions—which were all one question: Why?

A Memory:

He met Nancy. She worked in a storm-door factory. He had no job at the time. He liked to go to the Art Institute on Thursdays, when there was no admission cost, and, Nancy, once a week, on her lunch hour, went to the Art Institute, because, as she explained later (when she knew he would not laugh), she wanted to be in a building that held all those pretty things.

7

NEW MOON ON THE WATER

A *Good* Memory:
A Realization:
The Truth:
I love Nancy.

℘ • ℘

"Johnny, you can't die.... Oh, please, baby, oh baby ..."

He thought if she knew just how terrible the pain was, she wouldn't ask him to go on living. It would be so easy, an end to pain, to die, to die now but he was afraid

—*No, son*

The Old Man's voice came to him from the light

—*Do not be afraid*

℘ • ℘

Old bastard, old sonofabitch, you're dead

—*Yes*

dead and in hell, right where you belong

—*No*

in hell

—*Son, it's not hell, not*
heaven. I don't know
what you'd call it,
Beyond
or Eternity
or maybe just someplace else.
It's a better place, Johnny.
There's no time here
so there's all the time
in the world. That's how
it is.
There's time to think about things,
to realize all you did wrong
and how to set
things right.
Listen to me, Johnny.
I want to help you.

Help? Your idea of help was always to give me shit and shove me in it.

—*I said I did a*
lot of

8

things wrong. I know that now.
I wasn't a good father....
You weren't a good father? Christ! You were a drunken, rotten, rat-fucking sonofabitch
—Johnny, get it all out
of you now, all the
poison so you can
leave it behind
forever.
I hated you.
I hate you.
—I know, Johnny, I know. But that isn't what you wanted, is it,
Johnny ...

ᘓ • ᘓ

—Johnny?
No
—Say it, Johnny
I wanted to love you
—I know
I wanted your love
—There's something I want
to tell you, Johnny, something
I can say and mean—now
—Johnny, I'm sorry,
I am sorry

ᘓ • ᘓ

He floated up and away from the pain, from his body, nearing the light and the promise of a timeless time and peace and reconciliation

ᘓ • ᘓ

"Johnny!" Nancy cried

ᘓ • ᘓ

—I love you, Johnny
The Old Man stretched out his arm.
—Take my hand,
Son.

NEW MOON ON THE WATER

He wasn't afraid
   Not anymore
   He took The Old Man's hand

He died

and he was screaming in agony as the marrow of his bones (though he had
no bones, though he had no body) boiled and a thousand whips lashed his
back and razors slit his eyeballs (though he had no eyes, though he had no
body) and corkscrews twisted into his skull into his brain
   and all about was the cacophonous shrieking chorus
souls in hell
   and flames, tinged with black
we are souls in hell
   and the stink of suppurating
wounds and shit
   And The Old Man laughing like crazy
—It's a pisser, huh, Johnny?
laughing his ass off
"You lied to me!"
laughing
YOU LIED!
—Guess I'm just a
goddamn liar
is
what it is.

HENDERSON'S PLACE /
THE GIRL WITH THE SUMMER EYES

He carries The Place with him always, but it is at night, in dreams, that Henderson sees it most vividly:

A secret place, a hidden-away place, a place far from this universe that has gone to concrete and neon and plastic.

A time-out place, a time-slowed and time-melted place.

Dew-gleaming grass. Sky a layered blue. Tall trees. The easy slope to the brook where water flows snake-softly over flat stones.

This is Henderson's Place.

It is his, his alone.

Except for the one with whom he is meant to share it. Who is:

The Girl with the Summer Eyes

Who is—

—in dreams—(And Henderson knows that dreams are dreams and

that dreams can tell you so much if you know how to be in the dream in just the right way)—

With Henderson, in Henderson's Place

Who is:

of The Place ...

So Henderson sees The Place in his dreams.

But dreams end with, "For Chrissake, I've called you three times. Will you puh-leeze get up?"

Will he get up? He asks himself that question as he opens his eyes. Another beckoning from down the hall, the kitchen: "Come on!"

Henderson rises. In his pajamas, he goes to the window, raises the shade, almost expecting to see summer, but though the sun shines, there is a flatness to the day that tells him this is autumn.

In the bathroom, he lets the shower run, very hot, while he stands naked at the vanity, razor in hand, face lathered with aerosol-propelled cream that smells like burnt plastic. The mirror fogs. He erases an oval

11

of mist, erases another patch, sees stubbly cheek, shaves it. Another clear spot, the razor again, and so until his face is smooth. He sees a cut on his chin, a line of blood. It does not hurt at all.

A few minutes later, he is dressed and in the kitchen. His wife, in housecoat and slippers that snap against her heels when she walks, gives him a paper plate with two breakfast tarts on it and places a cup of coffee on the table. She says it is harder to wake him than it is to raise the dead.

Henderson's teeth crack the tasteless toaster-tart. He looks at his wife's eyes. They are hard and lifeless.

"Going to the office, or do you have calls to make?"

A salesman for Educational Enterprises, Incorporated, Henderson goes to the office on some days. On other days he visits schools. He doesn't recall where he is to go today.

"Well?" At the counter, his wife pours herself coffee. She yawns. "I swear, I don't know what's gotten into you. You act like you're missing half of what's going on."

Henderson smiles, enjoys his so secret, so-special knowledge of The Place.

Soon he is on the tollway, going to, going to … *The office.*

That's right.

In the rush hour traffic, he pulls into line at a toll booth behind a new blue Chevrolet. The sun's reflection on the Chevrolet's bumper is a blazing fireball that pulses in a steady, insistent rhythm.

Suddenly a horn blares. Now there are three lengths between him and the Chevrolet. Henderson pulls up. The Chevy is under the toll booth's concrete column supported roof—in the shade.

The flashing, compelling fire-eye is gone.

ↄ • ↄ

When third period ends, Linda and Karen, her best friend, go to the "safe" restroom where teachers seldom bother to check for smokers. "God!" Linda says, "Wagner's class is a total bore!"

She stands at the mirror combing her long blonde hair.

"For sure," Karen agrees. She lights a Kool, rests her blue-jeaned backside on the edge of a sink. "School is one big bummer. Totally."

"Yeah," Linda says. "How come if school's supposed to be for kids, we all hate it?"

"'Cause it sucks. That's the American way," Karen says. "If it's big-time dumbass and boring and all, it's supposed to be good for you." She waves her hand. Her cigarette is a baton and she is conducting an orchestra, singing, "My country misery, you keep on shafting me …"

12

Linda giggles. She looks at the mirror. She decides she is pretty. Well, not pretty exactly, no brag, just fact, but she does have nice even features and pretty eyes, big and green.

And so if she is young and pretty—almost pretty—and she is—if she is exactly the way an American teen of her American time ought to be—and she is, she thinks, all things considered: Upper-middle class family. Way upper. Ten-years-older brother far away and gone in San Francisco doing something with spreadsheets and probably wearing ties and (how the hell would she know? Ten years after all. Maybe he's a queer for all she knows). Her college education guaranteed by parents' careful financial planning (What college? I don't know. I should start thinking about it except I don't want to think about it.)

So everything is Boring! Better than the Brady Bunch, right?

Then just why does she feel so damned shitty so damned often? What it is, she gets up, you know, goes to school, comes home, breezes through homework. She doesn't have to work some dumbass job at Greasy Arches or Fashion Fart or anything, not with the Parental Units agreeing that Teen Time is the Time to focus on studies and self-identity and shit like that.

She dates on weekends, guys she likes "okay" and her parents don't much dislike, and all in all, she has what is supposed to be a "pretty fun time."

And usually she feels like a shuffling-along zombie in a grade-Z horror movie, just shuffling through it, shuffling on through all of it.

Feeling nothing. Nothing.

"Hey, Kar?"

"Hey what?"

"Want to ditch next hour? I don't feel like my daily dose of American history."

"Yeah. Okay."

"We can stay here and smoke a little. You got herb, don't you?" Karen laughs. "For sure."

They light a joint as the bell rattles the washroom windows.

ℰℬ • ℰℬ

At the desk in the office he shares with four others, Henderson takes invoices from a wire basket on his left and transfers them to a basket on the right. Henderson is a "paper man." The computer thing, sure, he learned what he had to learn when computers came along, but, thank you, pencils and paper.

More and more pencils these days. Not pen. There's a sound made by a pencil point that is subtle and real that you cannot get from a pen.

Henderson glances at a brochure for Educational Enterprises' new United States history text and discovers that not one word in the first sentence of the copy is related to any other word.

He looks around. It's as though everyone and everything in the office were pressed between two sheets of glass, flat, two-dimensional, like television cartoons.

"Henderson, what are you doing here?"

Tom Beamer, sales manager, has suddenly appeared. "Nothing," Henderson says.

"You were supposed to ... Say, Henderson, something bothering you?"

"Oh, no," Henderson says, "everything is fine."

Yes, yes indeed. Everything is fine. He has The Place. *And it comes to him that, why, whenever he wishes, he can go to The Place, flee this drab, silly, and oh-so-strangely-flat world.*

Yes. The Place.

"... appointment, Henderson. It's big. They want to toss out all the texts they're using and kick in a whole new line across the grades, one through twelve. And Henderson, there's the multimedia ..."

"Yes," Henderson says. Multimedia. He might remember what that is. It's possible. He might.

"... That is one school district with serious money. No tax caps for those suburbs. Mom and Pop want the fruit of their loins to go to Harvard and Brown and Yale so they can be just like Mom and Pop who went to ..."

Henderson folds his hands on the desk. Beamer glances at his wristwatch.

"... get moving, right? Don't want to be late."

Beamer is still talking. Henderson can see the mouth open and close in the flat face. Beamer's voice fades away and then ...

is gone—

And Henderson hears:

the bubbling of water skipping across stones.

Henderson pushes back his chair. He stands and smiles at Beamer.

Beamer's open mouth stays that way. "Now," Henderson says, "I forget. Where is it I am supposed to go?"

Henderson forces himself to hear the sales manager.

Tom Beamer says, "Christ doing cartwheels, Henderson ..."

water over stones

"Look, we can send Martelli out on this. I can go myself. It's okay."

"Oh no," Henderson says. "That's all right. That's all right. I'm already on the way."

He has The Place. Its serenity fills him, and he pities poor Beamer, Multimedia Beamer, who does not know, cannot know, has nothing.

Blue sky
tall trees
water over stones

A minute later (time) Henderson is on his way

"Pine Forest High School." Yes, he is on his way.

But before he leaves, he gazes back where everyone has become trapped in a gigantic ant farm, sandwiched between the transparent glass walls.

Henderson laughs pleasantly.

೮ • ೮

They are sitting on the window ledge, passing the third joint. A serious joint. Reggae-ska-ganja express el bomber *grande*.

From time to time, others have come in, some to sneak a cigarette, most to use the facilities, a couple to share a hit with them. No teachers have spot-checked, though, and while some of the "goody-pies" have given them nasty looks, there is no need to worry about anyone ratting them out. Pull that shit at Pine Forest High and poof! Ostracism—instant exile.

"I don't know," Karen says. "Guess it's sixth period."

"Huh?"

"See, you asked me what time it was, well, what time it is, really was, I guess, 'cause time takes a while, you know how it is with time. If you think about it, it's funny. Really."

"Oh," Linda says. "I am totally destroyed. This is good shit."

She takes the joint from Karen and decides she doesn't like or dislike being destroyed. It's just another way to be, that's all.

But to be ... what?

That is the question. Nothing. That is the answer.

That is the answer most of the time and it makes her sad as hell when it gets to her at all and sometimes she wishes she could really sob about it, really cry, big gulping nose-running sloppy sobs ...

"Let's play," Karen says.

"Play what?" Linda shifts her weight. The window ledge is hard.

"What do we play when we're stoned?"

"Nah, I don't want to."

"Sure you do."

"Sure I don't." Linda has a chill.

"Come on," Karen says. "The only time you can really talk is when you get stoned, right? It's no bullshit time. Let's play the Truth Game."

"Uh-uh," Linda says. She is colder now, and she has a sudden moment of absolute clarity, of shining frozen vision. They must play the Truth Game.

This is what is meant to be.

"Please," Karen says. "I want to talk and we are best friends and everything."

"Okay," Linda says, "but you have to start."

"True-true-true," Karen says. She whispers, "You know that party last Saturday? You didn't go."

"Yeah." Her period. Cramps making her pull her knees up to her chin.

"Well, everyone got real crazy. Drinking and smoking. There was this guy, Marty. He goes to Ridge. He's a senior. He's pretty nice, I guess. I don't know. I was kinda stoned."

A pause for air. "So anyway, it was him. Definitely. Marty."

Then the words rushing together, true-true-true: "So I guess I'm not a virgin, anymore."

"Oh, Karen," Linda says. "Oh." She knows she should ask the right stuff: "Did you take precautions?" and the stuff she should want to know, like, "Did it hurt?" and there should be all sorts of things to say and ask. Instead, she says it once more: "Oh."

Karen sighs. "Now it's your turn."

℃ • ℃

As Henderson drives, all color is fading. At last, he sees only black and white and gray. A world of dim, shimmering outlines.

Henderson amuses himself by blinking. In the fraction of a second that his eyes are closed, The Place springs magnificently into view, into life.

The grass is a throbbing green. The brook is a billion diamond encrusted hearts, beating, beating, beating. The life force of the trees roars through the veins in their leaves.

A horn screams behind Henderson as he drifts into the left lane.

He swings back. A Toyota passes in a blur, the faceless driver—no more depth to him than to a sheet of paper—gives Henderson the finger.

Henderson's hand moves to the radio

then

the song of the breeze through treetops

water over stones
and now—so complete the vision
The Place.
And The Girl with the Summer Eyes
who waits for him
Now
who sings her song, his song, the Song of The Place
Henderson, Henderson, Henderson
Come now Henderson …

Soon, then, soon Henderson will make the certain journey to The Place.

Where she awaits
The Girl with the Summer Eyes
Henderson, Henderson, Henderson

But there is yet something he must do, something to be taken care of in the flat world, this world without color, this dead world.

Lines wriggle and take on a rectangular shape. For an instant, there are letters: PINE FOREST EXIT.

Henderson slows and pulls onto the exit ramp.

ల • ల

"True-true-true," Karen says.

"Okay," Linda says. The memory comes welling up from so deep within.

It has been with her a long time, buried, and re-buried, and it is only now, the Truth Game, that she can dredge it up, vomit it out.

Yes, the dope has opened the door to understanding. All is clear. She can perceive the wispy connections between things that were and things that are—and things that will be and won't be.

Now she understands. She sees herself not as she appears to be but as she is. The real Linda. Someone so different.

Someone so bad.

"You know how down from our house it's so woodsy and everything?"

She is talking. No, the fake Linda, the go-to-school, big-eyed, nearly pretty Linda is talking. That is not who she really is …

"I was six years old, I guess."

She is stalling. She is not playing the Game. She is keeping the Truth inside.

"I was playing down there. By myself. Dad said I couldn't go there alone, but I did. The ground was all rough, and I could have gotten hurt, I guess. I found this nest that fell out of a tree. There were three baby birds."

Linda closes her eyes.

She tries not to see it, tries to see her father's face as he warns her about where she is never to go alone, that place that is going to get her something she won't like if he ever catches her down there—

She tries to imagine Karen and the guy screwing, Karen eye-rolling stoned with her legs up and that guy ramming it into her while the worst retro-disco trasho is playing somewhere in the background.

But she sees it all again as she knows she has to:

Because it rushes at her and happens again. It happens as it happened. It happens.

The bird nest. The baby birds are ugly, scraggly heads tipped back, beaks open impossible wide in constant, noisy demand. She stoops, takes a bird in her hand. Its heart beats like a frantic moth at a lighted window.

"Stop that," she says. It continues its cry. She is so much bigger than the bird but it will not be quieted.

She tightens her hand, squeezing.

The baby bird's body makes the small noise of potato chips being crunched or of autumn's dead leaves underfoot. Something oozes from the bird's beak and the bird is silent.

Linda is crying.

"Hey, come on, kid," Karen says. "It's the grass, Lin. It's got you paranoid or something. It's no big deal, okay? Really!"

The bell rings.

ↄ • ↄ

Henderson pulls into the parking lot as other cars like faint pencil strokes pull out. He parks in a space for "Visitors" and has a feeling of anticipation and irony. There is a rushing all about him as he walks to the two-dimensional building.

He goes in and finds the office. "May I help you?"

Squinting, Henderson is able to discern an outline, empty, like a hurried cartoon. A woman.

"I'm Henderson. Educational Enterprises."

The woman consults an appointment book on the desk. "Mr. Henderson, Dr. Thompson, that's the curriculum director for the district, you know, thought you weren't coming. You are two hours late, after all. Mr. Thompson is gone for the day. School's out. Everyone is going home now."

"Oh," Henderson says.

It is time for Henderson to go, too.
To The Place.

⌘ • ⌘

"Hey, that was the last bell, Lin. We've got to move it to catch the bus."

Linda has finished crying. She is free and weightless. Now she wants to be alone, just for a little while. "You know, Karen, to get my head together. Go ahead. I'll catch up with you."

"You okay?"

"Sure. You go ahead." Karen turns to leave, then looks back. "Linda ..."

"Don't worry," Linda says. "It's all right."

Then Linda is alone. Shit, that grass did a number on her, she thinks. Crazy thinking; paranoia-plus! Baby birds and a six-year-old kid and it was just something that happened, that's all.

That's all.

⌘ • ⌘

Henderson wonders why he has wasted so much time in this vanishing nowhere when he has always had The Place. He will not delay another moment. He steps out of the office. He is on his way.

Color explodes before him. Green. Golden. Warm pinks.

In this world of flat and gray, Henderson sees life.

Sees:

The Girl with the Summer Eyes.

Eyes of wonder and excitement. Eyes meant to gaze upon the forever beauty of The Place. The Place.

And that is why—She is here—He is here—Now. It is here that she has been awaiting him, It is here they are meant to find each other

Now

Henderson

And The Girl with the Summer Eyes.

⌘ • ⌘

Well, shit, she could wait for the activities bus, another hour and a half, but God! All she wants to do is get home, lock herself in her room, and sleep until there's not one single scrambled-up thought left rolling through her mind. She'll ask him for a ride. He's got to be a new teacher. He's got a suit and tie. There are more than 190 teachers on the staff so you can't know them all. This guy might be one of the poor dudes who gets stuck teaching the nerds in the remedial classes. He looks like it. Like he is one

19

of those guys who holds out his hand and the shitty end of the stick goes there automatically. Check out that half-ass smile, will you?

"Say, I missed the bus. I live close. Could you give me a ride?"

The way he's looking at her makes Linda wonder if the guy can tell she's still pretty stoned. "My name is …"

"I know you," he says.

It is so weird with teachers. They always seem to know everyone whether or not they've had them in class.

"You come with me," he says.

છ • છ

Henderson is surprised that she has to give directions. He thought he'd be able to find the route to The Place simply by listening and following the sound of water over stones.

But she says, "Left," and "You go right here," and he drives.

When the car turns onto a narrow gravel road, he know—she knows—that they are close.

Ahead, colors glow, there, where the branches hang heavy.

He gives it more gas.

Then

છ • છ

"Why are we stopping here?" Linda asks.

She doesn't want to be here.

Here is where a baby bird dies.

છ • છ

"This is The Place."

છ • છ

She understands that he knows, knows everything.

This is where it has all been leading, has always been leading, the end of the path found in dark woods when she was six years old.

They get out of the car. He takes her hand, leads her into the trees.

છ • છ

Something is wrong. Henderson does not see the brook, does not hear the water over stones. Something is wrong.

Yet he is here.

He is here with The Girl with the Summer Eyes.

He touches her.
She screams.

ભ • ભ

She knows it is all crazy. It is something that should not be happening. Goddamned marijuana has made her think crazy.

She has to get away from him.
He touches her.
She screams.

ભ • ભ

She has to stop. She *must* stop screaming, the Girl with the Summer Eyes.

It is all going wrong.
He touches her.
She screams.

He feels the grass wither beneath his feet. The trees are disappearing, growing dim. The color, the color drips away.

He touches her.
She screams.

"Please," he says, "please stop." His hand covers her mouth. He holds her and pushes her and tips back her head.

ભ • ભ

Something breaks inside her. She knows the sound: autumn's dead leaves underfoot.

He is touching her.
She is trying to scream.
There is more breaking.
She cannot scream.

ભ • ભ

She lies on colorless grass. Her eyes are closed. Henderson is confused. Something has gone wrong.

Henderson has—somehow—made a mistake.
This is not The Place.
It is only
Her Place.

NEW MOON ON THE WATER

A CIRCLE OF MAGIC

Thank you, to me you have been so kind, very kind. Living, I did not wish to continue, no, no more, but my life, you preserved my life, returned it to me. So please, I will repay you, as I am honor bound and in accordance with the customs of my land. I will truly repay your goodness, I will. All must be repaid, to me you have been so kind, very kind. Living, I did not wish to continue, no, no more, but my life, you preserved my life, returned it to me. So please, I will repay you, as I am honor bound and in accordance with the customs of my land. I will truly repay your goodness, I will. All must be repaid.

Therefore, do you see how upon the paper scrap, I draw the circle of magic as it is done in my country? No, it matters not upon what surface we place our circle. Ha! How foolish to think so, even. Magic is magic, it is so, and we do not need a good or better quality bond paper, of course not.

The source and power of Magic comes from intention and my intention toward you, oh, my uncalled-for friend, why, there is no end of the gratitude which is mine for that which you have done!

Thus, I draw the circle! There! The circle of magic, and thus, with sincerity and humility of the utmost, I do present it to you!

Of course I shall explain! Upon the circle of magic, please to gaze. And as your eyes focus upon it, then think of the one person in your life responsible for bringing to you the most pain.

This might be the love of your youth, a love which was unrequited.

Might it be the cruel parent or worse, the absent mother or father?

Might it be, oh, just might it be someone you hate because this someone is someone you cannot stop loving?

Think of this someone, please, yes, this individual who burned your heart until it became a hard glowing cinder the smoke of which still comes from your lungs when you remember.

Oh, I cannot this answer for you. You must answer for you.

And now, friend to me of the most unselfish graciousness, all you need do is place your finger within the circle and the magic will occur: Never

again, not ever again, will you think of this person!
　　Here, take the circle of magic.
　　It is my thanks to you.

THE W.W. II PISTOL

The tavern smelled of coal and of the drying sweat of men who worked in the mines. The jukebox's neon glow and the illuminated face of the Budweiser clock over the plastic Imperial sign behind the bar provided the only light. It was the end of the work week and the men seated at the six Formica topped tables and at the bar were drinking beers and boilermakers and highballs. There had been no accidents in the mines for seven weeks and no one had bought a new car; there was little to talk about.

Even Lori, the barmaid, fat, a bleached blonde, wasn't kidding around with anyone. She greeted new arrivals with "Hey," or "How're you?" and then brought beer or whiskey.

Joe Heane threw the door wide when he entered. It took a long time to close; the sunlight that followed Joe in made everyone blink. Joe's head swiveled on his tight neck as he looked around.

Curley Raymond, at the end of the bar, bottle of Stag beer in hand, moved his stool a quarter turn and said, "Guess who?"

Ron Adkins sipped beer. He sighed. "I'm getting tired of him. I'm getting real sick and real tired of him."

"Yeah," said Curley. "Me too."

Joe Heane's eyes again made a circuit of the tavern. He put his hand in the pocket of his blue vinyl jacket. He walked to the bar and stood behind Curley and Ron. They said nothing.

"How're you, Joe?" Lori said.

"I just want a beer," he said. "I want a Stag."

"Look, Joe," Lori said.

He interrupted. "I just want a beer. All I want." His lips were tight. "Know why I only want the one beer?" The light of the Budweiser clock shone on his face. His teeth were widely spaced. A spot of dried blood where he'd bitten his lower lip glittered like hard coal.

Curley circled his fingers on the neck of his nearly empty bottle. Ron took another drink.

"I drink too much," Joe Heane said, "screws up my eyes. Makes

25

everything all soft, fuzzy like and I can't see so good. I want to see real good, though"—the tip of his tongue touched the scab on his lower lip—"so I can see straight every goddamn sonfabitch in this place for the goddamn sonfabitch they are."

Ron shrugged and turned on his stool to face Joe Heane. So did Curley. "No need for trouble, Joe," Ron said.

Joe Heane stepped back. He looked at Ron, then Curley, then back to Ron. "No," he said, "no need for trouble. Just 'cause you're all goddamn sonfabitches." He smiled and his mouth got tighter. "Not scared of you, Ron Adkins. Not scared of you, Curley. You're sonfabitches the both of you."

Curley laughed. "Okay," he said, "you called us what you want to, so it's time you get out of here. Or you can sit down and have a beer with us."

"No," Joe Heane said, "no, no. Don't drink with sonfabitches. Got something better for you. Got it right here in my pocket."

"Yeah, Joe," Ron said. "We know."

"Yeah, yeah," Joe said. Then the words came quickly. "Got my World War Two pistol. Ought to take it and blow away every goddamn sonfabitch in here. Blow you all to hell. Carried this gun in the big war. I know what killing's all about."

"Yeah, Joe. We know."

"That's what I should do. Make you sorry for the first day you and all the other goddamn sonfabitches thought to make a goddamn fool out of Joe Heane."

There was silence and then Ron said, "Then do it, Joe. Just you do it, okay? You take out your pistol and let's see what happens."

"No," Joe Heane said. "Won't do it now. Get my World War Two pistol half out of my pocket and you and all the other sonfabitches jump all over me."

Joe looked like he'd just said something clever. "I won't do a thing. Not now. But I killed men in the war and I know what killing is. Every sonfabitch can stand some good advice ought to remember that."

"Okay, Joe," Curley said, "so what you do is take yourself and your pistol home now. Your pretty little wife is probably missing you, missing you real bad. So you go home."

"Curley, you are a sonfabitch and I'll settle it all with you someday."

"Maybe so and maybe no, but for right now, you go on home," Curley said.

Joe Heane said nothing. The hand in his jacket pocket moved so that his knuckles took on a layer of blue vinyl skin. Then he turned and left.

Ron and Curley swiveled their stools back toward the bar.

"A couple more beers here," Curley said to Lori. Then he said to Ron, "We're going to have to do something."

"Yes," Ron said, "I think so."

જ • જ

Duane Sellers sat behind his polished desk. A stray lick of black hair had fallen onto his lined forehead. He brushed it back, then folded his hands on the green desk blotter. "All right," he said, "what do you want me to do?"

Curley rubbed his chin. "I don't know. Getting to be some kind of problem."

"That's right," Ron said. He slid forward on the upholstered armchair. "That's why we came to you, Duane. You're a big man now. Assistant State's Attorney. But you never forgot who you were."

"That's right," Curley said. "You know folks around here. You know how they think."

"I guess so," Duane Sellers said softly. "I guess I do, that's right."

"Look, Duane," Curley said, "Joe Heane's getting crazier and crazier. He's carrying that goddamn pistol ..."

"Yeah," Duane Sellers said. He smiled. "The World War Two pistol. Lots of kids in town used to want to see that pistol. Getting out of high school, thinking about joining the marines or the army, they'd go talk to Joe Heane. Want to see the pistol he carried in World War Two. Wanted to hear what he did over there. Sometimes he'd let 'em look at the medals and everything, but then, after a time, he stopped doing that. Still tell the stories, though. Sometimes."

"Joe's not telling war stories anymore, Duane," Curley said. "All he talks about is how everyone's a goddamn sonfabitch and he's going to take the pistol and put a round in every one of us. Tell you, Duane, he is getting crazier and crazier every day goes by."

Duane Sellers nodded. "Guess that's so. Guess it is. I know he is a problem. Started acting crazy right after he got that pretty little wife from up in Decatur. Pretty little thing like that in a town like this.

"He goes off to work, and all the time he's chopping coal he's thinking about that pretty little wife. That would be fine if his thinking stopped right there. But next you know, he's thinking how maybe everyone else, all the men he works with, the men in town, are maybe thinking about that pretty little wife of his, too. Then he's dead certain that's just what they are thinking. So he goes a little crazy, thinking about what everyone's

27

thinking, and then he gets real crazy and figures maybe some men are doing more than thinking about that pretty little wife of his." Duane Sellers nodded again and said, "So, that's it all right. He starts in thinking crazy and now he's acting crazy, carrying that World War Two pistol all the time and making threats and the like."

"Wants to be crazy, he's welcome," Curley said. "I don't want him coming up behind me some night and blowing my head off. And I'm not the only one that feels that way, Duane."

Duane smiled. "I see your point. I don't want anything like that either. That would be bad trouble, a real mess."

Curley laughed. "Yeah," he said, "especially for me." Duane Sellers laughed with him. "Especially for you."

"Can't he go to jail for a while, Duane?" Ron said. "Give him time to cool down and maybe start thinking right again."

Duane Sellers shook his head. The stray lick of hair dropped onto his forehead and he did not push it back. "No, no," he said. "Around here you don't put a man in jail for talking crazy. Lots of people talk crazy. Lots of people carry guns. Can't have them all in jail. The asylum's no good for Joe, either. Be a lot of folderol to get him in there and he's nowhere near crazy enough for them to keep him more than ten days or so. And then he gets out, he won't be all that amiable, if you see what I mean."

Duane Sellers frowned. "Of course, he does sometimes beat that pretty little wife of his."

"I know," Ron said.

"No good," Duane said, shaking his head. "She won't press charges. I asked her a time back. Hell, my daddy used to hit Mom when he was feisty and she said it was nobody's damn business and certainly not the law's damn business even if the whole town knew all about it.

"Shit fire and save the matches, boys, but Joe doesn't make enough racket beating and she doesn't make enough noise hollering so that we could jug him for public disturbance. Even so, throwing Joe in jail wouldn't help. The man has gone crazy in the mines. Let him out of jail and he'd be twice as crazy. Then he'd sure come after all us 'goddamn sonfabitches.'"

"Well, then," Curley said. "So what do we do?" Duane Sellers thought a moment. "Kill him, I guess."

"Are you sure?" Curley said.

"Yes, I think so," Duane Sellers said. "Just do it right so there won't be much trouble about it. Maybe use his World War Two pistol and stick it in his own hand. Or knock him goofy and put him in the river.

"Don't want a lot of trouble about this. None of us do. Thing is, we just can't have a man running around town with a pistol ready to shoot everybody he thinks has been thinking about, or seeing, or messing with his pretty little wife. This is the only way I can figure."

"All right, Duane," Curley said. "Thanks a lot."

"That's all right," Duane Sellers said. "People expect me to take care of problems. That's my job."

"Thanks, Duane," Ron said.

๛ • ๛

It was Sunday afternoon and Joe Heane was seated on a wooden bench in the town square. Curley sat down on his right, Ron on the left. Joe Heane's old Chevrolet was parked in one of the marked spaces at the curb.

"I talked with Duane Sellers," Joe Heane said. "Called me in to his office. Said he had to talk to me."

Joe Heane licked his lips. His right hand was in the pocket of his blue vinyl jacket. He did not look at Curley or Ron. He kept his eyes on the old Chevrolet.

"You are all of you sonfabitches, you know."

"Yeah, Joe," Curley said. "We know. You told us all about it."

"Joe," Ron said, "that record has been spinning around too many times on the phonograph. That's just about enough of it, okay?"

"I don't know."

"What did Duane Sellers tell you, Joe?" Ron said.

"Said it was open season on Joe Heane. Said that's what he told you. Said it was going to get known around here that there wouldn't be a whole lot of trouble if I got killed. No trouble's, what he said." Joe Heane's voice was flat. "What he said was that it's all right to kill me for carrying my World War Two pistol, and marrying a pretty little wife, and calling you all the sonfabitches that you are. That's what I heard from Duane."

"Guess you heard right, Joe," Ron said.

"What I ought to do, goddamn it," Joe Heane said, "is take my pistol right now and kill you both. Kill you dead right in the middle of the Town Square here. Then I ought to just keep on killing until they kill me and it would mean something that way. Maybe I could get to kill that sonfabitch, Duane Sellers, and, goddamn it, that makes just as much sense as anything, I would say. Hell, I killed men in the war with my pistol."

"You won't do that, Joe," Curley said quietly. "We know you won't. Whole thing is just about done. You know that."

"Yeah," said Joe Heane, "I guess I do." He sounded tired.

Curley said, "See, you talked about it too much, so you can't do it. You talked about it the way you talked about all those men you killed in the war. And so now it's just like a story and it doesn't mean anything. It's over, Joe, and you know it."

"That's right," Joe Heane said, "so I guess what happens now is you kill me. Is that it?"

Curley laughed. "No," he said. "No need to kill you now. Sitting here and chatting like this, you are making good sense. I talked this over with Ron. We decided if you got in your car, just you by your own self, and drove on out of here, say maybe a couple hundred miles south, there's big mines there and you could get work just you going off by yourself and never coming back, then we don't have to kill you. Killing you is nothing we want to do, you see."

"You'd like that, wouldn't you?" Joe Heane said. "That's the way you sonfabitches are."

Ron laughed. He said, "Best thing for you to do, Joe."

"Is it?" Joe Heane said.

Neither Ron nor Curley answered him. Joe Heane looked at his old Chevrolet. "All right, that is what I'll do then. I won't ever come back."

"That's right," Ron said.

"One more thing, Joe," Curley said. "Before you go, you'd better give me your pistol. It's made a lot of trouble for all of us."

"No, it didn't," Joe Heane said. But he took the .38-caliber pistol from his pocket and handed it to Curley.

Then he rose, walked to his car, got in, started the engine, and slowly pulled away.

When the Chevrolet was out of sight, Curley hefted the pistol and said, "Gun like this has been through a lot."

"Guess that's so," Ron said.

"Genuine World War Two pistol like this," Curley said, "might be of value. Could even be worth a lot of money."

"Might be."

"We don't have a right to this gun," Curley said. "Joe Heane's wife ought to have it. Might bring her some money. She'll be needing money now with old Joe gone off to who knows where."

"That's right," Ron said. "We ought to drive on out there and see that she gets Joe's World War Two pistol, pretty little girl like that."

"Yeah," Curley said, "I think so, too."

POP IS REAL SMART

Lonny gazed at Jason. He loathed him with all the egoistic hatred of which only a five-year-old is capable. He was supposed to be happy he had a new brother. He was supposed to love him. Oh sure. Right. Damn.

Lonny's eyes measured the baby's length and studied the pink fingers curled in tight fists at the top of the blue blanket. He watched the fluttery beating of the soft spot on Jason's head as, under skimpy down, it palpitated with the tiny heart.

"Damn," Lonny said. Pop said "damn" a lot, like when he was driving and everybody else was driving like a jerk, or when he was trying to fix a leaky faucet or something. And "damn" is just what Lonny felt like saying whenever he looked at Jason. The only thing the baby could do— this ookey-pukey brother!—was smell bad. Jason always smelled, no matter how often Mom bathed him or dumped a load of powder on him.

Jason wasn't good for anything!

Now Scott, down the block, Scott was lucky. Scott had a real brother, Fred, good old Fred. Yessir, Fred was a fun kid. You could punch Fred real hard, he wouldn't even cry. And Fred didn't go running to tell, either. Uh-uh.

But Fred had these clumpy cowboy boots and if you punched him, then he would just start kicking you and kicking and maybe you would be the one who wound up crying!

Fred, that was the kind of dude you wanted for a little brother. Not Jason. This damn baby, hey, he couldn't do anything.

And this was the kid Lonny had helped Mom and Pop choose a name for? Jason. That was a good name for a good guy.

Damn!

Jason—this stupid thing with that stupid up and down blob on its head going thump-a-thump, thump-a-thump. No way, José!

Somebody must have fooled Mom. When she'd gone to the hospital, Mom had somehow got stuck with this little snot instead of a good brother for him.

31

Lonny wondered how Mom could be so damn dumb. Well, she was a girl, even if she was a grownup, and girls could be pretty dumb sometimes. But damn, how did they put one over on Pop? Pop was real smart.

Lonny reached through the crib slats. He lightly touched Jason's soft spot. At the pulse beneath his fingers, he yanked back his hand.

Damn, this baby was just no good. No. Good.

He left the room. There had to be some way to get rid of Jason. He would ask Mom to take the baby back to the hospital, tell her she'd made a mistake. Oh, he'd have to say it just the right way so she didn't get pee-owed, but he'd figure it out. Then she could go get him a really good brother, like Fred.

Yeah! He knew just how to say it. He'd talk to Mom right now.

"Mom!" he hollered, running down the stairs. He hoped he would wake the baby.

Mom did not answer. Jason did not cry. "Mom!" Lonny went to the kitchen. The linoleum buzzed beneath his Nikes and he heard the muffled thud of the washing machine in the downstairs utility room.

Mom was doing the wash. Damn, it was never a good idea to talk to her about anything when she was into laundry.

Lonny decided he might as well make himself a sandwich or something. He dragged a chair from the table over to the cabinets. He climbed up and took down the big jar of peanut butter. He got the Wonder Bread from the breadbox.

He set the bread and peanut butter on the table. He hoped he could open the new jar by himself. No way did he want to ask Mom for help when she was doing the laundry.

Okay! The lid came right off. "Yeah," Lonny said. "She's gonna have to take it back. It's no damn good, and if it's no good, you just take it back."

Hey, sometimes he wondered how a smart guy like Pop got stuck with Mom, anyway. For real, it was Pop had the brains.

Like once Lonny had goofed it. He had spent his birthday money on a rifle at Toys"R"Us and damn! It was wrong. It wasn't a Rambo assault rifle. It was a stupid Ranger Rock rifle. No way did you want a Ranger Rock rifle. Who ever heard of Ranger Rock?

So he and Pop took it back to get the Rambo rifle.

"No refunds on sale items, sorry." That's what this real dipstick at the store had to say.

Then Pop showed him how you couldn't even pull the trigger and the way the plastic barrel was all cracked and everything. No problem, man! They got back his birthday money, went to another store, and bought the

Rambo rifle.

And you know what? That nerd at Toys"R"Us never even had an idea that Pop had busted up the stupid Ranger Rock rifle himself!

That's how smart Pop was.

With his first finger, Lonny swirled out a glob of peanut butter. He popped it into his mouth. Yeah, peanut butter was great. He could live on peanut butter all the time.

He'd make a nice, open-faced sandwich, and then maybe Mom would be done with the laundry and he could talk to her about getting rid of smelly Jason.

He went to the drawers by the sink. He opened the top one.

Mom always spread peanut butter with a dull knife. It was the sharp knife that caught Lonny's eye.

NEW MOON ON THE WATER

HEALERS

1. WHAT IS

He peered down at the child who lay in jockey shorts on the twisted sheets of the daybed. The living room of the housing project apartment was close with the smell of sickness and grease and poverty.

"Mister, he dyin'," the boy's mother said. "Maybe gone by mornin' tomorrow, maybe next day, and then my baby boy ain't no more."

It was not yet 11 o'clock at night and it seemed the mother's "mornin' tomorrow" might well be optimistic. The boy's skin was the color of putty, stretched taut on a body bloated with its own poisons. His eyes floated in poached-egg yellow and each time he breathed, a tiny bubble of spit burst between his lips.

"Not yet seven years old," the mother said, "and it's not right. You tell me, Mister. Is it right a boy like him should get no more time than that to walk this Earth?"

He shook his head. "I can't tell you. I long ago gave up thinking about what is right and what is wrong."

"What is it you do think about, Mister?"

He said, "Only what is."

The boy's mother said, "Mister, I tell you what is. My boy dyin', that's what is. Dyin' cuz he's black and dyin' cuz we're poor. They says 'Money can't buy health,' now that's a damned lie and a double-damned lie. You a rich white boy needin' a kidney transplant and you get a kidney and you live. Don't work that way for poor niggers, Mister. We ain't like them, cuz they got and we don't, and we ain't like them, cuz we're black and they are white. And they hate us cuz we different, and what you hate you afraid of, and what you hate you try to pretend ain't there, an' more than anythin', what you hate you don't never give no help to—and if it goes away, goes away like my boy goin' away, forever, well you damn glad of it."

She paused. "I guess I talks a lot, but Mister, I guess maybe you know all about bein' different. So you tell me ... Am I saying what is?"

35

"Yes," he said. Then he asked, "What do you want of me?"

She pointed at her son. "Don't let him die, Mister. Please." He bent and his fangs found the boy's jugular.

When he straightened, the child's mother said, "Thank you, Mister. My boy's gonna live."

He said, "He will not die," and he left.

2. A BILLION MONSTROSITIES

It was so late that it was early when Rafael Martinez returned to his home, but when one visits the city, as Martinez did more nights than not, a Mexican *turista* city built to cater to the needs and desires and whims of wealthy gringos, there is much to do, much pleasure to be found and taken in places that are devoted exclusively to pleasure finding and taking. Martinez felt greatly welcome in the city, and why not? He was wealthy, BMW, Mercedes, Jaguar wealthy, Rolex watch, IBM computers, and Pierre Cardin suits wealthy.

When he turned on the light in his bedroom, Rafael Martinez felt a flash of surprise—but half a moment's appraisal convinced him that he had nothing to fear from the stranger who somehow had invaded his home and now sat in the arm chair by the balcony window. Rather than fright, Martinez felt anger that his privacy could be impinged upon—but no less did he feel a reassuring familiarity.

Had he not seen many who looked like this—and had they not brought him a fortune? The stranger looked old, but it was not the natural aging that mankind is heir and prey to; rather it seemed the result of grievous wasting sickness that had stripped away layers of flesh to leave only a parchment-skinned skeleton, with a bald head the color of old ivory and too-bright, fever-glittering eyes.

"Who are you?" Rafael Martinez asked sharply. "What are you doing here?"

"You don't know me?" The stranger's voice sounded the way his eyes looked, a fever-glitter sound. "You should. I know you, Rafael Martinez."

"*Dr.* Martinez ..."

"Rafael Martinez, you are no doctor."

Rafael Martinez sighed. Whatever this was, he was tiring of it. It was time to summon the police, he decided, and because he saw no threat from the stranger, Rafael Martinez, as he reached for the bed-stand telephone, announced such an intention.

36

But the stranger was out of the chair, and he gripped Martinez's wrist, and his fingers were remarkably strong and no less remarkably hot, and Martinez could not pick up the telephone.

"I've come because of the clinic," the stranger said.

"I see," Rafael Martinez said. "But this is quite irregular. We can make the proper arrangements if you will come tomorrow directly to the clinic ..."

"To Rafael Martinez's famed clinic," the stranger interrupted.

"Where I treat the afflicted ..."

"With purges that twist their guts and foul-tasting elixirs that make their heads spin, with hot baths that draw their tiniest bits of remaining strength streaming from their pores in rivers of sweat, and cold baths that freeze their pain within them, with brutal massage and spinal re-alignment that bends their already bent bodies into bizarre postures of screaming misery.... I know the work of your clinic, Rafael Martinez, and I know you do all this—and you do that which is far worse: You sell false hope to the hopeless."

With the stranger's strong hot grip on his wrist, and the stranger's eyes unblinking and piercing, Rafael Martinez began to feel fear.

"Who are you?" he demanded.

"You know me," the stranger said, and he let go of Martinez's wrist.

And it was now that Rafael Martinez felt within his blood, within his bowels, within his lungs, within his bones and the marrow of his bones, the peculiar movement of a billion and a billion times a billion multiplying monstrosities.

The pain swelled inside him, waves of pain without diminution, as his body inexorably began to consume itself.

Rafael Martinez fell to his knees.

"You know me," the stranger said once more.

Rafael Martinez looked up through curtains of thick red and screamed the stranger's name. "Cancer!"

3. MISS HAZELTINE'S MIRACLE

Lord Jesus, blessed Jesus, merciful Jesus, my own sweet Jesus, help me.... Heal me—this time! That was the silent prayer Lois Anne Hazeltine prayed as she hobbled into the tent on her two canes, her bent body vibrating with the always pain, the pain that filled her so that she thought on the worst days (there were no good days: only bad days, worse days, and worst days) that she would burst with it.

NEW MOON ON THE WATER

The diagnosis, made five years previously, when she was 32: rheumatoid arthritis. The prognosis: Pain for the rest of her natural life, pain that would cripple and twist her body, that might be (sometimes) alleviated (slightly) by aspirin, by anti-inflammatories (indomethacin, cortisone), but pain about which medical science said, "Well, quite frankly, Miss Hazeltine, there's not a great deal we can do for you."

No question then that she needed a miracle. And she'd prayed for one ("Ask and it shall be given"), and sought one ("Look ye to the Lord"), but though she avidly watched and prayed along with TV preachers, putting her clawed hands on top of the Sylvania console and opening a humble heart to the Holy Spirit, and though she'd gone to faith healers in 33 counties in Kentucky, and Missouri, and Illinois, and though she'd sent in coupons from supermarket-sold tabloids, receiving for a dollar, two dollars, or ten dollars, miracle beads, miracle statues, miracle crosses, miracle pictures, miracle water, she had not yet received a miracle.

But she would. (I believe) Lois Anne Hazeltine did not doubt. (I believe) Her faith was real and unwavering and it would be her salvation. (I believe I believe IbelieveIbelieveIbelieveIbelieve!!!)

This time!

Because Jimmy Smalley had a reputation. He was the man who could work miracles.

There was no organ playing as the miracle seekers found seats on the wooden benches. No choir sang hymns to God.

There was just Jimmy Smalley striding to the platform, moving like a tall man and not a pudgy five-footer, Jimmy Smalley raising his arms, the jacket sleeves of his polyester leisure suit riding up to reveal a good three inches of none-too-clean cuff, Jimmy Smalley greeting everyone in the piercing voice of an amphetamine-fueled munchkin:

"Well y'all, hello, hello, hello! We're gonna get movin', right here and right now and right away, 'cause you come here for miracles, and miracles you're gonna have. Get some lines here, and bring your sick and wasted and twisted selves right on up here, why doncha? Got some cancer in your co_on? We'll clobber it! Take care of epilepsy in an instant and scoliosis in a second. Gonna mash your miseries, heal your hurts, and pull the pain plumb out of you and throw it on over the moon. Maybe you was born deaf, but tomorrow night you're gonna be singin' along with the theme from *Love Boat*. Maybe you was born blind, but tomorrow morning when that pesky blue jay wakes you up with its squawk, you can pitch a bit of chat and knock it right square in the head. Come on, come on, come on! Get a move on! Got us some mircalizing to do—and I do mean NOW!!"

38

Lois Anne Hazeltine wanted to hurry, to claim a place at the head of the line, but she was barely capable of movement, let alone rapid movement, and so, far back in the line, she had plenty of time to pray (Oh Lord, let it be, this time, my sweet Jesus, grant my prayers!) and to watch:

As Jimmy Smalley put his hands on the shoulders of a man in a wheelchair, a man who had muscular dystrophy, and commanded: "Now you just get on up out of that contraption." And the man did. Jimmy Smalley, his hands still on the man's shoulders, walked backward and the man, who had not walked in four years walked, walked forward, walked without a lurch or stumble or hesitation.

"Now on your knees, friend," said Jimmy Smalley, and the man knelt easily, Jimmy along with him, and Jimmy Smalley whispered in his ear and the man threw up his arms and screamed: "I believe! I do believe!"

Jimmy Smalley said, "You are healed."

And the man was.

And in more or less the same way ...

—so was a woman who had a short leg (and the leg grew, right there, with everyone watching ...

—so was a man who could not speak, whose first words—ever—were "I believe! I do believe ..."

(And getting closer now, closer to the miracle that was waiting for her, Lois Anne Hazeltine prayed to God and told Him she believed, had never stopped believing during her trials and travails and torments.)

—so were all those who came to Jimmy Smalley for a miracle

—until at last it was Lois Anne Hazeltine's turn, her moment for her miracle.

With Jimmy Smalley's hands on her shoulders, she felt the power, a buzzing glow, spreading through her, (Yes! Oh, yes dear God, at last!) and when Jimmy Smalley said, "Drop those canes, you're not needin' those silly things no more!" she did—and she felt herself straighten, felt an incredible life-rightness within her, as though she were a springtime plant bursting from the dark and cold of the ground.

"Now claim your cure, woman!" Jimmy Smalley commanded. "On your knees now!"

She fell to her pain-free knees (hurt gone—the hurt is gone—Jesus, this is my miracle!).

Jimmy Smalley was kneeling with her.

(Thank you, Jesus, Oh, thank you, dear Lord ...)

Softly, so softly, Jimmy Smalley whispered in her ear, whispered a promise of radiant health and a promise that brought her the most profound pain she had ever experienced:

"Woman, now you know what he can do. This is the Devil's work, woman; believe in him and be healed."

And Jimmy Smalley asked, "Do you believe?"

BUCKEYE JIM IN EGYPT

Prologue

In the beginning, there was darkness.
  Then came light.
  That is the beginning of everything.

I

The more mundane among us contend Southern Illinois
is called "Egypt" or "Little Egypt" because of its southern-
most town, Cairo, on the Mississippi River.

More probable is that the term came into usage
because we are still waiting for a Moses to lead us out of
here right to the Promised Land, although every time one
appears on the scene, we kick him flush in the backside
and tell him to let us tend to our own affairs.

—Brian Robert Moore, weekly columnist, 1920–1973, "I'll Tell You
What!" for the *Sesser Sentinel*, Eads St. Publications, Sesser, Illinois

Way up yonder, above the sky,
  white bird nests in a green bird's eye.
"Buckeye Jim"
An American folk song, usually performed on the banjo

Monday, July 12, 1925

Sometimes he forgot who he was.
  Sometimes he forgot what he was doing here.
  It was just past 7:30 in the morning, and already the thermometer

41

had hit a swampy 80, but it was not the temperature or fatigue that caused the man in the lightweight suit coat to set down his straw valise and banjo case and lean on the rail of the half-mile long bridge. He needed to think. Gazing down at the rippling, sun reflecting waters of the Washauconda River helped to bring about a mind calming focus.

He reached into his pocket. He found it: a lucky buckeye. Every time he reached into his pocket, there would be one—and one only. The seed of the horse chestnut was brown and brittle; it felt as though there were something magical and off-center within it. It was exactly like the world.

His smile came slow and easy. Nobody would ever mistake him for handsome, but when he smiled, it made most folks like him.

He knew who he was.

He was Buckeye Jim.

This time.

He knew what he had to do.

Buckeye back in his pocket, he hoisted his grip and banjo. Just then a new, deep-green Oakland All American Six pulled up, the powerful Phaeton model. Of course, in this weather, the windows were down. The driver, in a straw fedora, tie knotted in a half-Windsor, a prominent American flag pin on his collar, leaned toward Buckeye Jim. "How do."

"How do," Buckeye Jim answered, bending down, face framed by the window. "Your automobile is a beaut."

"I do thank you. Might I offer you a ride into Ft. Lorraine? I assume that is your intended destination."

"Yes, sir, " Buckeye Jim said.

"The Devil is always hiring fiddlers and banjo pickers in hell, but if you're after employment in the mines, Mr. June Legrand's got a one-hole privy operation in Ft. Lorraine that is likely to oblige. If you don't mind working next to niggers. And if you don't mind being forced to join the union."

Buckeye Jim said nothing as he stowed his gear in the back.

The driver added, "Not saying Legrand's a Bolshevik. Not saying he's a nigger-lover. I do wonder if he's a true-blue American."

The auto felt massive. Buckeye Jim wondered if he would ever get used to cars. He did enjoy the smell of new cars. He liked the smell of gently flowing rivers and hot sun on steel bridges ...

He suddenly remembered the strong and surprising odor of light, a smell that was itself pure radiance, shattering and banishing the darkness.

The driver's name, said the man who wore his nation's flag on his collar, was Mark E. Dupont. ("Thank you for the ride, Mr. Dupont, and people call me Buckeye Jim.") He seemed a friendly fellow, not too jolly or too serious.

Not too much one or the other ... He could be a dangerous man, Buckeye Jim reckoned. On several occasions, Buckeye Jim had been killed by just this sort of man.

Mark E. Dupont casually mentioned he was assistant superintendent up to the new strip mine owned by Illinois Coal and Power north of Herrin. A new process, strip mining would be the wave of the future, and it was swell. It meant more profit for everyone. Also, Mark E. Dupont mentioned (casually), he'd been elected to Herrin's town council. There had been talk—casual, but who could tell—about his running for mayor.

He started to say something else casual when Buckeye Jim said, "Sure a fine automobile. A real ace."

Dupont chuckled. "Well, I would have been most happy and satisfied with just your standard model, but my boys would not have it."

"You have sons?" Buckeye Jim asked.

Dupont said, "Well, I do have a family, and I do have boys. Two boys, a girl, and a fine, Christian wife who dotes on me.

"But I was not referring to my offspring. I meant the boys in the Klan."

"Clan," Buckeye Jim said quietly.

There were times when his mind became a tedious and troublesome thing.

So many memories ...

He did remember clans. The MacEldoes? The McCutcheons? In Scotland. He recalled Scotland as a land of thistles and foggy mornings more gray and ominous than anywhere else on earth. And cutting through the grayness, he could remember the swirling-squeal of the pipes, eerie and mysterious, a summons to war and death....

He remembered ...

"... I'm the leader. What you call a Cyclops," Dupont said.

"'Course they have to inflate it some, call me the 'Grand Exalted Cyclops' and what not." Mark E. Dupont sounded like he didn't mind that "his boys" wanted him to be "grand" and "exalted" and to drive a Phaeton.

"Well, I don't know," Buckeye Jim said.

"A lot of people don't know," Dupont said, "and among 'em is one Mr. C. Cooper Legrand, Jr. I'll be jawing some with him today. Rich man like him, what he can't realize is this was hard-scrabble, bare-bone, poor country 'fore the mines come. And if all the really big companies from out east choose to leave because Legrand has a head full of foreign thinkin' and a heart that beats pure nigger time like a shufflin' pickaninny ..."

Buckeye Jim said nothing. He was confused. Not infrequently, people thought him dull-witted.

But if you live many lives, and you don't know what you should know and you do know what you shouldn't know ... My, oh, my, and wasn't it a perplexing business?

Mr. Dupont was talking about—

"... the Klan is four-square for the Bible. I'd imagine a right-looking American fellow such as yourself, why, you wouldn't be having any moral or spiritual argumentations with that, would you, Mr. Buckeye Jim?"

With all his poor head had to tote, sometimes Buckeye Jim felt he had no room left over for a sense of humor, but doggone! That did make him laugh!

"Mr. Dupont," he said. "I would testify in any court of the land or on Judgment Day that I have no dispute with the Bible."

"Well, good, good," Mr. Dupont said. He went on to tell how the Ku Klux Klan defended Americans from foreigners and Communists and Catholics (especially those "Eye-talian Catholics but also Bohunk and Polack" Catholics), and he went on to tell how it brought true Christianity to those as needed the Gospel Truth, and he went on to tell how it put the fear of God in the bootleggers, like those East St. Louis Shelton Brothers, or that Jew Charlie Birger with his roadhouse, the Shady Rest, and he went on and he went on and on and on ...

Buckeye Jim said, "Looks like we're here."

Like virtually all Southern Illinois town squares, Ft. Lorraine's was a circle. In the center, an imposing island of civic sanctity, stood the municipal building, new red brick, with broad, white concrete steps. Merchants on the town's center hub included Walker and Sons clothing, the Vick-Cline Pharmacy (where the forty-cent size Fletcher's Castoria was on sale for twenty-nine cents), and Ulricht's Shoe Store.

Buckeye Jim got out and pulled his gear after him.

"Good luck," Dupont said, shaking his hand through the passenger window portal. "You find Ft. Lorraine isn't exactly to your liking, that maybe it smells too niggery, you come on up north of Herrin way and perhaps I can do you some good."

"Why, thank you," Buckeye Jim said. You know, Buckeye Jim felt altogether humorous today. "Mr. Dupont, you are the very first Grand Exalted Cyclops I have met in my entire life and I am likely some older than you take me for."

Mark E. Dupont waved a "Pshaw" hand in pleased self-deprecation. "And by the way," Buckeye Jim said, "I'm a Jew."

II

With Britain's defeat of France in 1763, the dreams of a French empire in Illinois ended. In the south of the state, such lasting place names as Vincennes, Prairie du Rocher, Bellefontaine are usually so mispronounced in southern Illinois twang as to be unrecognizable to any Frenchman.

But today, in Ft. Lorraine, Illinois, in Union Grove County, "an experiment in planned living" is being conducted that makes many of the local citizenry proclaim their community "a heaven on earth."

The "social scientist" responsible is C. Cooper Legrand, Jr., who owns the Old Legrand and Washauconda River Mining Corporation, one of the smaller operations in the region—"but one of the safest," Legrand stresses. A childless widower, C. Cooper Legrand is usually addressed good-naturedly by his employees as "June," or "Juney." With enthusiastic forthrightness, he states, "Yes, we are working together to create a utopia, an earthly paradise if you will. After all, my father created hell."

In addition to owning the mines, the Legrand family built and owns much of the town of Ft. Lorraine itself, renting living quarters to its laborers. But these houses are a far cry today from what they were in "the not-so-good old days." According to the Illinois Coal Report for 1898, these dwellings "lacked central heating and running water. One outhouse privy served six homes. Workers led 'joyless, brutal, dangerous lives,' and had little opportunity to 'even dare to dream of bettering themselves.'"

"My father died in 1910, and I bear him no grudge, and I hope others do not. He was not cruel, merely unenlightened," states Legrand. "I was 22 at his passing, and I felt myself ready. I had studied in Europe, in France, England, and Germany. I had visited Russia. I knew that if capitalism did not change, it would be brought down, that there would be a revolution in blood and fire. History would condemn those who reaped inhumane profits from the sufferings of the masses. I envisioned a decent, compassionate capitalism, one that has at its root the understanding that the human experience is one we all share."

Upon assuming the mantle of leadership, Legrand immediately instituted new safety features in the mining operations, and transformed the workers' "squalid huts" into real homes. He opened negotiations with the United Mine Workers of America and his operations today are 100% union.

Not infrequently, C. Cooper Legrand, Jr. is asked if he is a "leftist," or even a Socialist or Communist, and in this part of the country, these are damning labels.

But Legrand laughs at such allegations of "Un-Americanism." "What I am is a progressive," he maintains. "I believe in people. I'm working for a better world for all of us, without the invisible walls that have kept people apart for too long."

From "Utopia in Illinois?", a feature article by Roy L. Potts, *St. Louis Tribune-Leader*, May 10, 1924.

"Horseshit."

Mark E. Dupont, Grand Exalted Cyclops of the Knights of the Ku Klux Klan; a private response to the above article.

The Knights of the Ku Klux Klan stand for the purest ideals of native-born, white, Gentile four-square Americanism:
The tenets of the Christian religion.
The protection and nurturing of white womanhood.
The freedom, under law, of the individual.
The "right to work" of the American working-man; his individual liberty to enter into such business negotiations and private and personal contracts as he chooses.

From a two-color handbill entitled "The Fiery Cross: America's Guiding Light," written by Mark E. Dupont and the Rev. James E. Scurlock, January, 1924

"Horseshit."

C. Cooper Legrand, Jr., in a private response to the above quoted handbill, prior to his ripping it to pieces as he laughed.

III

He liked it.

By that afternoon, he'd walked here and he'd walked there, and after a time, he knew Ft. Lorraine was the right place.

A little girl on the east side sold him a one-penny lemonade, ferociously cold and snapping with lemon.

He saw a blue jay.

A negro woman on the front porch of a neat little house in a neighborhood of neat little houses called to him.

"Sir?" She held her little boy by the hand, a child of perhaps five or six.

Buckeye Jim went up the walk. He liked the way she sounded, not the "hiding away" voice black folks often use for white people.

"You lost?"

No.

No one is lost; no one is forsaken, were the words that came to his mind.

There were flowers in the yard. Impatiens. Pink and yellow roses. And tulips. July, and so hot, and yet the tulips were still here and lovely.

A happy perplexity filled his head, and he felt a small grin growing that he knew to be silly. Maybe at last, at last, it was coming around! Coming around here, in Ft. Lorraine, and maybe this town would be a light unto the nations ...

He was, he said, just sort of scouting the territory, and he told her his name.

She was Mrs. Willoughby. Her little boy was Paulie Jason. The child drew closer to her. "My Paulie can't talk. He can hear, but he can't talk. Doctors don't know as to why it is."

Buckeye Jim put his small straw suitcase down on the walk. He reached into his pocket. "Yes! I thought I had me one. And it's an extra special lucky one!"

A snap of thumb launched the buckeye. At the top of its arc, it hung there ...

... and there it hung—

Then Paulie Jason let loose his momma and slowly, slowly, his hand swam out as the buckeye dropped through weighted depths of air to land on his palm and his fingers closed over it.

Buckeye Jim turned and walked away.

Paulie Jason said, "Goodbye, Mr. Buckeye Jim."

IV

Socialism, communism, and other doctrines have played no part in the violence and murder which have brought such ill fame to the "queen of Egypt."

—William L. Chenery in *The Century*

... respect to Mr. Chenery, this self-proclaimed Sage of Sesser holds that we are just as willing to kill for doctrines as your most radical, bearded, bomb-toting, Eastern European anarchist. Many of our law-enforcement officials and politicians are willing to kill for the doctrine, "Under the Table and in My Palm," while our bootleggers resort to violence to enforce the "Right of Americans to Get Drunk." Our Kluxers, of course, will take up arms in defense of every town's prerogative to conduct festive lynching bees, while I personally know at least two Methodist churches whose congregations load the cannons if you try to take away their covered-dish potluck dinner, which they hold as a sacrament.

Of course we Egyptians, when we lack doctrines to kill for, will quite happily kill because a) we've nothing more interesting to do and b) our nation expects us to act like savages.

—Brian Robert Moore, "I'll Tell You What!"

ლ • ლ

Son of a bitch! Mark E. Dupont, THE Grand Exalted Cyclops, did not hold with unnecessary violence, but at this particular instant, he could violently put a new Montgomery Ward steel-toe work boot all the way up that man's ...

Mr. C. Cooper Legrand, Jr., "Call me June," trying to be "plain folks," but oh, the man was just so full of himself!

48

Talk reason to him. That's what the Illinois Coal and Power Company wanted its designee (and rising member of the management team!) Mark E. Dupont to do.

Illinois Coal and Power would like Legrand to sell them his enterprise. Not that Legrand was real competition, not with I C and P's far-cheaper strip mining process and non-union operation ...

—But I like having a coal mine, Mark! It's fun!

Negotiations could begin immediately. Accommodations could be reached with the union. Mr. Legrand could play a role on a board of directors ...

Mr. Legrand, whether you know it or not, there was trouble stirring; many of Egypt's citizens did not hold with white and colored living and working together like that—

—Mark, when they come off their shift, all you see is eyes, so you can't tell a colored coal miner from a white one!

—this union thing, well, in the long run, it might DE-stroy individual incentive ...

—meant no one was cheated and everyone got what was coming to him. Do unto others and all that, Mark ...

(Like to give you what's coming to you! Like to do unto you until you're done for certain, chucking Bible at me when nobody ever sees you at church!

(Hmm, could be some of the fancy learning you got overseas included how to spurn the Lord your God? You an atheist, Juney-Bug? By the way, how long your wife's gone and you still single and no lady around but that giant mammy house-keeper? Could be you more of a Jane than a June, Mr. Legrand?)

At sunset of a frustrating day, Dupont pulled up in front of his home in Herrin. If Dupont had been able to get things moving right, he'd been virtually promised the super's position at the Illinois Coal and Power's Ft. Lorraine mines!

But ...

Say, what the hell?

He picked it off the seat of his new Oakland All American Six Phaeton.

A buckeye.

That guy this morning, that sort of mush brain ... The buckeye felt damn bad, he thought.

That's when lightning hit.

Lightning did not blast down from the heavens.

It burst from deep within him, and he felt the searing anguish in his eyes, felt his blood boil, felt his heart blaze and burn and turn to hard, black coal. And he felt a hellish hand wrap around his soul and squeeze!

The power of it threw him against the car door with enough force to spring it. He did a back somersault, losing his hat in the process. He pushed himself up to his hands and knees.

"Aaaaah! Aaaaah!" he shrieked, but it was a thin shriek, all breath and tightness. Jesus! Jesus!

Save me!

In spiritual and physical agony, his American flag collar-pin falling into the disgusting Niagara as he vomited and vomited …

…in the fetid black and green foaming spew from his guts, he could see incredibly tiny frogs, obscenely clean and shining-eyed…The Devil had him! He could not doubt! The Devil …

In his anguish, he comprehended it. The Devil could don many guises …

Buckeye Jim! Oh Lord, deliver me, Dupont begged, for The Devil has laid his fiery hands upon thy servant!

Somehow, somehow, Legrand, atheist nigger lover DEVIL WORSHIPER! had arranged it all. He understood that without any evidence but the revelation of his tormented spirit.

Dupont staggered to his feet, slumped against the car. A sudden cramp, and drool and frogs—he could feel them on his tongue and palate!—leaked out of his mouth down his clothes.

Up at his house, he heard the commotion.

"What is it? What?!?"

What it was was he was DAMNED!

He lurched into the car. He needed God's help.

"Please, God, please …" he whispered. The automobile jerked away, as he squinted to see through his tears.

He had to get to Granny Gunger!

☙ • ☙

Give me that old-time religion!
It's good enough for me!

Granny Gunger had a regal and hideous demeanor as she presided at the rickety table in her hovel out near the tracks at Whittington Curve, a prime location because, when a train slowed for the turn, coal would tumble from the tender and she'd reap the bounty of Luck and the Illinois

Central Railroad.

Granny Gunger came from the hills. She knew dowsing and how to draw fire out of wounds. She could stop bleeding or set bones. She could not re-grow an eye, however, and so there was the mucus-and-muscle rippling empty socket where her drunken father had accidentally thumbed her when all he'd meant to do was punch her.

"You stink, Mister Dupont. You stink like you crawled up a OH-possum's ass," Granny Gunger said. Granny Gunger was known for plain speaking.

Dupont told her why he'd come.

"Frogs," she said. "Frogs is bad. You got strong enemies doin' Satan's bidding. Mister Dupont, the Old Deceiver wants you. You're in sorry shape now, and I don't think you'll like eternity in hell much better."

"Help me, Granny!"

"You got faith, Mister Dupont? You got true faith and the courage of it?"

"Yes."

"You got a RE-solve for God A'mighty to put you to the test?"

Dupont shivered. "Yes," he whispered.

"You got five dollars?"

He nodded.

Granny Gunger slouched over to the black box, unfastened the chain, opened the padlock and reached in. Mark E. Dupont prayed as he had never prayed before.

At just under three feet, Sweet Mercy was not the biggest diamondback rattlesnake in the universe, but he was a lovely one, with radiant coloring and perhaps the snakiest eyes ever to grace the mean triangle of a rattler's head.

Granny Gunger kissed Sweet Mercy right at the bony ridge of his nose.

Sweet Mercy rattled happily.

"They shall take up serpents," Granny Gunger quoted scripture. Then she improvised, as she hobbled to Dupont. "For if they be a generation of vipers, what profiteth a man to dwell far from the tabernacle as he goes up to the Land of Goshen?"

Mark E. Dupont thought, prayed, and entreated the Lord.

"Pucker up now," Granny Gunger said. "Let the kiss of salvation come to you."

Dupont closed his eyes. He puckered. He heard Sweet Mercy's rattle. He felt the snake's subtle breath—sugary, like the breath of a baby.

Then Sweet Mercy's forked tongue flicked against the dry, chubby, pursed lips.

Dupont flew to the floor, landing on his heels and the back of his head.

And when he could rise, he did not doubt.

He knew it—because he FELT it! HALLELUJAH! Free! Saved! Praise God!

Delivered! he thought, as Sweet Mercy got delivered back to his box.

"Now, Mister Dupont," Granny Gunger said, "we got to do us some plannin'! We got to take some precautionary actions. We got to make sure. We must confound your enemies."

"Yes."

"I got somethin' special," Granny Gunger said. "It's got nightshade and a bloody thorn and the lips and eggs of a stone-blind fish in it."

"What does it do?"

"You'd best believe it does just fine."

After Dupont's departure—preceded by her reminding him of the five dollars he owed her—Granny Gunger sat with Sweet Mercy in her lap, petting the diamondback like a tabby. "Well," she said, "told him the Old Deceiver wanted him, and now the Old Deceiver's got him."

She laughed. "Don't you?"

Sweet Mercy rattled in a way that sounded almost exactly like Granny Gunger's laugh.

V

Prior to beginning another insightful commentary on our ever-interesting Egypt, I wish to thank those who have been kind enough to write the *Sentinel* comparing me with Mr. H. L. Mencken, and offering to tar-and-feather us both as soon as we can find the time for this singular honor. While I greatly admire Mr. Mencken's writings, I find him far too optimistic about the future of the allegedly human race.

Now, let's talk about the pride of Egypt: A true crime lord.

With the passing of the years, it becomes more and more difficult to distinguish Charlie Birger from the "legend of Charlie Birger."

I knew and liked Charlie. On occasion, I bought him an illegal beer at his illegal roadhouse, and he bought me one. We told one another jokes, few of which could be printed in this newspaper.

As his acquaintance, then, I will tell you I do not believe that the shady owner of Shady Rest rode the rodeo circuit with Tom Mix, but I have seen him on horseback and cannot doubt his formidable skills.

I do not believe that, following an argument in a St. Louis speakeasy, Charlie fought to an impromptu bloody draw with Jack Dempsey, but I believe he would go to the line against anyone of any size because I have seen him do just that.

More folks liked Charlie than not, and they had reason. The poor of Harrisburg knew his charity. A good number of men found employment, if not necessarily of the legal variety, because of Birger. He had wit, grace, and courage. He was a man's man, and on occasion displayed a streak of sentimentality that would have been derided in a less masculine fellow.

Above all, Charlie Birger was the steadfast friend.

If Charlie liked you, he'd kill anybody for you.

—Brian Robert Moore, "I'll Tell You What!"

ɞ • ɞ

Tuesday, July 13, 1925

A slow afternoon at Shady Rest, so, nothing much else to do, the boys wanted to see him shoot. Charlie felt frisky and in the mood. They went out back, behind the pole barn.

Though a Tommy was his weapon of choice these days—you had to stay modern and keep up with competition, to say nothing of your enemies!—he took his old Winchester. The boys tossed beer bottles and he snapped off shots from the hip: Eight shots, eight hits.

"That's the way it is done by a shootist, ole hoss," Charlie said. Born in New York City, Charlie Birger spent his youth in the west as a cavalry soldier, a wild-horse breaker, a gambler and a gun-fighter, and he still often spoke the palaver of the range. It had been a good life out there; folks played you straight. You were what you were, what you said, and what you did, and that was all that counted.

Here in Egypt, well, let's just say it was considerable different. You couldn't count on all the cards being on the table. But Charlie had done well; they called him the "King of Egypt."

Now the King needed a suitable chariot.

So after a beer, Charlie and some of the boys drove off to West City, where Joe Adams, mayor, gin-mill owner, and proprietor of a Stutz dealership, was working on a new conveyance for His Royal Majesty!

ↄ • ↄ

Buckeye Jim got hired by the Old Legrand and Washauconda River Mining Corporation.

In the weeks following this uncelestial event, there were other happenings that might be viewed as more interesting or even "curious." One of them involved K. J. Pritchard. One afternoon, when, as usual, he was standing on the square, dark glasses and a tin cup, a cardboard sign around his neck saying—

A VETERAN

I WAS BLINDED FOR LIBERTY'S SAKE

—he sensed someone standing in front of him. He said, "The big war. I was in the big one."

"I was in that one, too."

"It was gas. They didn't have to gas us! It was NOT FAIR!!!"

"Nothing ever is, not in war."

"Help me?"

K. J. Pritchard heard something drop into the tin cup. It didn't sound like a coin. Cheap bastard.

With his left hand, he took it out. It felt like … It felt like a buckeye! He held it up. Yes, that was just what he was looking at, a …

He ripped his dark glasses off, shattered them on the pavement. The bright sunlight burning his eyes, he wept.

ↄ • ↄ

There was a car wreck late one night out past Crenshaw Crossing. A rattle-trap Ford full of young boys and younger girls who were full of shine. In the moonlight, you could see the silvery white of bone punching through flesh, and a head squashed the way you'd swear a head couldn't be squashed, and a bloody mess in which you could not tell twisted metal from human meat.

One of the victims, fifteen-year-old Anna Beulle Diggs, would later say, "I had this strange dream. I heard a voice, kind of like Daddy when he's disappointed and angry both. It said, 'This is foolish, but children ought not to die for being foolish. So all of you, you live. And sometimes you think about just how precious life is.'

"Well, we all did live. Maybe it was plain luck, but such a great big lot of luck like that might be a miracle. I think, anyway …

"I don't know why I've kept it, but when they found us, I had this buckeye in my hand, and I have had it as a lucky piece ever since."

എ • എ

It was heavy dark, the frogs and crickets and night sounds, loud, so loud in his throbbing head. Out in front of The Jolly Sports roadhouse, Sam Washington had a gun and no options. With just the one arm, the other blown into sausage in the explosion at the fireworks factory where he had worked, he couldn't find a job, not anymore. He was colored and he couldn't read and he was as tapped-out as a man could get.

Once he'd been a pretty good gut-bucket piano player. Not a real professor like Jelly Roll or Willie The Lion, or even the white boy, Art Hodes, but he might have had the makings of a tickler. He used to dream, one arm ago, of going to New York and making records and playing for the swells, just like Mr. Jelly Lord.

Once he had a dream and now he had a gun.

Then there was a white man standing in front of him. He seemed to pop up just like a haunt, but his smile was a man's.

"Mr. Washington, let's make a trade. Let's swap death for life. You give me the pistol. I give you …"

Washington knew it was all right …

The man said, "Now what you do is take your dream and go on and live it. Play the piano, Mr. Washington."

"I don't know, sir. You need ten fingers to play piano."

"How many you got?"

"Five."

"So move the five twice as fast."

എ • എ

… strange reports that none other than Jesus, formerly of Nazareth, is paying a visit. Call me a doubting Thomas, but I fear our Egypt an unlikely locale for the Second Coming. Our civic-minded Kluxers (and clucks!), enforcing the Volstead Act, will not tolerate His turning water into wine, the unions will move if He attempts to practice His carpentry without getting a card, and few of our churches will listen for five seconds to this "foreigner's" ludicrous doctrines of compassion, charity, and tolerance.

—Brian Robert Moore, "I'll Tell You What!"

ɔ • ɔ

Tuesday, August 17, 1925
First Shift at Old Coop #3

He had on his British design helmet (the best and safest) and his Davis lamp. Like always, he stepped into the cage first, before the others, all of them: Oren, Dicey, Connie, The Buds (Little Bud and Hey Bud), Hezzie, Luka, a team of 26 men.

No matter how many years they'd been in the mines, the other fellows knew that moment's hesitation, that instant of fear when you understand it is possible for the blackness to engulf you forever.

Buckeye Jim knew darkness. He was summoned forth from the darkness.

Don't fear, don't fear. That is what he wanted to tell them, what he wanted to tell everyone. Love one another and do not be afraid.

But they were not ready to hear it yet.

So he smiled the smile that made the others think him a "nice fella," though "no winner in the Mental Olympics, if y'know what I mean." Not that you had to be a chess champion to heft a shovel in a coal mine, and he certainly was one for that!

Buckeye Jim liked the work. He liked the feeling of using his muscles, his back, arms, and legs. He liked the idea that darkness, the coal, became heat and flame.

There was much for Buckeye Jim to like these days. He lived in Spartacus House, one of two company-owned residences for single men. It was a lot like an Army barracks: clean, fresh sheets every week, showers with limitless hot water, and detective and science magazines, and a Victrola and a player piano, and pretty pictures on the walls; he paid two dollars a month room and board. He liked the men he lived and worked with. Tonight, he'd go on out with them and have him a beer or two.

And of course he liked to play the banjo—

ɔ • ɔ

… one hell of a picker! Carrying his Thompson submachine gun, Charlie Birger walked over to the table of Ft. Lorraine miners at his roadhouse, The Shady Rest. After 11, but the joint still had a good crowd, even though tomorrow was work day. White and colored drank at the Shady Rest—and if somebody purple showed and had a nickel for a beer, he'd be welcome, too—and there was even a gigantic Ojibway Indian, Big Tommy Tabeshaw, and so at the place, you might hear Italian, Polish, Lithuanian, Rumanian or Ojibway. (When he was really lost in the firewater, Tommy talked to himself and to the "Ojibway ghosts" in his head.)

Charlie told the banjo player that he plainly admired the way he could fram away on that five-string.

The banjo player said he appreciated the compliment, but hoped Shady Rest's owner wouldn't get to framming away on his instrument.

Charlie Birger laughed like hell. No, no, no, his Tommy meant protection for himself and his guests. There were some shitheels, Kluxer bastards mostly, didn't like his catering to a "mixed clientele." And, for that matter, they weren't too delighted with Mr. C. Birger, Esquire, being a co-religionist of Moses.

"My name is Buckeye Jim." The banjo player offered his hand. He said, "*Shalom Aleichem*," the traditional Hebrew greeting, "Peace be unto you."

Charlie Birger blanched. "*Aleichem Shalom*," he said softly. "And unto you, peace." The gleam in his eyes might have been tears. "You're …"

Buckeye Jim shrugged. "*Vuden?*" Loosely translated, the Yiddish term meant, "What did you expect?"

"I'll be damned," Charlie Birger said. "A hillbilly Yid! A Yid-billy! Well, me, too, I reckon!"

Birger bellowed to the bar, "This gentleman and his friends drink free! Tonight and every night."

He turned back to Buckeye Jim. "You have yourself a friend in Charlie Birger."

"Thank you," Buckeye Jim said. "A man needs all the friends he can get."

VI

Sunday, September 12, 1925

God forgive me, Opal Rae Brown thought. If He did, it would be long before she forgave herself.

Opal Rae puttered about, a huge woman who seemed to fill up all the space in the vast kitchen that had so long been her domain. Oh, Lord, he was a good man and she had to …

He was a white man, she tried to tell herself, and if every white man in the country America decided to swallow a Mason jar full of iodine, lye, and turpentine, now wasn't that just too bad? Besides ...

Besides, she was scared, she was scared in every one of her 280 pounds. That man, that Mr. Dupont, had never raised his voice as he told her this, and told her that, as he asked her this and then asked her, "You ever smell black skin burning? You are sort of heavy-set, so I imagine it would take a long time for the fire to bubble and blister and cook all the meat right off your bones."

He gave her orders and the "secret potion" she was to add to the food (Now don't you worry, just some fish eggs and stuff) and a hundred dollars. The money would take her north, she vowed. Nobody burned colored people in New York, not as she had heard, anyway.

She took a deep breath, then another.

Then she took Mr. C. Cooper Legrand, Jr. his evening meal. The next day, he was in Ft. Lorraine's hospital, condition—critical.

☙ • ☙

Buckeye Jim couldn't sleep. He went for a walk, moonlight his guide. At midnight, that empty moment that is neither one day or another, he was far from Ft. Lorraine, deep into the rolling woods. He relished the coolness and earth smells, the myriad night sounds, the eternal celebration and affirmation of life.

Oh, he did not want to die. Not again.

Ahead, on the path that wasn't a path but simply the way he chose, he saw the gleaming eyes. The rattler's precise, gorgeous diamond patterns shone hypnotically. It rose up like a cobra, shifting left and right, the forked tongue a flicker-blur.

Surprised?

"Not hardly," Buckeye Jim said. "Sure you're here. You're everywhere." He took out the lucky buckeye and flipped it, caught it, flipped it. "But you're not going to win, you know. Each time, we get closer."

Fool!

"Fool? Maybe. But God needs His fools."

Do you not see? Each time and every time Man is given a chance to damn himself, he says, "Yes, thanks, and might you have a few extra opportunities for my friends?" The victory will be mine!

"No," Buckeye Jim said, "Man is not born to lose." The buckeye flew up high and then higher and came down in his palm. Buckeye Jim grinned.

"Man is born to win."

ↂ • ↂ

On Wednesday, condition now "serious/guarded," Legrand had visitors, representatives of the Illinois Coal and Power Company—Mark E. Dupont among them. They did not want to tire him out, to do anthing that might slow his recovery.

Inside of 15 minutes, C. Cooper Legrand sold them everything.

VII

Buckeye Jim, weave and spin,
 Time to go, Buckeye Jim.
"Buckeye Jim," American folk song

There will always be questions, but I knew C. Cooper Legrand, Jr. I drank coffee with him, went to New York with him to hear Emma Goldman, and spent a long, memorable, mentally exhilarating night, arguing with him over the Nihilistic philosophy of Bakunin; both of us agreed that the man had to be an idiot if all he would allow to go undestroyed would be Beethoven's Sixth, the closest the composer ever came to failure.

Juney Legrand was all right.

So to my dying day, I will not accept that he willfully betrayed the people of Ft. Lorraine or his dream of a world of brotherhood and harmony.

They did something to him. I know they did. As incredible as this may sound, coming from a man who is reputed to be sane, if surly, I have come to believe there are conspiracies meant to stifle and suppress Mankind as we struggle to attain the next step on the moral and ethical evolutionary ladder.

A conspiracy of ???

The Left will tell you it is a wicked collusion of Capital and Government. Too-imaginative pulp-magazine fans will offer you theories based on a wicked cabal inside our hollow Earth. Then there are preachers who will tell you it is all the work of the Devil ...

—Brian Robert Moore, "I'll Tell You What!"

NEW MOON ON THE WATER

❧ • ❧

Monday, September 27, 1925

In the basement of Ft. Lorraine's Masonic Temple, they argued and argued, called each other names, threw about the words, "scab," "fink," and, a phrase frequently used in the American labor movement: "Dumb son-of-a-bitch!" They would march on the state capitol! The nation's capitol! A splinter group said there was a case for assassination—if they could figure out who to assassinate.

They waited to hear from the president of United Mine Workers of America, John L. Lewis. Last time, he said the wrong thing; it provided impetus for the Herrin Massacre of '22.

This time he said nothing.

The Illinois Coal and Power Company meant to take possession of the mines—the town. But damn all and double-damn, it was not the property of I C and P; Ft. Lorraine was their town! The mines were their mines. It was their labor that gave them ownership, their muscle and sweat and not a capitalist's dollars!

It was theirs, damn all! They meant to keep it! If it took guns to …

It went on and on, until, at last—

Now they are ready to listen, Buckeye Jim said to himself. He was sad. He liked these men. He did not want to leave them. He thought about bitter cups. He thought about the Lord's will. He thought about what he had to do.

Then Buckeye Jim said he wanted to talk. He talked easy and slow, flipping a buckeye.

He talked and they heard him.

Funny, how a guy you don't figure all that equipped with smartness can talk to you in a way that makes you say, "Why, yes indeed! That is what we have to do."

That is what they did.

They barricaded the northern approach to Ft. Lorraine. They left their guns at home, but they turned over worn-out tin-can cars, piled up bales of hay, and strung barbed wire the way some had learned in the War to End All Wars.

Behind their barricade, they linked arms, the black men and the white men.

They were a living chain across the Washauconda Bridge.

They were ready.

❧ • ❧

To assist in the I C and P's taking possession of its properties were men in smart-looking uniforms, all duly deputized, bayonets on their rifles.

From Sesser and Marion and Ina and dozens of other towns came non-union miners, needing work, armed with baseball bats, shotguns, pistols, and pitchforks, determined to get these sorry niggers and Bolsheviks out of their way.

Mark E. Dupont led the largest delegation, the stalwarts of the Klan. The Grand Exalted Cyclops, in his robes of flowing white, a regulation Army Springfield under his arm. Now he'd claim ... his!

His, damn all! Mr. Mark E. Dupont, the new General Superintendent of ICP's Ft. Lorraine holdings, had the might and purity and right of the Klan stepping smartly behind him, armed with everything from a Quackenbush boy's model single-shot to a log chain!

The forces of the Illinois Coal and Power Company tramped onward.

The men of Ft. Lorraine waited.

The army of the Illinois Coal and Power Company came closer, ranks tightening as they trod upon the vast length of the Washauconda Bridge.

Waiting for them, someone called out, "Stand firm! Union men, comrades in the war!"

Men with bayonets, men in miner's hats, men in KKK garb, moved forward.

The men at the barricades sang:
Hold the fort,
Brave union miners!
Show no fear,
Be strong!

❧ • ❧

At the other end of the bridge, taunting voices called, "Let's kill us some niggers!"

"Turkey shoot! They ain't got a gobbler's chance!"

The I C and P troops drew closer. The bridge shook with their out-of-step march. The collage of sounds was sinister and portentous: muttering and shouts, the hiss and whisper and bubblings of the Washauconda below, the click-ready sound of firearms.

You could smell oil and gunpowder.

"You are an unlawful assembly, blocking a public thoroughfare!" Dupont called out. "Give way immediately or perish!" He liked the formality of his proclamation.

He did not like the roared response it drew from a defender of Ft. Lorraine: "You get up on your momma's shoulders and kiss my ass."

When less than a hundred yards separated the men of Ft. Lorraine from the I C and P forces, Buckeye Jim suddenly appeared between them.

Quizzical, because nobody really saw him walk there, but there he was. It stopped them all.

Buckeye Jim wasn't flipping a lucky buckeye. Not this time. He had his arms up and out, as though he were Moses helping God push back the walls of water to part the Red Sea. There are some still living who, even to this very day, will tell you the man was transfigured.

Buckeye Jim had something to say.

ↇ • ↇ

Nothing happened he didn't know about. Not in his kingdom.

Because—you'd better know it and you're mighty well told!— Charlie Birger was the King of Egypt!

Ft. Lorraine? Good boys, there, and his Yid friend, Buckeye Jim, so …

Time for damned sure to hitch the horses to the king's chariot. Except he didn't need horses.

ↇ • ↇ

Everyone stayed quiet. Everyone heard him.

He said, "Some of you don't know me, and some of you know me as Buckeye Jim. But years back, years and years and years ago, I was the one they talk about in the Bible. They call me 'The Widow's Son.' I was dead, just as dead as Mr. Lazarus, but then Jesus called to me and said, 'Come forth from your tomb.'

"Well, I was grateful and such, and I politely thanked Him, but I asked him why He had summoned me from the ever-dark of death into the light of life.

"Didn't I like being alive? Didn't I want to do the work of the living God, the God of the living?

"I thought about that and thought about that—

"Until I said, 'Why, yes, I guess I do.'

"Now this is what Jesus told me. This is what He wants me to tell you.

"Jesus came to bring hope. He said it was my job to be hope, because I'd been dead and now I was alive.

"We are all the children of God. The Devil and the darkness will never defeat us!

"Jesus told me something more.

"He said He would come again.

"He said He would return—on the day after He no longer was needed!

"That means it's up to us to set it all right.

"And we can start to do that. We can start now."

There was silence.

And almost everyone stood frozen.

But not Mark E. Dupont, who thought, *The Devil can quote scripture for his own purpose*. Dupont slammed the stock of his Springfield into his shoulder and fired.

The bullet caught Buckeye Jim just to the left of the heart. He flew backward, slammed into the bridge railing a slice of an instant after his blood and fragments of bone did, and, loose-limbed, flipped over. If his body splashed as it plunged into the river, no one heard it.

The I C and P forces let out a collective yell that drowned out a sudden roar of thunder in the clear sky above.

They charged.

☙ • ❧

"Give it all you've got," Charlie Birger commanded. The driver of the brand-new armored car obliged. The powerful Stutz engine thrummed. The heavy sheet metal riveted and welded to the auto slowed it and guaranteed nothing could stand in its way. Instead of a windshield or windows, the car had gun slits. Except for treads, it was a tank—and its solid rubber tires weren't about to be knocked out by any varmint hunter's firepower.

It was the lead vehicle of three. Two cars loaded with Birger men followed.

Charlie might have been confused, once they hit the bridge, but with the KKK bastards decked out like Monday wash on the line, why, he knew who to shoot! So Charlie popped the heavy hatch, and rose up to let loose with a quick spray from Mr. Tommy. One blast felt so fine, the gun a roaring quiver in his hands, that he fired off another. He heard the guns of his army behind him. He saw the befuddled I C P men turn, trying to figure what the hell. There was sporadic return fire, slugs pinging off the metal around him.

"Welcome to Egypt's O.K. Corral," Charlie yelled. He laughed and fired off another burst.

Then another.

With the next one, he totally hem-stitched Mark E. Dupont.

Inside of three minutes, 43 men lay dead on the Washauconda bridge, most of them Kluxers; another 75 or 81 or 58 (depending on which account of the conflict you believe) were wounded and conveyed to area hospitals.

Most historians cite the "Battle of Washauconda Bridge" as the end of the Klan's power in southern Illinois.

Charlie Birger and his warriors retreated to Shady Rest and drank beer. The King could not figure where Buckeye Jim might have disappeared to. He hoped he would turn up. He wished him luck.

˜ Fellow played one fine banjo.

Epilogue

Mark E. Dupont received one of the most elaborate Klan funerals in the history of the organization. A vice-president of I C and P gave the eulogy, saying Dupont was one of the company's finest assistant superintendents; after the funeral, he presented Mrs. Dupont with a check for 50 dollars.

Virtually everyone employed by the Old Legrand and Washauconda River Mining Corporation was fired and had to leave Ft. Lorraine. The union did not regain any foothold in the region until FDR.

Charlie Birger had a falling-out with Joe Adams, who'd built "The King of Egypt's" armored car, and was convicted of arranging the man's murder.

Charlie was hanged on April 18, 1929, the last man legally executed in this way in the state. Legend has it that the night before his execution, Charlie had a lanky visitor, who talked and joked a while with him, then handed him a buckeye.

Perhaps that is the reason that, on the scaffold, Charlie's last words were, "It is a beautiful world.

"Goodbye."

AS OTHERS SEE US

My passion is the killing of *Homo sapiens*, sub-genus, female: the chirpy, the flirty, the pouty and the perky; the tarnished dove with the heart of brass who masquerades as the good pal, the desperate dame desiring what hapless hubby cannot provide, that comely cupcake at the midnight clambake, etc., etc. If in order to be true to your essential nature, you must skirt, flout, ignore, and abhor the laws of Man, why, then it's a matter of reason that you must be extraordinarily clever so that your dastardly doings, your evil enterprises, your many, many, many murders are not detected.

No joke, Jake. They find you out, you get a fried fundament, a bullet in the brisket, or hemp-enhanced height.

You do not have to be Nietzsche to comprehend this Philosophical Principle: If you would murder with impunity and joy, you must assume suitable disguises so that you seemingly become Callow Calvin or *Monsieur* Mundane or Andy A. Nonymous. You must adopt camouflage that makes non-entity Seymour Citizen and Clint Common Clay declare you Guiltless Guy, Norman Normal, Ordinary Orville. their peer and pal and *compadre*.

By chance and Mendelian genealogy, I have a countenance neither ugly nor handsome: the proper number of features in a fairly symmetric arrangement; mine is a generic faceless face of the Man of the Crowd, the visage of the ice-man virtually indistinguishable from that block on his shoulder, or the mug of the elementary-school janitor the principal wouldn't remark were that custodian sweeping the halls with a large cat tied on a mop handle. Your Everyday Egg, Just Plain Bill/Joe/Uriah, I Yam What I Yam and 'at's All What I Yam—with one exception.

I am big.

Oh, by no means sideshow-sized, no competition to Cardiff, nor to the latest Packard to roll off the assembly line, but heavy-boned and heavy-bodied, with weight ranging between 230 and 250 and height at six-four. My feet are only elevens but my hands, if not quite hams, are assuredly not slender strips of bacon. And yes, I am strong, bucking barley or shoveling cow flop on the farm, toting sofas and sideboards as a furniture mover in the city, hooking and hustling crates on the longshore, why, I tender an honest day's work for your Depression-day dime.

Of course, my strength has other uses. That little lady in Misanthrope, Maine, ah, she would not put an end to her peep-peep-peeping prattle, so I put a single, cautionary punch to her vocal cords, and her throat swelled shut and she was gasping for breath, so I held her nose and she died.

Metaphysical Meditation: Women are not strong; is it because they are both the representation and reality of weakness that it is so pleasing to kill them? Once there was a woman—Road Apple, Rhode Island? Ignorance, Indiana?—who dared to slap me three times. I allowed it, novel sensation that it was, and, in truth, I felt the last slap, felt the line of her fingers below my ear and on the hinge of my jaw, felt a burning and anger and a thrumming energy that made me hurt and hurt and hurt her for a quite some time before she died.

But I digress. The point you are no doubt pondering is how can I veil my vastness, minimize my massiveness, tone down my tonnage? An irony: You notice big people because they attempt not to look big. Conversely, you notice little people because they seek not to look little: Napoleon, oh, he was that short guy who conquered the world. "Ah, he eeze one eensy-weensie maybe Emperor, *mais non! Sacre bleu, le* shrimp, *le* minuscule megalomaniac, what he lacks in height, he makes up in lack of height!"

Sizable though I am I do not slump, I do not slouch, I do not thrust my mitts majorus in my pockets, do not plaster my enormous elbows tight to my floating ribs as though apologizing for intruding on more planetary space than I should be allotted.

Big, I am so big I allow myself to be—but with a difference. I give you a diversion, a distraction, a sleight of self so that you take no note of my stature.

Call me Railroad Red. Was it in the town of Despond, Delaware or perhaps North Jesus, New Jersey that I took on that identity? Surely you radio and record connoisseurs of hillbilly music, that three-chord slough of whining sentiment and stupidity, remember old Railroad Red?

A pause ... Why, you remember Jimmie Rodgers, the consummate consumptive, the Yodelin' Brakeman, jug ears on a jug head and the weary adenoidal voice? Jimmie's the Pappy of Country Music, and Railroad Red was none other than Jimmie-Bub's best bindlestiff buddy, a rail-rider, freight-car commuter sans ticket du passage.... Sho', I played GIH-tah on "Blue Yodel #7, #12, and # 17" ... #17, the one he recorded jes' three nights 'fore he coughed out his left (or was it the right) lung and died ...

'Course, I wouldn't be playin' for a while, you know, 'cause … My left arm was a-hangin' in a cast in a sling, you see, 'cause I took a fall when that train come on to a curve and I tried to grab my Gibson Tennessee flat-top 'fore it flew out the … (I did indeed have a Gibson flat-top; the original owner currently plays harp in the Celestial Enesemble.)

No, little girl, I'm not used to askin' for he'p. Jes' not comfortable or suited for it. Well, thank you. Well, I don' know what to say. I've not had that much kindness come to me, no, and so I don't …

Oh, you do sing pretty, girl. I wisht I could set to strummin' my GIH-tah; I'd play a G minus chord and then sorta ease on in and …

Why, yes, I surely do understand why you want to be a-singin' on the radio, little lady.

Dense Dora, Dim Dora, Double dose of Dumb Dora. I couldn't play guitar if you gave me a graft of Eddie-goddamned-Lang's hands, but I sure as hell can bash your pretty head with my busted arm so that pink and gray brainless brain comes oozing and dribbling out of your eyes, nose, and ears.

Wa'l shucks, honey britches, yuh gone and got yerse'f all kilt to death, my li'l cornpone possum pie …

What it is, you see, is that *Americanus moronus* tends to take a man at his word, so my word has made me a river-leapin' stump preacher (during which tenure I brought several young ladies right to the Lord!), a Pennsylvania organizer for the UMW (Call me Big Biff Beidermann!), a carnival patch on the Riggaby and Tells circuit, a salesman for Regal motion picture projectors, a doctor whose kindness toward those in need of getting out of the family way cost him his license to practice (you can do quite interesting things with a doctor's kit), and once a negro journalist from 126th Street in Harlem ("Why sho' 'nuff, Mistah Kingfish, an' lawdy lawd, I'se de highest high-high-high yaller you ever done seed!), traveling the country to report on race relations (I am without prejudice in matters of skin pigmentation; I killed two dusky darlings, sisters they were, in Pie Crust, Tennessee—or was it Offal, Alabama?)

Hither, yon, and likewise over there, I became for others what I chose to *appear* as and no one ever discerned the duplicitous, murderous ME!

Yet there is more to earning a PhD of Disguise than limping on alternating legs or whistling "God Bless America" when people expect you to play "Making Whoopee" on the kazoo or calling yourself Jack Dempsey when someone asks if you are Wallace Beery.

The best disguise is other people.

It was little … Little Sarah from Flat Tire, Florida or Susan from

NEW MOON ON THE WATER

Misery, Michigan or ...

She was an "S," of that I am positive. I have a mental link between her "S" name and spine, which is what I planned to break. I recollect that precisely, see her / hear that thick, satisfyingly spread-out thump as I slam her bloody face into the wall and swing and then make myself miss so that I hit the wall and not her sacrum and ...

Epiphany! Revelation! *I have a use for Miss S!*

Do I terrify you, baby cakes? Do I bring on fear like you've never known fear, a coldness vibrating from your core? Do you doubt in the slightest that on whim or worry or want I will cut your pit-a-patting heart out of your chest and stuff it down your still-screaming mouth?

Why, of course you will cooperate with me. Thank you. Appreciated. Your assistance will aid me and will also keep you alive. Symbiosis, what?

Call me Blind Otto Kuhlberg, and wasn't he fortunate that his doting sister treated him all right, you bet, 'cause you don't have family, you don't have no one is what that talkative cuss Blind Otto says, because, why, blood is thicker than water (there's an insightful observation), and after all, in unity there is strength, and it's Sissy helps big brother get around and sees that he gets on in the world and there's an old uncle in California who's got a ranch (a farm but all those Pacific Ocean Paupers call their pathetic patch of dirt a ranch!) and that's why they're hitching cross country 'cause they'll have a place with him ...

One day, alas, after "S" had played her not-inconsequential rôle in providing prey as well as serving as attentive, if not exactly enthusiastic witness, she simply collapsed, flew all to flinders: could not stop crying, could not stand up, just sobbed and sobbed, "I can't anymore ..."

Certainement that was the end of her.

But the concept is viable, and thus do I take to disguising myself with other people.

Up to Alaska (Mush you huskies and hush you muskies!) and down to Florida (An alligator in every pot!), in the company of a nineteen-year-old named Annie (I remember the name because, like comic-strip Annie, there was a blankness to her eyes) I killed with invisible impudence, Annie aiding my finding killables, luring them in, watching as I did what I did.

One day, it came to me that Annie was boring.

Au revoir, auf Wiedersehen, and 'at's all she wrote, Annie.

An irony: Womankind is born to dissemble, to be Dame Deception, but somehow cannot withstand the pressure of maintaining the lie created for her by another—or at least a lie created by your most obedient servant, mine own self, toot sweet and notary sojac.

A man, then, I decided. A young man, youth providing malleability, a child of fifteen tender years ...

It felt wrong from the first. My intuition goes fried-radio-tube, all hiss and spark and black smoke smell. You could see him working at it, trying to find a fit for the skin I'd commanded him to assume.

Call me Silent Sylvester, supposedly deaf and mute and he was my nephew; we communicated with flamboyant hand signs, manic gestures, groans, grunts, and sighs. It would have been quite the show had the wee laddie been up to it.

"There's somethin' real queer about you two birds"—everyone's a critic!—this review from a shopgirl who otherwise possessed bread pudding in place of brain cells. She commences to ki-yi-yodel, crummy kismet summons off-duty flatfoot with on-duty revolver drawn and the boy and I amscray, abscond, and head for the hills, post-haste.

Farewell, budding boyo and down you go tender youth (really quite tender, I observed when I ripped him to pieces).

George Tidwell, however, is working out ever so much better. George Tidwell: grinning when something's funny, eyebrows knitting together when reflective, etc., etc. Just one of the fellers, you know, hey, "no stupid sluggo but nothing special, either," nose clean, shoulder to the wheel, and visit to the church every other Sunday and the cathouse maybe every six weeks. Uh-huh. Definitely. Takes one to know blah-blah, and Tidwell, discerns I, is the kind of guy who sees himself one step and maybe two toes ahead of everyone else, the kind of comrade who knows when to lead and when to follow—and when to steal a car and light out, leaving you sucking up the spoiled buttermilk.

Ah, *Monsieur* George Tidwell, prior to our initiating a mutually beneficial partnership (for me!), I must disabuse you of the notion of your innate cleverness. I do so by employing the pedagogical technique of intense pain, which begins with my pinching an ear lobe until George loses consciousness (and can't tell where to find it). When he rouses, he's naked and I hurt him in places afforded me by his nakedness and in so doing I humiliate him, I would venture, to no small degree.

Since then, all has gone well with my unequal partnership with Toady Tidwell. There are nine or ten *femmes* from Itch, Idaho to Crumb Bum, Connecticut who might so testify were the dead capable of voice.

Still, every relationship has its rocky patches. Two months back, I had to provide Georgie Porgie a measure of pain pudding and anguish pie, a refresher that made him cry, and he lay there sobbing, somehow still daring to say, "If I get my hands on a gun," which prompted my doing some things to his hands and then to other areas of his *corpus* until all that came out of his yap was bubbly drool.

Now, California, here we come.

One of my more endearing traits is an endless ability to create for myself a persona who truly fascinates me even as it bamboozles the baboons. This time I've taken to speaking ever so slowly as though I'm painfully searching my vocabulary of perhaps one hundred or so primarily single-syllable words. I let my jaw hang often, particularly when chewing food. If I look at something, I turn my entire head rather than merely shifting my eyes. If I manage to stumble on an idea, I stay on it until it's squashed near to death.

Voila! Here I am: Your All-American Idiot!

Tidwell, I tell him, why, *you* are the bright boy, the brains of the outfit, the top-kick, the kingpin, and the Major-Domo Muckity-Muck! While you'll keep your first name, so that you'll always be sure to respond naturally, I'll arrive at a new last name for you that subtly hints at poetic insight and understanding: Blake? Wordsworth? Ah, let us dare grandiosity: Milton.

And I? Irony.

Big old dumbbell ME? Call me Lennie Small.

FATHER AND SON

It can't be all work and no play, is what my father says. So last Friday he tells me, "Time to take a break. Come on, son. Put on your hat. We're going to the crucifixions."

All right, I think. I always get a kick out of watching Romans at work. Anything and everything is just another job to a Roman. Doesn't matter if it's road-building, nation-conquering, crucifying, Romans do it right.

But these crucifixions aren't as much fun as some you see. The crowd's not into it. Nobody is kidding around with the two thieves, and I'll bet at least half the people up there on Calvary are crying or about to when the Romans get to hammering Jesus onto that cross.

All in all, pretty dull, really. Now, I was at this one crucifixion, and here's the condemned man doing a whole routine. "Nice view ... Hey, my nose itches ... Yo, Jerome, you're going bald ... I never noticed that before."

But you know what Jesus says when they get his cross planted?

"Father, forgive them for they know not what they do."

My father leans down to whisper in my ear, "The hell we don't." I laugh softly.

"Fix your hat, son," my father says.

I pull my hat down lower, making sure the horns on my forehead are covered.

Not long after that, we leave.

Playtime is over and we've got work to do.

NEW MOON ON THE WATER

BIRD'S DEAD

There's a sign with a tipped top hat out in front.

It's got nothing to do with nothing because this is The Commodore's Blue Note.

You walk in. The smoke encircles you and drags you in. Drags you into the music. And there's always music, even when there is no one on the stand. There's a Rockola juke box. There's a phonograph. There's a battered-to-hell Steger and Sons upright piano in the corner—It's Mr. Jelly Lord mainly tickles that one. There's a violin on the wall, supposedly carrying with it a Gypsy curse, but when Stuff Smith comes in and he's feeling all right, he takes down that fiddle, says, "Curse of the Romany, I defy you!" and he sets to hard swinging, and though the notes do not always come in tune, the man is pure virtuoso.

Here. That is right where you are.

The Commodore's Blue Note can be like staying high all the time.

The Commodore's Blue Note can be like when you are under the lowest. This is it, the place, the joint, the saloon, the pad, the locale of … hipsters and shysters and mooches and backsliding preachers. And tailgatin' muffaletta-chompin' juke-jointers and swingers and malingerers and zoot-suiters and add in a shouter and a professor and a half dozen unclassifiable unreconstructed originals.

In The Commodore's Blue Note you sometimes find Ben Webster. Ben Webster at the bar, floating on reefer and slugging down Scotch and there is something pinning those eyes that isn't Scotch or reefer and Ben Webster looks for all the world like an obsidian statue of a gorilla. An ugly gorilla. An acromegaliac, brow-bone-bulging, lantern-jawed, lowland gorilla. But did anyone ever play a sweeter horn? Could anyone do that sweep up the register into nothing but breath and heartbreak like Ben Webster?

Ben Webster is the Ugly who plays so beautiful.

However, unless you want your next suit of clothes to be made out of pine, you do not wish to give insult to Ben Webster. You do not want to hurt Ben Webster's feelings in any way, because Ben Webster is sensitive. He is a soulful man. He is a man who can all too easily take umbrage.

I saw this once. We were at a rent party. Ben Webster came in, sax around his neck, Scotch fumes trailing him like Mighty Clouds of Glory. And some damn fool, this little bit of a country boy, with his hair all country parted down the center, this hayseed, this rube, this chicken plucker, happened to give offense to Ben Webster.

What Country Boy said to Ben Webster was, "Sir, even with that saxophone hanging on the neck, you look like a statue of a gorilla. Obsidian." Ben Webster's feelings were hurt. Ben Webster sort of whispered sometimes when his feelings were hurt and he wanted to sound like Dexter Gordon. Ben Webster whispered to the country boy, "I take umbrage."

The he took Country Boy to the window. What he said was, "I am so full of umbrage that I feel like throwing you out the goddamned window."

Well, if you know anything about Ben Webster, then you know for Ben Webster to feel was no different than to do. He threw Country Boy out the window.

Did I mention that we were about 14 or 15 stories up? As I said, Ben Webster was a sensitive man.

You know who else you might find at The Commodore's Blue Note? Damn near everybody, that is who. One night in walks Miles Davis with Billy Eckstine. Billy was trying to get back into Miles's good graces because Miles had tried to punch him out over five dollars he had tried to cheat Billy out of and Billy had raised up several major lumps beneath Miles's eyes. (He never hit Miles in the mouth. Billy Eckstine was a good friend to Miles and he also understood commerce.) Now Miles was sulking.

Miles's father was a dentist. This shaped Miles, you see. The offspring of dentists are likely to become architects or abstract painters or Existential Christian theologians. Anything but a goddamn dentist.

On any given night at The Commodore's Blue Note, this could be your—

Roll Call!

Behind the bar. It is The Commodore. They call him that because some years ago somebody who claimed to be Wallace Beery gave him a pirate hat. "This here, matey, be the very *chapeau* I was a-wearin' in the movie *Treasure Island*. Now, if you could give me a drink on the house ..."

Nobody drinks on the house at The Commodore's Blue Note. Forget it. But the Commodore liked the hat. He gave the man who claimed to be Wallace Beery a drink for it. He perched it on his head. "Avast, lubbers," the Commodore would say. "Keelhaul the bilges. Mizzen the poop deck." Even bartenders dream of the sea.

Roll Call:

Billie Holiday, *here*. That gardenia in her hair. Oh, doesn't she think she is the stuff?

That is because she *is* the stuff. Ethel Waters did not like her. Ethel Waters said, "She just thinks she's the stuff, don't she? And when she sings, she sounds like her shoes are too tight."

Ethel Waters. This is the real Ethel Waters. This is not the Ethel Waters who got to being the Godly Negro Lady for the Billy Graham rallies in Madison Square Garden and The Cow Palace and Comiskey Park and Ecuador and the South Sea Islands. This is the Ethel Waters who starred in *Blackbirds of 1928* and quite possibly coined the legendary bit of advice, "Walk softly and carry a big razor."

Roll Call!

Roll Call!

Roll Call at The Commodore's Blue Note.

Buddy Bolden?

Present.

Jelly Roll Morton.

Here. Jelly Roll? Where the hell else has he got to go, now that his career is in the toilet and the hoo-doo is on him?

Eddie Condon?

Present and drunk as Cooder Brown. Bix? Bix? Biederbecke, you here, boy?

Yeah, I'm here … That smile. Jesus, that smile. That smile was so shy and easy, you knew he came from Indiana.

Yeah, Bix is here. He is *luftmensch*. He is here and elsewhere. He is lost in a mist.

You know who smiles like Bix?

Chet Baker. A man utterly lacking in guile. Mr. Innocence. Right. My ass in two parts. Baker the Faker swiped the smile along with about three-quarters of Bix's chops.

Not that Chet Baker smiles like that anymore. Drug thing, you know. He burned some people, you know. People who were called names like The Bear, and Perpetual Scar Tissue, and Emergency Warning Buxton, and Guido and Fat Tony, and Big Tony, and Large Tony, and Tony Kick Your Ass Esposito. What happened was the people he burned in this drug thing—and this is just something I heard, okay?—they got together and knocked every tooth out of Chet Baker's mouth.

It did nothing for his looks.

Of course, with what he had picked up from his father, Miles Davis could have fixed Baker right up, but Miles hated Chet. Miles hated everybody.

And of course, there at the bar, tonight and every night, it is The Detached Cop. He is Webster's size. He wears suits that make you think of Bulgaria. Some nights, he sits and drinks and listens to the music and he weeps. Sometimes someone tries to talk to him. Usually, the Detached Cop says, "Get away. I am undercover." You want him to say more. You want him to confess all, become maudlin and confidential. You hope he will reveal, "I am investigating the Lindbergh baby snatch. I am investigating crop circles and Judge Crater and those mysterious strangers and the celebrated rain of frogs that would have been the clincher for anyone except that dumbass Pharaoh. I want to know if Ambrose Bierce and Pancho Villa changed their names and became a tag team on WGN's *Wrestling from the Marigold*. I'll sure as hell find out who threw the overalls in Mrs. Murphy's chowder. And who was it played poker with Pocahontas when John Smith went away."

The Detached Cop never says anything like that, though. I think he's afraid it would make people like him.

Every night, every night, you will find the Two Metaphysical Wineheads at their table.

They are good luck for the joint.

They somehow always have money for Dago Red.

They have discussions which are so laden with insight and all that that the Dalai Lama would instantly give them his Rolex and autographed picture of Marilyn Monroe and one of those funky Sherpa hats if he heard them talking.

Consider this conversation:

Man, what time is it?

Now.

Yeah, now. What time is it?

Now.

Yeah, I say now. What the hell you think I say? What time is it now!

Now.

Oh, hell with you. Just drink some wine, that's right.

I will, says a profoundly philosophical Metaphysical Winehead. I will drink some wine ...

Now.

Thing is, everyone is alive. Everyone who ever was in jazz, everyone.

Alive! They're alive, I tell you. 100% guaranteed and bona fide and assured by an electrocardiogram on record.

They are alive. Right.

Now.

Except for Bird.

Charlie Yardbird Parker. Yardbird is dead.

That is why The Commodore's Blue Note is down tonight.

Nobody wants to believe it. Nobody believes it. Paul Whiteman is alive, for Chrissake, and he is so lame nobody even thinks he should be, and Fats Navarro is alive and Bill Evans is alive and Benny Goodman is alive and Robert Johnson is alive.

Robert Johnson. Poisoned and shot and stabbed and chopped up in a cotton baler and with his head caught in a punch press! Acid thrown on him by one old girl, ice pick stuck in his nose, ear, and ass by another, but Robert Johnson is alive.

But the word has spread throughout the community.

Bird is dead.

Naw, says one Metaphysical Winehead.

He be dead, says the other Metaphysical Winehead.

Bird joking. Bird always one for the jokes. Bird, naw, he ain't dead.

I sure hope dead, says the other Metaphysical Winehead, 'cause they done gone and buried him. Oh, my, ain't I a stitch? Ain't I a caution?

Naw, says the other winehead.

It is precisely then …

That a touch of the mystic and unexplainable, of the awesome and of the pure enters The Commodore's Blue Note.

The door swings open. It opens though no one sees a human hand upon it. And if there is no human hand, then there is no human being attached to that no hand and so it is that no human being enters The Commodore's Blue Note.

What flies in is a white dove.

Get it?

A bird comes flying in.

Say what you want about the brilliance of Yardbird, the creative genius, the inspired lunacy, but the man was not always subtle.

Everyone is silent. Even Jelly Roll Morton stops noodling on the battered old upright in the corner of the joint. That's about all he can do these days, about all that gives him comfort. He is convinced that there is a serious curse on him and that is why nobody wants to hear his music anymore. Mr. Jelly Lord's music is called "moldy fig" music. Moldy oldie.

Moldy Mush and Moldy Gramma. Aw, that is stale, that is square, that is … Moldy. The A and R man at RCA told him, "Well, you and your Hot Peppers, you ain't so hot now. So toot sweet, and write if you get work, but I bet you won't."

Whoo! And how's that for a hurt? Whoo! And who was it that just plain *invented* jazz? Why, none other than Jelly Roll Morton, and if you don't believe it, just ask him.

But now we are back to smoky silences and a white dove winging its way to the bar. For a moment, it hangs motionless in the air. Some that were there that night swore the dove glowed brilliantly, as though it were becoming a halo, needing only an angel beneath it to complete a religious experience. The Commodore, trying to remember lines his mother and her faith used to inflict on him, thinks The Kingdom of Heaven has come, and he says, in a reverential whisper, "Blow me down."

Then the dove alights on the bar. He is strutting as though he is the literal cock of the walk.

Everyone is saying it, not quite simultaneously, but saying it. "It's Bird. Bird's here. Bird lives."

"Horse manure," is what Jelly Roll Morton says.

Now what some folks don't know, because Jelly told a lie or two in his time, is that Mr. Morton's claim to have been a sharpshooter with the carnival was 100% veritas.

These days, not knowing if the hoodoo would come at him like a Swamp Dog or a Dhambala bat, Jelly Roll has taken to carrying around an 1873 Colt Peacemaker.

Which is what he yanked out. He let fly.

And anyone who saw that shot does not dispute the Jelly's claim to have been a carnival sharpshooter. Because in one bang and one burst there is nothing but some splatter on the bar and a feather in the air.

Then Jelly Roll Morton says, "Bird's dead."

He sets the Colt on the piano and, grinning his diamond-tooth grin like he has not since being given the RCA heave-ho, he starts in playing "Graveyard Blues."

And there ain't one moldy thing about it.

THE RUNNING HORSE,
THE HIGH, WHITE SOUND

Some strange things have happened to me lately. That's why I'm writing this. It seems things make more sense if I put them on paper, then, later, read over what I wrote.

I think writing's okay, even if a lot of jerks at John Dewey High think it's for creeps and faggots. I get A's on all my themes, and Miss Bertello says I could maybe be a writer. We're not doing themes now, though. Miss Bertello is trying to teach the morons not to say, "I have went."

English is probably my best class, a lot better than Civics with old Neederkorn the Nosepicker who's always yapping about how we have to be involved young adults, knowing current affairs like if Ike shot a three under par or had another coronary. Frankly, school would be a real douchebag if it weren't for English class.

Problem with getting all this on paper, though, is I'm not sure where to start. Okay, "Begin at the beginning and end at the end" is what you get in English class, but I just don't know for sure where the beginning begins.

I guess I should probably just write about the rumble we had with the nigger gang, the Del-Sonics, when my brother Vince got killed. It was at the baseball diamond in Douglas Park. Rangers and Dels were spread out all over, beating on each other. It was tough, but clean, no bats or blades or aerials like a lot of the gangs. That was the way Vince, he was the chief man in the Stilton Street Rangers, always set it up and you could count on the Del-Sonics, with Beau Dooley—he was their warlord.

Vince and I were back to back on the pitcher's mound. That was the best way. Nobody could get behind us. I think Vince was looking out for me; he made sure that was how we always fought.

It worked. Soon as a Del got in close, I had him or Vince had him.

The Rangers were doing all right. Monster, who looks like he was born in Dr. Frank N. Stein's lab, had a headlock on Beau Dooley and was clouting him in the middle of that niggery curly wool with a bowling-ball-sized fist. Colored guys are supposed to be hard-headed, but you could tell the way Beau was kicking and yelling that Monster's message was getting through. In center field, Lonny and Ron were doing a number on a tall skinny Del. Lonny'd clip him, spin him, Ron would nail him, and give him right back to Lonny for more.

Of course Mumbles, who's just as smart as your average head of lettuce, was getting his ass stomped. He was flat on his back with three Del-Sonics kicking away. That kind of thing never got to Mumbles. He'd show up the next day, bragging and mumbling, "Man, did they kick my ass, man."

Seven or eight Dels got smart and made a circle around Vince and me. "Get set," Vince said, so I picked my target, a dude about my size. I'd let him have the knee, slam him one in the mouth, then grab him and use him for a shield. As soon as Monster finished creaming Beau Dooley, he'd see what was going down with Vince and me and come charging like the Seventh Cavalry to the rescue.

Vince and I just had to stay cool, keep on our feet, and pound away. No Del or anyone else was going to stop the Monster, not unless they used a cannon.

It didn't work that way. A sawed-off guy broke out of the Dels' circle and came running right at me. He swerved at the last second and I missed with a left. "I got him," Vince said.

Then Vince grunted. He fell back against me and nearly took me down. I swiveled my head to see what was happening and got tagged under the left ear.

Then Vince screamed.

Once I saw this scabby-looking dog get scrunched by a beer truck. It pulled itself to the curb, dragging its hind legs, letting out a pinched yip, yip, yip, until it died.

That's kind of the way Vince's scream sounded, only it didn't last so long.

The Del-Sonics ran for it. They piled into their cars in the parking lot and took off, tossing gravel.

Most of the Rangers beat it, too, except Monster, at second base, his jaw hanging.

When I lowered my hands and turned around, Vince was on his knees, hands inside his Ranger jacket. Blood poured down his white chinos.

"Man," I said.

I was going to touch him, I think I was going to touch his face, when he looked at me. "Ah, shit, Jimmy," he said. Then he pitched onto his face and died.

So, that's the beginning, I guess. I could write about the cops, coming on with questions like they watched too many Dragnets, but who the hell tells cops anything?

Like usual, the old man was soused at Vince's funeral.

My little sister, T, and I stood there wearing new clothes. Father Zeranti did his bit about dust to dust. Aunt Carmella, her slob husband, and Suzie and Liz, her pain-in-the-lower-neck kids, were there. Aunt Carmella filled up a couple handkerchiefs with her bawling, same as she did when my old lady died.

And sure, the Rangers were there. That night, I got loaded with them on Tango and Budweiser.

It's weird, but it wasn't until four weeks later that it hit me that Vince was really dead. It was a Saturday morning and I was in bed, halfway between awake and nowhere. The furnace in the basement is about ten years past tired out, but I had a couple blankets so I was warm and kind of drifting.

I kept thinking that I ought to be feeling good. There was no school today. Maybe tonight I'd take my sometime-steady, Cookie Bamonti, to The Grand. Last time they had a horror movie, I got her bra off just when the giant lizard was eating the scientist's Oldsmobile.

But I wasn't feeling good. I wasn't feeling anything. Keeping my eyes shut, watching the red and purple blobs fly around in my skull, I finally got it.

Vince wasn't singing.

Vince was always the first one up. He left our room quietly, but when he got in the shower, he let loose. The first thing I was supposed to hear on Saturday was the water rushing in the tub, the pipes clanging and knocking, and, right in the middle of all that, Vince.

Vince had a great voice, a lot like Dion or Neil Sedaka, only much bigger. He could hit notes that were way, way up there. It was a pure, high, white, sound. He knew all the hits, line for line, "Runaround Sue," "Valerie," "Duke of Earl," "The Wanderer," you name it, and he made even the drippiest words sound like absolute truth.

Vince always used to say he was going to be a big recording star.

"You know, man, they're always grabbing Italian guys off the front porch and wham! Next thing you know, you're a Frankie Avalon with three gold records and a Cadillac."

Vince used to joke about it, but I think he believed it.

It came to me slowly, but I got it. Vince wasn't going to make any records or own Cadillacs. I'd never again hear him singing in the shower.

He was dead.

I didn't want to get up, but staying in bed when you're wide awake is a drag. I tossed off the blanket. When I sat up, the cold grabbed me.

In my underwear, I stood in front of the dresser mirror. My hair stuck out all over. I'd have to wash it before I gobbed on the Brylcreem and combed it into a solid DA.

I turned to snatch my robe from the hook on the back of the door, but I stopped to take a look at the picture Vince had scotch-taped over the mirror. You could make out a dark horse's head and a wild mane in the center, but all the rest was swirling black lines. T drew it last year in her sixth grade art class. It was supposed to be the way a horse felt when he was running across the plains or something like that; that's what T said, anyway. Vince used to kid T, tell her she was going to be the famous artist in the family just like he was going to be the famous singer.

After a hot shower, heavy on the shampoo, I went back to my bedroom and put on my regular Saturday clothes, jeans and a black t-shirt, and fixed my hair right. Then I went downstairs.

The old man's bedroom is just off the living room and his door was closed the way I figured it would be. The old man was snoring like a choir of chain saws. He always brags he's never missed a day's work, but every other hour of the day is his boozing time.

He was sleeping off another Friday night so that when he got moving at three or four in the afternoon he'd have plenty of energy to slurp down the whiskey.

T was at the kitchen table with the cornflakes and a package of Hostess gunk-filled cupcakes. T eats about a zillion Hostess cupcakes but she stays a toothpick. She still looks like a little kid, with big brown eyes and pale skin, and nothing at all round to her body. She even has a little kid's mouth, bright pink, with no real shape to her lips.

I boiled water and put together a cup of instant. T was halfway through the white squiggle on cupcake number two when I sat down.

"Aunt Carm's picking me up," she said. "She's taking me and Suzie and Liz to the show." "Okay," I said.

Suzie and Liz are little creeps, but it was probably better for T to be with them than to sit home and watch the old man pickle himself.

I sipped my coffee. T dabbed at chocolate frosting on the tabletop. Without looking at me, she said, "Whatcha gonna do today?"

"You know," I said. "Mess around."

"With the Rangers?"

"Yeah, I guess."

T mashed more chocolate dabs. "Jimmy?"

"Yeah? What?"

"Oh, nothing."

T was real quiet. She even looked quiet. That rattled me somehow, so I said, "Hey, you haven't brought home any pictures for a while."

"I know," T said.

That was the end of our breakfast talk. When I left out the kitchen door, wearing my Ranger jacket, T didn't say anything; she gets like that sometimes. She just went on squishing chocolate.

It was cold enough outside to freeze both cheeks off your ass. I walked slowly down Stilton Street, watching the tips of my roachkicker boots. The scenery wasn't worth looking at, nothing but two story frame houses, every one of them the same.

Twenty years ago, this was supposed to be a "class" neighborhood. Now it's a worn-out island of white, surrounded by all the blackies in the high-rises the city built. My old man, when he isn't too bombed to talk—which isn't that often—says it's a very big deal how we're keeping the "goddamn jungle bunnies" out.

Ron and Lonny were at the schoolyard, sitting on the entranceway steps. I sat down and Ron handed me his pack of Luckies and a book of matches. I lit up. "Wanna do something?" I said.

"Yeah," Ron said. "I want to milk a coconut."

"Not me, man," Lonny said. "I think we ought to wash a reindeer."

"You guys are incredibly funny," I said. "Shit."

We sat there shivering and smoking. I had three Luckies, one right after the other, lighting the fresh one off the old butt.

After a while, Monster showed up.

"Hey, man," Lonny said. "What's shaking?"

Monster nodded at me. He jerked his thumb over his shoulder.

"Lonny and Ron," he said, "you guys take a hike."

"Yeah, man."

They disappeared like they'd had lessons from a magician. I didn't blame them. Monster is a frightening guy. It doesn't matter if he's on your side, he can still make you mess your pants because he's the kind of guy that busts heads just because he likes to, the way some guys go bowling or something.

Monster sat down. I took the cigarette he gave me. My throat felt blow-torched already, but I didn't want to get Monster hacked.

"Look, man," he said, "I been doing some talking with Beau Dooley.

That nigger, he knows, Jimmy. The Dels, they know. It was supposed to be straight."

"Piss on Beau Dooley," I said.

"No," Monster said. "Listen. See, Beau Dooley's been laying it on his guys. It was a bad scene and 'cause it was Vince it's even worse. Beau Dooley knows that."

"So?"

Monster sunk a meathook in my shoulder and made me look right at him. "Man," he said, "what I got to know is could you break the guy's ass that got Vince?"

I didn't even have to think about it. "Yeah," I said.

Monster said, "Sure, you're his brother. You got balls."

"What're you saying?"

Monster said, "The Dels will hand us the asshole, man. He's not one of theirs. Just a punk. Some guy's cousin was with them, that's all. He had a knife. He was showing he was a hot shit."

"Okay," I said.

Monster told me the rest. He had a cousin who'd done time for liquor store and gas station stick-ups. His cousin had a friend who could get ahold of a piece. That was it.

"You got it, man?" Monster said. I did.

He told me a couple more things—where to meet him and when and all—and then he took off. I sat there wishing I'd bummed a few smokes. I never buy my own; I don't want to get into a heavy habit. I just hit on the guys when I want a butt and I make it up with money for gas when we go cruising or buy the guys Cokes or something.

If I'd had a weed right then, I could have concentrated on lighting it, taking the first drag, feeling how the second drag tasted a bit different, feeling the heat get closer to my fingers, studying the black mark it made when I ground it out on the concrete. I wanted to think about something like that, something simple.

My ass was starting to freeze to the concrete, so I got up and went over to Cookie's. Her old man and old lady were both home, a double treat. Cookie's mother made me a salami sandwich and gave me a Pepsi. Cookie, smelling of hairspray and Juicy Fruit, sat across from me in the kitchen while I ate. Her mother rattled on about Vince and what a shame it was and how sad and all.

I kind of wanted to tell her it was okay, no sweat, because I was going to kill the guy that did it. That would have shut her up.

Mr. Bamonti was sprawled in a stuffed chair in his guinea t-shirt, sucking a Pabst as I followed Cookie upstairs. "You kids keep that door open. Ha, ha, I know what it's all about. I was young once myself, you know."

Ha, ha, I thought, as Cookie gave her cute little behind an extra wiggle, maybe for me or maybe to say that she knew her old man was a real jerk.

When we got to her room, Cookie kissed me. She tried to get some tongue action going, but I wasn't in the mood.

"What's wrong?" she said. She backed off. Her eyes were like dimestore marbles circled by Bozo the Clown blobs of mascara.

"Nothing," I said. "Maybe I'm on the rag. You ever think of that?"

"Jimmy!" Cookie dropped her chin. You could tell she was trying to be shocked—just like a movie actress or something. "You shouldn't talk to me that way."

"Hey, man," I said. "Shut up, okay?"

"Jimmy, if something's wrong with you, you know you can always talk to me."

"I know," I said. "You're a regular Dear Abby, except she never lets me feel her tits."

"Jimmy!"

I sat down on her blue bedspread under this picture of Vince Edwards tacked to the wall. Cookie turned around. She was very hacked off or pretending to be, but I was also sure she wanted to remind me what a sweet little ass she had. Even standing still, she kept it bipping a little as she fooled with a stuffed toy on her dresser. Then she picked up a bottle of cologne and set it down.

She was reaching for a tube of lipstick when I said, "All right. Shit. I'm sorry, okay? Forget it. Just forget it."

Cookie turned back to me, all smiles. "Okay," she said. "You know, you got moods and so do I and everything. It's okay as long as we understand each other. We've always got to do that, Jimmy. Something's wrong with you, you know you can count on me. That's what true love is, Jimmy."

"Okay," I said.

"Hey," Cookie said, "I bought a new record. Want to hear it?" "Sure," I said. Really, I didn't give a damn. Cookie's new record was usually something everybody had already had for a couple of months. Cookie didn't really dig music the way some people did. I think she tried to dig it because you were supposed to dig rock and roll and that was it with her.

She slapped a black-and-red-labeled 45 on the spindle of her portable phono on the shelf by the window. The record player clicked and the tone arm lifted and the disc dropped. The needle sissed in the opening grooves.

Then the music started and it screwed into my head like a dentist's drill. It was Frankie Valli and the Four Seasons:

Walk Like A Man. Frankie's voice took off like a wailing police siren on a summer night when the rain is pounding the pavement and it got louder by the second.

"Turn that goddamned noise down!" Old man Bamonti was hollering downstairs.

I stood up. "Stop it," I said.

Cookie was snapping her fingers and shimmying her hips. "Huh?"

"Turn the fucker off," I said.

Cookie slashed the needle across the record, nearly slicing it in half. Then she turned on the waterworks. "You are crazy, Jimmy! You are crazy and you're mean talking so nasty and dirty to me. You are just nuts."

"Yeah," I said.

"You don't know how to act with a lady. You don't even know what true love is."

I got out of there.

Frankie Valli screamed in my mind all the way home.

It was later than I thought because, when I stepped into the kitchen, the old man was already drinking supper. He had his big hand wrapped around a water glass and he was staring at the half-full bottle of Ten High on the table.

I picked the bottle up by the neck.

"Hey Jimbo? What's this? What you doin'?" The old man sounded like he was chewing a sweatsock.

"I'm taking your booze, man," I said. "I want to practice now so I can be just like you when I grow up. Dig it, Daddy-o?"

"Hey, Jimbo? Don't be like that, huh?"

I just stood there with the bottle in my hand. "Are you going to stop me, man?" I said. I waited until I knew for damned sure he wasn't, and then I went up to my room and slammed the door.

Sitting on the end of my bed, I unscrewed the top of the bottle. Then I had a drink, the lip of the bottle clicking on my teeth.

The first swallows burned like I was gulping down hell, but they went to work right away. Frankie Valli was getting fainter by the second.

I was sure old Ten High could do the trick, so I didn't drink so fast after that. What I did do was drink a hell of a lot.

It was some time before I passed out that something weird happened, something like on the Twilight Zone TV show. I was looking at T's picture. I was trying to follow one black curving line from where it started to where it ended but I kept getting lost.

Suddenly, it was like the picture was getting closer and closer, dragging me into it. Did you ever stand on a tall building and look down? You get this feeling that there's something below, something with a power working on you to yank you down. It is scary as hell.

That's pretty much what it was like, except nobody I know ever went off the building but I got pulled right into the picture.

Now this gets wilder, crazy even, like something a guy in the booby hatch dreams up. For about a second there, I was a horse. I was running wild and free and all alone, running so fast I was a part of the wind.

Then it was just T's picture again and I was so plastered I was seeing two of it. I flopped back on the bed. I slept and I didn't dream.

It didn't take an alarm to wake me. I left the house without checking on the old man.

The moon was bright. You could see gobs of pigeon crap on the statue of the Douglas guy the park is named after. Monster leaned back with his elbows on the pedestal.

"You okay, man?" he asked.

"Yeah," I said. "I'm cool. Give me a weed."

I watched my hands as I struck the match. I wasn't shaking. The cigarette tasted good. Monster put a hand on my shoulder.

"Don't do that, man," I said. "Don't touch me, okay?"

Monster took his hand away. "Jimmy, man," he said, "you sure you're okay?"

"No sweat, man," I said. "I'm fine." I smoked, taking deep and easy drags. Then I said, "Got something for me?"

He took the gun from his jacket pocket. It was small, a .22 or .25. I took it. It felt like part of my hand. I slipped it into my pocket. It felt right, knowing it was there.

"Walk like a man," I said.

"Huh?" Monster said.

"Nothing."

We went to the diamond. Where else? It all made sense right there. We waited by the backstop. I watched the parking lot. Monster checked his wristwatch.

"They'll be here," I said. "It's cool. It's all cool. Don't sweat it."

I bummed another smoke. Just as I was grinding it out in the cold dust, a beat up Ford pulled up. Beau Dooley got out on the driver's side. The passenger door in the front opened and another Del stepped out. He reached back into the car and pulled a guy out. The dude came tumbling out and fell onto the gravel.

He was the one.

Fine.

Walk like a man.

Beau Dooley, walking cool-tough, circled the car and he and the other Del-Sonic stood the guy up. They even had him tied, arms behind him, and there was a white gag in his mouth. The dude's eyes were as big as the moon. Beau Dooley clipped him, open hand to the back of the head.

"Here we go, man," Monster said. They marched him over, the guy who killed Vince, and Monster and I walked to home plate.

They were three shadows. I could smell the guy in the middle.

"Hey, man," Beau Dooley said, "this ends it, right?" "Yeah," Monster said.

I didn't say anything.

Beau Dooley and the other Del-Sonic leaned on the guy, made him drop to his knees.

"Man," Monster said, "do it!"

I was cool. I stuck the gun in the guy's face. His eyes went crossed. It was pretty funny.

There was no reason to hurry. There'd be all the time I needed. I could feel myself smiling. This was so easy.

Then I blinked.

For that little bit of a moment when my eyes were shut, it was just like I was back in T's picture again. There was nothing to me. I was only air.

Then I heard this choking noise slide through the colored guy's gag. It was a strange sound. It reminded me of something I'd heard before. It might have been on a record. It might have had something to do with a ratty dog hit by a beer truck.

It might even have made me think of a pure, high, white sound. Now this is where everything gets weird, real weird.

Sometimes, when I think about this, I figure I'm ready for a trip to the funny farm. What happened was, I stopped being me.

I was Vince and I was Monster and I was Lonny and I was Ron. I was Beau Dooley.

I was a nigger on my knees on a cold night.

It was just a flash like that, but it stayed with me. I blinked my eyes a couple of times, real quick, but nothing changed.

I was ... Everyone.

"Kill the fucker!" Monster said that. I think he yelled, actually.

I gave Monster the gun. He took it with both hands. He held it like he couldn't figure out what to do with it, and then he put it in his pocket. His face told me he didn't understand what had happened.

"All right," he said to Beau Dooley, "get this asshole out of here."

"No more, dig?" Beau Dooley said. "We call it done and settled and over."

"It's done," Monster said. "Just get him out of here."

I went over by the backstop. Beau and the other Del didn't even take the gag out of the guy's mouth or untie him. They just dragged him back to the car, tossed him in, and took off.

Monster came towards me, shaking his head. "He was your brother," he said.

"Yeah," I said.

Then Monster said, "You goddamn pussy!" and he punched me in the gut. All the air exploded out of me. Bent double, I wrapped my arms over my stomach. "You fucking faggot!" Monster said.

I squeezed my eyes shut, saw red and black pools seeping into one another. My head was filled with bad radio static. I didn't try to breathe, not yet. I hugged the hurt into me, pressed it in deep and held it there.

A little later, all shaky but pretty much okay, I straightened up and Monster was gone and I was alone.

I guess that's the end of it. I don't understand that nutty scene in the park when shit got in my blood. I don't know why the hell I went chicken. I don't know what the hell happened to me. It just doesn't make sense.

So maybe I ought to quit writing right here and go off to get measured for one of the white coats that ties in the back.

But there's another thing that happened, too. I don't understand it either, even though it's not as goofy as the other stuff, but I have a feeling it goes along with everything else so I'll put it down.

The next few days, all I did was hang around the house. I didn't go out. I didn't go to school. The old man and I had nothing to say to each other. Maybe I gave a "Hello" to T a couple of times but that's all.

I had no energy. I stayed in my room, sleeping, getting up to eat a little something once in a while, and then going back to my room to look at the ceiling.

Then it was Wednesday, late afternoon, and there was this knock on the door. I didn't answer.

"Jimmy?"

I started to say, "Go away," but what the hell. When I sat up in bed, it made me dizzy. "Come in," I said. The door opened. T had on her school cloches. She was carrying an envelope. "What is it?"

T licked her lips. "Jimmy, I got a note. Dad's supposed to see it." "So show it to him," I said. "Don't bug me, okay?"

"You know Dad," T said.

Yeah, I knew Dad. Old Ten High Dad. I told T to give me the note.

It was from T's art teacher. T hadn't turned in four drawings. She was going to flunk. Her teacher wrote, "I am worried about this drastic change in attitude for a student who has always done so well."

I said, "You know what this is?"

"I guess," T said. "Yes."

"Then what the hell's wrong with you? You want to flunk?"

T looked down at the floor. "I don't care," she said, "It doesn't matter."

That's when I stopped being tired. I got mad. I think I was madder than I'd ever been in my whole life.

I slapped T.

Her head jerked. Instantly, the lines of my fingers were bright red on her cheek.

Then I grabbed her and I held her. "Goddamn it," I said. "Shit."

T was so awfully skinny and she was crying. Not loud, but this deep, awful shaking crying. I put my face close to hers. "I'm sorry, I'm sorry, I'm sorry," 1 said. "Oh, man, don't cry, don't cry, okay? Don't."

I was crying, too.

That's it, I guess.

Yeah, I don't always know where to begin, but I know that has to be the end.

UPSTAIRS, DOWNSTAIRS,
AND ALL ABOUT VAMPIRES

Upstairs

The time is our time. Death Rock and The Doors still worshiped, Jim Morrison into being dead before almost anyone realized how cool it was. At the MegaMall Movies (ninety-six screens—no waiting!) *The Crow*, starring dead Brandon Lee as a dead avenger. Unlife and varieties thereof, that is where it's at.

And in the room the women have rather unoriginally chosen to call "The Dark Room," candles hiss and flicker and shadows waver and pulse on walls lit by sickly yellow light.

Three women in black. Black cowls and flopping black sleeves, black gowns blacker than the somber shadows of The Dark Room.

Ambiance. Mood.

Style. Style is all. Or nearly everything, what the hell ...

This is their thing, you see.

Three women, with black hoods and faces white beyond ghostly and white beyond ghastly. Three women with heavy black circles beneath eyes that make you think of Edgar Allan Poe and Death (Death Tangible, not Metaphor), or German Expressionist cinema, or severe sinusitis.

Three women, one young, and two who would say they are ... "older," if they would condescend to say anything at all about a matter that is none of your concern—really. The young one, let's risk being politically incorrect, and call her "The Girl." But one of the older women is only, let us say, "big sister" older (and from now on, let's speak of her as Big Sister), and the other older woman is, well, "Old enough to be your mother" older. (It would be impolite, even an unintentional double entendre, to call her "Mother," and we won't, but we can call her leader, that is, The Leader, and, truthfully, that is the way she thinks of herself.)

Now, in jaundiced arid pallid light, in light that brings to mind cigarette coughs and stories of bleak winter in America's Great Depression, three women in black touch fine-stemmed glasses, glasses that hold a liquid dark and purple and every bit as red as it is purple and dark.

A delicate ting. Smiles. Three white and cold smiles, so serious beneath raccoon-from-hell eyes. Smiles intended to be jaded and decadent and insouciant.

Smiles you might consider casually cruel for this familiar toast:

"Blood!" says The Girl, in an exultant whisper.

"The blood is the life!" says Big Sister.

The Leader draws out the moment, her moment, appreciating drama, timing, style, yes, style, and, like a jazz musician (be-bop-a-re-bop!), cool ...

The Leader says, "To ... Life'"

(Which is what you might hear at a bar mitzvah, but there wouldn't be any incongruity.)

Laughter.

And three women in black in The Dark Room drink deep.

Downstairs

Damn! Rat bastard! Damn! Argh! Dazed, defeated, drained as he is, he understands Eternity because he is in it up to his hoo-hah and hairline and honker, and because he understands it, you bet he would tell you, "Eternity sucks!"

The dark is upon him like suffocation, infection, and telephone solicitors, as he lies in unending absence of light, the cold and hard circularity of chains at ankles and wrists securing him on the rude altar or heavy table or what the hell.

He has been a prisoner how long? He does not know. Eternity screws your sense of time, and it's so damned dark he couldn't see his Timex even if a) he had the freedom to move his arms and b) they hadn't taken his watch.

The Timex along with everything else. So long to the Florsheims and the Levi 501s. No receipt for anything they boosted when they stripped you buck NAY-KED!

Oh, yes, it is his skinny bare butt on the tabletop. Hey, fellas and gals, forget the physical your HMO recommends once a year, forget standing in the shower going rub-a-dub-dubby on all your private, personal, and very own! places, you do not understand bare-assimo ultimata until you are a) wearing chains and b) one hundred the hell and twelve extra percent at the mercy of ...

MORT CASTLE

Those!
God!
DAMNED!
BITCHES!!!

Upstairs

The Dark Room is close with the smell of wax and the scent of perverse excitement. (Think Calvin Klein perfume and Lust Potion Number Nine …) Arrowheads of candlelight are distorted reflections in the curved bowls of empty stemmed glasses on a dresser top.

As though mocking that which is round, near the glasses is the gleaming angularity of a single-edge razor blade, a proud, if disposable, member of the Wilkinson clan.

"And so, which of us this time?" The question is posed by The Leader. Her tone tells you she is, without a doubt, the kind of "go for the throat" modern woman who frightens many men in the business world—and likewise causes strong, if not always welcomed, arousal, in others. (Same rsponse for / from women. Check out your Kraft-Ebbing, under the topic, "Nothing New Under the Sun.")

"Please, me!" says The Girl. Her excitement is what you'd expect from a high school sophomore, one both overly dramatic and hormonal.

"It was you last time," says Big Sister, although she sounds every bit as peevish and *nyaah-ayaah-nyaah* as would only a slightly older sister who might run to rat out her sib, in hopes that the sib might get grounded or even whacked a good one.

The Leader orchestrates the scenario. (Got that, girlfriend?) She arches an eyebrow. She touches a long and filed-to-murder-weapon-sharp fingernail to her chin. Her head tips. This is all done so casually that you know the pose has been well and frequently practiced. It is what you'd expect of an actress in a made-for-cable film—if the cable network were USA or one equally chintzy and tawdry.

As authoritative as the curriculum developer for "Assertiveness Training for Sumo Wrestlers," she says to The Girl, "Yes. You."

Big sister's "Oh," is disappointed, but then, in just a micro-moment, you can see the feeling of "let down" vanish to be replaced by "worked up."

As The Girl pushes back her flopping sleeve to reveal a slender and ivory-pale left forearm, with pinkish and whitish marks, scars old and new.

And now she concentrates, the Wilkinson blade poised, delicately held between thumb and forefinger.

93

NEW MOON ON THE WATER

And now she draws the diagonal line with precisely modulated pressure. The tight flesh of her forearm parts. Purple-crimson beads appear, swell and pulse, dots grow and connect to create a slender, rippling worm of blood.

The youngest woman in black proudly offers her arm and her blood. The mouth and tongue of The Leader touch and taste.

The Girl smiles.

In The Dark Room, two women in black taste the blood of another, who then kitten-licks and sucks and then drinks her own blood, and then, there is what we might call a "collective sigh," as well as several similar, if not exactly shared, psychological and physiological reactions.

Then The Girl, Big Sister, and The Leader, three women in black, go downstairs.

Downstairs

Uh-oh, is what he thinks when he hears the door hinge squeak above him in the darkness. He is more than a bunch bonkers and so, all kinds of whacked out things shoot across his mind:

I tawt I taw a puddy tat twee puddy tats ...

There's been a mistake, really, a *bad* mistake ...

Okay, we have had it with the preliminaries! Howzabout I call the law, tell 'em you're like a cult of weirdified lezbo crazykopfs or something, that you're so rutabaga you make the Jehovah's Witnesses seem like 4-H, and then, well, you'll go to jail and Oprah won't even have you as guests because you're so goddamned icky ...

You are such bitches!

You are goddamned Bitches!

You are. I am not kidding.

YOU ARE BITCHES!

Yes. I'm calling ... THE AUTHORITIES!

With the cellular phone I just happen to have in my ass ...

Tell you what, how about I plead? Very pleadingly, okay?

Please ...Oh, please. Oh, please. Oh, please.

Will you please, will you, please, willyouplease ...

Hey, that's what he is saying. Saying it right out loud. As out loud as he can, anyway, which is not all that loud, considering how thoroughly thrashed, bashed, and trashed he is.

"Puh-leezzz...PUH-leeee ..." He feels the plosive pop on his dried and burning lips. Feels the gritty rush of air up his windpipe and the searing slice of it on his tongue.

Three women in black surround him.

And one of them, the oldest, and most vicious, The Bitch Boss / Boss Bitch is putting on the demands. She is as friendly about it as a cement mixer, but her volume is a tad higher.

He *will* tell them.

Oh, yes.

He *will* do what they demand.

Oh, yes.

Does he think he has a choice? Does he think they can be fooled? Does he think …

He thinks: If he knew how to spin window putty into a goddamned free-monthly-lease Lexus, he would tell them. If he knew how to destroy his favorite Aunt Mildred in a lingeringly painful way, he would tell them. If he knew the position for the Cringing Ostrich Trick, supposedly taught to Jack Kennedy by Marilyn Monroe (film rights optioned by Oliver Stone), he would tell them.

He would tell the bitches anything.

Anything.

But he has told them.

They do not believe him.

Ladies, ladies, ladies, listen up! No kidding, honest Native-American, forget the fiction, all the bull by that one lunatic woman and her imitators, most of whom have three names, with or without hyphens. This is the *emmis*. If I am lying, I am flying (and I sure ain't, in case you didn't notice). The truth? Say, does the Pope poop in the woods? Tell the truth and have no regrets. I swear to tell the truth, the whole truth, and here we go:

I cannot help you. I cannot.

Not me or anybody else.

It's kind of like being black.

It's a birth thing.

You are born like me, okay?

Or, in your case(s), you are not.

You cannot sign up for classes. It's not like converting to Judaism. No one can teach you the secret handshake. You are wasting your time with personals in the *Village Voice* or semi-literate e-mail and computer message board. No way. Uh-uh. Won't happen.

Pay Miracle Momma Wombat to brand your behinds with a Big Voodoo "V." Learn to diatonically fart the 100 Arcane Names of The Devil. Combine the cookbooks of Countess Bathory and Famous Amos.

And it *STILL* won't mean *A THING!*
(Even if you got the swing!) Because …
You is. Or.
You ain't.
And I is.
And you ain't.
That's rationality, if you please, good women.
Okay?
Over and out.
"You want us to believe you."
Why, yes, compared to, say, your sawing off my manly-thing with the only Ginsu ever to be sold without a warranty…
"You'd like us to free you, to send you on your way."
I guess so. Go figure. Yeah, that would be okay.
"You will teach us. You will. We have patience."
They have patience—
—and they have blood.
The young one. She puts her forearm to his split lips. He laps greedily at the coagulating cut line, feels blood liquid and good in his mouth, sucked up by his system.
And he feels something like—no, not life—but a weak and dreamy energy that will sustain him for now—
—barely—
—until the Three Women in Black come again—
As they now leave him, as they vanish in darkness and distance …

Upstairs

A SOMEDAY MOVIE

Someday I'm going to hit it, it, hit it so big. The policy, maybe. Put my buck on 9-7-2 or 4-6-8, or maybe shooting craps some night and fall into a run of real good luck, nothing but sweet 7s, and lls, and all those easy 8s! Yes! These big old black fingers around all that green, all those dream dollars, and won't that be something, now, won't it just.

You know what a lot of the brothers would do if they scored that way, don't you? Go after that Cadillac with the tiger-skin upholstery and the closets full of 800-dollar suits and a different pair of shoes for each and every one of them. Sure, they'd blow the whole roll in a week and there wouldn't be one real god-damned thing to show for it.

That's not for me. I'm a serious man and I've got a serious plan.

I guess this plan of mine first came into my mind when Mama and I came north. I was about nine years old, so that would be 1942.

Now Mama was a church woman, a strict one, so damned near anything that was any fun at all was something she'd whip my behind for doing. Mama had this terror that I'd be in trouble with the police. She feared policemen like they were devils right from Hell, so she kept one eye on me always—and usually had the other eye keeping it company.

We were getting some money from the county relief, so Mama didn't have to work full days, and when she went off to clean white peoples' houses, she left the same time I was off to school and she always seemed to make it back before I did, so she was able to watch me real close nine months of the year.

But in summer! Summer was trouble time for a child and Mama knew that. All the kids playing in the open hydrants in the streets and pinching stuff from stores and sometimes sneaking on the streetcars and going off to the Loop where there was more to see and a whole lot more to steal.

So in summer, Mama used to drop me off on her way to work at my Aunt Lorinda's. Aunt Lorinda lived a couple blocks away. She didn't have a job and she never went to church.

Years later, I learned Aunt Lorinda had enough boy-friends giving her "gifts" so she didn't have to work. I'll bet it bothered my Mama's soul plenty to leave me with a woman like Aunt Lorinda but she must have thought it was better than my running with all those "trashy niggers"—that's what Mama called them—who were always getting into it with the Law.

Aunt Lorinda had a Victrola in the living room, not like Mama's wind-up one she was always playing church songs on, but a real electric phonograph that never got slow and shaky when the spring ran down. She must have had three or four hundred records, too, the kind Mama wouldn't allow in our house because they were "sinful": Louis Armstrong, Big Bill Broonzy, Petie Wheatstraw, Victoria Spivey, Bessie Smith, people like that.

Sometimes now when I'm working in the warehouse shoving this crate over here and lugging that one there, I start singing something like "Whiskeyhead Buddies" or "Diggin' My Potatoes" and it comes back to me that I learned it sitting on the floor by Aunt Lorinda's Victrola with my ear up close so that the sound went boom-a-boom inside my brain and stayed there ever since.

I used to play a lot of cards with Aunt Lorinda, gin rummy and casino mostly and once she was going to teach me poker but she changed her mind. "'Cause your Mama kill us both, sugar," is what she said. She was probably right about that.

Anyway, one day I was over at Aunt Lorinda's, drinking a bottle of Nehi orange and listening to a new Jazz Gillum record. Aunt Lorinda was at the table, reading the newspaper. After a while, she said, "Sugar, you want Aunty take you to a movie?"

"Yes'm," I said. I jumped right up. I was so excited I dumped the Nehi all across the floor. If I made a mess like that at home, you can bet Mama would go on. But Aunt Lorinda didn't. She just took a wet rag, cleaned up the spill, and then we were off to the show.

The Paradise Theater on Madison Street was the most beautiful moviehouse there ever was. There was deep red carpet in the lobby, and pictures like in the museums on the walls, and this big fountain squirting water under different-colored lights. They didn't have any kids for ushers, either. There were all these fine-looking older gentlemen in uniforms that made them look like generals or admirals. Oh yes, the Paradise was really someplace!

This usher that could have been a five-star general took Aunt Lorinda and me down the middle aisle. Aunt Lorinda told him, "Don't want the stiff neck from sittin' too close," so he pointed out two seats in a center row with his flashlight.

It was just early afternoon so there weren't many people in the show.

The movie wasn't on yet and in that cool darkness I sat there trying to think of an extra-special way to say, "Thank you" to my aunt. I didn't see too many movies, not real ones. Oh, once in a while Mama would drag me off to something at church, movies that showed you what fine work our missionaries were doing for the savages. And there was that time I tried to sneak in with some other kids to see *The Wolfman*, but a man grabbed us and threw us out and said if we ever tried anything like that again we'd be off to jail for a thousand years.

So, you know, going to a movie show was a real big deal for me. The picture Aunty and I saw was *Gentleman Jim*. Errol Flynn was in it and I liked it a lot. There were plenty of good fights. Oh, there was some of that love stuff, too, the kind you don't want to see when you're nine, but just when I'd start thinking there was too much kissing and silly talk, whoop! Errol Flynn would be whipping hell out of someone.

But watching that movie got me kind of mixed up, so when we were riding the streetcar home, I asked Aunt Lorinda about it. "I thought Joe Louis is the champion," is what I said. Every kid knew about Joe—and every colored child and grownup, too, loved our Brown Bomber.

"He is, sugar."

"Then that was just a story. I mean, it's something someone made up. There isn't really a Gentleman Jim."

"See, Sugar," Aunt Lorinda said, "Gentleman Jim, he used to be the champion a long, long time ago. He was a real man and the movie tells you about some of the things he really did. Oh, I don't guess it's all true, but there's lots in it that is pure gospel."

It was right then I knew what I was going to do someday.

I was going to make a movie.

I was nine years old.

I'll be 41 next October.

You know how it is. Like just about all of us, I've forgotten about most of the kid dreams I used to have.

But I'll be damned if I don't someday make my movie!

Of course, I don't know a thing about the mechanics of movie making. But when I have my bundle, you can bet I'll hire the best cameraman and the best sound man you can find. Then all they're going to have to do is exactly what I tell them, because I've been through my movie a couple million times in my head and I know just the way everything has to look and sound.

Now I've got to tell you I haven't figured out a name for my movie yet. And I'm not quite sure how I can let the people in the audience know that everything that happens takes place in 1938 down in Mississippi. I've seen movies that put white lettered signs right over the picture to tell you things like that, but I think that looks wrong and there can't be any one single thing looking wrong in my movie.

My movie starts like this:

There's a dusty road leading up to a small wooden house. There are these big trees behind the house and more trees on both sides. It's the kind of house poor farm people used to live in, but it's not all run-down. It's painted a nice fresh white and the porch doesn't sag in the middle. It's just a nice little house.

Then there's this black boy that walks out of the house. He's got no shoes and he's not wearing a shirt and his overalls are held up by just one strap. He's saying something to himself, you know, the ways kids do when they're trying to sound like grownups. He says, "Sure a fine day."

Then he goes to the edge of the porch and sits down.

Now this is going to be really hard to show in a movie. That's why I've got to get the best cameraman there is. See, the sun is shining real bright, and the boy feels it on the back of his neck. The movie has to make the audience feel just exactly what it is that the boy is feeling, right there, where there's that little knob on the back of his neck. I guess that camera is going to have to be right inside that boy so we know just how it is when his skin drinks up all that sunshine.

Okay, the door opens again. A tall man comes out. He's got on a white shirt and there are suspenders holding up his pants. The boy turns and looks at him.

Did I say the man and the boy have to look a lot alike?

They do, they surely do.

The man steps on over to the boy and the boy has to lean his head way back to see him because the man is so tall he's near like a giant.

"I'm goin' to the store, Son," the man says. "You go with me?"

The man and the boy walk down the road. The man looks like he always takes great big steps but now he has to walk slow because the boy is with him and you can tell the man doesn't mind. After a while, the man takes hold of the boy's hand. Then the man starts singing:

I'm gonna leave, gonna go off to France.
I'm gonna leave, gonna go away to France.
Gonna go to France
Jus' to give the ladies a chance!

The boy laughs. It's only when the man and the boy are off on their own that the man sings songs like that, and even then the boy has to promise he won't say a thing about it to Mama.

The man sings that song and then another one and they keep walking until they get to the crossroads. There's a store there with a sign in front that says: "Cooper's Groceries, Sundries, and Supplies."

That's where the man and boy go, but, before they get there, the boy asks, "Daddy, can I have a Hershey?"

The man says, "Every time I take you to Cooper's you 'spect a Hershey."

The boy says, "Ain't been to Cooper's but four times."

Then the man says, "We ain't come to buy candy, Son." He looks a little sad, like he wants to buy the boy a treat, but these are hard times and there's no money for candy.

Then they're in the store. There's a big fat white man in an apron behind the counter and he's drinking a Coca-Cola. That's Mr. Cooper. He owns the store. There's two more white men over by the window near the rack that has the magazines, and they're looking at the *Police Gazette* and *The Shadow Mystery Magazine*. The man on the left is skinny and he's got an Adam's apple about twice as big as a real apple. His eyes are always moving back and forth, back and forth. The other man, well, he doesn't look like much of anything.

"'Lo, Claude," is what the skinny one says. His big Adam's apple goes bouncing.

The man still holds the boy's hand and he says, "Afternoon, Mister Winthrop." Then he looks over at the other white man, who doesn't take his eyes off *The Shadow*, and he says, "Afternoon, Mister Deland."

The man and the boy go to the counter. Mr. Cooper sets his soda bottle down next to a box full of plug tobacco. He says, " 'Lo, Claude. What can I do for you?"

"I come about my bill, suh," is what the man says.

"Oh yeah, yeah," Mr. Cooper says. "I told your Essie about that."

He messes with some papers that are stabbed on a spike alongside the cash register. "Here it is. Nine dollars and 30 cents. Want to pay all that now or you give me just some of it and settle up as you can? 'Course I don't like to let these things go on too long."

"No, suh, Mister Cooper, suh," the man says.

Mr. Cooper acts like no one's said anything at all to him. "Bein' you a good customer, Claude, and you always …"

"No, suh, Mister Cooper," the man says. He's not talking loud, but he's talking in a way that gets heard.

"What's that, Claude?" Mr. Cooper says.

"No disrespect, Mister Cooper, but the bill's wrong. I don't owe but six dollars and 87 cents."

Mr. Cooper says, "What's that you sayin'?"

"These are hard times, suh, and I can't afford to be payin' what I'm not owing."

"Claude," Mr. Cooper says, "you sayin' I'm out to cheat you? You watch that kind of talk."

Now we take a look at the white men by the magazine rack. They're still holding the magazines, but they're watching what's going on.

Then we look at Mr. Cooper. He's got both hands on the counter and he's leaning way forward and every time he opens up his mouth to say something, we feel like he's going to swallow up the whole theater full of people watching this movie.

"Goddamn it, boy! I figured out your bill. I never cheated nobody, no white man or nigra, in my entire life."

"Ain't sayin' cheat, Mister Cooper," the man says. "I jus' think you mistaken in your figurin'. I can't do nothin' with a pencil and paper, but I'm good with numbers in my head. You made a mistake ... Mister Cooper, suh."

Mr. Cooper shakes his head. His face is red. He looks like he's run twenty miles using only one leg. "Goddamn it!" he yells—and then he really starts hollering. "Well just goddamn it and *double* goddamn it all to hell! You just get your black ass outta here!"

Now the little black boy looks like he doesn't know what's going on. He's never heard anyone talk that way to his daddy. Mr. Cooper keeps on hollering. "You don't owe me nothing no more! You surely do not! And I don't need your trade and I sure don't want you taking up space that ought to belong to customers who know I'm a fair man."

He aims a big, fat finger at the boy. "Get on out and haul your little nigra with you."

The white men are a still over there by the magazines. Mr. Cooper looks at them. Then he smiles like he's going to tell a secret joke just for the three of them. He says, "That is, if he is your little nigra."

Now here is where the man doing the sound for my movie will have to do a very careful job. I want the whole store to fill up to bursting with the laughter of those white men. I want the two magazine men laughing, and Mr. Cooper laughing, and it gets louder and louder and louder, and then, all of a sudden, there's no sound at all.

Nothing.

And everything happens slow from now on, and we see it all just the way the little black boy is seeing it, as his daddy's black fingers go around the neck of that Coca-Cola bottle on the counter, and he picks up the bottle and swings it back and then that bottle is going Crash! right across Mr. Cooper's big, fat, laughing white face.

Green chunks of the Coca-Cola bottle hang in the air.

Blood that looks like a red hand stretching out its fingers is all over Mr. Cooper's face and one drop makes a big, thick splat on the counter.

Now it's outside and the boy and the man are walking away from the store. There's yelling and screaming behind them, but they keep on walking down the road like there's never been any trouble at all.

And they walk on home.

That's it.

I guess there can be some music or something there, but that is the end of my movie.

No, we don't have men coming round with guns. We don't have a black man grabbing his chest and falling off the porch and layin' there kicking on the ground with the blood making a puddle on his clean white shirt and shooting out of his mouth like a fountain.

We don't have a black woman waving her arms and screaming, "Sweet Jesus, sweet Jesus, help him!"

No.

There's no little black boy looking down like he doesn't know what's happening as he watches his daddy die on the Mississippi dirt.

No.

That's not in my movie, not that part. It doesn't happen this time.

No.

Not this time.

NEW MOON ON THE WATER

14 SHORT HORROR STORIES

1. THE MUSIC OF THE NIGHT

The wolves howled.

"Listen to them, the children of the night!" Dracula said to his guest. "What music they make!"

"It is terrible, but I will try to work with them," said the Phantom.

2. MIND CONTROL

In the next sixty seconds, think of those horrible, depressing, painful, miserable, flat-out and utterly wretched experiences you've lived through; come up with as many as you can.

Good.

Now think of the words: If only ...

Okay. All through. Don't think of any of this stuff. Okay?

Just don't think of it. Simple, huh?

See you around.

3. OF COURSE THEY SAVED THE BRAIN

Hitler's brain. And of course the head made such a practical and aesthetically pleasing container, that it, too, was saved.

And the brain decided it was time. And the eyes blinked. And the Chaplinesque mustache wriggled like a mildly palsied caterpillar.

And the men of science, Japanese and German and Russian and Korean and Cuban and Saudi and American, waited.

Then the mouth issued the command: "*Ja! Der Tag!*"

And simultaneously Japanese and German and Russian and Korean and Cuban and Saudi and American fingers pressed their buttons.

And every cell phone in the world exploded.

4. KIP'S QUESTION

kip was four years old and like nearly every day had been hell on jet-skis all day

aluminum foil in the electrical outlets and see what happens when you turn on every faucet in the house and let's play bowling with cantaloupe in the supermarket and

she had thought about smacking him and smacking him good but as a kid she had been smacked good too many times for too many reasons she usually had not understood and

now even if kip should be in bed she did not want to fight with him to get him to bed and he was just sitting there about three-quarters of an inch from the television and the news was on and kip was watching because he would watch just about anything that moved for about 30 seconds or even a minute sometimes

and

then a story came on with a lady being taken away by police and the lady was a mom who had been telling lies about someone stealing her car with her two kids in it because what really happened was she was the one who killed her kids and

now kip was big-eye-riveted to the television and

then kip turned his head and very quietly asked why did that mom kill her kids

and even though she did not want to say it something low and mean and insistent made her say it and

what she said was

because they were bad

5. WEDDING GIFT

Belittle me, will she? Hah!

The Shrew! Call me feeble and weak, will she? Hah!

Dare to laugh at my ... stamina and demean my technique? Call me fool, will she? Dare I think—her words, mind—"I could even hope to provide her the least satisfaction?"

Hah!

Very well, then, my dear. Oh, very well—but perhaps not so well for you.

On the night of our … nuptial celebration … I assure you, you will receive a quite special wedding gift.

Call me mad, will she?

Hah!

I have created life, do you hear me, LIFE in the laboratory!

Hah!

Let us see what our most singular wedding guest can do for you.

6. THE CHILD MOLESTER REVEALS THE SECRET OF SUCCESS

I know how to listen.

7. HEADLINE: AGENT OF BIOLOGICAL WARFARE FOUND IN IRAQ

They brought him in.

They sat him down.

They made him confess.

WMD?

No, he had a URI, upper respiratory infection.

His orders?

Sneeze or cough on as many Americans as possible.

8. ADVICE

Why don't you just ask that nice colored man to bust up the chiffarobe for you?

9. INSPIRATION

Couldn't come up with anything. Zero. Nada.

Went outside. In the garden, he heard the roses singing.

Went inside. Sat down at the animation table.

Walt Disney created *Silly Symphonies*.

NEW MOON ON THE WATER

10. URBAN MYTH: HALLOWEEN

Got to love the Internet.

Hey, razor blades in apples, Ex-Lax chocolate pumpkins. Peanut brittle with needles. LSD gum (talk about double your pleasure).

All those Halloween horror stories, why, that's all bogus. You know that, don't you?

Because you know how to find answers fast and you have checked out all the Latest BS and Vintage BS dot-coms, the Urban, Suburban, and Rural Legends websites. No murderer on the extension phone upstairs, no hook hanging from the door handle, no fingers in the Doberman's mouth, no beehive hair-do providing condominiums for all manner of biting, boring, breeding insect …

And you've got a built-in BS detector, right? Trick or treat.

Treat or trick.

I look forward to a visit from your kids this Halloween.

11. AMERICAN ICONOGRAPHY IN A SOUTH AMERICAN REVOLUTION

"… able to leap tall buildings in a single bound!" Miguel's English is accented, naturally, but enthusiastic. A pause, not all that long really.

"No," Juan says.

Miguel laughs. "*Que lastima.*" Such a pity.

"*A mí me toca,*" Juan says. My turn.

High above the verdant jungle, Juan grips Sister Consuela's arm and hurls her from the helicopter. "The Flying Nun!" Juan says.

12. IN THE NURSERY

Stop it! Stop that screaming at once!

Put something in his mouth!

Do not twist about like that! Stop your carrying-on!

That's better. Now, hold him more tightly. His arms, John.

There.

Sit on him, Michael.

We shall soon have this shadow sewn back on, Mr. Peter Pan, Esquire, shan't we just?

108

13. REST FOR THE WEARY

No, no, sit down please.

You're safe here. Tomorrow, you can tell me everything about the people chasing you …

They're not? Well, whatever, tomorrow we can discuss it. You're exhausted, aren't you?

Your drink? Please, just diet soda. Why would I want to … That's it, stretch out.

Here, just let me slip this nice pod under your head.

Sleep.

14. EXPIRATION DATE

Monday. June 6, 1985

And so you sit down to eat breakfast.

The clink-click of the cereal in the bowl is almost more than you can bear, but you have to eat because … You have to eat.

And you take the carton of milk and on the side is a picture of a child. Your child.

And on the top of the carton is a date: June 8, 1985.

And on the wall by the telephone is a calendar you don't have to look at it to know the date that is circled is June 1 and within the circle is a clearly written lone word in your handwriting: *Funeral.*

Then you pour the milk on the cereal.

You have to eat.

You have to eat.

NEW MOON ON THE WATER

PARTY TIME

Mama had told him it would soon be party time. That made him excited but also a little afraid. Oh, he liked party time, he liked making people happy, and he always had fun, but it was kind of scary going upstairs.

Still, he knew it would be all right because Mama would be with him. Everything was all right with Mama and he always tried to be Mama's good boy.

Once, though, a long time ago, he had been bad. Mama must not have put his chain on right, so he'd slipped it off his leg and went up the stairs all by himself and opened the door. Oh! Did Mama ever whip him for that. Now he knew better. He'd never, never go up without Mama.

And he liked it down in the basement, liked it a lot. There was a little bed to sleep on. There was a yellow light that never went off. He had blocks to play with. It was nice in the basement.

Best of all, Mama visited him often. She kept him company and taught him to be good.

He heard the funny sound that the door at the top of the stairs made and he knew Mama was coming down. He wondered if it was party time. He wondered if he'd get to eat the happy food.

But then he thought it might not be party time. He saw Mama's legs, Mama's skirt. Maybe he had done something bad and Mama was going to whip him.

He ran to the corner. The chain pulled hard at his ankle. He tried to go away, to squeeze right into the wall.

"No, Mama! I am not bad! I love my Mama. Don't whip me!"

Oh, he was being silly. Mama had food for him. She wasn't going to whip him.

"You're a good boy. Mama loves you, too, my sweet, good boy."

The food was cold. It wasn't the kind of food he liked best, but Mama said he always had to eat everything she brought him because if not he was a bad boy.

It was hot food he liked most. He called it the happy food.

111

That's the way it felt inside him.

"Is it party time yet, Mama?"

"Not yet, sweet boy. Don't you worry, it will be soon. You like Mama to take you upstairs for parties, don't you?"

"Yes, Mama! I like to see all the people. I like to make them happy."

Best of all, he liked the happy food. It was so good, so hot.

He was sleepy after Mama left, but he wanted to play with his blocks before he lay down on his bed. The blocks were fun. He liked to build things with them and make up funny games.

He sat on the floor. He pushed the chain out of the way. He put one block on top of another block, then a block on top of that one. He built the blocks up real high, then made them fall. That was funny and he laughed.

Then he played "party time" with the blocks. He put one block over here and another over there and the big, big block was Mama.

He tried to remember some of the things people said at party time so he could make the blocks talk that way. Then he placed a block in the middle of all the other blocks. That was Mama's good boy.

It was himself.

Before he could end the party time game, he got very sleepy. His belly was full, even if it was only cold food.

He went to bed. He dreamed a party time dream of happy faces and the good food and Mama saying, "Good boy, my sweet boy."

Then Mama was shaking him. He heard funny sounds coming from upstairs. Mama slipped the chain off his leg.

"Come my good boy."

"It's party time?"

"Yes."

Mama took his hand. He was frightened a little, the way he always was just before party time.

"It's all right, my sweet boy."

Mama led him up the stairs. She opened the door.

"This is party time. Everyone is so happy."

He was not scared anymore. There was a lot of light and so many laughing people in the party room.

"Here's the good, sweet boy, everybody!"

Then he saw it on the floor. Oh, he hoped it was for him!

"That's yours, good boy, all for you."

He was so happy! It had four legs and a black nose. When he walked closer to it, it made a funny sound that was something like the way he sounded when Mama whipped him.

His belly made a noise and his mouth was all wet inside.

It tried to get away from him, but he grabbed it and he squeezed it real hard. He heard things going snap inside it.

Mama was laughing and laughing and so was everyone else. He was making them all so happy.

"You know what it is, don't you, my sweet boy?"

He knew.

It was the happy food.

NEW MOON ON THE WATER

LOVE, HATE,

AND THE BEAUTIFUL JUNKYARD SEA

It wasn't until the third grade I learned I could love. It was in third grade I met Caralynn Pitts.

Before that, seems to me all I did was hate. I had reason. As everyone in Harlinville knew and let me know, I was trash. The Deweys were so low-down you couldn't get lower if you dug straight to China and kept on going. My daddy was skinny, slit-eyed, and silent except in his drunken, grunt-shouting, crazy fits that set him to beating on my mother or me. Maybe it was the dark and dust of the coal mine—he worked Old Ben Number Three—that got inside him, poisoned him to turn him so mean like that.

My mother might have tried to be a good momma, I don't know, but by the time I was able to think anything about it, she must have just given up. In a day she never said more than ten words to me. At night, she cried a lot.

Trash, no-account trash, bad as any and worse than most you find in southern Illinois, that's what I was, and if you're trash, you start out hating yourself and hating your folks and hating the God Who made you trash and plans to keep you that way, but soon you get so hate filled, you have to let it out or just bust and so you get to hating other people. I hated kids who came to school in nice clothes, with a different shirt everyday, the kids who had Bugs Bunny lunchboxes with two sandwiches on bread so white it made me think of hospitals, the kids who lost teeth and got quarters from a tooth fairy, the kids whose daddies never got drunk and always took them on vacations to Starved Rock State Park or way faraway, like Disneyland or the Grand Canyon. I hated all the mommas up at the pay laundry every Monday morning, washing the clothes so clean for their families. I hated Mr. Mueller, at the Texaco, who always told me, "Take a hike, Bradford Dewey," or "Boy, jump in a hole and pull it in after you," when I wanted to watch cars go up on the grease rack, and I hated

Mr. Eikenberry, the postmaster. Mr. Eikenberry had that breeze-tingly smell of Old Spice on him. What my daddy smelled like was whiskey and wickedness.

If you hate somebody, you want to hurt them, and I thought of hateful, hurting things happening to all the people I hated. There wasn't a one in Harlinville I didn't set my mind on a wish picture for, a hate-hurt picture that left them busted up and bleeding and dead. I imagined a monster big as an Oldsmobile grabbing up Rodney Carlisle—his father owned the hardware store on the square—and ripping off his arms and legs, a snake as long as the Mississippi River swallowing Claire Bobbit, Patty Marsel, Edith Hebb, and all the girls who used to tease me, and an invisible vampire ripping the throats out of all the teachers at McKinley School.

You might think, then, that I really did try to hurt people, I mean, use my hands, punch them in the nose or hit them on the head with a ball bat or something like that, but that's not so. Never in my whole life have I done that kind of hurt to anyone.

What I did was to find another way to get people. I started lying. You tell someone the truth, it means you trust them. It's like you got something you like them enough to share with them. Doesn't have to be an important piece of truth, either; it can be a little nothing: "I went to the show last night and that was one fine picture they had," or "It's really a pretty day," or "My cat had kittens," or anything at all. You tell someone the truth, you've given them something and it's the same as liking them.

So when you lie to a person, it's because you got no use for them, you hate their guts and what makes it so fine is you're doing it without ever having to flat-out say what you feel.

So I lied, lied my head off.

I told little lies, like my Uncle Everett sent me five dollars because I was his favorite nephew and I did so have a wonderful birthday gift for Rodney Carlisle but I wasn't giving it to him because he didn't ask me to his party, and I told monster whoppers, some of them crazy, like I was just adopted by the Deweys but my real parents were Hollywood movie stars, or I had to kill this 300-pound wolf with just my bare hands when it attacked me out at the junkyard.

I didn't really fool anyone with my lies, you know. That wasn't what I was trying to do. All in all, I'd say Miss Krydell, the third grade teacher, was right when she used to say, "Bradford, you are a hateful little liar."

But all that changed when Caralynn Pitts came and showed me th-beautiful junkyard sea.

You've probably had to do it yourself, stand in front of the class and tell who you are and all because you're the new kid, and you're supposed to be making friends right off. It was the first week in May, already too hot and too damp, an oily spring like you get in southern Illinois. The new girl up by Miss Krydell's desk was Caralynn Pitts. She had this peepy voice about one squeak lower than Minnie Mouse. Her eyes and hair were both the same shade of black and she was wearing this blue and dark green plaid dress.

Caralynn Pitts didn't say much except her name and that she lived on Elmscourt Lane, but in a town the size of Harlinville, everyone knew most everything about her a week before she'd even moved in. Her daddy was a doctor and he was going to work at the county hospital and her momma was dead.

Well, Caralynn Pitts wasn't anything to me, not yet. I went back to drilling a hole in my desktop with my yellow pencil.

A week later I talked to Caralynn Pitts for the first time.

It was ten o'clock, the big Regulator clock up near the flag ticking off the long, hot seconds, and that was "arithmetic period," so, like always, Miss Krydell asked who didn't do the homework, and then she started right in on me: "Bradford Dewey, do you have the fractions?"

"No, ma'am."

"Please stand, Bradford, and stop mumbling. Didn't you do the homework?"

I actually had tried to but, when I was working at the kitchen table, my daddy came up and popped me alongside the head for no reason except he felt like it, so I lit out of the house.

I wasn't going to tell Miss Krydell any such thing. "Ma'am, I did so do the homework. I don't have it is all."

"Why is that?" said Miss Krydell.

I felt this good one, a big, twisty lie, working its way out of me. "I was on the way to school and I had my fractions and next thing I knew, the scurlets come up all around me and that's how I lost my homework."

"The *scurlets*," said Miss Krydell. "Please tell us about the scurlets."

There was a laugh from the first row, and someone echoing it a row over, but Miss Krydell swept her eyes over the classroom and it got dead quiet real quick.

I said, "The scurlets aren't all that big. No bigger than puppies, but they are plenty mean. There's a lot of them around every time it gets to be

Spring."

"Oh, is that so?" Miss Krydell said.

"Yes, ma'am. It was running away from the scurlets so they wouldn't get me that I dropped my homework and I couldn't go on back for it, could I? See, the scurlets have pointy tails with a stinger on them and if they sting you, you swell up and turn blue and you die. And when you're dead, the scurlets eat you up ..." I was really running with it now. "They start on your face and they bite out your eyes the first thing ..."

"That will be enough, Bradford."

"... I guess for a scurlet, your eye is kind of like a grape. It goes 'pop' when they bite down on it ..."

"Enough, Bradford."

I stop right there. Miss Krydell says, "You are a liar, Bradford, and I am sick and tired of your lies. You'll stay after school and write 'I promise to tell the truth,' 500 times."

I sat down, thinking how much I hated Miss Krydell and how bad my hand was going to feel when I finished writing all that.

The day went on, and, it was strange, but every time I happened to look around the room, there was Caralynn Pitts looking at me with those black eyes that were big as the wolf's in "Little Red Riding Hood." I didn't quite know what to make of that.

After school, I wrote and wrote and wrote, each "I promise to tell the truth" sloppier than the one before it. With my hand feeling like someone had taken a sledgehammer to it, Miss Krydell finally let me go. I cut back of the school through the playground to take the long way home. I heard this *shh-click* like someone running on the gravel, and then, she was calling my name—somehow I knew it was her right off—so I stopped and turned around.

She ran up to me and before I could say anything, she said, "You can see things, can't you?"

Not knowing what to make of that, I said, "Huh?"

"See things," she says.

I figured Caralynn Pitts had stayed around school just to tease me like Claire Bobbit, Patty Marsel, Edith Hebb did, and so I answered in kind of a nasty way, "Sure can."

I pointed over at the monkey bars. "You go hang by your knees and I can see your underpants. What do you think about that?"

Caralynn said, "You can see the things other people don't, can't you, Bradford? Like the scurlets." Then she started whispering, "Bradford, *I* can see things, all kinds of things, too. I can see tiny people living under sunflowers and I can see giants jumping from cloud to cloud and I can see bugs that fly in moonlight and spell out your name on their wings and once I saw a stone in the sunshine trying to it turn itself into apple jelly!"

I said, "What are you talking about?"

"Both of us, we can see things, so that means we ought to be friends."

I said, "No sense to what you're talking, Caralynn. I can't see anything much, nothing like what you're saying, and if you can, then you sound crazy."

Caralynn said, "I can't tell my daddy about what I see because he says it's only pretend and I'm too old to pretend that way. I used to tell Momma, before she died. She said I had imagination and sometimes, when there was nothing worth seeing in the whole world, all you had was your imagination. When Momma was so sick, she was dying, I guess, it seems like it rained every day. I used to sit with her, and we'd look out the window and every day, Bradford, every day I could see a rainbow. It had 12 colors, that rainbow, colors like you don't ever see in a plain old rainbow. I used to tell Momma how the sun made the colors change from second to second. Momma said that was our rainbow. That was the rainbow over the graveyard the day we buried Momma. It wasn't even raining, but I looked up and there it was, and where it bent and disappeared on the other side of the world, I saw Momma and she was waving to me."

"I don't know," I said. "I don't know anything about that or rainbows."

"Bradford," Caralynn said, "there's something I want to show you. Something beautiful. Can I?"

"I guess," I said.

I'm not a bit sorry about saying that, and haven't been since the words slid off my lips, but in these years gone by, I sure have asked myself why I just didn't tell Caralynn to go on and get lost.

Maybe the reason is, I was small and my whole life was small but packed inside was this big hate and hate is an ugly thing, and so I guess I was tired of all that ugly and ready to be shown something ... beautiful.

Not that I believed Caralynn Pitts had a thing to show me, but I did go with her, all the way past the edge of town, through Neidmeyer's Meadow, and then along the railroad tracks until we came to the curve, and there, by this rusted steel building that I guess the railroad must have once had a use for but didn't anymore, was the old junkyard.

It wasn't the kind of junkyard where you go to sell your falling-apart car. It was an acre or so where everybody dumped the trash that wouldn't bum and was too big for the garbage men to haul off. It was all useless, twisted garbage: a three-legged wringer washer with the wires sticking out the bottom, and a refrigerator with the basket coil on top, and an old trunk without a lid like maybe a sailor once had, and a steam radiator, and a bathtub, and hundreds of pipes, and a couple of shells of cars, and thousands and thousands of tin cans. Everywhere you looked were hills and mountains of steel and glass and plastic, all kinds of trash that came from you didn't know what stuff. Flies swarmed in bunches like black cyclones, and over it all, hanging so stink-heavy you could see it, was the terrible smell.

That was what Caralynn Pitts had to show me.

Not more than a spit away, a rat peeked from under a torn square of pink linoleum, its nasty whiskers quivering. I chucked a stone at it. I told Caralynn Pitts maybe she thought she was funny but I didn't think she was funny and I started to run off.

I didn't get a step before she had my elbow. "Bradford, can't you see it?"

"It's the junkyard. That's all it is."

"It's the sea, Bradford, it's the beautiful junkyard sea. You have to look at it the right way. You have to want to see it, to see how beautiful it is. Please look, Bradford."

So I did. And Caralynn Pitts started talking to me in this peeping voice that seemed to crawl from my ear right into my brain.

"Look at the water. Can't you see how blue and green it is? See the waves ..."

... the water goes beyond nowhere, the waves gentle as a night breeze, the rippling tiny hills rolling in to wash against the diamond-dotted golden sands where we stand ...

"... and a sea gull ..."

... its wings are made of air, its eyes magic black ...

"... and way out there ..."

... there, at the horizon ... a whale ... there ... whales, the song of the whales, placid rumbles unearthly and eternal ...

"Bradford," Caralynn said. "Can you see it, the beautiful junkyard sea?"

"No," I said, and that was the truth, but in the moment before I said it, I almost saw it. It was like someone had painted a picture of the junkyard on an old bedsheet and the wind catching that sheet as it hung on a line was making everything ripple and change before my eyes.

It was because I *almost* saw it—and because, I know now, there was a fierce want in me to see it—I came back to the junkyard day after day with Caralynn Pitts.

120

On a Wednesday, in the afternoon, a week after school let out, it happened.

I saw the beautiful junkyard sea.

The forever waters, sunlight slanting, cutting through foam and fathom upon fathom, then diminishing, vanishing into the ever-night depths. The sea gulls, winged arrows cutting random arcs over the rippling waves. A dolphin bursts from the sea, bejeweled droplets and glory, another dolphin, another and another, an explosion of dolphins ...

Far off, a beckoning atoll, a palm-treed island. Far off, a coral reef, living land. Far off, the promise of magic, the assurance that a lie is only a dream and that dreams are true.

Good thing you don't have to learn or practice love, that it just happens.

In the fine sea spray
in the clean mist of air and salt water

I kissed Caralynn Pitts on the lips.

I told her I loved her.

I loved her and I loved the beautiful junkyard sea.

ᥱᥣ • ᥱᥣ

Every day that summer, Caralynn and I visited the beautiful junkyard sea. It was always there, always new, always wonderful.

Then late in August, Caralynn Pitts told me she was moving. Her daddy was joining the staff of a hospital in Seattle. I said I would always love her. She said she would always love me.

"But what about the beautiful junkyard sea?" I asked her.

"It will always be ours," she said. "It will always be here for us."

She promised to write to give me her address once they were settled in Seattle. We would keep on loving each other and when we grew up, we'd get married and be together forever.

The next week, she moved. Months and then years went by and there was no letter.

But I had the beautiful junkyard sea. And this is the truth: I never stopped loving Caralynn Pitts or believing she would return to me, return to the beautiful junkyard sea.

ᥱᥣ • ᥱᥣ

She did.

I was 22 years old. When I was 12, my daddy got drunk and drove the car into a tree and killed himself. What with his miner's benefits, and no money going out on whiskey, Mama and I got by. I'd scraped through high school, pretty bad grades, but I learned in shop class that I had a way with engines. Pop the hood and hand me a wrench, and chances were good to better yet that I could fix any problem there was, and so I was working at Mueller's Texaco.

On a sunny day in late April, Caralynn Pitts drove her white LTD up to the regular pump and asked me to fill it up, check the oil, battery, and transmission fluid.

Stooped over, I just kind of stood there by the open car window, jaw hanging like a moron. There was a question in Caralynn Pitts's big eyes for a second and then she knew.

"It is Bradford, right?"

"Yes," I said.

"You've changed so much."

"I guess you have too," I said. That was probably the right thing to say, but to tell the truth, she hadn't done that much changing. It was like she was still the kid she had been, only bigger. "You came back, Caralynn," I said.

She gave me another funny look, and then she laughed. "I guess I have. I work out of Chicago—I'm in advertising—and I was on my way to St. Louis and, well, I needed gas, so I didn't even think anything about it … Just pulled off 1-57 and here I am."

"You came back to our beautiful junkyard sea," I said.

"Huh?" Caralynn Pitts said. She laughed again. "Oh, I get it. I remember. The beautiful junkyard sea, that was some game we had. I guess both of us had pretty wild imaginations."

"It was no game, Caralynn," I said. "It isn't."

"Well, I don't know …" She tapped her fingers on the steering wheel and looked through the windshield.

"Could you fill it up, please? And do you have a restroom?"

I told her, "Inside." I filled the tank. Everything checked out under the hood. When she came back a minute later, I said, "Maybe we could talk a minute or two, Caralynn? It's been a long time and all and we used to be good friends, special friends."

She took a quick look at her wristwatch. Then, in her eyes, I saw something like what used to be there so many years ago.

"We were, weren't we?" she said. "Maybe a quick cup of coffee or something. Is there someplace we could go?"

"Sure," I said, "I know the place. Just let me tell Mueller I'll be gone awhile."

I drove her LTD. She told me she had gone to college, Washington State, majoring in business. She told me she and a guy, I forget his name, were getting serious about one another, thinking about getting engaged. She told me she hoped to be moving up in advertising, become an account executive in another year or so. When we got out past the town limits, she said, "Bradford, where are you taking us?"

"You know," I said.

"Bradford ... I don't know what's going on. What are you doing? You're acting, well, you're acting strange." I heard it in her voice. She was frightened.

"There's something I want to show you," I told her, and I drove to the junkyard.

She didn't want to get out of the car.

She said, "Bradford, don't ... don't hurt me."

"I could never hurt you, Caralynn," I said.

I took her arm. I could feel how stiff she was holding herself, like her spine was steel.

"Here it is, Caralynn," I said. "Here we are."

We stood on the sun-washed shore of the beautiful junkyard sea. She jerked like she wanted to pull away from me but I held her arm even tighter. "I don't know what you want, Bradford. What am I supposed to say? What am I supposed to do?"

"What do you see, Caralynn?" I asked.

"I ... I don't see ... anything, Bradford."

"Don't say that, Caralynn. I love you. Don't make me hate you."

"Bradford, I ... I can't see what isn't there. This is a junkyard. That's all it is, just an ugly, stinking junkyard! Please ..."

They never found Caralynn Pitts. I left her car there and walked back to town. The police did have questions, of course, since I was the last person to see her, but like I said, I know how to lie, and so I made up a few little lies and one or two big ones that made them happy.

I haven't gone back to the beautiful junkyard sea. Maybe I never will.

But I can't forget, won't ever forget, and don't want to forget how Caralynn looked

when the waters turned black and churning and the lightning shattered the sky and the sea gulls shrieked and the fins of sharks circled and circled and the first tentacle whipped out of the foam and hooked her leg, and another shot out, circled her waist, and then one more, across her face, choking off her screams, as she was dragged toward that thing rising in the angry water, that great, gray-green, puffy bag that was its head, yellow eyes shining hungrily, the

corn-colored, curved beak clattering, as it dragged her deeper, deeper, and then
she disappeared and there was blood on the water and that was all, until,
    at last
    the sun shone
    and all was quiet in
    the beautiful
    junkyard
    sea

I AM YOUR NEED

I

August 4, 1962
The Brentwood Section of Los Angles

Marilyn Monroe lies naked and dying.

You can see it there, at that spot on her forehead where electrolysis permanently removed her widow's peak. Just beneath the skin's surface, a blue-black flower grows.

It is Death.

There is the promise of finality in her every tentative breath, the sporadic sighings, the intimation of ending.

Marilyn Monroe is dying.

I am her death.

And I will die, too.

That is, when she dies, I have to assume I will also cease to be.

Marilyn Monroe. She was born in the flesh and of the flesh.

Like you.

And I?

I was born of her need.

I *am* her need.

II

February 6, 1961
New York

I could not bear it. I could bear no more, anymore. I wanted to die.

No, I *need* to die. That is what I thought.

The address of the Lonesome Capitol of the world is East Fifty-Seventh Street: The Millers' apartment, now my apartment. His typewriter was gone, his *Oxford Unabridged* was gone, his leather-bound copy of *Madame Bovary*, the first "quality book" he ever bought, his underwear, his Schick electric shaver, the silk tie he wore when he testified before HUAC … He did not take the picture of me I had given him, the one in which I wear white gloves (hiding my ugly hands, my ugly, ugly, *ugly* hands) and a hat that Mamie Eisenhower might have worn. I looked "demure" in the picture, he said. I looked regal and contemplative and lovely, he said. I kissed him regally and demurely and even contemplatively, and then I fucked him until his eyes rolled back in his head and he screamed some things none of his characters will ever be allowed to say on stage.

I stood at the living room window. Below, the city. (The Asphalt Jungle! The Naked City! Broadway, the busiest and loneliest street in the world! All the clichés of popular culture are true!) It was a perfectly cold, perfect blue sky February afternoon. You cannot be more alone than that.

It seemed Death was summoning me. My marriages were dead. My marriage to Jim Dougherty, Just Plain Jim, the sweet Irish merchant marine. To the jealous and sweet and mean Yankee Clipper, my slugger, my Joltin' Joe.

And now, to the New York Jewish Liberal Intellectual, Arthur. I called Arthur "Pops" or "Popsie." I consider *The Crucible* his best work. He was surprised, you know, that I understood the play so well, that anyone as blonde as I could possibly comprehend metaphor and symbol. I got mad when he told me that. I cried. I told him I wasn't stupid. I told him I understood metaphor and symbol, understood better than he, because I goddamned good and goddamned well was metaphor and symbol and the way he looked at me then, the way he looked at me, that clever observing way, I knew the bastard someday would use what I had said in a play.

I loved Arthur Miller. Arthur Miller loved me, but, when you realize something like that, that all you might say or do or think, that you are likely to become grist for the creative mill … No, you cannot stay married to a man.

There were other voices beckoning me, calling me to the Nation of the Dead.

My children. I don't know how many had been scraped out of me, poor little blobs, you have to force yourself to lose track of statistics like that, but all those children died and they cursed me: They cursed my tubes so I could never have sons or daughters. They left behind a dead womb.

The dead call out …

There, the insane contralto of Della Monroe, dear old Gram, who muttered she smelled strange smells in the house that nobody else could smell, burning silk, fish oil, lye soap, and something she called "the putrid stink of black flowers." There were men in wool suits, men with gray hats and well-shined shoes, they had to be men from "the agency, that's who they were," and they followed her. They sat behind her on street cars. They held the door for her when she stepped into a department store. They had accents, but the accents kept changing, French, Spanish, Eastern European …

You know, it's weird, but if you really try, I bet you can remember everything, everything, no matter how young you were, and I can remember Gram's lopsided determined smile as she pressed a pillow down on me. (I can still summon that wet-feather taste—in my nightmares I taste it) I was maybe 14 months old or so when Gram tried to kill me.

Someone stopped her. Mama? That I can't remember for sure. Maybe I have not tried hard enough. I might need more analysis. It might have been my mother. Poor Gladys, and sometimes you think she had to be doomed because she was named Gladys (I chose my name, I choose my names, Marilyn Monroe, Zelda Zonk, Journey Evers, but I cannot run away from what I am!); not all that long after Gram played "Baby want pillow," my mother went crazy herself; one day, instead of just looking nervous, with her hands flying this way and that, she sat down and started crying. "I can't, I can't, I just can't …" She kept saying that and she went off to the asylum and that's where you will find her today.

Family tradition: Gram got packed off to the insane asylum and died there.

(Was the Monroe Madness my inheritance? I've frequently discussed that with my psychiatrists. We talk about "nature and nurture," genetic tendencies, then they prescribe new drugs—I give the Demerol four stars, but forget that Seconal: leaves you with a cotton brain and the flavor of a day-old Dr. Scholl's corn pad in your mouth—but mostly my therapists want me to talk about fucking. A couple have wanted to do more than talk.)

Oh, and by the way, my movie was dead.

It was/had been called *Something's Got to Give*. I had insisted on a tasteful swimming-pool nude scene, so tasteful that tasteful stills had tastefully been carried in the always-tasteful *Life* magazine, pictures which tastefully showed my tasteful tits, the top of my tasteful tush crack (a far cry, don't you think, from such digest-size stroke mags, wherein my image used to appear, as *Caper, Dizzy Winks,* and *Hotcha Babe!*) but the production was all shut down, *boomthudboom*. Studio lawsuits against me. Countersuits against the studio.

NEW MOON ON THE WATER

All right, the script was *dreck à la dreck*. Definitely. That did not matter. It often doesn't. Consider *Some Like It Hot,* the kind of "filmic vehicle" that might have starred Gale Storm with Moe, Larry, and Curly, had they had a better agent, some luck, and the ability to read. As it is, *Hot* was perfect for me: I became a respected comédienne (accent it properly, if you please), a "luminous and gifted comic actress with impeccable timing and commanding presence," said Archer Kellbourne in the *New York Times.*

Something's Got to Give could have been my salvation. No. I did not want salvation.

Something's got to give and the something is me.

Okay. Grandiose, I know. Self-pitying shit. Solipsistic.

Does it surprise you that such a word is in my vocabulary? I have, after all, despite its aging, what has been appraised as a "million-dollar ass" by no less an authority than Hollywood raconteur and celebrated ass connoisseur Groucho Marx. With an ass you can take to the bank, why, mercy on my Pie O My, why ever would you even *need* a brain?

Pay attention, *s'il vous plaît* (she said multilingually, which has nothing to do with giving you a blow job): Here are other words I know and can properly use: insouciant, ontological, non sequitur, dialectic, moribund, phlegmatic, truculent ...

May I not say, "Seurat's pointillism never descends into perfunctory technique or mannerism"? Do you think, "That guy sure painted pretty with those little dots" is the MM style?

Maybe you are right. Maybe I am a dumb blonde. After all, I did give Yves Montand a blow job. Stupid, huh?

Oh, the hell with it.

The hell with it already.

It was time to die, time to stop concerning myself about what I truly was and what people thought I was and ...

Time to die.

My first thought was to step out onto the ledge, to take that deepest of breaths as I sucked in clean winter air, to look up at the sky and to see it with the utmost clarity and then to leap.

Step out onto the ledge...

My god, that would be like a scene from *I Love Lucy.* "Looseeee, choo get back in *la casa muy pronto!* You got some 'splainin' to do."

I wanted to die.

I did not want to be ridiculous.

So I opened the living room window as wide as possible. And then I backed up.

I would run and hurl myself out. A swan dive (just like Esther Williams—to her credit, she never attempted to act—or think), only sans water. I had heard that jumpers lost consciousness before they landed and there was an appeal in that.

I clenched my fists.

I licked my lips. They were dry and rough. My mouth felt cottony. Nembutal and Dom Pérignon and chloral hydrate, an always interesting aftertaste.

I could hear my heart beat but not feel it. That was curious, I thought.

And then I ran but it was not so much running as floating, and I didn't know if I could really do it, if I had the force of will to kill myself.

Then just before the jump, I looked down, and there was someone out there, someone down below on the sidewalk, someone looking up at me

—and I knew him, I could see his face, despite the distance, and I knew him even though I did not know who he was—

—Daddy?

—(you have had the feeling, haven't you, maybe just once in your life, but you have experienced it and so this is not a delusion of mine or a paradox for you, is it?)

—and I said, "N- ... Nuh-No-No."

(I stuttered as a child. Sometimes, even though I am now all grown up, I still do.)

I changed my mind.

I made a rational decision: I did not have to die. I was meant to live. I was a survivor.

But momentum or destiny or something worse carried me on, carried me toward the cold and the window and then I thrust my arms out, locking my elbows, and the heels of my hands smashed hard against the window sill and the shock went all the way up into my teeth and I went reeling backward.

I did not die.

A day later, I checked myself into the Payne Whitney Psychiatric Clinic at New York Hospital, where I was classified as "suicidal," which was neo-Jungian, post-Freudian, Harry Stack Fucking Sullivan bullshit.

Fuck that, Freddy.

Marilyn Monroe is a survivor.

III

If it can be said that I am capable of surprise, I am often surprised by all that I know and by all that I do not know:

For example, I can intelligently discuss existentialism, possibly win an argument with Jean-Paul Sartre himself if need be. (Existence before essence, yes, albeit not in my case.) Let the subject turn to the aesthetics of cinematography, and I will explain the importance of the Eisenstein montage and the Gance panorama. Shall we focus on the universal themes of Osip Mandelstam's modernist poetry or the immensity of suffering in Picasso's *Guernica* or the myriad subtleties of vocal shading in the performances of June Christie?

Marilyn needed me to be smart, to be intellectual and artistic. You were no dunce, Marilyn, no dim-bulb bimbo, no sack-ready starlet with a *VACANCY* sign on her forehead and *HOT TO TROT* on her round heels. You needed intellect and that is what I became (in part!) and what I am.

I am your need.

Yet I have no idea how to write a check. That is because you had others to take care of that. On an afternoon kiddy TV show, I heard the word "hygrometer"; I have no concept of what it is, what it does, why it is needed, anymore than do you. You thought Sukarno was the president of India, not Indonesia; you had no idea of the history, the culture, or even the location of either country and so, neither do I.

And of course I had to be "political" because you were involved in your own way in politics. I guess you would have to call me a Democrat. Here I always defer, Marilyn, to your reasoning:

Jack is a damned clever politician and progressive thinker and not such a bad lay, say a six or seven, but he's more in love with himself than he could ever be with anyone else (poor Jackie, poor, poor Jackie), or with the country for that matter, and Bobby Kennedy is a good man, usually, even if being Catholic has made him nuttier than most Catholics, and he is so smart that he doesn't feel threatened by a smart woman and so it's good to talk to him and he is a good politician and maybe he will be able to help people the way he wants and maybe Jack can help him, if Jack's ego will permit IT, and you know what is really nice is that Bobby really does love his wife and kids, so no matter how bad he wants to put it to Marilyn! Monroe! and wants to even more because Big Brother has greased the gears, no matter what, Bobby probably won't do it—and you do have to respect a man who won't fuck you …

Here is what else I know, Marilyn.

You needed me.

And when the need was powerful enough, when it was pure ferocity of need, then, like magic, like dream, like aneurism or lottery, like the roll of the dice, the whirl of the Great Mandala

I am.

With no burden of personal history, with no more clue to my beginnings than had any fleabite scratching caveman, there I am!

I am

your need

I AM

IV

September 4, 1958
Early afternoon

San Diego is the best city in California and perhaps in the United States. The weather is always so near to perfect that you do not think at all about the weather. The youth are golden and smell of sea water and lotions and if you see one of them frowning it is noteworthy. Old cars have no rust, no wrinkles, no dents, nor do old people. Dos Picos Park is the favorite park of San Diego's residents. The oak trees are majestic as only oaks can be and the shadows cast by their limbs are not frightening. And there are the ducks waiting in the pond. The ducks like visitors.

She liked being here, squatting at the water's edge, tossing oyster crackers to the appreciative ducks. She should have been in makeup and costume, should have been on the set at Coronado Beach, but she had decided to be difficult, a star turn and how do you like it, you assholes. She could not stand to be with Mr. Billy Wilder, a certified prick (figuratively speaking) but without the sensitivity of a prick (literally speaking); and she couldn't stand to be with Curtis, who told her, "The script says I kiss you, but kissing you is like kissing Hitler."

Curtis probably would delight in kissing Hitler. The uniform and the leather boots and all. Curtis definitely thought he could out-beautiful her. She thought he'd look like a mummified drag queen when he got old, and that wasn't in the least ironic because ...

Oh, God, she was so afraid, she was so afraid. The mind was going: *Tilt! That's all, Folks!* Right into the Mad Mad Monroe Maelstrom.

"It's me, Sugar." That was her part, her only line, for yesterday's scene. "It's me, Sugar."

Here is the *Reader's Digest Condensed* version of what she said:

I ... i- it's sugar, me.

Sugar me

It is I! *Cigar!*

It's just me, sugar pie.

It's just fucking sugar shit fuck fuck ...

It required 37 fucking takes for her to say, "It's me, Sugar," 37 takes to synch brain with mouth to get out words that Lassie could have managed with one hand cue from trainer Rudd Weatherwax and the promise of two Gaines biscuits.

And there was Billy Wilder, looking like he hadn't had a dump in three weeks and had no hope for the future, and Mr. Tony "I Feel Pretty" Curtis throwing his hands in the air.

She had to get away, had to, had to be alone—

—did not want to be alone, so alone—

Incognito time. Easy, surprisingly easy. Forget Max Factor and Maybelline; slip on the kind of dark glasses that sell three for a dollar at the Texaco station and tie a scarf over the blondeness, and a far-too-big UCLA sweatshirt (Tits? Tits? In this potato sack?) and the kind of shapeless skirt that would embarrass a Jehovah's Witness, and you disappear, you become nobody

I'm nobody. Who are you?

I'm nobody but I need to be somebody and I need to show them show them all that I am somebody and I need to be loved and need to be somebody's and I need and I need and I need

V

I take her elbow, feel that tremor within like a too-tightly wound clock spring. She is not surprised that I am here.

I am her need, corporeal, need now made manifest, though I have always been with her.

We sit on a bench. "The crackers," she says. "Whenever I go to a restaurant, I always take the crackers for the ducks. I love animals."

I know.

I know she needs to tell me about her love for animals, needs me to hear about this goodness in her.

"I've always loved animals."

I know.

"Want to hear a funny story?"

She needs me to hear a funny story, needs to remind herself of a time when her life could be safely compartmentalized in funny little stories, mundane events no larger than life and nothing in the least crazy.

"My first husband, Jim, it was when we were first married. We went off on this weekend. He had friends near Van Nuys and they had this small farm. They called it a ranch 'cause everything's a ranch in California, but it really was a farm.

"So we went out to their farm and they were our age, well, Jim's age, he was five years older than me, you know, and we played gin rummy and danced to the radio. We were drinking Blatz beer. I remember that 'cause it was the sponsor of the radio remote we were listening to, 'Live from the Congress Hotel in Chicago,' with Eddy Howard and his orchestra.

"Anyway, then we went off to bed and it had started to rain and, next thing I knew, I heard a calf outside, it was mooing, you know, and it was so lonely-sounding …

"I told Jim we had to get it, had to take it out to the barn."

"He laughed at me.

"I never minded when Jim laughed at me. If that fuckface Tony Curtis laughs at me, if that fly boy even dares, I'll pull his panties up around his neck and strangle him, but I liked it when Jim laughed at me.

"'Babe,' he said, 'don't worry about that calf. Little guy will be all right. He's covered in leather.'"

Marilyn was silent.

She thought she needed silence.

But I knew otherwise, of course, because I was her need. She had to tell me—

—the worst, the most tragic and horrible animal story she knew.

She needed to tell me the story—

"No."

No?

I am her need and a need is patient, patient but insistent. She had no choice, not really: One must acquiesce to need, always, always.

She began to cry then.

So many tears, Marilyn, so many tears so many times.

Then she said, "I had a dog once, Cinders. I was in a foster home then. Cinders was only a puppy, a very sweet puppy, and funny, and like puppies do, Cinders barked a lot. A neighbor got mad about it, just really furious and what he did, I saw it, he picked up this hoe and he chopped Cinders in half. I saw it."

Again, a silence. A needed silence.

"Maybe it was then I started to go crazy."

NEW MOON ON THE WATER

VI

August 4, 1962
The Brentwood Section of Los Angles

Marilyn Monroe is dying.

Her diaphragm has quit working and her breathing is now all from the stomach. The color of her aureoles is fading. I touch her hand, then her wrist. I can find her pulse but only with difficulty, regular but slow, so very slow and thin. There is a tranquility to her flesh that morticians strive for and never achieve.

She is dying because she needs to die.

And, curious, so curious, I do not understand it but I, I feel no abatement of my selfness, no ebbing away of my consciousness.

I who have never been alive feel no less alive than ... Than previously. I am her need.

And to myself I am becoming an enigma.

VII

You need to hear about the sex, don't you?

I know what you need. After all, she fascinates you, compels your ever so avid interest, Mr. and Mrs. Main Street America:

—you regular fellas at the Tip Top Lounge who with the wisdom imparted by the old after-work boilermaker know you'd have her *wailing* once you gave her the old Jack Hammer John.

—you Lutheran housewives in Michigan who have begun to get the hint from her this hyperbolic persona that is MM: women are supposed to like it, too.

—you, the 13-year-old horn-rimmed smart boy who's been a whiz with his slide rule but is now discovering there's something about Marilyn Monroe's gyrating buttocks that puts lead in the little pencil.

—you, the desperate 19-year-old, selling ribbons at Woolworth's, just a little orthodonture shy of being beautiful, dreaming of love, dreaming of Hollywood, dreaming of magic

All of you, all of you, I understand your need. How can I not?

So, addressing the topic of Marilyn Monroe's womanhood, I speak with a degree of expertise, a PhD, if you will.

Marilyn Monroe not infrequently needed fucking and I am her need.

And so, on occasion, I fucked her the way she needed to be fucked,

fucked her hard and then harder, knowing she relished the sensation at the spot just above her anus where the testicles go *slapslapslap*, the hot juices flowing along mounds and fissures, fucked her with her hips doing the comma-wriggle bump and pump, fucked her with the exact length and girth and temperature of cock her need demanded at that particular time for that particular fuck, fucked her saying all the amorous vulgarities she needed to hear: You beautiful, wild bitch, you hot cunt, you whore, you sweet pussy, you …

I fucked her.

And so many times, when she came (came because she needed to come), she cried and she cried out, "Daddy!"

I am her need.

she needed daddy and she needed fucking and she needed home and she
needed sanity and she needed respect and she needed dignity and she needed
she needed she was a sucking vacuum
she was an endless deep need
at the core of the universe she was
she needed limits and laughter
and kindness and concern and
gentleness and daddy oh god
she needed daddy she
needed she needed she needed
love she needed love she needed
love she needed love
she needed love she needed love
she needed love she needed love
she needed she needed she was

All Need. All Consuming Need.

and i am

VIII

August 4, 1962
The Brentwood Section of Los Angles

I am often surprised by all that I know and by all that I do not know.

I have told you that, haven't I? I must be telling you again because it is something you need to know.

I heard the wet rattle within the V juncture of throat and collarbone.

It was a death rattle. I had never heard it before (how could I?)
but I knew it.
Marilyn Monroe was dying.
She would die and I would be no more.
Then I was startled, that's what it was, I was startled at the sudden
slow movement, as her head lolled on the pillow, and white-tinged mucus
bubbled at the parched corner of her mouth.
She sat up. It was melodramatic but no less comic and grotesque, like
an inexperienced vampire in a Universal Studios monster film.
Her eyes sought focus and found it.
She looked at me. She smiled.
"No," she said. "Not this time. Not ever. No."
I am her need.
I have always been her need.
I understood her, understood her even when she did not.
Lie down now, I told her. You need to die.
I know.
I am your need.
And I made her die.

IX

August 4, 1962
The Brentwood Section of Los Angles

Marilyn Monroe is dead.
Her heart has stopped. Her blood no longer circulates. Lividity
discolors and distorts her features. You might no longer know who she is.
She isn't.
Marilyn Monroe is dead. And I?
?
A mystery, if you need a mystery.
I am here.
Marilyn Monroe is gone and I am here.
And if I do not understand, then, very well, that is the way of it, I
suppose, I assume, I would think, I surmise: who attains full understanding?
Jesus, Buddha, Mohammed, Joseph Smith, Mary Baker Eddy, Norman
Vincent Peale, Bishop Fulton Sheen ...
But I think I am beginning to realize, to know:
you
you are alone in a lonely night and you cannot bear the sound of your own

heart cannot tolerate the touch of your mocking breath as it leaves your nostrils to brush your upper lip and the weight of your existence offends you

you

you are at the city's busiest intersection on this busy day and the sunlight that pours down is weighted and cutting and you feel it slice away the flesh slice away your protection slice away all that protects and keeps you hidden

you

you have children and they hate you and you hate them

you are watched all the time watched by secretive men who know what uncle did and know how dirty you are and though they are biding their time for now they will act they will

you are lies covered over with lies covered over with lies and all covering the truth the terrible impossible unendurable truth

you are 52 years old and you still cry for daddy

you have no satisfactions

you have no joy

you (all of you) you are unloved and you are unlovable and you are cursed (all of you forever children alone in the dark) and you cannot try cannot dare cannot hope (all of you the forever lost

you and you and you

and you cannot hope and you need you need you need

and you need

you need death

and

I am

your need

NEW MOON ON THE WATER

MOON ON THE WATER

Jazzmen make it ten or 20 years after they die. Fats Navarro, Yardbird, Coltrane … Sure, there were people who dug them while they were here to lay it down, but it's now, years after the final bar, and gangbusters, right?

So I'm thinking it's soon going to be Breeze's time. The past year, there've been a couple reissues of sides we cut years ago, decent sales and good reviews in *Downbeat* and even—hip to this?—*Rolling Stone*.

And Breeze's trip is the stuff that makes for a cult following. He was a junky, you see. Good box office there—check with Lady Day. And Bird and Chet Baker.

And they did fish Breeze out of Lake Michigan one cold autumn day in '59, found him with his fingers on the keys of his sax.

❧ • ❧

Any city's a rough-old, tough-old dues-paying time for a jazzman, but Chicago was better than New York for Breeze and me. That's why we blew the Apple Major, where cool and post-bop and hard bop pretty much ruled, and where, pre-Coltrane revelations, if you were into something new, and you were Ofay besides, it was guaranteed nowheresville.

And Chicago was a better scene, too, if you were in "the life." If you kept your cool, the heat did not jump all over you when you went on the prowl in search of white powder.

And Chicago had the lake. First time he saw it, Breeze said, "Yes." I knew what he meant. Looking one way, all you'd see was city. Then you could turn your back on it, forget it, and there was endless water, frozen in two-a.m. moonlight, making you understand loneliness and eternity. And maybe you had the kind of thought that's like smoke, curling and disappearing, thinking about magic and just how small we all are and maybe you even dreamed the kid-dream of dream monsters that swim and slither just under the surface of water and just out of sight.

Yeah, for the good solid citizens of Chicago, the city that works is also the city that sleeps and when the square johns were doing Morpheus,

139

there were many times when you could find Breeze and me by the lake. Breeze would have his horn. Most everywhere he went—then—the sax was with him. Sometimes when it was really right, the heroin rushing through you and turning your vision incandescent, you could see the radiance, the notes shining on the water, perfect and pure for an instant before they shattered and changed into foam.

So, for us Chicago did indeed make it. We had a two-room dump just off Wells Street. We scored scag, did not get strung out, did not get burned, did not get beefed and we swung enough gigs to pay the freight.

It was Chicago that we found Micah and really started to get it together. Micah was stand-up bass. He was shadow-skinny and yes, he had the hands, long, long fingers and fast. Micah was younger than we were, a dude who'd dropped out of college to do the jazz thing, but there was a monkey on Micah's back, too, so we got music-tight, junky-tight and it was like it was all supposed to happen.

And we were working on and getting to and sometimes touching, really *touching*—close to the sound.

Uh-huh, the sound. What was it we wanted? What we were after?

What we did not want: tired-out, straight ahead swing. Not spit-it-out all flash and fingers be-bop. Not thud and boom and stretch it so they think you're saying something when you're only blowing smoke.

A moment for metaphysics, okay? A moment to direct your eyes on what those Impressionist painters, Renoir and Monet and Degas and Caillebotte and Cassatt and Manet, the masters of the moment, were doing with hay stacks and rivers and sunrises and railroad stations.

We wanted morning light coming through the clouds the second before the sun goes orange-pink. We wanted not a dream but the way you feel when you almost remember the dream. We wanted it be a little bit like you think maybe God is.

And looking back and thinking back and sometimes, oh, way down there, really going back, I wonder if we didn't want the moon on the water?

Maybe that.

Maybe.

Breeze played alto. I was guitar. Micah, on the bottom, was the heartbeat. We didn't have drums, didn't need them with Micah. Here's the root, here's the core, here's the *center*, that was Micah on bass. No reason to make a clash and clatter.

Of course, Mulligan, the Jeru, with his quartet gigging out in Citrus-land, did not have drums, either, but he was going his very own horn-rimmed academic-glasses way and we were into something entirely else.

There were times when we laid it down, the calm and the ease and the gentle. There were times when we found the song inside you that you didn't even know was there.

There were good times.

☙ • ❧

And then she came out of the lake.

☙ • ❧

It was summer, around three in the morning. There were "No Trespassing—Keep Out" signs, but there was also a six-foot section of chain-link fence that was down. We'd left Micah at a restaurant, soothing his junky craving for sweet with Danish and coffee with lots of sugar. It was just Breeze and me and his horn.

It was not a beach for people. Rocks, great lumping boulders, and smaller ones, smooth here and jagged there, making walking something entirely else, an unearthly experience best appreciated when seriously high. Ahead of us, the beach curved. A long, falling-down pier stabbed into the moon-gleaming water like a giant, arthritic finger pointing your way to nowhere.

We drifted, the two of us and the muggy quiet, our steps taking us close to the waterline. We stood on the rocks. Spray splashed our shoes. Breeze squeezed the mouthpiece between his lips. He shut his eyes, doing some key-flipping to clear the horn. Then he let a few notes slide out of the bell, full of breath, just on the verge of breaking. There was no set time to what he laid down. It was just this shaky, brute insistence to continue, like an old man marching heavy-footed to the end.

Then he went to this riffing thing, kind of a squeak-jump-around, like the feeling you get when your arm's tied up, you've got the bubbling hit, *your* bubbling hit, in the dropper, and you know in just one eye-blink you'll spike that vein for the big rush.

That was when I saw something in the water and that was when Breeze's tune changed. Way out there, way beyond the pier, someone was swimming.

Breeze's horn was going slow, notes rounded with a tired-moan edge, like a bad morning when you've got to reach for the white port to kill the pain. Sure, I knew Breeze's stuff—knew where he was coming from and how he got there—but he was putting down a sound I had never heard before. It went way back to the beginnings, to swirling fog of wishes and visions. His sax was luring and welcoming. It was the curved Viking horn bringing the far-traveled dragonship into the bay, to safe harbor and warm greeting and balance.

What was out there was a lady, a lady in the lake. She came swimming toward shore in rhythm to Breeze's music. Behind her was an ever-vanishing trail in the water. From second to second, the connection from where she was to where she had been was disappearing.

When she reached the shallows, she stood up, came walking out. She moved sure-footed on clicking pebbles, like a dance.

Breeze lowered the horn, let it swing on the cord.

She did not look frightened or surprised. All she looked—here's a word so tired it sags—was beautiful.

The moon was a halo behind her head. Her long lake-gleaming hair hung tangled like tree snakes on jungle branches. She had magic-cruel eyes and her mouth was the soft passion of a bitch-goddess.

And I remember thinking she should have been naked. Oh, she wasn't, had on bra and panties made translucent with wetness, but she should have been.

She came up to us and, in the moment before she spoke, I felt it.

You get tight with a dude, hang with him, do good times and bad, there are flashes when you know you're touching just what the other cat feels. That was how it was with Breeze and me.

She was working on Breeze, doing a real number.

How? Cannot say. The old bluesmen sing about the hoo-doo. The square heads write songs for square heads about enchanted evenings and crowded rooms. But, when it all comes down, who the hell can really say?

"Hey, what are you guys doing here?"

The spell—and that's no real word for what it was—was gone. I heard the over-control in her voice that hipped me she was pretty well juiced, confirmed by a heavy slash of booze on her breath.

"We're jazzmen," Breeze said, like that explained everything. In a way, maybe it did.

"Jazzmen ... You know what I am?"

"A chick." I shrugged, always cool, even though, well, you never did feel cool around her.

"I'm a chick who got in the car and went cruising. I was looking for something, God knows what. I don't, not anymore, if I ever did. But you know, it seemed to make sense that I'd find it in the lake, so I went swimming. There were a couple times when I nearly reached that place where the moon was right on the water. But then it moved. It always moves just when you're there."

"That's the way it goes," I said, thinking about drunk talk and crazy ladies, neither of which is supposed to make sense but both do if you think about it when you're not really working at thinking.

Her eyes did three beats on me, then triple that on Breeze; she was deciding something. "Jazzmen," she said. "I want you to come with me."

Maybe this is just "years later" wisdom talking, but I think I was a little afraid. But hell, cool means you go the way it goes and you flow the way it flows.

She'd left her clothing under the pier. Without any attempt to dry off, she slipped into a beige dress, and then we followed her to her car, parked not too far away. She had a dark blue Lincoln.

We went to an apartment building on the Gold Coast. The doorman lamped Breeze and me with a look that said it wasn't his business what kind of whatevers rich people hung with but that didn't mean he had to dig us.

She lived so way up there in the ozone that she could have gone next door to borrow a cup of flour from God. Massive furniture that made you feel like you'd disappeared when you sat down. Windows providing a view of the city that half-convinced you everything was all right down below. And the bar at the end of the living room was a juice-head's dream of heaven.

The three of us, two jazzmen and a crazy lady, sat sipping wine, and on the hi-fi set—she had a solid classical collection—was Respighi's *Pines of Rome*. And then the mood, whatever it was, was broken by the click-click of the closing grooves of the record. The crazy lady smiled and said, "Which one of you is going to bed with me? Or is it going to be both?"

I shook my head. Sorry, lady, but even before H kills your ability, it knocks out your interest. But Breeze nodded and he went off down the hall with her, leaving his sax on the sofa.

I drank more wine. I put Vivaldi's *Four Seasons* on the turntable. I listened to that fine baroque sound from that time when music and the world were tight and structured and I heard something else. Breeze and the crazy lady were definitely getting it on, the old push-rub-tickle.

Weird, huh, because, like I said, dope is guaranteed to *un-do* your ability *to do*. All I could figure was that the chick had really gotten to Breeze and that no chemical negativity could out-do what she had done to him.

Think enchantment or conjure or sex magic or as Screamin' Jay has it, put a spell on you.

The solid truth? The *emmis*?

In the end, it doesn't much matter.

NEW MOON ON THE WATER

හ • හ

Who was she?

Some of this I picked up pretty quick and other stuff I only fell onto later.

Name: Lanna Borland. Heiress of a family that made many, many coins mainlining their chocolate bars into America's super-sweet tooth.

Occupation: Full-time fun-seeker, liver of the good life, from Port-au-Prince to the Riviera. Three divorces. Notch the bedpost to kindling with all the affairs. A bullfighter in Madrid, a member of the Dutch royal family, a sometime starving charcoal artist in New Orleans, a Hollywood alleged actor who never did figure out if he dug women, men, or both.

Goals in life: Something new. Something different. Kicks. Philosophy of life: Get what you want.

Call it the classic poor-little-rich girl riff: You get everything, you get it all, and none of it really does it to you, nothing ever quite manages to knock you out, to wig you, zonk you, and knock you over and so, maybe after a while, nothing means anything and you just keep on looking for something.

This time around, figures me, Lanna Borland's something was A Jazzman.

And, man, she had him. Righteously. Breeze was solid gone on the crazy lady. Dead solid gone.

She just started being there, being there all the time. She was a bring-down and a hangup to the music. Breeze and Micah and I trying to work up new charts, she was there. While we were blowing on-stage at the Fickle Finger, she was there at a stage-side table, those eyes lamping and vamping, doing a back beat on Breeze and his style. And when Micah and I tried to put it back together, to get it right and tight and true like it had been—sometimes—just the three of us grooving to the sounds inside we used to share, uh-uh, it wasn't three of us—it was four.

No. Not four. Split that. It was two and two. Micah and I. Breeze and Lanna.

She had Mr. B, one hundred and two percent, had him so that she was it—and there was nothing else.

There are women like that.

And sometimes I'd get into this off-the-wall mind *shpritz* about her, how she came out of the lake, and how, oh yeah, every little kid knows it before you teach him otherwise, way, way out in the water, way deep in the water, that's where the real monsters live.

Lanna drained Breeze. She zombified him. And she slipped this dream into his head and blood to take the place of everything that was meant to be there. "Lanna's Song." He was going to write a tune for her. His mind was exploding with it, that's what he said, but that song didn't happen for a long time, and for sure not then.

Breeze tried, tried like hell. And sometimes he thought he had it, asked me to do a minor slide-and-drift thing behind him. Then he'd shut his eyes and lay down a few notes. But those notes were never part of a song. They were always unconnected and alone.

Fact: The music went to hell. We fell into routines, repeating ourselves, re-tracing paths we had already worn out. When jazz is making it, it's as real an exploration as what Christopher Columbus pulled off; it's a voyage to a new world. But when you are not making it, uh-uh, you've got a nowhere trip on the city bus.

It was wrong. It was wrong for Breeze and Micah and me.

And naturally, Micah and I wanted Lanna Borland *G-O-N-E*—

Gone. We did not hate her or anything like that. When you're cool, you do not hate.

Gone was just the way it had to be for her and for her to be gone was cool, okay?

ლ • ლ

Take it to the starting days of cold autumn. It was a Saturday afternoon, the kind of dragging-slow time when you don't feel alive because most of you isn't. We were at the pad Breeze and I still shared but where he was spending less and less time.

We were there. Micah and I. Breeze and Lanna.

She was next to Breeze on the Salvation Army-reject sofa. She wasn't wearing makeup and she had on jeans and a black turtleneck. Maybe she thought she was a beatnik.

"Look," Micah was saying, "we've got to get it set, and get it down, and soon." He was moving jerky all around the room, staccato steps and twitching. He wasn't long for needing to fix.

"Okay, man," Breeze said. "Stay cool, okay?"

"Cool is cool and fool is fool," Micah said. A junky will say something like that and another junky will take it for profound.

The A and R man at BACA Records had been riding us for a while, pressing to get us into the studio to lay down some new sides. This time around, looked like there'd be real distribution, thanks to a push we got from a critic at Metronome.

145

But Breeze was making bad kibosh on recording. We had to be ready. We wouldn't be ready, so sayeth the Breeze, until we had "Lanna's Song."

"Go slow, go slow," Breeze said. He stayed cool, but Lanna came on *mucho* cooler. She was turned toward him, knees up on the couch, and she was eyeballing him like the Amazing Kreskin.

"Go slow," Micah said. Indubitably.

"Hey," Breeze said softly, "you're like some strung out. Why don't you unlax yourself?"

It was a good idea. Micah looked as though he were ready for the crawly-shakes. He was in need of a calm-down, slow-down trip to the no-nerves-a-jangling Beyond.

Micah nodded. "Yeah."

He said to me, "I'm carrying but I'll need your works."

Call me your Eagle Scout with a merit badge in Heroin: I was prepared. He started to follow me into the bedroom, but Lanna said, "I want to watch." There was something pretty wild working in her face. It was more than curiosity. Maybe it was hope.

Sure, she had known all along that the three of us were in the life. That's not a number you can hide from someone who's always there. But she had never seen any of us fix.

You see, it was different then. The needle and you, that was a private thing, your time of prayer with your private god.

Breeze shrugged and said, "So she sees. So?"

So she saw. And dug what she was seeing, you could tell.

Micah was one smooth and careful user. He did the cooking slow, the tip of the flame caressing the bowl of the spoon. Dr. Kildare couldn't have been more precise drawing up the junk through the thin, sterilized needle.

Micah had me tie up his arm with my belt. He worked his fist to pump up the vein. I kept glancing at Lanna. The princess watching Rumpelstiltskin spin straw into gold.

"There we go. Nice one," Micah said when a clean and fat vein popped up, ready. He dabbed the inside of his elbow with an alcohol wet cotton swab. He raised the needle. He hit perfect the first time, and the fiery good news was on the way.

He didn't even have the needle out when it hit him.

"Christ," Micah said. "*Beau*-ti-ful." And you could see the transfiguration.

"Yeah," I said. I was getting a sympathetic rush off him. He began bobbing his head, drifting with music only he could hear.

"That's what I want," Lanna said.

"Uh-uh," Breeze said.

Micah came out of his bipping-trance scene. "What you want, baby?" he said. "Huh? You tell Papa Micah what you want."

She pointed at his arm where a drop of blood was a ruby on the blue river of the vein. "I want you to fix me up."

Nothing had to happen. I mean, there's no script in the skies that shapes your life. Lanna Borland did not have to suddenly come up with a new want, did she?

Or maybe she did. Maybe she had to because of the same reason she went swimming way out in the lake, trying to reach the place where the moon lay on the water. Maybe she thought the needle had that promise— and could deliver.

Breeze got up and walked to the window. He stood with his back to us. "How about it, Breeze?" Micah said. "She's your chick."

On the couch, Lanna was rolling up her sleeve. Breeze said nothing.

"Come on," she said.

"Right," Micah said. "Initiation time." Then he said to me, "The works, if you please."

All the time we were getting the fix ready, there wasn't a word from Breeze, not even a glance from him. We tied her up and watched the vein rise, bulging and ready.

"Give it to me," she said.

"You got it," Micah said. He swabbed her arm and my eyes met his.

The thing is, I think I knew. I think I could have stopped him.

Maybe.

But the other thing, the bigger thing, is that I did not want to.

And so he popped her. And then he said, "There you go. Now, kinda walk around and feel it."

She stood up and Zoop! Oh, yeah, she felt it. Her face went white. Her eyes rolled back. She dropped to her knees. She made one short sound that was not a word, and she flopped down hard on her face, and she was dead.

Breeze had turned around by then. Mouth hanging open, he just mechanically shook his head from side to side.

Nobody did anything for a minute, and then it was time for somebody to do something, so I did. I got Breeze seated on the sofa. It was like moving a dude with a brand new lobotomy. I told him to stay put, not to move muscle one.

The way he was, I was sure he wouldn't.

And then Micah and I straightened up. I had to fix before I could get thinking the way I had to think, but we took care of it.

NEW MOON ON THE WATER

Life is not *Dragnet* with the cops solving everything just before the last commercial. Lanna Borland was found a week later in a forest preserve near one of the city's northwestern suburbs. It was not front-page, prime-time news, not in those days. Back then, if you had money, you could buy "hush," and so, when a chocolate-bar heiress makes an OD exit, there are things happening behind the scenes to guarantee, ultra-cool, no muss, no fuss, no scandal—and what we have here is "death by misadventure."

Micah split for the coast.

And Breeze and I stayed together. That is, we kept the pad. But the way Breeze was, I could have been the oily character in the turban taking care of the mummy in one of those antique Universal flicks.

Like you might figure, music was out. Until one night, a few weeks later.

The temperature had dropped, not yet winter, of course, but a promise of certain winter. It was down in the 20s and there was that knife-slice of wind that is exclusively Chicago's own.

Breeze left our place at midnight. His horn was with him. I was with him. I don't know if he wanted me, but there I was.

We went to that rocky beach that belonged to the summer. With the wind doing its work on the lake, the water looked as jagged and tearing as the rocks we stood on. I kept my hands in my pockets, wished my jacket were warmer. I wondered if I'd ever be warm again. I was high. I had the feeling I knew everything that was going to happen, everything that had to happen.

"She is out there, you know," Breeze said. His voice and the wind were one.

I started to say something. I didn't.

The moon was full. Far out there, where the world ended, the moon lay on the water. It was a place where you could maybe find monsters down deep in the lake, or maybe the exact spot on the earth where dreams died, or maybe the one point where you'd expect a crazy lady to be.

Then Breeze had the mouthpiece between his lips and he was playing. And he played warm as your own breath when the blanket's up over your chin. Then he turned it cold, and his cold was the midnight cold when you're alone in the house and every tick-tick of a pipe and the slow drip of a leaky faucet remind you of that aloneness.

And finally, he played a curling mist that was every dream that never will be.

He was playing a song. And I knew it was "Lanna's Song."

He was still playing, variations on an end theme, as he walked stiff-legged into the waves.

That was how it had to be. So I let it be. And it seems I heard "Lanna's Song," the echoes of it, even when there was no reason to hear it anymore.

There are times I know I hear it still.

NEW MOON ON THE WATER

THE CALL

How do you answer their questions?

How do you answer the question?

Just a smile, a "hello and how's it going" kind of guy down the block. Fourteen years a husband, ten years a father. He had a mortgage like the rest of us, okay? His kids seemed like sweet kids, pretty much, nice but not all that outgoing. For that matter, he wasn't that outgoing, not him or the wife.

Pretty wife. Remember back to the old kiddy shows on TV, the live ones when you could turn on the set and they'd have somebody playing kid games and showing cartoons and all? Beth Morgan had that sort of "live-TV kiddy-show host" smile. Not perfect, Just pretty. But you saw her, you figured you'd probably like her.

Back to the question—

Well, Marv was pretty much a guy just like the rest of us, okay? You know what I mean.

What else can you tell the police or the reporters?

Marv Morgan. Mr. Enigma and a hell of a lot worse than that. But, okay, the reporters and the cops will go away after a while, and most likely, even the documentary TV videotapers will be gone and that is that. *El Fin.* All he wrote.

Written in ...

So what you do is tell the kids they'd damned well better always let you know where they are and how long they're going to be there.

It probably is time to get deadbolts for all the doors. Hey, this old world is not what it used to be. Fact of life, and it sucks, but that doesn't make it any the less a fact.

And, you know, okay, you're a bullshit liberal but might not be a bad idea to have a gun in the house and you and the wife take some lessons in firearm usage: "How to Kill the Ass of Anybody Fucking with You ..."

Might not be bad to—

—quit hammering your very own personal head with the question,

151

NEW MOON ON THE WATER

What in the name of God and/or the Devil makes a guy do something so ...

—because you do not have a clue, Mister. Not doodley, not Jack, not nothin'.

You don't know about the telephone call that began it, that started it all ...

༭ • ༭

He left the dinner table at the ringing and walked down the hall. He went to the small stand at the foot of the stairs and picked up the telephone.

"Hello," he said. "Marvin."

He felt it then, the trill of the heart, the sudden onrush of vertigo and joy. He was confused and happy. "Yes," Marv Morgan said.

"Do you remember what was done?"

"Yes," he said, and his lips moved as though he were praying.

"It is now the time, Marv. It is now *our* time."

"Yes," he said. Yes, yes, yes! Then he put down the phone. He took in a breath, held it for a count of five, released it. He went back to the dining room and stood a moment in the doorway.

He looked at the two girls. His children.

Beth Morgan. His wife.

"Something wrong, dear?" she asked. His wife. "You look ..."

He realized he was smiling, the kind of smile you have when you leave the dentist's office, nitrous oxide still bubbling in your brain and Novocain freezing your mouth. His daughters—*his*—chewed and swallowed and ignored him.

"No," he said, "everything is fine."

Then he sat down at the head of the table. His table, the head of the table. He looked at his wife, he looked, in turn, at each of the girls.

He laughed and didn't give a damn how it sounded. Then he began to eat ravenously.

༭ • ༭

There has to be a reason. Has to be, has to...People just don't...Well, shit, yes, they do. Obviously they do. We've got the goddamned proof.

Okay, then, so we can't find a reason in the present, can't even find him, then it's time to go bopping into the past.

Talk to his high school teachers. His grade school teachers. Talk to his relatives. His parents.

A good boy. A shy boy, sort of. Liked to be alone with his thoughts.

152

Hey, you could probably say all of us were like that, even those who pretended not to be.

Well, there was the "thing" with the dog when Marv was ten, but that didn't seem all that much. He said the dog ran off. Said it slipped the leash. Said he couldn't find it.

It was a pretty nice dog. Golden retriever, mostly. Had a happy face. Marv didn't cry or anything. He wasn't much of a crying kid, all in all.

But the dog never got found.

Marv Morgan. A kid like all the other kids. Average grades.

Bicycle for Christmas. Helped with the household chores if you stayed on his back about it. Didn't really find anything all that funny in jokes, but he wasn't any kind of ...

You know, if you try right this minute to picture his face in your mind, there's going to be sort of a blankness there. He just wasn't the kind of kid or, later, grown-up, that you would notice.

Oh yeah. He went to summer camp when he was twelve. Camp Totem Pole. (Try that for stupid-plus names!) It was sponsored by an affiliation of suburban churches. Didn't cost too much.

Something did happen there.

ℰⅈ • ℰⅈ

He had just finished stowing his gear under the steel bunk's frame when cabin three's counselor walked in. He had seen counselors for other cabins. They looked like over-aged campers themselves.

The man who stood at the door of the wood and wire mesh was different. His black hair was long, almost to his ears, his eyes were deep-set and dark.

"Hi, guys," he said. "I'm Peter. Peter Revson."

"Hi, Pete!" squalled the fat boy sprawled like a skin full of suet on the bed next to Mike's.

The counselor looked at the fat boy with a look that said nothing.

"I'm your Camp Totem Pole counselor." He smiled for all of them then. "I'm supposed to teach you things."

The fat boy clapped his hands "Way to go!" His voice was a yip, like that of an injured dog. That was what Marvin thought. "Pete is neat! Pete is neat!"

Peter Revson pointed. "You."

It became quiet. He had that kind of voice. Outside, boys marched to their cabin by a counselor who was leading them in an off-key but spirited "Onward, Christian Soldiers."

"Me?" Fat boy was blinking.

Peter Revson nodded. "You," he said. "Stand up."

Bed springs squeaked. Fat boy's shorts were stretched tight over his watermelon gut and hung down to his baggy, elephant-skin knees. His Camp Totem Pole t-shirt stopped over an inch above his navel.

"What's your name?"

"Albert." Blubber lips shaped the syllables. "Albert Quanstrom."

"All right," Peter said. "Sit back down now, Quanstrom."

Peter's dark eyes went over the other boys one at a time. He looked at Marvin.

He smiled.

And Marvin Morgan smiled back. Peter said, "Okay," and he left.

৩ • ৩

Who was there who really knew him, was really like tight with him? Not the neighbors, but somebody, though, someone along the way. Best friend or something. Has to be, right? Like when he was a kid. Uh-uh. You wouldn't call him unfriendly, but he wasn't best friends with anyone in particular, and that's a matter of record assuming anyone ever thought there was a reason to keep a record on a bland-o, ho-hum, so what and who cares non-entity like Marvin Morgan.

Best friends? A real *Kemo Sabe*? Blood brother. Secret handshake and spit?

Nah, no one like that—

—that we know about ...

No one ...

৩ • ৩

It was Sunday afternoon. He'd slipped away from the hymn-singing in the "long house." (Indian words. Respect for Native American Culture. "We are all God's children." Sure. Smoke-um peace pipe and then slaughter your red asses.) He lay on his bunk, arms behind his neck. Overhead, a spider wove a web in the corner where two beams joined.

Maybe if he watched long enough, he would see a fly get trapped. He'd like that. It would give him a funny feeling in the base of his spine and his belly and brain.

The screen door creaked. He heard steps. Then Peter Revson stood over him. "You're supposed to be singing right this very instant. Don't you like to sing praise to Him from Whom all blessings flow, verily, verily?"

"It's okay. I just didn't feel like it."

"What do you like to do better, Marv?"

"I like to think."

Peter sat down on the side of the cot.

"Oh, I understand, Marv. You think about our world and all the people in it, that's what you think about. There's something else you like to think about, too."

"What?"

"How you're going to keep on fooling them, pretending you're just the same as they are."

Marv sat up. "I don't understand what you mean."

Peter Revson nodded in the direction of the long house. "You can hear them all the way over here. Make a lot of noise. It doesn't mean anything, though. They don't mean anything."

"Peter," Marv said, "well, hey! I don't get it. What are you saying?"

"Thing is, they think they have it all. 'The meek shall inherit the Earth.' They really believe they've got it already."

"Yeah," Marvin Morgan said. "That's like something I heard in Sunday school, I guess."

Peter put a hand on Marv's shoulder. His voice was soft, like a woman's. He spoke gently. "Our day is coming. Wheels turn. That is what wheels do. 'To everything there a season.' Maybe you got that in Sunday school, too."

"Maybe," Marvin. "I don't remember. What are you getting at, Peter?"

Peter Revson tapped himself on the chest with his thumb. "I'm not one of them and I know it. I've always known it. They have names for those who are like us, when they occasionally recognize our existence. They don't want to consider Nietzsche. They don't want to consider the 'Myth of the Superman.' They just try to pretend we don't exist." Peter's thumb rapped again on his chest. "But I exist." He touched Marv's forehead, his index finger like the tip of a gun barrel. "You exist."

"I don't ..."

"Don't fuck around, okay?" Peter Revson said. "You fuck around, you play the stupe from beyond Stupeland, it makes me want to knock your fucking head in. You know who we are, you do. You've always known."

"We're different," Marv said.

"That is right. We are different. And soon there will be a lot of us. You can feel it happening. When our time comes, we will be together and we will be strong. It will be our turn then. It be our world."

"Peter, are you sure I ..."

"Yes, I'm sure. I'm as sure about you as I am about me. That is my gift.

155

I look and I know."

Then he rested his hand on Marv's shoulder. "You knew, too, didn't you? Knew me when you first saw me."

"Yes," Marv said, "I hoped ..."

He started to cry.

ఌ • ఌ

So let's search the past. Go over it with a microscope. Logic. Deduction. Let's hope that hindsight has a value. The shrinkers want to know about nail-biting, bed-wetting, try to seek unresolved Oedipal conflict Ego locked in battle with Id.

Then we get the "spiritual philosophers, " hard to distinguish from the phony-miracle-prayer-cloth assholes on the Christer programs, and they talk about the breakdown of family values, the turning away from belief, the ... You know.

No way to figure. Not really. Violence is now part of the 100-percent-homemade, all-American pie. Don't think so? Try taking a walk at night on a city street. You'll have your throat cut because you scratched your nose and it looked like a "gang sign" to some degenerate asshole with a machete and a 70 IQ.

Catch the news a week or so ago? That kid who took daddy's assault rifle (AK-47) and dusted four of his classmates. Not like he didn't have a reason. Hell, they gave him some shit about his Air Jordans. No sir, you can't dis a guy's athletic shoes and get away with it.

But you know it used to be better when we were kids. It was a less dangerous time and an easier time.

Remember sitting around a campfire or something, late at night, dreaming about how terrific and just different it would be when you grew up?

Remember?

ఌ • ఌ

The fire crackled and pinpoints of red and orange flew wildly into the night sky. They were in a small clearing, on the other side of the lake. They had hiked all day. They were many miles from Camp Totem Pole.

Albert Quanstrom's pudgy hand slapped at the back of his neck. "Got him," he squealed. It was a moment of triumph for the fat boy. He rolled the mosquito's gooey remains between his thumb and index finger.

Peter Revson laughed. "All right, you killed him! Way to go. Now is it fun to kill a fucking mosquito or is it FUN to kill a fucking mosquito?"

Albert's doughy face was puzzled in the firelight. "Hey, you're not supposed to talk like that!"

Peter Revson smiled. So did Marv. "Like fucking what? How the fuck am I supposed to fucking talk?"

"Well, you know …" Albert said. He blinked stupidly.

"Oh, I think I get it!" Peter said. "You mean because I'm a counselor at a fucking church camp I shouldn't say fuck. It's not a fucking Christian thing to do, huh?"

Marv laughed quietly.

"I mean," Peter said, "most good Christians wouldn't say fuck if they had a mouthful."

Albert scratched the side of his neck. "This is weird. How about …"

"Weird? What's weird, you fat fuck?" Peter Revson said. "Marv, do you think this is weird?"

"Definitely not weird," Marv said.

"Definitely not," Peter said. He opened the flap of his pack. slowly took out the knife. The five-inch blade gleamed with the reflected fire.

It looked beautiful, Marv thought, and he could smell the steel of it. His heart beat fast.

"You see," Peter said, as he rose, the knife at waist level, "what's going to happen, Albert, is that we are going to kill you. Trust me, there's not one fucking thing weird about that."

Albert's eyes filled his entire face. He snapped a horrified look at Marv. "Marv, hey! Tell him to quit kidding around."

"Okay, Peter," Marv said. "Peter, quit kidding around."

Peter smiled. "I'm not kidding."

"He's not kidding," Marv said to Albert. "I'd say that one of the things Peter is not doing is kidding." Marv shrugged. "That's my opinion, anyway."

Peter moved toward Albert. Albert shuffled back on his hands and heels.

"What it is, " Peter said quietly, "is I want Marv to see just how it is. Nothing to it, really. And it feels so … It feels so fine!"

"No!" Albert rolled, pushed himself up, tried to run.

But Marv was in front of him, grinning. He kicked him right the balls.

Albert whuffed and made moist gagging sounds, doubling over. And then Peter was behind the fat boy, locking his left arm around Albert's neck. Now there was a snuffling sound and gagging and snot and drool and tears were wetting the boy's big-eyed face.

Marv moved closer. He wanted to see everything. He wanted to feel it. Albert's arms were waving spastically. Peter pressed him down, brought him to his knees, squatting behind him. He moved his left arm to cup a hand under Albert's blubbery chin. He pulled back the boy's head. He brought up the knife.

"Yes, " Marv whispered. "Yes. Yes …"

The fire-shining blade lay across Albert Quanstrom's neck. Peter pressed the knife down hard and drew it across the boy's throat.

Albert's mouth opened wide. He looked surprised. A thin dark line appeared on his throat. It quickly thickened and bubbled and then gushed. Dark spray hit Marv's face and sizzled in the fire.

"See, Marv," Peter said, "nothing to it."

Peter and Marv talked late into the night. They spoke of a day, the day, that would come. It would be a while yet, but it would not be forever. There were others like Peter, right now, finding others like Marv.

And they were all of them born to kill.

Until their time—our time—until then, Marv would have to go on pretending, acting as though he were one of the others. His whole life had to keep on being a fake, but he must never stop believing in the promise of their bloody day, their killing time, their victory.

Peter would not forget him.

They were brothers. Blood brothers who found each other here at Camp Totem Pole.

Marv realized it was a joke so he laughed.

Later, they hid Albert Quanstrom's body, disposed of the knife. Peter Revson was good at cleaning up. Nothing to worry about; he told Marv he had done this sort of thing 30, maybe 35 times. Kids, men, women, each one was different and each one was "exquisite." Yes, that was the only and right word.

Marv understood.

The next morning, they returned double-time to Camp Totem Pole. Albert Quanstrom had just wandered off. They spent the whole night searching, but couldn't find him.

Their story was believed.

"Of course," Peter said later, "this is what they want to believe, you see. If we told them, well, we took that puddle of puke out in the brush and cut his fucking throat, they would have a bitch-kitty of a time believing that."

Rangers, campers, and counselors, along with the town police, looked long and hard. The woods were dense. Dragging the lake revealed nothing.

It was a shame. Why, you could see how awful that poor young man, Peter Revson, felt. "It's all my fault," that's what he said again and again.

And Marvin Morgan, well, he must have been really good friends with poor Albert Quanstrom. The kid just lay on his bunk sobbing, and you could hardly get him to eat anything.

So the disappearance of Albert Quanstrom was a dark blot on the otherwise golden summer of the children, all the fine youngsters, at Camp Totem Pole.

ల • ల

Really, what's there to say? Just one of those things that happen and there is no way you, Sigmund Freud, or Dick Tracy can figure it.

What happens is just that your ordinary dude goes *el bonkers grande mucho-mucho*, and does something incomprehensible and horrible.

What you try to do, then, is just forget it, or forget about it as much as you can. Hell, with time, everything passes and all that bumper-sticker-philosophy BS. And as you're working at forgetting it, you of course do think about it, right? Maybe you are watering the lawn or sitting in the tub wishing the kids had not used up all the hot water, and then you ask yourself, Jesus H. Christ on a Harley, just what could have been going through that whackadoo's mind before he did that? You get a little shook, then, hoping to God you have never had thoughts like that—whatever they were—in your very own skull ...

ల • ల

Marvin Morgan checked his Timex. It was two-thirty in the morning. He studied the small room he used as his office. It was neatly organized. There was a place for everything and everything was in its place.

Morgan smiled. This was not his room. It belonged to the pretender.

The pretender who had died with Peter Revson's telephone call. The pretender who, that night, had hugged the two children he fathered, had tickled them, laughed with them for a half hour at the "Tasmanian Dev-il" cartoon special on the Nickelodeon station. The pretender who had made love, slowly and gently, with Beth Morgan, who now lay asleep and unaware of his pretending.

No pretending.

Not anymore.

Not for him.

Not for any of them.

Marvin Morgan clicked off the light as he left the room. He walked down the hall, past the girls' bedroom. He listened to the special breathing sound made only by sleeping children. A few more steps took him to the master bedroom at the head of the stairs. Beth was a blanket-covered mound on her side.

He went downstairs. In the kitchen, he opened the drawer nearest the sink. The knife he chose was a good one, a Sabatier.

Then he went back up the stairs.

ⓔ • ⓔ

So, to sum it up, to give it definition and pretend that understanding comes with it, let's say Mr. Marvin Morgan (wherever he might be!) went ultimate psycho, okay? Let's say the elevator went all the way to the top and kept right on going. Let's say ...

Nothing that you don't pick up on every day.

Ten-month-old baby gets pitched into the incinerator. Says Momma dearest, "I just couldn't take her crying anymore, y'know? She was trying to drive me crazy, she really was, an' what she done was drive me crazy ..."

A screwball senior citizen gets tired of pissing and moaning about the lumps in the mashed potatoes and so he takes a pump 12-gauge and goes at it on the entire first floor of the retirement center.

Junior-high kid in Texas gets paddled three good whacks on the butt for smoking, so he puts three .38s in the principal's head: that's an equation that makes sense to him.

Wife says she wants the carpet cleaned and next thing you know, hubby is giving her a pseudo-Sassoon haircut with a Black and Decker chainsaw.

Our world, ladies and gentlemen. A world in which we do have these awful insanities. These hideous, but isolated instances of homicidal dementia.

But it sure as hell is a damned good thing these lunatics are too warp-o to ever get together with one another.

Damn, they could really raise hell then, couldn't they?

HANSEL, GRETEL AND THE WITCH:
NOTES TO THE ARTIST

Dear Aline,

Your letter flatters me, even as your preliminary sketches honor me. (Just "silly scribbles" you call them, you modest young woman. And I can call you that, child, in that I am a far-too-boastful *old* woman!) I am certain our collaboration will be a marvelous success! After our discussions last summer, I cannot believe there is the slightest disparity in our most deeply held convictions regarding literature for young people. Moreover, though miles by the thousands are between us, I feel it is important that in our undertaking we demonstrate in our own way that people who know and hold to the True and the Good are the same in many nations, is it not so?

I pause now to positively blush as I read the paragraph I have just written, so stodgy and pompous I am!

Deliberately I began this note without a conventional heading, so that it might be no more formal than the many good "chats" we had last year when I visited your country. But, my dear Aline, it is possible that formality, even a rigidity of manner, is our national curse!

Perhaps it is because your nation is so young, a child among nations, really, that you can, like children, candidly express your enthusiasm without undue social restraint.

I will soon send by postal air the opening of the book.

I am excited over our working strategy, for with my submitting to you sections in sequence for your illustration as I write them, I will thus have your art to inspire me as together we grow a book for the beloved young people of a nation.

As I have heard in your country, "Let us put the show on the road."

NEW MOON ON THE WATER

ᘓ • ᘓ

Our beginning is as old as stars and sweet things, or maybe even older. I am certain you know it.

Once upon a time, a woodcutter and his family lived in a simple hut just beyond the town and just this side of the ever so deep woods. The woodcutter was a good man. He loved his country and he loved his God and he loved his wife and he loved his two children.

It would not surprise me any more than a potato pancake if you knew the names of the children.

The boy was named Hansel. And the girl was named Gretel.

Ah-ha! Is that what you say? You know this story, then?

Fine, you may *ah-ha* now, and even *ah-ho* or *ha-ha-ha* if you wish, but sadly, dear children, though you think you know the story of our precious Hansel and Gretel, I must tell you that you do not.

Oh, no!

You do not, that is, know all of the story. But you should.

And there are some parts of the story that are ever so much more sad than you could even imagine.

But that means, of course, as surely as sun shining down, that the ending of our story is destined to be gloriously, magnificently, and wonderfully happy.

To know the true story of Hansel and Gretel is to know and to understand how Good must always, always, always, always triumph over Evil.

Then let us ask a question:

You know, of course, that the mother of Hansel and Gretel died.

But do you know how it was that she came to die?

You see, three days before God embraced her in His loving arms, she journeyed to the town to do her marketing. Times then were hard, and so she had to shop ever so very carefully, buying only what she absolutely needed. She admired a dainty thimble for her little Gretel but could not afford it. She regretfully regarded a shiny metal whistle on a chain for her little Hansel, but could not buy it. She felt unhappy because she could not give her children special gifts. Yet at the market, even during these so hard times, there were to be seen a very few people clothed in the finest, most gaudily expensive garments. They spent lavishly on this and on that, and on that and on this, and on two of anything else beside. Sometimes they talked among themselves in a strange language that sounded like a wicked song, a song like a frog might sing if it wanted to sound like a vulture.

Hansel and Gretel's mother became ill at ease when she noticed these rich ones gazing at her, gazing in a furtive way that was not meant to be noticed, their dark faces all pinched at the eyes and their heavy, purple lips too wet.

Hurriedly, she concluded her shopping, thinking how glad she would be to be gone from town and back again safe in her own home. And oh, if only she had returned to her loving home straightaway.

But she was hungry and she was thirsty. She could afford no food, but water was free at the well, and she drank deeply ...

ఴ • ఴ

Dear Aline,

If I have any quibble (quibble, this is the word?) with your memorable rendering—and this quibble is hardly even of such a nature as to be termed a "true quibble"—it is in the way you give us the "little man who looked as much like a troll as a man, who sneaked and slipped around at night like a great rat, who sputtered in the daylight and muttered in the night's dark ..." This character is a vassal of the Witch, of course, yet he delights in doing evil for its own sake. He was born to it. So at midnight, when he is poisoning the well, you have a perfect opportunity to make his grotesque visage still more bizarre and vermin-like ...

ఴ • ఴ

... clever, and when cleverness is bent upon wickedness (let all good people be vigilant and resolute!). The poison was a terribly cunning concoction of a nature most peculiar.

Upon a sturdy or robust person, it might have no effect, or cause only the slightest of stomachaches or headaches. But upon those of a delicate constitution, or upon those who were very young or very old, or upon those who had been weakened by the unnatural physical rigors and mental strain caused by poverty, this hideous poison had a far more grave and morbid result.

Thus did our poor Hansel and Gretel come to be bereft of their good and loving mother.

Thus did an overwhelming grief seize the poor woodcutter. Now he worked harder than ever, setting his mighty ax to ringing on trees deeper and always deeper into the endless deep that was the deep woods. He worked until he could no longer raise his long-handled ax, until he could no longer raise his arms, until he could no longer raise his head. Only then, too weary to work and too weary to weep, would the sorrowful man return to his home.

But one day ...

ℭ • ℭ

I wish even a hundredth part of your artistic gift were mine, my dear Aline, so that I might share with you in a drawing, no matter how crude, the missing quality I feel needed here, but the truth is, I appreciate your talent not just for its own sake but because I can do nothing with pencils, chalks, watercolors, or oils. Even as a very young child, I was berated by my teachers who would say that if I drew a simple stick figure, it would be too round.

So, let me remind you of a woman we greatly laughed about when you were so kind as to take me to the game of baseball at the Wrigley Field. Surely you will recall her, sitting behind us in the stands, with her loud and overly exuberant family.

She could have been thought quite pretty in a haughty way, but you had the right of it to say she doubtless had to wax her mustache at least three times a week! And when she spoke in that voice that could curdle milk or etch glass, there was no question of what she was ...

ℭ • ℭ

... a short distance from the hut.

"Father loves her," Hansel said.

"Very much," Gretel replied.

"She does not love him," Hansel said.

"No," thoughtfully replied the good Gretel. "It is as though she says the words of love, but they are not true. It is as though she wears a mask of love, but it fools him. It does not fool me."

"Nor am I fooled, dear sister," said Hansel with a sigh, "but I cannot speak to Father about this. I have tried and he will not listen. He gets a sad and unbelieving look on his face and asks me why I hate so much a woman who loves us so much."

Gretel nodded, saying, "She pinches me. She scratches me. I have marks. She slaps me. I do not cry." Then with firm, if sorrowful, resolve, she added, "I will never cry before her."

164

"She wishes to do us great harm, I have no doubt," Hansel said. "Last night, she thought I was sleeping, but, though my eyes were closed, I lay awake in my bed as she stood over me … She was whispering in the way a serpent might whisper. She said, 'My mistress will be pleased with you, my little Hansel. Ever so pleased with you!' I do not know what she means, Gretel, but I fear her."

"As do I," Gretel said. "Brother dear, what can we do?"

"We can pray to the good God above that He will notice our plight and come to our aid."

And there, my dear children, trusting in the Lord … our Hansel and Gretel knelt and folded their hands, and a narrow sunbeam from the holy sun of heaven fell upon them and it seemed to silently speak a golden promise …

ɞ • ɞ

Perfection itself! So cunning the trap! This is the house of the Witch! In their innocence, feeling betrayed and abandoned, there is no wonder that this gilded palace of wickedness beckons them and they heed its call …

ɞ • ɞ

… for as great as were her magical evils, no less formidable were her talents as an actress. "I am Judith," said the Witch from the doorway, a claw-like hand gesturing to entice Hansel and Gretel closer. "I am alone and I am lonely because of my ugliness. Grown-up people are cruel, but children have hearts pure and good. It is to your hearts, pretty ones, that I appeal as I entreat you to come into my home, to be happy and end my loneliness …

ɞ • ɞ

… hoped by now to see Judith the Witch; I am so certain she will be a memorable horror indeed, far more terrifying than Mr. Disney's witch in the cartoon movie you took me to see, *Snow White and the Seven Dwarfs*.

If, however, you are having difficulty "designing" her (Is that the proper term? What an artist might say?), let me suggest that you give her a prominent, beak-like nose. It would be good, too, I think (and I know I am not an artist, so if this is foolish, forgive me) to make Judith's eyebrows wild and fiercely black, like the rough fur of a predatory animal and …

℘ • ℘

... the unknown letters, if indeed they were letters, twisted and evil, almost as though they were diabolically squirming upon the ancient pages.

This book, little Gretel thought, was the source of Judith's power! If only she might learn the secret language of the old book, she could free Hansel from the cage and they would flee this dreadful house and the horrible witch!

"You little fool!" Judith's shout made Gretel spin about. The Witch had sneaked up on her, and now stood, cackling insanely and joyfully, waggling a bony, long-nailed finger at her. "My magic is in the book, that is what you think!" Judith's voice made a bubbling and breaking sound, like a cauldron on a fire. "But what of all my other magic? Look there!"

Judith the Witch pointed to the entrance of the house, where, on the doorpost was a foreign-looking charm adorned with a wavering, three-fingered design like the mark of a crow's foot in the dirt.

"Look there!" Judith the Witch pointed to an upside-down crucifix over the mantelpiece, and Gretel seemed to see Our Dear Lord writhing in anguish, and seemed to see Him dripping blood from his hands and feet and side, and seemed to see Him dripping blood and tears from His endlessly patient eyes, and seemed to hear Him say, "And still they kill Me, and still these perfidious people murder Me!"

"Look there!" Judith the Witch pointed to the far corner of the room where Hansel, his eyes big, a filthy cloth in his mouth, and heavy ropes wrapped all about him, lay in the cage. "Oh, yes, pretty little girl, your brother's blood will be upon my doorposts and upon my lips. And then when he is emptied like a pig-peasant's wineskin, into the oven I will pop him, and cook him for a feast that I will prepare for the Elders ...

℘ • ℘

... waited and waited, checking the post faithfully. I attempted to telephone you yesterday, but, as you can understand with world events being what they are, it was impossible to have the connection made.

I do hope you are not ill, my dear Aline. I so look forward to your presentation of Judith's demise, as Gretel hurls her into the oven, and she is consumed by flame to become smoke and ash and vanish forever from the face of the Earth ...

℘ • ℘

... a warrior. He was a great man, and so it goes without saying (although, the chatterbox that I am, I say it to you, my dear children) that he was also a good man, for only a good man can achieve greatness.

It was not mere happenstance nor anything as foolishly unreliable as luck that guided his steps through the deep woods. Our Good and Eternal God had heard the prayers of Hansel and Gretel, had heard the prayers of millions, and so ...

ల • ల

... shocked and sad, I truly thought we had commenced a long-lasting and artistically gratifying collaboration.

It is not impossible I misunderstood your comments during the time we shared while I visited your country.

Still, I thought your remarks about "those people," particularly your comments about their, let us say, over-representation, in the fine and performing arts, the medical establishment, and, most importantly, the world of finance, to indicate that you were not in disagreement with the views the majority of us are free to openly express in my country.

Life is strange, as we both know, and I can only hope that, despite the vehemence of what you call your "final note" to me, there will come a time when we are again creating together, when we are again friends.

Though you request I destroy your art, this I cannot bring myself to do. I will instead return it so that you may do as you choose.

It is my plan to seek out an artist in my own country, one who understands (your word) my goals and aims as I continue to write for the dear children, dedicating my work to the youth of today, tomorrow, and a thousand years of tomorrows.

NEW MOON ON THE WATER

BONDS

Perhaps all cats are telepathic, but Lyra, yellow, with six toes on her left hind leg, was especially so. Robert decided, one day, that Lyra had mentally told him to kill his wife, Ellen.

So Robert seized Ellen by the throat, and began strangling her. Ellen could not yell. She could only think.

At which time Maxwell, the Rottweiler, with a forehead that wrinkled when he was alert, bounded into the room. First he bit out most of Robert's throat. For good measure, Maxwell then snapped Lyra in two.

Perhaps all dogs are telepathic, but Maxwell was especially so.

NEW MOON ON THE WATER

OTHER ADVANTAGES

I walk into the store about one o'clock in the afternoon, and Mr. Rotello, the owner, is at the checkout, putting a quart of milk in a sack for an old lady who comes in every day. "Hello, Manuel." Mr. Rotello gives me a big smile, like he's glad to see me, you know, and he smiles at the old lady, too. Mr. Rotello, he smiles a lot and he most of the time looks happy. He's got that kind of face, you know what I mean? Like nothing ever bothers him.

The old lady, though, she's not smiling when she walks past me and out the door, moving slow like there's no reason to hurry home because there's probably nobody there waiting for her anyway. There's plenty of people in the world like that, I guess, but it seems like most of them live around here.

I go into the back room, limping a little, my bad left leg hurting from the long walk to the store. I take the apron down from the nail in the wall by the door that leads back out into the alley. I'm whistling as I tie on the apron. I'm feeling pretty good. See, I only have this job about a week, but it's nice, you know? Mr. Rotello is a friendly guy and he pays me okay and if my mother asks me to bring something home, Mr. Rotello lets me take it at cost.

Tell you, it wasn't so easy for me to get a job, either, with the short leg and the way I sound when I talk English. I mean, the truth is I sound a lot like that cartoon guy you used to see on the TV commercials, the "Frito Bandito." But, okay, no problem for Mr. Rotello, he tells me. He says it's good to have a guy working for him that speaks Spanish because we have plenty of Puerto Rican and Chicano customers. My short leg isn't any big deal, either, is what Mr. Rotello says, because it doesn't matter when you're pushing buttons on a cash register or setting cans of Ajax on a shelf. Really, if the store wasn't in such a bad neighborhood, I'd think I had the best job there could be—for me, anyway.

With my apron on, I go up front. The boss is sitting on a stool behind the register. He's smoking a cigarette and he's real careful to put the ashes in an ashtray. A lot of guys that owned their own store wouldn't be careful like that, you know? They'd just throw ashes all over the place and grind out the butt on the floor because they're not the ones that sweep up. But the boss, uh-uh, he's not like that.

"Well, boss," I say, "what do you want me to do first?"

Mr. Rotello scratches his head where there's not much hair anymore and says, "Oh, the usual, I guess. It doesn't look like rain so it might be a good day to do the windows. I think we're running low on cereals, so bring in a couple cases from the back and get them on the shelves."

I turn to get the cornflakes for aisle three, but Mr. Rotello calls me back. "You see the movie on channel eight last night?"

Sometimes I get the feeling that the boss hired me so he'd have someone around to talk to. Probably it got boring for him being alone in a grocery all day.

"No," I tell him. "I don't watch a lot. See, my mother, she gets on me if I look at a lot of television. She thinks it makes you lazy and stupid and all."

Then I realize what I said to Mr. Rotello, and how it sounds pretty snotty even if I didn't mean it like that, but the boss just says, "Your mother's probably right, Manuel," and he laughs and goes on, "but this was a good film. Lots of action. John Wayne ..."

It does sound like a good film. Mr. Rotello gets kind of worked up talking about it, telling me how John Wayne shot the bad guy off the porch and he got the one behind the water trough and how he turned just in time to blast this guy sneaking up on him.

Anyway, we talk a little more and then Mr. Rotello tells me he's going out for a while and that I should keep my eye on things. That makes me pretty proud, you know, the way he trusts me to watch the whole store and take care of everything.

In the next couple of hours, I get the windows washed, inside and outside. I roll in a carton of cornflakes and get the boxes on the shelf, real straight and right so they don't all come down if someone buys a box. A couple of customers come in but nobody buys too much. People around here don't have a lot of money to spend. Sometimes I wonder how Mr. Rotello makes enough money for himself and to pay me a salary both. I bet it's not easy.

After a while, I take a rest, sitting on the stool back of the counter.

I'm really pleased with myself. The store looks good, no dust on the cans, no dirt on the floor. That's the way stores ought to look. Now some of the places around here ...

There's this "credit jeweler's" across the street with a load of shining, glittery junk in the window that you can spend the rest of your life paying for. There's the corner liquor store that sells muscatel and quarts of beer for twice what they should be to people who are too broken down to go to places farther away where they could get fair prices. Tell you the truth, plenty of the stores here are in business just to suck the blood out of folks who don't have anything much but their blood to pay.

Anyway, I'm just sitting, not doing anything really, and my eye lands on the gun. It's hanging on a peg on the underside of the countertop, and seeing that ugly piece of steel makes me a little bit nervous, you know what I mean? Oh, I saw that gun first day I came to work for Mr. Rotello, but still, every time I look at it, it doesn't make me feel too good. It's a .38, I think, like the detectives on the TV cop shows have, and sometimes I think what a lousy thing it is that a really good guy like the boss, who runs a good, clean store and doesn't bleed people with big, fat prices has to keep a gun for protection.

Uh-uh, it's not a perfect world, but like my mother is always saying, it's the only one we've got.

So, I'm thinking about the world, and that can get you down, you know, but before I get too hung up on thinking, The Professor comes in.

The Professor's about a hundred years old. He's shaking more than usual, but he still tries to give me a smile before he goes down aisle four. He stands there a long time, hugging his brown overcoat around his poor old shaking body, and looks over everything very careful-like before he makes up his mind about what he wants.

Today it's a bottle of soy sauce that he brings up to checkout.

The Professor's mouth is working like crazy, like this time, today, he knows exactly what it is that he wants to say. It must be real important, too, the way he's trying to get it said, but he just can't do it. He mumbles something that doesn't come close to being words. Finally, looking really disappointed, he pays for the soy sauce with pennies, nickels, and dimes.

"That's okay, man," I tell him, to let him know that if he ever manages to say it, I'll be willing to hear it, and I put his soy sauce in a sack. The Professor leaves, and I'm trying to figure out why people call him the Professor and just what it is that he does with the stuff he buys. Every day he comes in and every day it's something different: One time crackers, another time stuffed olives. I guess The Professor is a crazy, but there's a lot of crazies in the world and most of them never do anything bad or hurt anyone.

The boss is back around three or so and he's in a real good mood, singing to himself. He tells me I did a fine job on the windows and then he goes in the back to hang up his coat. When he comes back to the counter, he asks me if there were a lot of customers while he was out.

"No, boss," I say.

"What?" he says, slapping his forehead and rolling his eyes. "You mean Mrs. Van der Rich didn't drop by to pick up her order of imported bamboo shoots? What about the squabs I special ordered for the Rockefellers?"

I tell the boss I don't know anything about those people and then I get the joke and we're both laughing. You laugh with a guy, it's a good feeling, you know, the kind of feeling that makes you think you can say anything at all and it will be all right.

So I decide to ask Mr. Rotello a question that's been bugging me since maybe the second or third day I started work. I'm pretty sure the boss won't take it wrong.

"How come you have a grocery store, boss?"

Mr. Rotello stops laughing and his face gets real serious, like maybe he's remembering something from a way long time ago. Then he wets his lips with his tongue and looks at me like he's going to tell me a real big secret.

"I guess everybody has a dream, Manuel," he says. "Do you think mine was to someday have my own grocery store?"

I don't answer his question, and it's bugging me that I didn't wind up really asking him what I wanted to in the first place. A lot of times, see, I'm thinking in Spanish and when I say it in English it's nothing like what I really meant to say.

"When I was a kid," the boss says, "I always thought I'd grow up and do something exciting. I mean, when I was eight, I wanted to be a cowboy. Cowboys were a big thing then, Manuel. Like Tom Mix or Buck Jones or Bob Steele. Then, a couple years later, I figured I'd be a cop. I'm not talking about the kind of cop who spends his life writing parking tickets, you know. A real gangbuster, a G-man, Dick Tracy or something."

I nod my head to show Mr. Rotello I'm following him, even though he's not answering my real question, the one that didn't get asked. I tell him, "My grandfather used to tell me how he wanted to be a matador. He was a farmer instead until he came to this country to pick oranges and grapes."

"Oranges and grapes," the boss says. "Yeah, me too. I work with the oranges and the grapes. And cornflakes, and pancake syrup, and cans of ravioli. You know how it goes. I got myself married right after high school. Then there were the kids, one right after another for the first five years there. A man's got to earn a living. You've got to be practical. You start being practical and you don't do much dreaming anymore."

He stops talking and even though his eyes are still on me I can tell he's looking somewhere else, somewhere way faraway.

Neither one of us says anything for a while and I get this feeling I can't explain but don't much like. To get rid of that feeling, and because I still want to know about the boss and this store and all, I ask, "But why do you have a store in a crummy neighborhood like this?"

Sure enough, my strange feeling goes away when Mr. Rotello laughs, and there's this happy wrinkle by his eye, and he looks like maybe there's still a Dick Tracy or a cowboy he keeps inside of him.

But the boss doesn't talk about dreams or anything like that.

"See, Manuel, I bought this store at a good price. It was what I could afford without getting up to my butt in debt. I don't have competition from the big supermarkets down here and I don't have to spend a fortune in advertising. Besides, this is only a half-hour drive from my house."

It's funny, but what the boss says doesn't seem to make a whole lot of sense to me. Okay, I can see a guy like the credit jeweler on the other side of the street running his business here because it gives him a chance to bleed people until there's nothing left but the crappy wristwatch they bought that quit working five years ago and a monthly payment book with a thousand tickets left to go. But Mr. Rotello, uh-uh, he's not like that, not that kind of guy.

So I say, "But Mr. Rotello, what I'm talking about is this crummy neighborhood and you know what I mean crummy, okay?" See, there are plenty of sad, lonely, broken-down people in this part of the city, but there are mean ones, too. Okay, the wineheads that cover themselves up with newspaper and sleep in doorways, they're too beat down to hurt anybody, but there are others, you know, like all the junkies that walk around looking like they just came out of the grave or the street punks that hang out on the corner just hoping for bad trouble. I mean some of the mean guys around here will cut your throat for a quarter. The junkies, well, they're crazy, and it doesn't matter how many cop cars cruise the streets. A junky goes crazy wild in the head when he needs his dope and he'll shoot you or slice you or hit you in the head if he thinks you've got any money or anything he can hock for money. It doesn't matter to a junky, you know, and then, there you are, dead in an alley or somewhere.

"I mean, Mr. Rotello, in some stores I bet you don't have to keep a gun under the counter. You don't have to worry about a stick-up every five minutes, right?"

Mr. Rotello gets a look on his face, like maybe he has a secret or something but it's going to stay just between him and himself. "I guess you're right, Manuel," he says. "This is a tough neighborhood, but I don't mind running my business. There are other advantages …"

But Mr. Rotello doesn't get a chance to tell about those "other advantages" because here comes Mr. Wood, a real old man, and he's yelling at the top of his lungs like it's us that's deaf and not him, and he wants me to show him where the cat food is. Of course, it's where it always is, but I limp down aisle three with Mr. Wood following, yelling about his new cat, real happy now that he's got 20 of them. Mr. Wood and I carry 12 cans of Hap-E-Cat up front and Mr. Rotello bags them all up.

The day goes on. People come and go, buy a little something, maybe say a few words to me and the boss. Somehow, though, as the day goes on, Mr. Rotello and I don't get to talking serious anymore.

Anyway, it's about a quarter to nine, near closing, and we're both standing behind the counter, and I'm about to ask the boss if he can give me a ride home the way he usually does, when we get trouble.

Two guys walk through the door. They're young, but they have an old, bad look, like poison's in their guts and running in their blood. One guy is short and he's got real thin blond hair that looks like a sick halo. The other one is a tall guy. His hair is slicked back and greasy. They both are wearing long coats that have to be seven sizes too big, the kind of clothes you buy at the Goodwill store for a dollar.

These guys walk down past the canned soda and they're standing there together talking in real quiet voices.

You know how the television cops are always saying, "I had a feeling of danger?" That's what it was for me, I guess, like I'd swallowed a brick or something, and, all over, I was cold like I'd been inside a walk-in freezer for a month.

"Mr. Rotello," I say, edging closer to him, "I don't like the way …"
"It's all right, Manuel," the boss says softly. "Nothing to worry about."

So I just stand there next to him, scared, thinking the boss is wrong. These guys are going to be something very bad. I can see it. The short, blond guy, he's a junky for sure. You can see the barbed wire under the skin on his face. The junkies lose their bones and get wire instead when they have to have their needle.

But Mr. Rotello isn't shook at all that I can tell. The two guys walk all around the store, and then the tall one goes over by the door and the blond guy is in front of the boss and me at the counter. He puts his hand in the pocket of that too big coat and comes out with a gun and he waves it at us.

You know, my mother's always saying I ought to go to church every

Sunday, and right then I'm thinking she's right and I'm making all kinds of promises to God and hoping I don't have to stand before Him real soon.

I sneak a quick look at Mr. Rotello and then I feel just a little better because the boss is so calm I don't half believe it. It's almost like this is all a movie he's seen a couple of times already and he knows that everything works out okay.

The blond guy aims the gun right at me and says, "You, put your hands on the counter and keep them right there where I can see them." He's got a squeaky voice, crazy-like, and it sounds like he's not all the way sure what he's doing but he's going to go ahead and do it anyhow.

Tell you, maybe guys on television are always looking into gun barrels and it doesn't shake them and they still talk tough and snotty and everything, but me, I slap my hands flat on the counter.

Then Mr. Rotello, sounding like he's just saying "Hello" or something, tells the guy, "There's not much in the register, friend. Why don't you and your buddy forget it and get out of here and save us all a lot of trouble?"

The gun gets pointed right at Mr. Rotello's head. "Shut up!" the guy says, and I hope that the boss does shut up. "Open the register and keep your big mouth closed."

Mr. Rotello hits the button. The drawer flies open and the register's "No Sale" flag goes up. The boss picks up the bills—there's not more than forty bucks, I guess—and hands them over.

The blond guy stuffs the money in his pocket with his left hand and says, "The change, too."

Mr. Rotello sniffs like he's going to laugh. I'm praying that he doesn't. The shooting could start any second. Then Mr. Rotello hands the guy the coins, too, and the blond guy starts backing to his pal at the door. The tall one opens the door and slips out and the blond guy starts to leave, too, when I feel—I mean, I don't really see—Mr. Rotello move.

He bends down, real quick, and takes the gun off the peg under the counter.

"Hey!" Mr. Rotello yells. The blond guy isn't outside yet. He turns and his eyes are real big. He starts swinging the gun back toward us, but there's this explosion and a flash of fire from Mr. Rotello's pistol, and the blond guy jumps straight up into the air like one of those dumb Saturday morning cartoon characters on television. He hasn't even hit the floor yet and Mr. Rotello is pushing past me and around the counter and out the door and then I get the idea: The boss is after the other guy!

I'm kind of ashamed of myself for acting like a big chicken and all so, when I can get my legs to stop shaking, I go running out, too. Maybe the boss will need my help or something. I have to step around the guy by the door, though, and what I see makes me a little bit sick. He's kind of in a heap, like dirty laundry, and some of his head is all punched in, and the floor that used to be so clean is real bloody.

With the short leg, I can't run too fast, but outside, up ahead, there's Mr. Rotello moving like he's after Olympic gold. He stops at the corner, under a streetlight, and he looks from side to side, and then he goes running to the left.

When I get to the corner, I see the boss turn into the dead-end alley that runs behind the store. I follow as quick as I can, and when I'm at the entrance to the alley, there's Mr. Rotello, standing still. His left hand is on his hip. He's turned sideways. His right arm is straight out. He's aiming.

The tall guy is racing down the alley past the garbage cans and piles of trash and tossed away old furniture. The way he's moving, it's like he doesn't even see the brick wall ahead of him and he's planning to go right through it.

The boss shuts his left eye. Something real funny comes onto his face, then, and for a second, it's like nothing is real. Mr. Rotello's not real, the guy running away isn't real, there was no hold-up , nothing. It's almost like I'm watching a movie or reading a comic strip, and everyone is—*flatter*—and less real than everything really is.

Then the gun makes a big bang in the boss's hand and his arm jerks up and everything is really real again.

The stick-up guy looks like someone invisible hits him with a flying tackle and knocks the legs right off him. He spins right, slams into a garbage can, and bounces off onto a pile of trash.

He's starting to get up when Mr. Rotello shoots again and then that's it. The guy isn't moving or anything. He's just sprawled there on the trash.

Back in the store, we don't have long to wait. The sirens are screaming real soon and I'm sitting at the counter and there's a whole bunch of cops coming in. I look at the gun on the peg under the counter, and there's this sick feeling in my stomach like you can get when you're afraid something is wrong and you're even more afraid that you know just what it is.

Two guys in white get the blond guy off the floor, cover him up on a stretcher and haul him away. A couple of policemen are asking me questions, and I guess I'm answering because I can hear my voice, but what I'm really doing is watching what's going on in front of the counter.

There's a big cop with a long face slapping Mr. Rotello on the shoulder and saying, "Man, you are something else. How many does that make?"

"Five, I guess," the boss says, "in the past 11 months."

"Damn," the big cop says, "Rotello, your killed-and-wounded record's better than any officer's in the precinct."

I guess I'm acting strange because the policeman who's talking to me keeps asking me to repeat answers to questions that I thought I'd already answered.

But, you know, I'm just not feeling good, no good at all. I'm remembering the way Mr. Rotello looked back there in the alley, and I think I'm understanding maybe why his face looked the way it did, and I have this idea why he has the store in this crummy neighborhood.

So I'm sick to my stomach, and maybe sad or something, too, but whatever it is I'm feeling, it's all squeezed up real tight in my throat, and I'm thinking I have to quit this job because I don't want to work here anymore.

NEW MOON ON THE WATER

FYI

This is not a confession. Confession might be good for the soul, but I do not believe in a soul. Confession with proper demonstration of remorse might save your life in a court of law, but I am not concerned with such matters.

Remorse? I do have regrets—heartfelt—and I anticipate more, but my stating that is strictly FYI, strictly for your information and not my benefit.

FYI. That is what this is all about.

This is what you need to know. This is what I mean you to know and it is being told to you in the way I mean you to know it.

So, then. So.

FYI. Yesterday, I killed my children.

I loved my children and I love them still in the profound and weighted echoes of their absence.

I loved them.

And I killed them.

℮ • ℮

Who were my children?

FYI. Bob. Adam. Tammy Lee.

Ages: Bob, eight, Adam, ten, and Tammy Lee, twelve.

Sometimes Tammy Lee used to ask, used to demand, "I am your favorite, right, Daddy?"

She was. Sometimes. Sometimes Adam was and sometimes Bob was and sometimes I could honestly answer, satisfying none of them, "You are all my favorite."

That's how it is with your children, isn't it? So, then. So.

I loved them and I killed them.

I killed them and I will never see them again and knowing that is an intense and angled emptiness within me. That is the pain. That's what this pain feels like for me.

NEW MOON ON THE WATER

They say nobody can truly know another's pain.

Perhaps not.

But you can get an inkling of it, can't you?

FYI.

ↄ • ↄ

FYI. This is how I killed my children.

They are at the beach. It is a perfect beach day. The water is shifting greens and blues and the sun becomes scooped out broken angles on the always-moving water.

It is only the three of them at the beach. I am not yet with them, not yet.

They wait, patient, on an old, green, pill-nappy blanket. They smell of sunblock and popsicles.

Adam and Tammy Lee. They are waiting.

They know I am coming.

They are waiting for Daddy.

This time they have no idea what I mean to do.

So, then. So. Then I am there. Inside me is a great sorrow and a great resolve.

It makes my movements solemn and slow.

Then I tell them what I will do. I do not attempt an explanation. This is nothing that can be explained. Not to them; they are innocent.

They submit, one by one, each in turn, Bob and Adam and Tammy Lee, fearing eyes, sick yellow paleness, give themselves to me without struggle, surrender to me and to death, as I will myself to be so strong, and then, one by one, each in turn, Bob and Adam and Tammy Lee.

I break their necks and marvel each time at the cracking sharpness of that breaking, at each body's frantic, senseless thrashing at disruption of signals from the brain, the furious seizures of disconnection and shutting down and dying.

They are dead. Beautiful children. I lay them side by side by side on the blanket. They look wrong, the heads are tipped wrong. I cannot set them right. Adam's eyes will not close. I shut the right one with a gentle thumb, then the left, but then the right pops open and then the left opens.

There is no accusation in Adam's eyes.

There is only death.

I recognize what I see and I weep.

ↄ • ↄ

FYI. This is how I killed my children.

This time, it is only my three children and me in the house, of course.

I fill the bathtub. I make sure the water is pleasantly warm. Not too hot. Not cold. There will be enough shock without that of the wrong water temperature.

Then I call Bob.

He doesn't know. There's no need for him to know, not really, and I don't need him to know, because I must do this in the way I must do this, building up from worse to worst to beyond that.

I tell Bob to take off his clothes.

Bob doesn't like to take a bath. He is eight years old. Eight-year-old boys do not like baths.

You know, I am sure. Little boys have no natural affinity for the tub. It is different with girls.

Bob argues.

I joke. I tell him terrible toe jams will come curling around his ankles, climbing up his shins, tell him kids will call him old Nasty Butt Bob, tell him the silly old stuff about potatoes sprouting behind his ears and mushrooms springing from his disgusting scalp.

He strips. I pop him in the tub, and slide skinny legs forward, scoot him along on his bottom, and then I tip him back and push him below the water and hold his shoulders, and he twists, head breaks the surface of the water, so the heel of my hand is on his forehead and my elbow is locked and then for a second's foolish comfort perhaps he thinks it's a game it's all a game it's a game.

But it is a game he does not like and he is such a skinny little boy, so bony, and he tries to wriggle free, to lift his head, to breathe, and he is making foolish and crazy sounds and bubbles and I hold him down in the water and hold him down and his eyes grow huge and there's a writhing snake of a blue vein in his forehead I've never before noticed and somehow a thin hand claws at my face, claws into my face, and I feel skin tear under nails, and I hold him and I watch him drown and I watch him drown and I watch him die and I kill him and I murder my Bob.

So, then. So.

Then I murder Adam.

FYI. I want it to be harder this time, harder for Adam and harder for me. We go to the backyard. The fence is high and there are no neighbors, inquisitive or otherwise. This is the place I have made for us, this place where we live, my children, my three children Bob and Adam and Tammy Lee. We have only one another here. That is the way it has always been.

NEW MOON ON THE WATER

Adam wants to know about the baseball bat. I don't like baseball, don't like sports and especially team sports, and my son, my Adam, of course does not like baseball and so we don't play baseball.

But now I have a baseball bat.

Because, I tell Adam, I am going to hit him with the baseball bat and hit him and I have set my mind to just keep on hitting him until he is dead. I am kidding. I have to be kidding, is what Adam says.

I told him because he had to know, because that was part of it, too. Then I swing the baseball bat, swing it hard, a low and whooshing arc and I catch him at an angle across the shins.

The shock comes all the way through the shaft of the baseball bat and my wrists thrum painfully and Adam screams loud so loud but of course there is nobody to hear screams.

Adam falls. Adam cannot run. His face is teary and he's gulping and there's a milky-looking wad of snot at his nostril as he rolls and tries to crawl, a crawl that's mostly with his arms.

So I bring the bat down. I have the incongruous thought that I probably look like a cartoon character chopping wood or something like that.

And I set to chop-chop-chopping and there are streamers of blood in the air and Adam looks dented and I think he's yelling *don't don't don't* and I find a rhythm synched to that yelling and then a wet and muddy noise and no more yelling.

He is not moving. Not now.

But he is not dead.

Not yet.

I want to stop right there, I want to undo it all, to save alive my Adam and my Bob and my Tammy Lee, but I cannot no I cannot.

So I use all my force and smash in his head and there's not all that much to it, just a rotten busting thump like a cantaloupe dropped to the floor in the produce department.

It is finished with Adam for now.

It is time to kill Tammy Lee.

We are in the kitchen. I tell her what I have done to Bob and Adam, tell her what I mean to do to her. I state it simply and directly, neither understatement nor hyperbole, just what has to be. I show her the serrated bread knife.

Tammy Lee's tears ball up and ooze out like clear oil. No, don't kill her, please don't kill her, please ... I have tried to avoid melodrama, to present only the reality of these situations, but we know children are theatrical

184

by nature, and so Tammy Lee begs and she does so on her knees, hands clasped together like a prayerful angel cliché.

No, don't kill her, just slap her, beat her with your fists or with your belt, don't kill her don't kill her don't kill, oh, she doesn't know exactly what it is bad men sometimes do to little girls, but she knows it is very bad, bur whatever it is, it is not death it is not dying so do that do that to her instead please oh please.

That is how she begs.

FYI. It makes me almost angry, I think I am angry, and I don't want to hear that anymore and maybe that's all it takes sometimes, do you think, the simple need not to hear anymore.

I yank her up by her hair. I bend her back onto the table.

I slash her throat, and I keep doing it as she stops making anything like intelligible sounds. I concentrate on the subtle flesh and steel interplay between the serrations on the blade and the coils of her windpipe.

When I stop cutting, Tammy Lee's head is held to her body by only a somehow-unyielding strap of neck skin.

Then I rest.

I need to rest.

හ • හ

So, then. So.

I rest and as I often do, I think about Mr. G. Gordon Liddy. In the quiet house of my dead children, I think about Mr. G. Gordon Liddy.

FYI. I'm not political, not at all. I think you need to be informed to vote and I don't seek to be informed and I don't vote nor do I imagine my vote might matter in the least should I cast it. I therefore do not concern myself with Mr. G. Gordon Liddy's politics or those actions judged illegal by the courts for which he was sent to prison.

In a book he wrote, a *true* book, Mr. G. Gordon Liddy tells how he held his hand over the flame of a candle until the flesh bubbled and blackened. He burned his hand and accepted the pain and he did not flinch.

Here is how I think he did it. I think he first saw himself doing it, saw it in a wonderful vivid place in his mind, and he held onto that scene seeing himself doing it seeing the flame tickle the palm of his hand and seeing the steadiness of his arm and seeing his own face as expressionless as a countertop. Then he made himself see that scene again and again and again, holding onto it, making it more real than ever dream could be and more real than most of the mundane and pointless moments of daily life.

And when there was no question, only an affirmation, when he did not doubt, doubting neither the reality of the pain nor his ability to inflict it on himself and to bear it, then he did in fact and deed hold his hand over the candle and I think, perhaps at least the first time, I think he might have had just a hint of a smile on his lips.

FYI. The title of Mr. G. Gordon Liddy's book is *Will.*

๛ • ๛

I'm sure you want to know who I am. Now you want to know that.

There's irony there. You never wanted to know me until I started telling you all this, FYI.

You know I am someone who has read a book.

I read a poem, too. I might have read more than just one, actually, but there is only the one I recall. It was years ago and the writer was named Emily Dickinson, a woman poet.

"I'm nobody, who are you?"

That was, I think, the first line of the poem, or maybe the first two lines.

I remember that because I am nobody. I'm the one who washes your windshield and through suds and squeegee blurs you take little notice of the name in the oval above the pocket of my blue shirt and do not see my face, not really.

So, then. So. I'm the bagger the supermarket checker signals to provide a "carry-out" but you don't want help, don't want my help, as you roll the cart past me into the parking lot. FYI. I'm the one you do not apologize to when your elbow strikes me as you board the 5:38 commuter train. I'm the telephone solicitor who doesn't even get the courtesy of a rude "Go to hell," just a quiet hang up, as you reach for the remote to watch a rerun of *NYPD Blue.*

I'm the one who never had a hand in the air in grade school or junior high or high school and the teacher never noticed and never asked and the other students never said anything about it, not even anything derogatory. I'm the guy across the way who lives in a neighborhood and has no neighbors, who gets pink-slipped with no mid-level manager picking up on the empty cubicle for at least a month, the one at the deli who holds Number 57 and listens to the call of "55 … 56 … 58 …59."

FYI. I am nobody.

That is who I am.

I think without even saying it, I am answering, too, the question implicit in Ms. Dickinson's poem, "Who are you?"

MORT CASTLE

FYI.

So, then. So.

Yesterday, I killed my children.

After I killed them at the beach, after I snapped the necks, drowned, beat to death, cut the throat of my children, after I killed them by these means, I killed them again and again and again, killed them with rope and shotgun and rat poison, smothered them with pillows, shocked them with electricity, locked them away and set them aflame, I killed them and killed them and stopped killing only when I no longer had imagination or innovation to conjure up a method.

I killed my Bob and Adam and Tammy Lee and it hurt.

And as I am sure you've realized, realized because you are so perceptive, so smart, wise even, the sort of person who is the pillar of society, a community leader, a true heart of the nation, a leader and a follower both as you choose, an upstanding, righteous citizen, you comprehend that my children were imaginary.

In a wonderful vivid place in my mind, I had three beautiful children.

So, then. So.

This is what you need to know. This is what I mean you to know and it is being told to you in the way I mean you to know it. FYI—strictly for your information and not my benefit.

I told you that at the beginning, didn't I?

With your discerning mind, with your keen intuition and highly developed interpersonal skills, you surely cannot believe this is merely a nasty shaggy dog story contrived as an ugly joke by a nobody.

FYI. No, not so.

Believe me, killing my children, my Bob and Adam and Tammy Lee, that hurt me. The hurt is not imaginary. It is agony and the promise of anguish without end; that is what it is to lose your children. You have to know that.

Maybe there is something else you understand by now, but if not, I will state it for you.

FYI.

I hate you. I hate you not for hating me but for not even acknowledging my presence on this Earth.

So, then. So.

FYI.

NEW MOON ON THE WATER

Yesterday, I killed my children.
FYI.
Tomorrow, I will kill yours.

IN THE GYPSY CAMP

Stanki Nashti arakenpe manushen shai

"Mountains do not meet, but people do."
—A Romani Proverb

I

Berlin, Germany
March of This Year
"No Boundaries" World Music Concert Series

The *Konzerthaus Berlin* stands in the *Gendarmenmarkt* square between two lofty cathedrals. Some would say this neoclassical edifice itself is not without an aura of the sacred. Within, as the applause diminishes, the other musicians comprising the Rom group called *Wortacha!* slip away: the double bass, the mandolin, and the two guitars. The name of the group means "Partners!," but now the lean young violinist stands alone. This is Tacho; he is the son of Tacho, who is the son of Tacho, and it is Tacho who concerns us for the present.

In true Roma fashion, Tacho wears an earring, and while many young and even not so young men do so in our time, the earring has meaning for Tacho, as does the *diklo*, the neckerchief knotted at his throat. He wears also a gold medallion of *Chon*, our Mother Moon, and resting upon it, a silver cross: silver for the ten silver nails the Romans had apportioned to pierce the hands and feet of our Lord. As you may know, Gypsies stole seven of these nails and were blessed by Heaven for thus reducing a little the agony of The Savior.

"*Nais tuke*," Tacho says. "Thank you, you are kind. You are most kind." Germans have always appreciated Gypsy music; had Hitler's plans come to fruition, a number of German Gypsy musicians, members of the

189

Sinti clans, might well have been allowed to live, perhaps even breed, in order to provide entertainment for the Reich.

Bengesko niamso ... Were Tacho less of a man, he might well be thinking this: *Cursed be the German.* But Tacho is *Rom baro*, a big man of generous spirit.

As is his father.

As is his grandfather.

Tshatsomo. This is the truth about Tacho.

"I should like now to play a song I myself have composed," Tacho says. "It is called 'The Gypsy Camp.'"

Silence as Tacho raises the bow. It will not be a Hungarian Gypsy czardas this time, nor an American swing tune and never would our Tacho play the arabesque schmaltz of the café Gypsy.

Tacho's song is *mulengi djila*, a dirge, a song of lamentations and memory, *brigaki djila*, a song of hardships and sacrifice but *Pachivaki djila*, also a song of celebration.

This is the song of *Puri dai* Melantha, Grandmother Melantha, the old *rawnie*, the wise woman who knew all manner of *draba* and *vila* charm, who could *dukker* with tea leaves and the lines of the hand and the Tarot.

This is the song of Tacho, the father of Tacho, who is the father of Tacho.

And this is the song of *Obersturmführer* Hans Kessler, officer, junior grade, of the *Waffen* SS, Division *Totenkopf.*

This is the song of Auschwitz-Birkenau. This is the song of the *Hitlari.*

This is the song of Tacho.

Listen, please, attend with your ear, permit the *djila* to take you to
The Gypsy Camp.

II

Auschwitz-Birkenau
June 1943

Arbeit Macht Frei.

This was the motto emblazoned over the entrance to Auschwitz. As they exited the cattle cars to the enthusiastic welcome of whips and jackboots and the shining eyes and gleaming teeth of vigilant German shepherds, some of the Reich's prisoners, mainly Jews but also Poles, Russians, homosexuals, and criminals from all the occupied territories, read the sign. Some sought to believe that "Work will bring you freedom," and thus to find a measure of hope in this gray and confusing world. Others only noted the irony.

From throughout Europe, Gypsies were transported to Auschwitz in "considerable numbers" in 1943, although estimates of those numbers range from ten to twenty thousand. (Though the German became renowned over the centuries for his historical and statistical record-keeping, somehow exact counts from the murder camps have not been found. Rudolph Hoss, commandant of Auschwitz-Birkenau, estimated the total number of Gypsies who lived or died at the camp as "roughly 16,000" in the memoirs he wrote before he was hanged.)

It bears mentioning that one of the Gypsies transported to Auschwitz in June of 1943 was 18-year-old Tacho. (*Puri dai* Melantha, the *gule romni* whose story this is as well, had previously come to Auschwitz at a time when, as she said, "Destiny determined I was meant to be here.")

It is reasonable that you wish to know of Tacho's family. One without family is little more than a *mulo*, a ghost, or an imposter.

Tacho's father, Rupa, played mandolin and knew horses as well as any Lovari. When war came, Rupa joined a band of partisans, was *lelled* by the Germans, refused to *mong* for his life, and had his brains blown out; his body was burned in a roadside ditch. *Akana mukav tut le Devlesa*; thus we leave him to God. Tacho's mother, Saro, and his younger sister, Keti, were sent to Ravensbruck where they abided a time until they departed in the form of smoke rising from a chimney.

Tacho and almost all the Rom from the trains took scant notice of the words *Arbeit Macht Frei*; most Gypsies could not read. Nor would they have believed such an adage because a) it was a saying of the *Gaje*, and therefore unworthy of trust, and b) it was obviously and foolishly untrue! You are born free of work and free to enjoy the pleasures of the world and to share those pleasures with others—if you are fortunate enough to be Rom. If not, well, who can understand the ways of the *Gaje*? The *Gajo* seldom understands himself.

The Rom did take note, however, of the barbed-wire fences and the hollow-eyed, shaven-head skeletons shambling about in their striped uniforms; they seemed comic, these Auschwitzers, like badly crafted and poorly operated marionettes. There was a ponderous stench over the place, a smell of human excrement and burning meat and hair and who could know what else. And there were electrical sounds and pounding sounds and sounds that had to come from machines but were like no sounds of any machines that belonged in this world. And all of it, sound and smell and sight, blended together in a powerful and terrible way that was much like the way of wicked dreams, so that some of the Rom wondered if they had journeyed into some Hell that God had abandoned and given over to *O Beng*, the Devil Himself.

Then a little of the strangeness and fear went away because a man in a dapper uniform stood before them on the railroad platform. He smiled, boyish and kindly. "*Naxdaran, Romali*," he said in their own language. "Do not fear, Gypsy friends. I wish to personally welcome you."

There might have been shouted questions and perhaps even curses from the men and the women, but here, where there were so many soldiers with guns and growling dogs and wires humming with electricity …

"I am *Obersturmführer* Hans Kessler," the man said. "You are not prisoners, *Romali*. You have been brought here so we may provide you refuge." The man made a weary-sad gesture with a gloved hand. "You are people of the road, and while there is war, the roads cannot be traveled. The danger is too great. Germany must protect the Rom in such perilous times."

There were mutterings at this. Germany safeguard the Rom? What nation had ever sought to protect Gypsies? What was it this *Gajo* was telling them?

"I am in charge of your well-being," *Obersturmführer* Kessler said. He nodded, as much to himself as to the Rom. "You will see. It will be all right here."

Then the Gypsies were loaded into trucks and taken to their camp at the edge of Auschwitz-Birkenau.

In the days that followed, many among the Rom began to think that, perhaps, perhaps … *Bater!* May it be so! Maybe the Germans meant them no harm. You see, prisoners in Auschwitz had their hair shorn, were dressed in striped uniforms, and assigned to prisoner barracks willy-nilly. But the Rom lived in family groups, in 20 barracks set aside for them. They were allowed to keep their hair and clothing and musical instruments. Yes, men were occasionally mustered out for "work details," but the Rom were incapable of taking seriously such a thing as organized labor, and the guards, not brutal camp-trusty *kapos* or monstrous Ustashi, but low-ranking SS troopers who reported to *Obersturmführer* Kessler, usually found themselves laughing at Gypsy ploys rather than punishing or threatening their charges.

In the evenings, the Rom were permitted small campfires, encouraged to play their instruments, to sing and tell stories. There was a hospital for their sick. They even had a canteen where they might purchase tobacco or sweets for the children.

Tshatsomo, there was little food and those who went to the hospital because of typhus or dysentery had slim chance of leaving alive. But, it was explained over and over, "wartime" meant shortages of food, clothing, and medicine. But the war would end someday and the Rom would again know a golden life.

Obersturmführer Hans Kessler seemed truly sympathetic to the Rom; was he a Romany *rye*, a *Gajo* fascinated by *Romali* custom and tradition? One might think so: frequently, the *Obersturmführer* asked, "How do you say this?" learning words and phrases. The German's pockets always held candy for the children, who called him "*Onkel*" whenever he entered the Gypsy camp.

One evening, *Obersturmführer* Kessler came to a gathering carrying a violin. "I play," he said, "*Eine kleines Bisschen.*" His eyes glistened and some of the impolite ones among the Rom would later remark how they'd smelled whiskey on the officer's breath.

Obersturmführer Hans Kessler waited humbly, as polite as any proper Gypsy, until he had an invitation. Agreeing, as though reluctant, he said, "*Patshiv tumenge Romali.* I offer this song as my poor gift to worthy people." Can we doubt that this German had beautiful manners?

Back as straight as if his spine had been replaced with steel, line of perspiration on his upper lip, *Obersturmführer* Hans Kessler seemed as nervous as a schoolboy on examination day. There in fire's glow he performed the "Allemanda" from Bach's *Partita Number II in D Minor*.

Not a note rang hesitant or untrue. Crescendo, diminuendo, the difficult double stops and the triplets, *Obersturmführer* Kessler played with logic and precision. He played with economy and efficiency. He was as exact as the workings of a fine Swiss (or German!) timepiece. He was no less mechanical. The *Obersturmführer's* performance was as alive as a tank tread.

And, it must needs be said, from his expression, he realized how utterly empty and spiritless was his song. No matter his other sins, *Obersturmführer* Hans Kessler did not practice self-deception.

What might have prompted the man to show his inadequacies in this way? Might he have wished to prove his appreciation of the music of the Rom by demonstrating his own shortcomings? Or perhaps, retaining a child's sense of how magic happens, had he dared to dream that at least a measure of melodious aptitude might fall upon him because of proximity with the Rom?

Regretfully, we cannot say.

The Rom applauded the *Obersturmführer*; it was a courtesy.

NEW MOON ON THE WATER

"*Danke,*" said *Obersturmführer* Hans Kessler, as was fitting. Then he nodded to Tacho, who, despite his years, had proven himself *Kralis* of all the musicians in the Gypsy camp. "*Bitte.*"

Well-taught by good Gypsies, Tacho possessed neither the foolishness nor impertinence of youth; *Rom baro* he was, despite little time on the Earth. And now, violin in hand, eyes modestly downcast, he spoke quietly, saying that he hoped he might create songs that would fill the hearts of the Rom with joy and their minds with precious remembrances.

With an artlessness wholly true to his nature, Tacho began to play: "Dark Eyes" to "Foolish Girl in the Woods," "Hot South" to Brahms's "*Zigeunerlieder,*" "The Good Road" to "*Szeleem.*"

So beautifully did Tacho play (on that evening that might well have decided the rest of his life!), that there was a silence more profound than applause when the final note disappeared into the sky.

"*Nais tuke,*" said *Obersturmführer* Hans Kessler in Romany. "Thank you." Then he repeated it. Then he said it yet again and left the Gypsy camp.

III

Auschwitz-Birkenau
August 1943

Even with the war, *Puri dai* Melantha might have escaped Auschwitz and the fate that befell her and so many others. So strong was the shriveled old woman's *draba* that she could have appeared to the *Hitlari* disguised as the lovely Emmy Sonnemann, the movie-star wife of Hermann Goring. Indeed, there were a dozen ways by which the *ababina* would not have known the distinctive hospitality of those German protectors of the Gypsies. Melantha could have worked *draba* charm to render herself totally invisible to the eyes of Rom and *Gajo* alike. There are those who say her talents were such that the gule romni might have summoned the flying *vurdon* of ancient days to carry her from cloud to cloud and then to somewhere far from wars and those who made wars.

Puri dai Melantha did nothing of the sort. How could she leave her people? Cut off from your own, without the memories they carry, oh, foolish *chavo*, foolish *tschai*, you might as well be a *balo*, rooting in the mud and standing in its own filth!

When a young SS trooper with a left eye that turned inward summoned her, Melantha went with him willingly enough. As she walked, she could feel an aura, a buzzing black hum enveloping the soldier. Another year, perhaps not quite, perhaps slightly more, and this German would be dead.

The first shot drops him. The Russian comes up and shoots him again and again. The last shot enters the eye that seems to want to look within himself and explodes a bucket of brains into the man's helmet.

Nothing to be done about it. No prayer nor charm against this poor unfortunate's death. This was *baxt*, inevitable and irrevocable.

The SS man who had a little more or less than a year to live conducted her to the office of *Obersturmführer* Hans Kessler. With one motion and no words, the *Obersturmführer* greeted her, dismissed the soldier, and showed her to a sofa near the window. *Puri dai* Melantha pushed back the *diklo* on her head, arranged her skirts and *poutsis*.

In craggy depths of aged flesh, her eyes surveyed the surroundings: a Grundig phonograph by the bookshelves, a music stand, a floor lamp. On the desk, a small plaster bust of Beethoven, the kind of cheap statuary awarded as a schoolboy's prize. Of course, there was a portrait of Hitler on the wall.

A very lonely place, *Puri dai* Melantha decided. A very lonely man. If she tapped the *Obersturmführer* on the chest, would there be a hollow sound?

Did she desire coffee or tea, inquired *Obersturmführer* Kessler; perhaps some other refreshment …

No, *gestena*, she thanked him.

He sat down near to her, turning so he might just as easily look into her eyes or away. She knew he wanted to speak but did not speak.

He cleared his throat. She said nothing.

He tried to smile.

She said nothing.

He said, "It is said you are an *ababina*."

"So it is said," Melantha replied.

"It is said you are a wise woman, a *gule romni*."

"So it is said."

"With your charms and your spells"—*Obersturmführer* Hans Kessler's voice became soft—"can you heal? Can you save?"

She heard his words and the words he did not say: Can you heal *me*? Can you save *me*?

She told him the truth: "I do not know." She needed to hear: From what disease did he need to be healed? From what peril did he need to be saved?

NEW MOON ON THE WATER

Obersturmführer Hans Kessler said, "I do not know." He told her the truth.

Then she took his hand, held it, felt pulse at wrist, studied whorls of fingertips, peered at lines in the palm.

"*Dukkeripin*," the *Obersturmführer* said.

"Yes," *Puri dai* Melantha said. "To determine if you can be healed, to learn if you can be saved, I must know you. This is the way of it."

"*Bater*," he said. May it be so.

IV

Gunzburg, Bavaria
1918–1937

Hans Kessler was born in the year the boastful Allies compelled Germany to sign the articles of shame and capitulation. His father was a mathematician of little creativity, no prominence, and cold temperament. He taught only the lower forms, earned a pathetic salary and perfunctory respect. Hans's mother, a frail *hausfrau*, never raised her voice and seldom her eyes to her husband. She doted on the only child she could ever bear if she wanted to live, said the doctors—*bloodsucking Jew doctors!*—consoled *Herr* Kessler, and so she gave Hans and got from him the sort of love that can sustain a needful woman too timid to seek fulfillment in any other way.

As an adult, remembering his early boyhood, Hans Kessler could honestly say in that unknowing time he was neither happy nor unhappy. A little somnambulist, like Caligari's Caesar as a midget, Hans thought, child automaton made of flesh ...

And then he awoke. He became a human being.

He was then eight years old. One afternoon, there was a special guest at school. A violinist, *Herr* Isaac Grosshandler, who had performed in Moscow, Vienna, Berlin, and even New York, gave a short talk about the glories of music and the life of Bach. He told the students "According to the philosopher Henri Frederic Amiel, 'Music is harmony, harmony is perfection, perfection is our dream, and our dream is heaven.'"

Some of the *kinder*, being potato-heads, did not understand that and most did not care. A few wondered in whispers why they had to listen to this dirty Jew, anyway.

Then *Herr* Grosshandler played the "Allemanda" from Bach's *Partita Number II in D Minor*.

The shimmering relentless beauty of it made Hans Kessler want to weep and he'd have done so had he not had a schoolboy's awareness of the consequences. The music made him dream and the dream was heaven.

He had to have a violin and lessons. He became a child obsessed and possessed. He begged and begged, and Frau Kessler, who'd have given her son the stars and the moon if he swore to love her always, yearned to grant his wish. *Bitte*, Mother, you will never need to remind me to practice. I will be dutiful and learn all that I can learn. I will become a great violinist, you shall see, and you will be so proud ...

Mathematician that he was, *Herr* Kessler had a reputation as a *pfennig-squeezer* of the first order. Thanks to the Jew bankers, a man could barely earn enough to put bread on the table, let alone a fiddle under the chin of a young fool! How Frau Kessler convinced her husband or in what ways *Herr* Kessler made her pay for every mark he had to spend, Hans never did learn. He began lessons with the church's assistant choirmaster, who, in addition to singing, played organ, violin, guitar, and tuba, all of them passably.

True to his word and vow to himself, Hans Kessler practiced and practiced and practiced. Thumb of right hand bent so, little finger just a gentle guide, left hand curled back from the neck of the violin, he moved from first to third position, from third to fifth and so on up the neck. He understood the cycle of notes and chord theory, the true and false harmonics, the sharp snap of pizzicato and the bounce of spiccato and the joining together of notes in legato ...

By age 13, Hans's playing could bring a smile to Frau Kessler's lips and a tear to her eye, sometimes both at once. Even his father acknowledged that the violin did not hurt the ears, though he wished Hans would learn more of the good old German folk tunes that made you want to whistle or beat a drum.

Then Hans Kessler heard Adolph Busch's phonograph record of the *Partita*. The music exploded from the record to sear his brain. The violin came alive and the music came alive and Bach came alive....

Hans wanted to smash his violin. He wanted to hurl himself from the church tower, dash his brains on the stones. He had sought Magnificence and was doomed to Mediocrity.

But *wait*. No! The world was huge and all he had known of it was Gunzburg!

There was a secret to the violin, a magic. Isaac Grosshandler and Adolph Busch, ah, they possessed the secret. What they knew, he could learn. What they had, he could have.

NEW MOON ON THE WATER

But because he was young yet, he did not know how. So he returned to diligent study and practice and cautioned himself to be patient, patient.

But we would be lying to say that Hans Kessler did so with a cheerful or even contented heart. As the American writer Ambrose Bierce observed, "Patience is a minor form of despair, disguised as a virtue."

When he was 15, two significant events set Hans on the path that led to Auschwitz and his becoming *Obersturmführer* Hans Kessler.

The first is so universal that we perhaps err in giving it overmuch emphasis: Hans Kessler fell in love with a girl and lost her.

Our second significant occurrence in the story of Hans Kessler is hardly a widespread experience and thus we may duly evaluate it as formative:

Hans Kessler ran off with the Gypsies.

Let us deal with these two not-necessarily-related events in order: Heidi Himmelberg came into Hans's life prior to the Gypsies, when, in late spring, her family moved to Gunzburg from Berlin because her father, a tailor, grew sick and tired of the unfair competition of the Jew leeches. As blonde as a Heidi should be, she had a sweet mouth and an overall properly placed plumpness that did not go unnoticed by the young and some of the not-so-young males of the town. She drew chalk pictures of horses and Rhinemaidens, studied flute, adored the poetry of Rilke, particularly "Love Song"—*How can I keep my soul in me, so that it doesn't touch your soul?*—and she laughed in a way that made you think of circuses.

They met at the library, where Hans was returning a book on violin crafting and she was borrowing *Melodien für Flöte Vol. I.* When Heidi learned he was a violinist, her sweet mouth went "O" (and his face went scarlet). She simply did not know how anyone could play so challenging an instrument.

Hardly outgoing, Hans initially became even more shy around Heidi, but she had the confidence of one whose laughter made you think of circuses.

To shorten even further what proved to be a very short story of first love, very soon Heidi was reading Hans favorite lines of Rilke (that she knew he would like):

"Music is closer to us, then; it streams toward us; we stand in its way but then it goes right through us ..."

And very soon, Hans was playing Heidi records of such virtuosos as Hugo Heerman and Leopold Auer.

And very soon, Heidi and Hans kissed and held hands and started to think of a future.

Then came summer and the Gypsies.

MORT CASTLE

❧ • ❧

Yet, here they are: With his trainer playing a recorder and a child banging a tambourine, the muzzled bear dances with clumsy exuberance in front of Schloss's Apothecary.

A Lovari horse trader extols the spirit of the dappled pony and gilded cart he would—reluctantly—sell to the interested Burgher ... Near the *rathskeller*, jugglers with flaming torches gather a crowd. And in the crowd, Choro Baro, of the magic hands and guileless face, picks a pocket, snatches a watch, expertly takes a silver chain from the neck of an unaware *fraulein*. "Read your palm, *mein Herr*?" entreats Madame Khaveri as she leans out the window of a *vurdon* decorated with pictures of saints and snakes, a transfigured Christ and the sun and the moon.

Everywhere, everywhere throughout Gunzburg, *Te phirav paoga*, the begging children, sad eyes imploring, palms thrust out: kind lady, please kind sir, help a poor Gypsy and may God grant you *satimasa*, good health and a blessed life ...

And everywhere, the music, the music, the music. The top-hatted accordion player's fingers dance unerringly on the buttons ... The gaunt man with Oriental features playing *tambal* ... Mandolinists dueling yet complementing each other ... Two balalaikas with a pinched klezmer-sounding clarinet between them ...

And everywhere, everywhere, everywhere, the violinists ... Their music fiery or sad or sometimes fiery and sad, their music hypnotic, luring Hans Kessler, filling him with visions he feared and embraced.

The music of the Romany fiddle called to him ...

Lured him to the Gypsy campground night after night after night.

And when the *kumpania* left the vicinity of Gunzburg, Hans Kessler left with them. He took no belongings. He asked no permissions.

He was gone three weeks. Though the proper officials were properly notified of Hans's absence, times and Germany were such then that a young boy could disappear.

And then, tired, crestfallen, and lighter in weight than he had been, he reappeared.

"I was with the Gypsies," he told his father.

"The vermin kidnapped you," *Herr* Kessler said. "They did heinous things to you."

No, Hans said, he chose to go with the Rom.

The Gypsies treated him well, if always as a foreigner, a stranger. And

199

in myriad ways, always politely, always with tact, patience, and subtlety, the Gypsies taught him that he could never play violin with the total heart and passion and devotion that was the *Romali* birthright.

This he did not tell his father. Why burden him with issues he could not understand?

Though Frau Kessler raised a timid protest, *Herr* Kessler beat Hans with a razor strop. Hans did not weep. He wished it hurt more.

Later that night of homecoming, he did cry. That was when his mother told him Heidi Himmelberg had died three days after Hans disappeared. It was the influenza. One moment, a laughing schoolgirl, the next, bloating and drowning in her own fluids—and the next moment, gone.

Music was dead for him. Heidi was dead.

When he came of age, Hans Kessler joined the SS, became an officer of Division *Totenkopf,* the Death's-Head troopers—

Warum nicht? He was a dead man and he appreciated irony.

—and the dead man went to his command in the camp of the dead …

He came to the murder camp.

—and the Rom.

—and their damned and damnable music, their sinuous songs casting webs of wondrous melody and of life again ensnared him, pulled him back to life, brought on those aching moments when he longed for beauty and love and longed for that which was inexpressible

except as music.

Gypsy music.

V

Auschwitz-Birkenau
August 1943

"I can help you," *Puri dai* Melantha said.

"Can you save me?" *Obersturmführer* Hans Kessler asked.

"I can help you, perhaps, so that you might save yourself."

"Please."

Puri dai Melantha calls on *O Del* and the spirits of her dear dead ones, each *mulo* aiding her as she casts the glamour, works the fascination: the *Obersturmführer* must look into her eyes, deep in her eyes, must seek her soul to find his own. She croons *draba* charm and invocation and Hans Kessler is entranced:

What never was now come to pass—
Bater! Bater! May it be so!

May your eyes now truly see—
Bater! Bater! May it be so!

He sees—
Heidi laughs. A laugh like a summer day.
Might I, *fraulein?*
But of course, *mein Herr.*
He plays the "Allemanda" from Bach's *Partita Number II in D Minor.*
He plays "Dark Eyes" and *"Drab l balo"* and *"Dzaf Me Dromeha."* A sweeping, endless legato weaves its way through "The Autumn Moonlight" and then he reels off a czardas and segues into the older *verbunkos.*
Heidi laughs delightedly. She is so alive, Heidi!
You play like a Gypsy.
Does she not realize, can she not know?
(And was there not a time when I did not know. ..)
Now I do know: *Son Rom!*
I am Gypsy.
A true heart has made me so.
From somewhere far, far off, *Puri dai* Melantha speaks:
Bater! May it be so.

VI

Auschwitz-Birkenau
August 1944

It upset Rudolph Hoss, commandant of Auschwitz-Birkenau. He was not without a sensitive side and his Gypsies, he wrote, "…were my best-loved prisoners, if I may put it that way." But there were orders direct from the office of *Reichsführer* Himmler and if one did not obey orders, then the world would be insane.

A pity, then, that Hoss no longer had the understanding help of *Obersturmführer* Hans Kessler; the SS Officer junior grade had inexplicably vanished—*Er hat von der Erde verschwunden.*

As had Tacho, who was the father of the father of our Tacho.

But so clever was Tacho's getaway that the SS guards never knew he was gone. One might even think Tacho had help from a German officer (junior grade) who had betrayed the trust of the Reich.

Nor did the *Hitlari* realize there was a "new Gypsy" in the camp. To the *Gajo* they all looked alike, these shiftless Gypsies, and one more or less meant less than a *Schweins weit* in the day-to-day workings of Auschwitz.

This new Gypsy played the violin and if he did not know all the Gypsy songs, no one could deny he played with a *Romali* heart and a Gypsy's passion.

On August 6, *Puri dai* Melantha and the "new Gypsy" and about 4,300 other remaining Rom marched to the gas chambers under the armed guard of their German protectors. In a surprisingly short time for so vast a murder, the corpses were ready for the crematorium.

The Rom became ash and air and dust and mist.

And their spirits became *mule*. They are the ghosts fettered to this place of death and endings.

And they are sensed even by those visitors to Auschwitz who pride themselves on their rationality.

VII

Berlin, Germany
March of This Year
"No Boundaries" World Music Concert Series

Tacho plays his violin.

He plays the *lied* of the murder camps. He plays Auschwitz. He plays Treblinka. He plays Sobibor.

Na bister.

Do not forget.

Do not forget.

He plays Ravensbruck. He plays Bergen-Belsen.

Na bister. Do not forget.

Chelmno … Majdanek …

Na bister. Do not forget.

Belzec … Jasenovac … Maly Trostenets …

Na bister. Do not forget.

And we hear and we are in the Gypsy camp and

Na bister 500,000.

We will not cannot will not forget the 500,000 Rom who perished in the *Porraimos*, who were consumed in the Great Devouring.

We promise this.

MORT CASTLE

Bater!
May it be so!

NEW MOON ON THE WATER

I'LL CALL YOU

The call comes at three in the morning. Maybe four. Some time in between.

That's what the bedroom clock tells you. You try to make yourself think, *Some jerk, some drunk, some wrong-number Drunken JERK* as a weighted fear presses down

on you and you have to say something: "Hello ..."

෨ • ෨

We wait in lines, all of us. The Dead.

There is something about this place that makes you think *airport terminal*. Part of it must be the lighting, cold and insistent, what fluorescent lights strive to be. And there are frequent announcements in a metallic pseudo-friendly voice: "Please maintain the lines. Do not worry: Everyone will have a chance to call. Your patience is appreciated."

Yet you do not think "airport terminal" when you take note (take note again and again and again) of the small clouds of fog swirling around your ankles, fog which is neither cool and damp nor humid: there is no floor, not tile or carpet or underlayment, *just no floor* beneath you. Of course, there are no clocks, nothing to indicate current time or to delineate time's passage: there is no time.

We have moved beyond the confines of Time. We have entered *The Twilight Zone* (cue the classic leitmotif). This is ... The Afterlife! Or at least *An* Afterlife.

Can you recall a theology or cosmology that had this scenario outlined?

And on this reincarnation, you will be a Brahmin but you will not wear a Rolex, nor will anyone else ...

...for I bring the Good News: In My Father's House are many lines and there you will stand until it is your turn to take up the telephone and call.

205

NEW MOON ON THE WATER

Again, we are instructed to "maintain the lines." Again, informed how very much our "patience is appreciated." A little philosophical wool-gathering:

What is patience: what does such an abstraction mean here? There is no time here, so there is no time passing here, and right now, whatever *now* means in non-time, you do not have anything else you could, should, or ought to be doing.

After a lifetime, *lifetimes*, spent queuing up, do the British find these lines the natural state of affairs? If so, then pity the poor Spanish ... of the lengthy *siesta* and the lackadaisical *por mañana*, pity this beautifully free people to whom straight lines and their illusion of imposed order/time and place are laughable.

But there are no Spanish here, nor British. Nor Italians. Nor French. Nor Irish. Nor Malaysians nor Japanese (not an airport: No Japanese!) nor Incas nor Hottentots nor Swedes.

There are only The Dead.

We are just as spectral as you might imagine—we could be all those ghosts you've ever dreamed or seen in films—and we are silent, because, well, because there is nothing for us to talk about—at least not with our Comrades in Death, not amongst ourselves, anyway.

But we do want to talk. Yes. We have to.

Perhaps not all of the dead need to talk. Perhaps other dead have gone on to a different place, a better place, perhaps, hallelujah and open the hymnals to whatever page you choose.

But we dead, we must talk and that is why we are here.

That is why we (Please) maintain the lines. That is why we are assured when reassured, Everyone will have a chance to call. That is why we are patient.

We are never stationary. Our spectral feet move on a spectral plane and the lines progress.

The lines move.

Everyone here will be able to call.

೮೨ • ೮೨

Telephone to your ear. Deep breath, held for a moment. "Hello?" Deep dread, held within. "Hello?" *Please, oh, please, please ...*

You would like to say, "Is this a joke? Is this something you think real funny?"

Of course you don't say that because you know this is not a joke and you can't pretend you think it is a joke and you know this is nothing that your caller thinks funny.

206

ଏର • ଏର

Lines progress.

Closer.

Of course, just because we get to make the call does not mean the call gets through, does not mean we will necessarily speak or be heard by someone.

Someone alive.

And just why is that?

We do not know. *That is how it is sometimes.*

You know: Like when your cable goes out.

But it's different, too. The cable goes out, we know there is cause and there is effect: a fiber-optic-eating squirrel or a satellite gone hinky or a Chevrolet plows into a utility pole and triggers a power failure.

In that other place, the world of the living, we have science and we have faith to explain what science cannot.

Here, no science. Perhaps no faith.

Knowledge, yes, we in the lines have that. We know if a call does not get through, there will be no explanation, but there will be another chance. Always another chance.

The unsuccessful caller moves to the end of the line.

Thus, begin again.

ଏର • ଏର

You hear that silence at the other end.

You hear that silence this time. You can hear your heart.

You can hear a rushing sound in your ears.

Oh. Oh, my.

You want to hang up hang the hell up—hang it up.

And you can't.

Because you know.

ଏର • ଏର

And so, everyone, each one, moves closer to the telephone. Each one of us moves closer to reach out in your night to call you. Each of us. Spectral feet move in silence through shifting billows of something like fog.

"Please maintain the lines. Do not worry: Everyone will have a chance to call. Your patience is appreciated."

We are the Dead and the Dead are patient. We have no time.

We have purpose.

NEW MOON ON THE WATER

꿍 • 꿍

Please. If you are there, talk to me. If you are here, talk to me.

What is this, you fool, you self-flagellating idiot! As oppressive and horrible as is the silence, why must you seek worse?

Do you understand—do you ever understand—why when your corkscrew-pain-to-the-brain midnight toothache at last quits pound *pound POUNDING*, you have to stir it with the tip of your tongue, poke away at the motherfucker, bring it back, no, not just bring it back but bring it back worse.

Talk to me. Talk to me.

Goddamnit.

Talk to me.

꿍 • 꿍

Then we talk.

Some of us get through on the telephone.

We call out, in the night, and are heard.

You abandoned me, you promised to love and cherish and promised forever and then I got sick and you abandoned me

… think I didn't know, think I didn't know what you were you doing with those men, your secret men, secret men and their secret diseases,
disease
you shared …

… never a daddy, never a father,
full-time absence, full-time betrayal …

Shame! The shame of it. The shame you brought me

there were crazy people there, they hurt me, you left me there with crazy people

a cigarette lighter and burned me and burned me and burned
made me confess though i had done nothing, with water and pipes you
made me confess though i was an innocent though i am an innocent

don't know why don't care why but know what you did and hate you
and hate you

208

MORT CASTLE

*I CAN TALK I CAN TALK NOW YOU BASTARD I CAN TALK
AND TELL YOU YOU BASTARD I CAN TALK*

I CAN TALK AND I CAN TELL YOU

We talk, the dead talk, and what we say, no matter what we say is always this:
We do not forgive.

ℰ ● ℰ

The call comes at three in the morning. Maybe four. Some time in between.

That's what the bedroom clock tells you. You try to make yourself think, *Some jerk, some drunk, some wrong-number Drunken Jerk* as a weighted fear presses down on you and you have to say something:

"Hello …"

ℰ ● ℰ

I'll call you.

NEW MOON ON THE WATER

THE DOCTOR, THE KID,
AND THE GHOSTS IN THE LAKE

I. INDIAN CAMP PART ONE

Many Years Ago
In the Ojibway Camp
at Ghost Lake, Michigan

Hey-aye-hey!
 Hey, Doc. Hey, kid.
 Kid get big. Ha! Kid play moccasin game plenty much?
 Ah, Doc bring Great Spirit! Cyrus Noble whiskey. Strong medicine!
Doc friend of Indian. No bullshit.
 Kid? Oh. You bet ghosts in lake. Why you think call it Ghost Lake?
No bullshit. Go where moon float on water. Look down. See plenty ghosts,
damn right.
 How get there?
 Hey-aye-yah! Red man tell story. True stuff. No bullshit. More Cyrus
Noble. Strong medicine, damn right. Indian got plenty stories for white
man.
 Long ago two braves fight for pretty woman. Name Winona. Braves
fight on shore. Winona in canoe in lake. Braves fight with knives.
 Blood flyin'. Winona clap hands. Say, "Ooh. Ah!" Have one damn fine
time, no bullshit.
 Braves cut each other all to hell. Plenty blood.
 "Ooh!" say Winona.
 Then big surprise!
 Neebanaw grab her! Neebanaw King Spirit of Lake.
 Neebanaw drag her down.
 Ghost? Hey, damn right Winona ghost.
 Winona *lonely* ghost.

NEW MOON ON THE WATER

Winona want sister ghosts.

Bitch ghosts just like her.

Tribe have bitch woman, man have bitch wife, bitch daughter. *Hey-aye-hey,* you just take bitch in canoe and send her to Neebanaw and Winona!

Plenty ghosts in lake. Damn right.

Hey-aye-yah!

—Gilby Edwards

II. NOBODY EVER DIES

1961
Mayo Clinic
Rochester, Minnesota

For many years, people had often called him "Papa" or "Mr. Papa" or "Señor Papa," and he often called himself in this way, although not all his children called him so, but now it was 1961 and he was 61 and in 1961 you were an old man, a "Papa"—*verdad!*—if you were 61 years old. He said, "The address, I can remember it. We lived there in 1923 and 1924. The first wife and I. In Paris. It was good then. Good wife for me then." He lowered his head. "Long time ago good."

He looked sad and confused, but more confused than sad. He also looked a little foolish because on his steel-rimmed eyeglasses was a clumsily wrapped and dirty wad of white adhesive tape on the nosepiece that he'd put there so the glasses did not cut into his flesh. He wore a much-washed flannel shirt, loose corduroy trousers, two pairs of white socks because his feet often were cold, even though he sweated a great deal, and leather bedroom slippers he had bought 11 years ago at Abercrombie and Fitch. Over this, he had on a red Italian robe he called "The Pasha's Imperial dressing gown" for reasons he could not recall and this also made him seem old.

"Now no good," he said.

"No good?" the psychiatrist said. He was quite a modern psychiatrist, so sometimes he was non-directive. "Your present life ..."

The old man ignored the non-directiveness. He was quite a famous writer who had written many famous novels and stories. One of them was about an old man and a great fish and some critics said it was a religious story. It was a parable. Jesus wasn't the only one who could make parables. That story, the parable, appeared in a magazine that sold many millions of copies. Motion pictures had been made of that story and others of his stories. Usually, the movies were not very good, but they brought in very good money, so he could sail his boat, a diesel-powered 38-footer christened *El Señor Santiago*, so he could go where he pleased in the world, and shoot big game in Africa, and pay considerable alimony, and the movies, even though no good, helped make him famous even to people who did not read his books or any books at all for that matter. Some critics of influence had pronounced him the best living American writer and sometimes he boasted publicly, saying much the same thing. Sometimes he thought it funny that he could be the best living American writer, making very good money and being so famous, and still be so profoundly sad.

"No, I cannot remember," the old man said. He shrugged, confused and sad. "It feels strange, you know. My address in 1923 was *54, rue du Corporal Lemoins*. I remember that. I can't remember my present address. I cannot remember my present wife's name. My present wife, I remember she's a nice person. Solid and healthy and a real trooper. She is a good shot. I think she came to see me yesterday."

"It is simple, really; it is the electro-shock," the psychiatrist said.

"Simple," the old man agreed. It was, really. For a brief time, your soul left your body; he understood that. It had happened to him before: he thought it had happened when he was a boy, and he knew it had happened when he was a man in the wars. Your soul goes away for a while and then your soul returns. Most of it, anyway.

The psychiatrist continued, "Your memory will come back after a while once you have completed the treatments."

"Memories do that," the old man said. "They come back. Just like ghosts."

"I wouldn't worry about it if I were you," the psychiatrist said.

"Well, then," the old man said. "Well, good. Nothing to worry about. No, no. Certainly I won't worry about it." He looked embarrassed. "I don't remember your name, either. You are my present psychiatrist?"

The psychiatrist smiled. He did not smile well because his lips were thin and his eyes were as cold as a trout's. But he did look intelligent.

"Dr. Koeller."

"Dr. Koeller," the old man nodded. "And are you a Catholic? I do remember that, that I asked that my present psychiatrist be a Catholic."

"Yes. I am a Catholic and a psychiatrist."

"Better if you were Italian," the old man said, dubiously. "Or a Spaniard."

"An Italian or Spanish Catholic is preferable?" Dr. Koeller said, non-directively.

"Yes, yes," the old man said. "They are deeply and truly Catholic. You can see their faith."

"I believe in the Holy Ghost, the Holy Catholic Church, the communion of saints, the forgiveness of sins, the resurrection of the body, and life everlasting," Dr. Koeller said.

The old man said, "Nobody ever dies."

"Here." Dr. Koeller leaned forward. "See my faith." He crossed himself very nicely. It was natural and not perfunctory. It made the old man feel better. Dr. Koeller said, "I believe in the Father, in the Son, and in the Holy Ghost."

"Father," the old man nodded. "Son." He nodded.

Then he said, "Ghost."

Señor Papa licked his lips. The medicine for his depression made his mouth and lips quite dry. He wanted a rum punch or a daiquiri. "Ghosts," he said. "I believe in ghosts."

"Tell me," Dr. Koeller said. "Tell me about that."

"Tell me a story, Papa," the old man said. He was teasing the Catholic psychiatrist, but for a moment his expression showed he, like all sentimental and tough men, could be cruel and a liar. "That is what the world demands of me."

"Is it?"

"Yes. No complaints. Demand it of myself. Long time ago, Papa newspaperman. Heap good un. Papa write-um truth. Now Papa make-um fiction. Make-um fables, fantasies. Make-um myths and allegories. Make-um parables." He paused, then tried to look cagey. "Catholic doctor, do you know the difference between writing the truth and writing fiction?"

"No, I don't," Dr. Koeller said.

"Shit. Me, either!" The old man laughed. "When it is true, it is *true!*"—the old man snapped his fingers—"It is a truth that is truer than true." He tipped his head. He would have looked cunning or even dangerous had there not been dirty adhesive tape on his nose. "How is that, then, Dr. Koeller? Lies reveal truth! Is that a paradox for you?"

"No."

"Don't you have to deal with paradoxes? My Catholic psychiatrist, can you reconcile Freud and Jesus?"

"I have no need to. There is no argument between them. They get along just fine. Both confront and proclaim the same thing."

"And that is?"

"Truth."

The old man laughed, a very natural hearty laugh. It sounded healthy, like the laugh of a drunken young man. "Good! That is very good! I think I would like to sit and drink with you. I think I might even like to fight with you. I think after drinking and fighting we might be friends. We could tell each other ..."

Dr. Koeller quickly said, "The truth. Would you like to tell me that, Señor Papa?"

"Yes," the old man said. "I will tell you a story."

III. FATHERS AND SONS

1935
On the Way to Michigan

You feel it on the back of your neck. In the way your scalp tightens. And just like that, you know: you are being watched.

Adam Nichols felt that. He had felt it for some time. Behind them, there are eyes.

The eyes had been watching for a while.

The eyes were The Doctor's eyes.

Toby said, "How is it, Papa?" Toby did not know about the eyes behind them.

"What's that?"

Toby had asked him something he'd missed. "An elephant. Is it like killing a man?"

"No," Adam Nichols said. "You do not need much of a gun to kill a man. Sometimes a man will die from a little wound that would not kill a rabbit. To kill an elephant, you need a big gun. Best I've had was the re-chambered Springfield '03. It had a kick as big as an elephant. It did the job."

The first shot drops the elephant after he has run only a minute or so. They find him easily. He is on his side. There is blood on his flank. The elephant could rise up and attack, but Adam doesn't care because this is his first elephant, this is a giant's death, and he has to be close to it if he is ever to understand. He looks into the elephant's eye with its impossibly long lashes and it seems that the eye is the most alive thing he has ever seen and that he himself is now entering a realm of loneliness that he must walk the rest of his life.

Then he shoots the elephant right in the ear-hole and when the bullet does what bullets do and the message comes to the elephant that it no longer lives, that it will no longer feel the earth shake beneath its great feet, that it will no longer raise its trunk to sample the breeze and its myriad scents, when the elephant gives up the ghost and all its great elephant spirit is fled to the Great Nothing, gone to that which is Naught, it lies a wrinkled heap without dignity: a hugeness of Death. There is nothing terrifying to it any longer.

"I think I would like to go to Africa."

"I think you would like it."

"Papa, would I be afraid?"

"No, I don't think so."

"I would hate to be afraid."

"I will be with you and teach you not to be afraid."

"You will take me to Africa?"

"Yes."

"All right. I will like that. Did your father take you to Africa?"

"No."

"Will you take my mother?"

"I think I would like to. But I don't think she would want to go with me. Not now. Maybe once, but not now."

"But I would be going!"

"Yes."

Adam slowed for a curve. He was cautious on curves with this car. The LaSalle had plenty of power but felt wrong on turns, the wheel off and stiff in his hands. Back in Arkansas, garaged in town, was a 1929 Ford roadster with a familiar dented fender, and the smell of his hands on the steering wheel, a car that suited him quite well, but Adam Nichols was a successful writer and it just would *not* do, said present wife, for him to drive such a proletarian motor car, certainly would not, agreed Mother Adeline (that bitch), and so, because he sought to please present wife and that bitch, he was driving a powerful, in-line-eight LaSalle sedan ($1700 goddamn it! $1700!) that smelled too new to be real and was about as long as a tennis court and about as responsive.

He looked over. Toby's head was turned away from him. On the trip, Toby had sometimes talked about his mother and then abruptly stopped talking as though talking about his mother confused him. Toby was Adam Nichols's first son. Adam thought he was a good boy, quite likely. He did not know him that well. Toby had come into the world via Adam Nichols's first wife in Paris. When Toby had been an infant, in a long-ago false spring in Paris, their gray-and-white six-toed cat, Mr. Pickle, had slept protectively in the boy's crib. Then Adam Nichols and first wife got a divorce and wife got Toby and Mr. Pickle and alimony. Mr. Pickle had been a very nice cat.

Now Adam Nichols was taking Toby, his son, so he could teach him things fathers teach sons. How to catch grasshoppers for bait when they are still wet with dew and cannot jump away. How to sense the right moment to shoot when you hunt quail. How to cook trout in bacon grease over a fire. How to make a bed of hemlock branches and a blanket. How to fish from the shore so your shadow did not warn the fish away. These were the things fathers taught sons and for which sons were grateful all their lives, as Adam Nichols was, having learned these things from his father, The Doctor.

There were other things for which he was not grateful. Some of those things that The Doctor had taught him made him pity his father and some made him despise him. One of the things The Doctor had taught him was a saying: "A man can be destroyed but not defeated." The Doctor also used to say, "A man can be defeated but not destroyed." The Doctor had yet another saying, "A man can be destroyed and defeated so fuck it and let's have a drink."

Adam Nichols thought about The Doctor. He thought about that which was good about him and that which was sad. He made himself not think about other things.

Adam Nichols smiled. He wondered if he smiled for the benefit of the eyes in the back seat. He knew he was not smiling a "rueful" smile. No one ever truly smiled ruefully or any such a damned thing. The *rueful smile* and the *happy thought* and such like were the clichés of bad writers who wrote for the pulps and would never understand that a smile was a smile was a smile and a thought was a thought was a thought, and that was that.

Adam Nichols checked the rear view mirror. Now it was no longer just the eyes he could see. Earlier, there had been only the eyes. Now he had another passenger: The Doctor.

His father rode in back. His father wasn't doing anything or saying anything. He was not asleep. The Doctor, his father, Chadbourne Nichols, MD, was dead, had been so for a pretty long time, and so, it could more properly be said that the ghost of Dr. Nichols occupied the La Salle's back seat.

—Your father's ghost was with you?

—True gen.

—That did not scare you?

—Nah, after all, he was dead. Dead can't do much, I guess. Killed himself, The Doctor, you see.

Besides, my good Catholic psychiatrist, we've all got ghosts with us, don't we?

And you know, I just did not scare all that much. Not then.

Before Adam Nichols went to war, back then, maybe he used to scare, but then he had been blown up and felt his soul leave his body and return to it, and then, some time after that, he had carried a dead man on his shoulders, talking to him and quite clearly hearing him answer and making good sense of it, while his boots filled with a heavy slush of mud and his own blood. You don't scare much after your soul has exited and returned, round trip, *lalala*, and after you've chewed the fat and talked all flap-a-dap with a dead man. Sometimes your mind, well, it goes *lalala, tickity-tick*, like an out-of-control flywheel in a clock, but you don't scare …

And how could it surprise Adam Nichols that The Doctor's ghost was with them? The cabin up in Michigan had been his father's favorite spot on Earth. It was just so pretty; it was just so goddamn pretty is what it was.

And it was ghost country.

"Papa?"

Toby was back. Maybe he'd talk about his mother and maybe he wouldn't.

"Hmm?" If you are a father, you say *Hmm* quite often. You learn to cock an eyebrow. It's better if you smoke a pipe. He did not smoke a pipe. He smoked cigars, sometimes, when he was in Cuba, where a man who did not smoke cigars was socially offensive and probably *maricón*.

"What is it, Toby?"

"Will we see any Indians there, up in Michigan?"

"I don't know," he said. "Maybe. Probably not, though. I think most of them, the Indians … The Indians moved away."

Gone, how could they be gone?

The Indians were real now. They were made real in his mind by the boy asking and by his memory which he could no more control than he could the rising of the sun. Gilby Edwards. Prudy. He could smell the sweet and biting smoky smell and the tired, too often washed flannel, and the whiskey. That is what his Indians and his father's Indians smelled like. And smelling the Indians, they became more real than present wife and this son he did not know. He remembered the totally silent, pigeon-toed way the Indians walked. He remembered how they laughed. Indians do not laugh much, ordinarily. Not in the way a white man would call laughing. But once you heard an Indian laugh, you never forget how it was.

"Aren't there any Indians left, Dad?"

Adam Nichols glanced into the mirror that showed what was behind them. The Doctor—his father's ghost—was smiling with his eyes. His father liked Indians. He understood a little of their sorrow. Perhaps he understood it better than his own.

Indians had taught them both quite a lot, father and son.

"Maybe some. Maybe ghost Indians."

Toby laughed.

Toby liked the little tick of fear it gave him to think about ghost Indians.

IV. INDIAN CAMP PART TWO

Many Years Ago
In the Ojibway Camp
at Ghost Lake, Michigan

Hey-aye-hey!

What are the ghosts like?

Nah, kid. Nah. That white man's question! They like nothin'. Ghosts in lake just ghosts. *Jiibay.* Spirit. Red man, white man, we all got spirit inside. Ghost, that your spirit. You know, *Jiibay.*

Soul? White preacher talk. Soul go to heaven. Wave bye-bye. Ha! Jesus dance cakewalk. Heap plenty bullshit.

Ghost like ... When you kid, spirit, ah, spirit go free in the night. Fly anywhere. See everything. *Hey-aye-yah!*

Long before White Man, First Ojibway boy travel in spirit through the Four Colors over the Earth. Fly to Moon. Look down. See everything. Everything good and everything bad. See everyone. Everyone good and everyone bad.

See Seven Grandfathers of the All the Nations in Sacred Sweat Lodge. See Comet, *ishkode*, burn across sky. See raven, *rgaagaagi*, pick out eyes of dead Rabbit. See black serpent Kena'beek twist in talon of Keneu' the great war-eagle. See men, *inini*, steal horses, steal clothes, steal wives. See fish, *giigoonh*, leap from lake and see bullfrog, *dende*, take piss in pond.

First Ojibway boy see everything.

Kid know. You know, right? *Hey-aye-hey!*

Damn right kid know. You born, you know.

Then you grow up. Still got *jiibay* spirit but feet heavy. Feet stuck on Earth. Spirit trapped deep in body. Spirit trapped on Earth. No can fly.

Worse for ghost. *Jiibay* got no body but ghost cannot go to Chief

NEW MOON ON THE WATER

Chibiabos in the Land of Spirits. *Jiibay* go nowhere. Must stay here.

Red man, white man, ghost, everyone remember flying free in night. Everyone remember and everyone sad.

Cyrus Noble Whiskey good medicine for sad man. *Jiibay?* Ha, nothin' for ghosts. No medicine. Ghosts heap plenty fucked up.

—Gilby Edwards

V. THE DOCTOR AND THE DOCTOR'S WIFE

Many Years Ago
Ghost Lake, Michigan

In the early afternoon, Adam Nichols knew there would be trouble. He and his father sat on the front steps of the cottage. The Doctor had a bottle of Cyrus Noble whiskey and from time to time sipped from the tin cup he used when they went camping. There was no breeze so you could not smell the lake. The sun was bright.

Just within, in the front parlor she called the "Salon," Mother Adeline was playing the Chopin *Études*. The *Études* were difficult. Mother Adeline played beautifully. Mother Adeline's touch was very delicate and very sure. She had to be exceptionally angry.

The Doctor said loudly, "What I wish is I had a harmonica. A good, ten-cent Hohner Marine Band mouth harp. I would play 'The Camptown Races.' *Do-dah, do-dah, 12 miles long. Do-dah-do-dah-DAY!* I would play it loud and at least 100 times. That is what I would do."

The Doctor was sweating and his face was red.

Then he said, somewhat louder, "I would play 'You're the Flower of My Heart, Sweet Adeline.'" He cut "Adeline" into three syllables, jagged and precise. His wife thought harmonicas common. She thought songs like "Sweet Adeline" lower than common. She thought such songs vulgar, contemptible, and somehow immoral, as were those people given to listening to or singing or playing such songs.

The Doctor and Mother Adeline had had words this morning in their bedroom. They often had words, though seldom in their bedroom, where they seldom found reason to speak to one another. Adam had heard them this morning, even with the door closed. Some of his mother's words he had overheard were "… filthy, a beast and disgusting. You are a heathen."

Mother Adeline sometimes called her husband a "heathen."

Several years ago, Mother Adeline had become a Christian Scientist. The Doctor was convinced she did it to spite him and medical science.

To spite her, he frequently said one had to have the highest regard and intellectual respect for a religion founded by a morphine addict.

The *Études* continued through the open window. The tempo did not change. If anything, perhaps the melody grew quieter.

Sunshine came out and leaned against a support column of the porch. She walked like she didn't wish to set the porch boards squeaking. A straw hat shadowed her round face. She was almost ten years old, a darling little girl, and her real name was Marcella Veronica, her mother's choice, which Sunshine thought an "astoundingly putrid name."

Sunshine was her pet name, what The Doctor called her. Mother Adeline thought it suited only for a nappy-headed pickaninny. Adam thought her a frequent pest but in a quiet way he loved her more than many boys love their little sisters and he admired her vocabulary for the countless words she knew that he did not know even though he had declared he would be a writer and had already published two stories in his high-school literary magazine.

The Doctor said, "Well, well." Like many stern men, he had a core of sentimentality to his nature which became more sentimental when he drank. "Sunshine." He said her name and you could tell he liked to say it. "*Hey-aye-hey,* Sunshine." He liked to "talk Indian"; Mother Adeline did not approve of The Doctor having Indian friends. She did not approve of Indians. Approval was not her strong suit.

Sunshine said nothing. Adam looked out at the bright glare of sunlight on the lake. He made it a challenge, to look hard at it without squinting. He wanted to see what was really there. He thought if he looked hard enough and long enough he would see just exactly what was and only that, nothing distorted, nothing made bigger or smaller by your thoughts or your vision than it truly was.

Adam Nichols was fifteen years old. It was an age when you feel like you might never understand anything. Sometimes he tried to tell himself he just did not give a damn. Years later, when he did give a damn and had a Catholic wife who gave a damn, he became Catholic.

The Doctor said. "Alas, I have no Hohner Marine Band harmonica. I don't have a washboard or a sweet potato. Or a damn tin whistle or a goddamn jew's-harp." With the thumb and forefinger of his left hand, he circled the neck of the whiskey bottle. "Fortunately," he said, raising his voice as he raised the bottle, "I do have Cyrus Noble." Cyrus Noble Premium Aged Whiskey was the name on the label. He poured his tin cup about half full.

He sipped. "Ah, now isn't that nice," he said. He sighed. "That is nice.

What a nice life! My oh my! Sitting here at my leisure and drinking this aged whiskey and listening to my own sweet Adeline's pretty piano playing, oh, my yes! Goddamn!"

Once, Adam had asked his father why he drank whiskey. His father said it was because whiskey was kind. He said Adam would understand soon enough and Adam thought he didn't understand now, though, and maybe he didn't want to, not ever.

The piano playing ended in the "Salon." The Doctor set his tin cup down hard. The brown whiskey sloshed over the rim. The Doctor applauded. "Bravo! Bravo!"

"Oh, Papa, "Sunshine whispered, "don't. Please don't." In some ways, Sunshine was quite a smart little girl.

"Music hath charms! Damn right," The Doctor said, rising. "Come on, Adam. Let's row on over to Indian camp. We'll go see Gilby Edwards, find out how the fishing's going."

The Doctor started to go inside. He had to get his knapsack, he said. Sunshine clutched at his arm, "Papa, please ..."

"*Hey-aye-hey*, Big Chief Doc, maybe him get-um peace pipe smoked," The Doctor said, loudly.

Mother Adeline's voice came out to them. "Do not think I am unaware of your heinous intent!" The music started then, not the *Études*, but Bach, as delicate as the edge of a newly stropped straight razor.

At the door, The Doctor winked at Adam. "Come on, then," he said. "Let us off to pursue heinous intent."

From inside, Mother Adeline said, "A heathen on his way to the heathen Indians." Her piano playing was exquisitely beautiful.

"Papa?" said Sunshine.

"I'm sorry," The Doctor said. He wagged a finger, telling Adam to "Pick up Mr. Cyrus Noble there, if you please."

"God sees all," Mother Adeline said, her voice quiet, the piano quiet.

"Good," Dr. Nichols said. "I hope he's got a Kodak."

☙ • ❧

Adam rowed and his rowing was strong and certain and The Doctor drank just enough to keep a little smile on his face.

"This is all right," Dr. Nichols said. "Do you think so, Adam?" "Yes," Adam said.

The Doctor took a gun out of the knapsack.

"That's Grandpa's gun," Adam said.

"Why, yes," said Dr. Nichols, "the very same. The Patriarch. Brave

222

Grandfather, a loyal follower of Father Abraham. He carried this weapon during the War Between the States. This is a .32-caliber Smith & Wesson, manufactured in Springfield, Massachusetts."

The Doctor took head-canted aim toward the middle of the lake. "Here comes one of Gilby Edwards' lake ghosts. Bang!" He jerked the gun up as though he had fired it. "Come on, ghosts." He mimed shooting again. "Come on, bitches!"

Adam tried to laugh because he guessed this was supposed to be funny.

The Doctor said to Adam, "You could not hit the broad side of a barn with this pistol if you were inside the barn. You could not hit a bull in the butt were you to crawl up the bull's butt.

"The only goddamned thing you can shoot with this gun is yourself. Just like Grandfather."

Grandfather had pressed the nose of the .32-caliber Smith & Wesson into his ear and blown out some of his brains. In the family, it was said Grandfather had accidentally died cleaning his gun. The Doctor amended that: He said Grandfather had died accidentally cleaning his gun with his ear.

The Doctor squinted as though he were really aiming. The gun jerked in his hand as though it had really been discharged. "Bang!" The Doctor said. "Got the bitch!"

− • −

"*Hey-aye-hey!*" Gilby Edwards took a drink from the Cyrus Noble bottle. "Son of a bitch," he said, happily. He and Adam sat on the sofa in the yard of Gilby's shanty close to the dock at the Ojibway camp. The sofa's cushions were torn and one end sagged, but it was very comfortable and it was much nicer to sit on something comfortable outdoors instead of indoors so Gilby kept it outside in front and not inside the shanty. The days he worked, Gilby fished and cut logs for a living. He did not work many days. He drank every day. He did not talk all that much but he talked more than most Indians. He wore his hair long and looked like the kind of Indian you would see on a coin.

Gilby took another drink. "White-man firewater, sweet son of a bitch," he said.

The Doctor and Prudy Edwards, Gilby's sister, who was 17 or a little older, were in the shanty. Even though it was a ways off, sometimes you could hear a little of what was going on in the shanty. It sounded like they were having a good time. Sometimes Prudy or The Doctor laughed or they both laughed together and sometimes Prudy made a sound that was like a laugh but wasn't really a laugh.

What Adam had noticed this summer was that Prudy was quite round in an interesting way. He had noticed that this time, and had realized that, in previous years, he had not noticed the roundness of her. In previous years, he had gone hunting with her and Gilby, sometimes with his father and sometimes not, and he had noticed Prudy was a good shot. He had noticed that her teeth looked very white when she bit into apples. He had noticed she could look into a bright sky with her flat brown eyes wide open and that she had a nice smell like woodsmoke and oranges and a little bit of sweat. He had noticed lots of things about Prudy Edwards in previous years, but he not noticed roundness.

Inside the shanty, Prudy laughed. Adam felt strange. Not bad, but strange. "Say," Adam said, "let me have some of that, why don't you?" He reached for the whiskey bottle.

"Okay with the Doc?"

"Sure, I guess so." Adam said, "You think I ought to go ask him?"

"Nah," Gilby Edwards said and handed him the bottle.

His father had let him drink beer a number of times, but Adam had never drunk whiskey. It tasted hot and mean and made it feel like his throat was pinching shut all the way down the center of his chest to his belly.

Then just like that he felt warm and good and bigger. "Son of a bitch," Adam Nichols said, happily. He took another drink. He felt very good. He thought he was about to understand something very big and important.

It was some time after that that The Doctor came out of the shanty.

He was not wearing his shirt. He was hairy across the shoulders.

The Doctor was smiling when he said to Gilby Edwards, "What did you do to him? My boy's got an edge on, Gilby!"

Adam laughed and said, "Son of a bitch."

The Doctor said, "Well," and his smile did not change and Adam did not remember getting to his feet but he was walking toward the shanty with his father alongside him and he was glad that his father was not saying anything and he said nothing and he was aware of the sunlight that filtered down through the gently fluttering leaves overhead and of the shadows and there was a gentle breeze coming off the lake and then he was going into the dark of the shanty.

He could see nothing but he heard his name and it took him a tick of time to realize it was Prudy Edwards saying his name and as that came to him there also came to him an odor that was of his father and of whiskey and of something mysterious and a little frightening.

Then Prudy Edwards called to him again and he went to her.

—And that was your, ah, sexual initiation?

—Damn straight, Dr. Koeller. Damn right, Dr. Koeller. Yer danged tootin' it was, Dr. Koeller.

That was it then. My father brought me to the woman he had been with and then I was with that woman in the way he had been with her and then I was where he had been and that was the way it was then. I think my father loved me very much then. I know I loved my father very much then.

—Well, how was it?

—Aren't you the good Catholic psychiatrist! That's funny. It really is. Are you seeking salient salaciousness of fornication's fine points? Prurient particularities? Did the virgin lad's manly member meet muster? True gen, libidinous Dr. Koeller …

And could you tell him that she was your father's gift and that she did first what no one has ever done better and can you bid memory speak of her good plump brown legs and the good roundness of her tight belly of her fine brown breasts of her round bottom and might you then tell of those well-holding arms and well-holding legs and of that quick searching tongue and the good taste of mouth and then uncomfortably, tightly, sweetly, wetly, lovely, tightly, achingly, fully, tightly, tightly, finally, unendingly, never-endingly, never-to-endingly, suddenly ended, and it was like your ending it was like your spirit flying free in twilight and then the moment that comes with your sigh when he knew that nothing not ever again would be so good.

He was right.

VI. THE MOTHER OF A QUEEN

For a day, Mother Adeline was silent. The next day, she did not speak much, but she did play piano: *Swan Lake*, which she had often said she loathed for its obviousness and melodrama and other "Slavic qualities." The third day, Mother Adeline was smiling and humming and she fed the birds and sat on the dock with her floppy straw hat shading her face and bare feet in the water and in the early afternoon picked berries and then made a pie and you would think her ever the contented housewife and sometimes she stopped at the piano to play something so delicate and melodic that it required only two fingers of the right hand and two of the left. Oh, my, Mother Adeline seemed ever so cheery, lah-de-dah. Why, boys will be boys, lah-de-dah. Like father, like son, lah-de-dah. They just go off to Indian Camp to do heinous things with savages.

There would be Hell to pay, Adam knew that; he was old enough to realize there always comes a reckoning. What he ought to do maybe was light out. Pack a tent, snitch bacon and flour, and take to the woods in the night, and, in the true first light of morning, keep on traveling. Light out for territories. Didn't he ramble? Canada. The Arctic Circle. Borneo. Africa.

And why in hell hadn't the Doctor lit out? How is it we get trapped?

—Even then, the old man says to the psychiatrist, even then I had the sense we're all bitched.

—Hmm, is the response, non-directive.

—Bitched and that's how it is. You just got to take it and not complain. Man's got to do what a man's got to do, says the old man.

—John Wayne. *High Noon.* Gary Cooper, Dr. Koeller said. You could show you knew and liked movies and still be non-directive.

—Coop's all right. He's my friend, Cooper. Damned good bird shooter. Good as me. Damned good Catholic. Better than me.

I am going to miss Coop. The Big C. Maybe Coop has got a month.

Maybe. Then he's heading for the barn. Should call him but you can't talk to Coop on a goddamn phone. You need to be by a trout stream, drinking a little whiskey and branch water ...

Goddamn, Cooper.

The old man feels his eyes tear up. Too many absent friends. Too many losses. Too many gone missing. The missing won't kill you, though. It's the despair. Too many gone oh our father who art in *pues y nada y pues y nada* hallowed be thy *pues y nada y pues y nada ...*

The old man knows he's talking talk that doesn't mean much but he's also thinking and thinking something that feels as though he might be thinking it for a first time: Maybe The Doctor was trapped because of Sunshine. Could not leave dear little Sunshine girl to Mother Adeline. Mother Adeline ate her young.

Or perhaps it is that The Doctor was no less trapped because of me ...

And now, it is after Mother Adeline's good dinner, and they are all of them in the parlor, the light soft and dusty with sunset more than two hours off. And Adam beneath the window, curve of back against the wall, with *Gallagher and Other Stories,* the adventures of a boy detective, a book he first read when he was much younger but still returns to frequently because Richard Harding Davis is such a crackerjack writer. And Mother Adeline reading Mrs. Mary Baker Eddy's *Science and Health with Key to the Scriptures,* and The Doctor and his *Sporting News,* clucking his tongue over "Frank Gotch retiring but damn, maybe it is time," and Sunshine on the floor with paper and colored pencils, drawing a horse, her tongue just at

226

the corner of her mouth, concentrating, lost in swirls and lines.

Sunshine is happy.

Mother Adeline cannot abide happiness.

"Marcella Veronica," Mother Adeline says, "I think I would like to hear you play Schumann, the 'Scenes from Childhood.' You play it well, dear. Yes, that would be quite pleasant."

"Oh," says Sunshine, losing her concentration. "Not now."

Oh, Jesus, Adam thinks, and The Doctor's *Sporting News* makes a fold-crinkling sound. It feels as if all the air has been sucked out of the room.

Mother Adeline says, "Excuse me? Pardon me? Excuse me?"

"We ..." Sunshine says, but look at her and you can see she knows she has somehow chosen the precisely wrong word: *We?* Why did she say 'we'?"

Mother Adeline hits it like a hawk on a rabbit. "We? Her majesty does not deign to grant a boon to her poor subjects?"

"I don't think ..." The Doctor starts to say something but only says that.

"*We* do not wish to play." Mother Adeline laughs in a way that could turn milk. "I am the mother of a queen. Should I have said, 'I humbly beseech you to play, your Royal Majesty?' Should I bend the knee and grovel so that you might condescend to play for us, Miss Marcella Veronica? Would you have your mother beg?"

"Mother Adeline," Sunshine says.

Looking at his sister, Adam thinks, *Sunshine's scared.*

"For Chrissake," The Doctor says.

"For Christ's sake indeed," Mother Adeline says. She quotes a lethal favorite by Mary Baker Eddy: "The entire education of children should be such as to form habits of obedience to the moral and spiritual law."

Sunshine gets to her feet. She looks miserable and confused. She looks like a cat in the rain. "I'm sorry. I just was drawing ... I didn't want to play. I just didn't want to ..."

Do not cry, Adam Nichols thinks. *Don't let her get you to crying that easy. You're probably going to cry, but make the bitch earn it.*

"Is that all, your Majesty?" says Mother Adeline. "Is that stammered foolishness your apology?"

The Doctor says, "The child did ..."

Mother Adeline gives him a look that is a warning and says worse than that because it says almost everything.

The Doctor says nothing.

Mother Adeline cites Mary Baker Eddy: "'A mother is the strongest educator.' I am about to educate Her Royal Highness."

Mother Adeline rises. "Come with me," she says. She takes Sunshine by the hand. She leads her down the hall. Sunshine walks without bending her knees.

—She beat her? The psychiatrist does not sound non-directive. He sounds judgmental.

—The world was more Calvin than Freud back then. Your parents hit you. It was what parents did.

—The Doctor had a razor strop. Mother Adeline's instructional instrument was the hairbrush.

Mother Adeline and Sunshine are back soon. "So, then," Mother Adeline says, "now, perhaps, Marcella Veronica will consent to play the Schumann."

Sunshine stands in the center of the parlor and looks like she has eaten something that had a too-strong smell and too-sharp taste. Her face is very white and her eyes are hard and shining.

What a good kid, Adam Nichols thinks. *What a real good kid she is.*

Because Sunshine says, "I would prefer not to."

"Marcella Veronica," Mother Adeline says, "think about what it is that you are saying."

"No," Sunshine says, "I would prefer not to."

I'll bet she could spit right now if she had to. Sunshine is just swell is what she is, Adam thinks.

"Very well," Mother Adeline says.

Adam Nichols looks to The Doctor. The Doctor's eyes are lowered. He doesn't say anything.

"Mary Baker Eddy teaches 'Children should obey their parents; insubordination is an evil.'"

The Doctor doesn't say anything.

"Come with me," Mother Adeline says.

This time, Sunshine and Mother Adeline are gone for quite a while and there is a good deal of noise: the sounds of hitting and the sounds a child makes when she's being hit.

The Doctor turns the pages of the *Sporting News*. Aloud, he reads, "Despite the shady nature of the mat game as it is practiced today, no one who loves the ancient sport dare cast any aspersions upon the quintessentially American athlete Frank Gotch. When he tossed his robe to his trainer-manager Jim Asbel, Gotch said, 'Keep this to remember me by,' though doubtless the faithful Asbel, who had seen Gotch in battles glorious against George Hackenschmidt, The Russian Lion…"

"Don't you think …" Adam Nichols says, just as a door squeaks open down the hall.

Mother Adeline and Sunshine return to the parlor. Sunshine's face is red and wet.

"Would you like to play Schumann's 'Scenes from Childhood' now?" says Mother Adeline.

"Goddamnit," The Doctor says, quiet.

"Yes, I would," Sunshine says.

"I thought you might."

"But I can't," Sunshine says, as she raises her hands and then takes the little finger of the left between her right thumb and forefinger, "because I'm afraid I've broken my finger." And she quickly bends her little finger back until there is bone snap muffled by flesh as the blood drains out of her face and she crumples down to the floor in a faint, smiling.

VII. NOW I LAY ME

Adam Nichols could not sleep that night. Usually, he felt tired and good at night up in Michigan and fell asleep quick and slept sound but tonight he felt heavy but not tired and did not feel good. So as he lay awake, he thought about the many places he had fished in his life and he thought about the many places he would fish and he thought about a big, two-hearted river but then he thought he saw himself wading in the water and all around him were dead trout, furry with white fungus, slapping uncaring against a rock in the meaningless way of death, floating belly up in the little pools and shadows beneath the trees and that made him sick.

Adam decided to stop thinking about fishing. He was just cold awake and he started praying. *Now I lay me ...* He prayed for all the people he had ever known, although he was not exactly sure what it was he prayed for those people. He probably asked for God's blessing for each of them, although he was not sure what a blessing was or how it might be deemed granted. He prayed for Jesus to take them all to heaven, which is what he thought he was supposed to do, although he imagined heaven to be little more than a clean, well-lighted place and was not in the least certain why anyone would want to go there. Now I lay me ... He mostly prayed because remembering the names of all the people he had ever known took up a lot of time and if you cannot sleep then you need something to take up the time. And if you cannot take up all the time with the names of all the people you have ever known, then you can try to remember the names of all the animals you have seen at the zoo, or you can remember all the names of birds from *Youth's Guide to Birds of the World*: canary and parakeet and stone curlew and quail and little ringed plover and oystercatcher and that's a funny name but what it does is catch oysters and the night is so heavy and you are never more alone than you are at night *Now I lay me* poor bird poor mourning dove poor whippoorwill poor Sunshine with her broken finger and two spankings in a single day *Now I lay me* and God granteth a blessing upon Sunshine and *Now I lay me* counting in the dark the sun gone down but the sun also rises and God bless The Doctor the poor Doctor and ...

He heard them.

He heard The Doctor and Mother Adeline. He heard their voices but not what they were saying.

He heard them moving quietly in the cottage.

Adam Nichols got up quietly. He had on his long underwear. He slipped his feet into leather slippers. He tried to walk in the totally silent, pigeon-toed way the Indians walked.

He followed Mother Adeline and The Doctor outside. He did not let them see him. There was a full moon. Mother Adeline and The Doctor were not talking now. The Doctor had grandfather's .32-caliber pistol. He held it casually at his side as he and Mother Adeline walked down to the little pier.

—This was a dream you had as a child? the psychiatrist said.

—No. You're a fool. You understand nothing. It was no dream.

This is what happened.

ლ • ლ

1961
Mayo Clinic
Rochester, Minnesota

There is an old man on a gurney and his belly is big and his legs are splayed and scrawny and a tired line of drool runs down at the left side of his slack mouth. You might think he looks like an old lion who could no longer hide from the hunters and has taken a bad shot but has not yet earned the *coup de grace*, but the old man would not say that if you asked him and he were able to respond.

He would say he looks like a tired old man.

They have just shot lightning through his head. It is like an electrical explosion in his brain. They have tried to blast away whatever has made him sad but something else has happened because he is no longer here not here and he is *Now I lay me* looking down at himself without pity nor irony

and *pues y nada* and now he goes drifting off drifting away
I'm lighting out.

VIII. THE STRANGE COUNTRY

—*Hey-aye-hey!*
  —Gilby Edwards. It is you.
  —Goddamn right, kid. Who else? Teddy Roosevelt? Buffalo Bill
Bullshit?
  —You're dead, Gilby.
  —Goddamn right.
  —You're a ghost.
  —Yeah. Hell, yes. Old Gilby gone *Jiibay* and that's a fact. No bullshit.
  —And kid, now you free like First Ojibway boy. You travel in spirit
and in the world of the spirits.
  —Look down. See everyone. See everything.

The moonlight made everything clear and black and white. Mother
Adeline and The Doctor were in the boat. The Doctor was no longer
rowing. The boat rocked gently and the water lapped softly against it. The
pistol lay by the Doctor on the seat.
  The Doctor said—and Adam Nichols heard him plainly—"This is
what the Ojibway say. Tribe have bitch woman, man have bitch wife, *hey-
aye-hey*, take bitch in canoe and send her to Neebanaw and Winona!"
  "You are drunk," Mother Adeline said. "Mrs. Eddy writes, 'The
drunkard thinks he enjoys drunkenness, and you cannot make the
inebriate leave his besottedness, until his physical sense of pleasure yields
to a higher sense.' You have no higher sense. You are a heathen and a
savage. You have chosen to be despicable."
  "Injun smart. Plenty ghosts in lake. Damn right." The Doctor laughed.
  "The Church of Christ Scientist teaches us about ghosts. '... ghosts
are not realities, but traditional beliefs, erroneous and man-made.... In
short ... there are no such things.'"
  You might think the ghosts in the lake had been listening. It was like
they were actors who had been diligent at all their rehearsals and were
now determined to give a superb performance. The *Jiibay* of Ghost Lake
rippled up through the black water. They were shimmering and glowing
white. They made a sound that was something like laughter but had no joy
in it. It was a dead sound and pinched. The women-ghosts had black holes
for eyes. They had black holes for mouths. They had no flesh. They were

231

horrible and ghastly and did a fluttering dance on the water all around the boat.

"What is it you intend?" Mother Adeline asked The Doctor. She sounded calm. She seemed to take no notice of the ghosts that had risen from the lake.

"I mean to take your life," The Doctor said. The Doctor raised the .32-caliber Smith & Wesson.

The ghosts encircled the boat. Their fleshless arms were waving and they moved in a parody of a dance. They sang a song that had no breath in it, no life.

Then the ghosts were a shimmering dome of dead white light that fell upon the boat and covered it.

Adam Nichols could see nothing.

But before he left the world of the spirits he heard the shot. It was sharp and had the flickering echo you hear when a bullet is fired over a body of water.

It sounded like a killing shot.

છ • છ

1935
Ghost Lake, Michigan

Each time Toby snapped off a shot with the .22-caliber Winchester, a black squirrel fell. He shot six squirrels with six bullets. It made for a good day. Toby's being a good shot surprised Adam Nichols because the boy's mother had not been a good shot, not anything like it, though she had tried to learn several times to please him. She tried to do a number of things to please him and never did, until at last she despaired of pleasing him and he grew weary of her attempts.

Toby pleased him a good deal. Toby seemed to do it without trying. Adam Nichols thought he would have liked Toby even if Toby were not his son.

In the early afternoon, they set up camp by the shore of Ghost Lake. They were hungry. Adam Nichols showed his son how to dress the squirrels, how to slip the furry skin down their legs as though you were removing little pants. Toby laughed at that.

In addition to all the squirrel, Adam Nichols cooked up a can of pork and beans and a can of spaghetti. It was not real camping food, but the kind of camping food he had eaten when he was a very young boy. And besides, Adam Nichols told Toby, "If we were willing to carry it, we have every right to eat it."

Toby laughed. "I don't think I've ever been hungrier," Toby said.

It came to Adam Nichols that he liked this boy quite a lot. He loved this boy.

And as he watched the boy eating, he wondered if the boy liked him or loved him.

Isn't that a question? The Doctor's ghost said that. *Isn't that a question you ask your whole life.*

Adam Nichols was not surprised that the ghost was here. If ghosts had a sense of smell, The Doctor always liked cooking over a campfire and had taught Adam. Though he saw nothing like it, Adam could easily imagine The Doctor's ghost as a wavering image just over the rising hot air of the fire.

Adam Nichols did not think Toby heard or saw anything. He could understand that. The Doctor was Toby's grandfather but The Doctor's ghost belonged only to Adam Nichols.

Adam Nichols had a good day with Toby.

That is why fathers have sons, The Doctor's ghost told him.

—And you believe this? the psychiatrist asked. He could not make himself seem non-directive. He sounded amazed. He did not sound Catholic.

—Yes, I believe.

—You believe your father's ghost was there and talking to you?

—I believe in my father's ghost who art or art not in heaven, depending on whether or not our Holy Mother Church teaches the truth about suicides, which The Doctor may or may not have been. I believe in the ghost of Gilby Edwards, who might well be drunk and whooping and dancing in the Happy Hunting Ground. I believe in the ghosts in Ghost Lake who are mean and bitchy and abideth a-bitching forever and ever amen. I believe in the ghost of the dead man I spoke to as I carried him to the dressing station in the war to end all wars that didn't end war not for shit, old son, not for shit. I believe in the ghost of the bullfighter Tonio Mendoza who twice had the horns pass through him and died calling to the crowd *I guess I have showed I can take it like a man!* I believe in the ghosts of Michigan and Cuba and the ghosts of Paris by night and the Serengeti by day and the glorious ghosts of the Abraham Lincoln Brigade ... *Viva la quince brigada!*

—I believe in the ghosts of all the people I used to be before becoming this broken-down human ruin with a rock-hard liver and bones that creak and a hollow vacancy in the belfry and nothing but memory which even now fades away like morning dew. I believe in the ghosts of wineskins and the ghosts of making love in the afternoon and of running with the bulls and of laughing and fishing for marlin and of drinking beer and the howitzers' great boom, the ghosts, all dead and gone, dead and gone, all ghosts.

—And if there are no ghosts, how is it that we carry them with us wherever we go?

I believe.

Help my unbelief, give me strength, I believe I believe.

—Let us pray.

—Now I lay me *y pues y nada* and I pray to ghosts my ghost to keep and welcome my ghost to the land of ghosts *y pues y nada y pues y nada* for *pues* is the kingdom and the power of ghosts forever and ghost amen my ghosts amen amen amen

ᑫᑭ • ᑫᑭ

Across the open mouth of the tent, Adam Nichols had fixed cheesecloth so there would be no mosquitoes and Toby was asleep in the tent. He slept the way boys sleep when they have had a very good day.

But Adam Nichols could not sleep. So he had a drink of whiskey from a silver flask. Then he had another. There was a three-quarter moon, but still he started a fire with chips of pine and he sat by it and looked out at Ghost Lake and saw a mist.

Then The Doctor's ghost was sitting beside him.

Adam Nichols did not have to look to know that, but he turned his head and there was The Doctor, a ghost.

I like it when you tell the boy about Africa.

"I will take him there someday," Adam Nichols said. "I will. He will like Africa. He will not be afraid. I will teach him not to be afraid."

I am sorry I never went to Africa, The Doctor said. *I am sorry I never took you to Africa.*

"You taught me to hunt and fish," Adam Nichols said. "You taught me what I had to do so I could begin to know Africa."

Adam Nichols smiled. He held out the silver flask of whiskey to his father's ghost. "Would you like a drink?"

I would, the ghost said, but did not move, so Adam took a drink.

Then he said, formally, "There is that which I wish to ask you.".

You may, the ghost of his father formally answered.

"I need to know the truth," Adam Nichols said.

There is a truth that comes at first light that is no longer true by noon, the ghost said. *That is a saying in Africa.*

"The Masai, it is one of their sayings, " Adam Nichols said. "Yes. But might you then tell me what happened that night?"

Adam Nichols and the ghost of The Doctor, his father, Chadbourne Nichols, MD, were both talking about the night on the lake when Mother Adeline and the Doctor were in the boat surrounded by all the ghosts and then the ghosts fell upon them and the gun was fired.

The ghost explained, *What happened that night was, she killed me.*

IX. THE END OF SOMETHING

July 2, 1961
Ketchum, Idaho

It was early and he was the only one up. It was a beautiful morning.

There were no clouds. There was sunshine.

Then he remembered that Gary Cooper was dead. Cooper had been dead for—was it a month?

Cooper, yes, Coop had beat him to the barn. Cooper him gone *Jiibay.*

He went to the gun cabinet. He opened it. There was only one pistol inside. It was an old .32-caliber Smith & Wesson, manufactured in Springfield, Massachusetts. It was his grandfather's gun. It was then his father's gun. His grandfather and his father had both used it.

When he was 30, Mother Adeline sent him the gun for his birthday, along with a note:

> *My Dear Son,*
>
> *I thought you might want this or have sentimental feelings for it.*
>
> *Though yours is not always a practical nature, I trust you will find some use for it.*

The note was signed: *With a Mother's Eternal Love.*

He did not take the pistol from the cabinet. He took the Boss shotgun he had bought at Abercrombie and Fitch.

He went into the front foyer. He liked the way the light struck the oak-paneled walls and the floor. It was like being in a museum or in a church. It was a well-lighted place and it felt clean and airy.

He whispered a prayer.

Carefully, he lowered the butt of the Boss shotgun to the floor. He leaned forward. The twin barrels were cold circles in the scarred tissue just above his eyebrows.

He tripped both triggers.

DANI'S STORY

August 15, 1994

William Raley, Editor
AFTER HOURS MAGAZINE
P.O. Box 538
Sunset Beach, CA 90741-0538

Dear William,

Thanks for asking me for a story for the last issue of
AFTER HOURS.

Sure, I've got a horror story. I have lots of them.

Don't we all?

Best,

Mort Castle

ᘉ • ᘉ

"I'm scared," she says. "You don't think so, maybe, but I am. I'm scared a
lot now, even when there's no reason."
 I tell her she'll get over it with time. I say, "It's all right."
 Scared.
 I do not tell her, I understand.
 I do not say, I think maybe we all are
 All the time.

ᘉ • ᘉ

Let's flashback. It's okay. The world is non-linear, right? One leads to two? No, sir, and once you realize Our Cosmic King has repealed the Law of Cause and Effect, you'll be less frequently disappointed.

So ... Flashback:

The city is Chicago and the time is Spring and dusk and the weather is just about perfect. You can taste Summer on the breeze off Lake Michigan.

Let's walk with her. We can do that, after all. This is fiction. I make the rules.

People and street lights and patterned reflections in store windows and random silica glitter in the sidewalk and sounds that are distinctly and distinctively city sounds:

A bus groans a turn onto Jackson and two Orientals laugh quietly behind her and she wonders if this is the first time she has ever heard Orientals laugh in real life and not in a movie or something. Overhead, the El train, metal on metal, comes to a stop.

You know, a night like this, you understand how it was the Impressionist painters came to see in the way they saw. It is only that instant of soft-focused precision that can capture this complete world within how many worlds, that can make you feel this

NOW

This

SUCHNESS of things.

And she is happy now. Her name is Dani. Well, her real name is Alison, and she does spell it with only the one "l," but this is fiction, so I can call her Eustacia Visigoth Marmalade if I choose. Dani is ON! HER! OWN! in the city, because she is All GROWN UP!

(Well, okay, there is some financial help from the folks, until she gets it all together, okay, and she will pay them back, 'cause how else, right now, could she afford an apartment in the ultra-slick, toney-clique Lincoln Park area?

(Hey, Dani works for a living, you know? Graphic design, a small but getting-noticed ad agency where a certain amount of goof-around—not goose-around!—is encouraged, part of the creative process ...)

Happy. Dani is happy because

it is Spring

now

in the city.

And let's get cornball, my friend, let's get sentimental and silly, because, hey, you are supposed to avoid diabetes-inducing sentiment in fiction, but goddamnit, *life* is loaded with sentimentality, ain't it, and this is, for real fellas and gals, friends and pals, the McCoy, the true gen, the *emmis*.

So, if this instant you peered right into Dani's brain, you would discover that right now she does indeed believe totally in Magic. Believes that everyone is entitled by birth to One Wish That Comes True. Believes That It is A Wonderful Life. Believes there is a Caring Celestial Eye on The Sparrow and You.

If Dani told you this, well, now that she is an adult, she'd probably feel stupid and say, "God, did I say that? That was dumb! I mean ..."

She might blush.

I think you might fall in love with her then.

ᑭ • ᑭ

Of course I am free to share Dani's thoughts with you. Dani is a fictional character in a work of fiction.

According to Webster's Dictionary, Fiction is Bullshit.

Phonius Baloneyus.

> *You just make it all up, right?*
> *It's all out of your head.*

Uh-uh. Out of my head. Yessirree,
Bob. Not that much to it, frankly.
Think it up and write
it down and when you're done,
stop.

And here is insight into the
workings of a fiction writer's mind.

I chose the name Dani
because it's sort of close to Demi, and
people used to tell our main character that
she reminded them of Demi Moore,
or, at least the way
Demi Moore looked in *Ghost*.

ᑭ • ᑭ

"Thing is," Dani says, "I never thought Demi Moore was such a much, okay? I mean, if I were lezzy, I would not want to go to bed with her."

239

Dani smiles, but it's the sort of smile that makes you feel wrong. She says, "I'm not pretty anymore."

Is she going to cry? Please, I hope not. I thought she was over that part of it, the tears that explode out of nowhere …

So, in that I am something of an obtuser, what I say is, "You are pretty. You will be even prettier. Today plastic surgery is no big deal, so you don't have to and you will never have to worry about yourself in the loveliness department, okay?"

"Okay," Dani says. Laughs. "Hell, you think any girl younger than you is Big Time Lovely."

My turn to laugh. Har-dee-har-horseshit.

Fact: I am forty-eight, and, starting last year, it felt like every girl and every guy and everybody who matters in the whole round world was younger than yours truly, Mort the *Moi*.

Sometimes I think about it.

Aging.

I guess I think about it often, probably.

Sometimes, sometimes it makes me sad.

Sometimes.

Often.

Often it makes me deeply and profoundly sad.

ↄ • ↄ

No.

Dani says she is really sorry, really, but she does not like most of what I have written so far. She says no way could she have been so Pollyanna-sweet, naive and assholic. I've made her just too nice.

"It's just bogus, you know."

Besides, why don't I just get on with it? Her story. Just charge into the beginning, chainsaw through the middle, and then, Tah-dah!

At last!

The End!

The End!

That will be IT!

That will take care of it. I know that is what she hopes in a vague and inexpressible way that manages to irritate the hell out of me.

So, hey, why doesn't she write it?

No, no thank you, Mort. I lived it. That takes care of my obligation, yes?

Dani thinks I have magic. Mort the Writer. Published and everything, published in languages I do not even speak.

Okay, maybe I reside at the Lower End of the U. S. Economic Ladder, but I am, to Dani, and a few others, Mort The Shaman

And I can do MAGIC

Get HER story into print.

That will give purpose to the horror.

Purpose. Not catharsis.

Catharsis? Doesn't happen.

And I cannot will not

will not tell her

that it is just there

the horror

the horror

will always be

the horror

she has known

the horror

we know

ↀ • ↀ

Let's go to that Friday night in early autumn.

We are done screwing around.

I ...

It's going to happen.

ↀ • ↀ

September 5, 1994
Dear William,

Sorry it's taking longer to get you a story for AFTER HOURS than I'd planned. Slow going and rough at this end of the mail chute.

But as you know, sometimes things have to come at you and come together in their own way.

And Raley, some of this is your own damned fault! Check out the resonant and evocative title you slapped on your magazine.

NEW MOON ON THE WATER

After Hours. Hey, pal, what is it we hear "after hours"? Who is it?

There are voices, you know, and they talk to me—after hours. Truth is, I'm hearing them more and more often. I don't sleep well, not anymore, and so, two or three in the morning, I'm up reading, trying to write, trying not to feel sad, whatever. And it is then "The After Hours Voices" (sounds like the name for the Chorus on an old Jackie Gleason album!) are keeping me company. Oh, they don't scream. They are soft, insistent, and regretful. They are not unlike the haze around a mountain peak in an Oriental painting, and just as real.

The After Hours Voices talk to me ..."Sing sorrow, sing sorrow ..." That is an English folk song, "The Lass From The Low Country," and I feel that sort of feeling as I listen to voices call from memory and from the peculiar nowhere that is the desolate realm of hopes gone to hell.

Voices you can hear only after hours.

They whisper intimations of horror.

And so, begin again.

Best,

Mort Castle

ᓂ • ᓂ

Because it did happen and so now it has to
    On her floor, the 16th ...
    Dani waits for the elevator. Waiting is not impatience. No foot-tapping. No running fingers along the strap of her purse.
    Horror waits for her.
    Not a monster.
    Not a demon.
    Not a ghost.
    You do not need a ghost to be haunted.

Horror is WHAT IF? Above all, and forget the bullshit metaphysics, horror is the impossible to control hurting we do to ourselves. If the toothache eases, hey, we just have to stab the old tongue in there to get it fired up and screeching again, don't we?

So—WHAT IF?

WHAT IF?

WHAT IF?

What if she had not decided to go out that night?

What if Cathy Lynn and Cathy Cole, AKA "The Two Cathys," AKA Cathy One (Lynn) and Cathy Two (Cole) had suggested they meet at the Hard Rock Café a half hour later? A half-hour earlier? It didn't matter, really. Cathy Two's boyfriend was working the door. They could always get in.

What if the elevators had been out of order? "I work out twice a week, but forget the free stress test, pal."

What if she had had a cold? "God deh snibbles, an' just wanna read a boog an' stay warm inna beddd."

What if *he* had never been born?

He ... What if Mr. Horror had been struck by lightning/run over by a Purolator truck/mangled beyond recognition by a punch press?

What if? What if? What if? What if? What if?

Let's push it over the top, to the utterly impossible, and ask, what if Dani had done what no kid in the history of the world has done, what if she had actually listened to her mother and father?

Her parents did not want her going so far away to the city.

Dani grew up in Monticello, just about the middle of Illinois, and what was so bad about it, anyway, answer me that, young lady?

Dad was the State Farm Insurance man with his office right there on McHemie Street—Like A Good Neighbor, State Farm Is There!—and Mom processed loan applications for United Savings and Loan of Monticello and Farmer City, and there was nothing wrong with the education Dani got in high school, was there (graduated seven, "lucky seven," in a class of 77), Dani had to admit that, what they couldn't understand, really not understand, was why she had to go study art at the Art Institute in Chicago, instead of, say, the U of I, or Illinois State University. You know, say what you want, a number of nationally known artists, like the sculptor Nick Africano, and the glass-blower, John Brekke (one of Mort's students when he was in high school!), they got all the art they needed right at ISU, not more than 50 miles away, okay, right there in Normal, Illinois.

Beginning of Dani's senior year:

"I do not want you in the city. No. I watch the news. I'm not paranoid and I'm not a hick, but I tell you, honey, I am afraid of the city."

"You're not afraid of a city, Dad. You are afraid of black people ..."

"It's not that they're black ..."

"Think about what you said, what you just said!"

"What I am thinking about is you! And you know me better than that, Dani. I'm no bigot."

"I know! I know. You always watch Bill Cosby. Why, some of your best friends would be Knee-Gah-rows, if there were any in Monticello."

Dad looks down, then, a hand to his brow so she cannot see his eyes. "I know you think this town is too little for you, okay? You're not going to be happy if the only major art exhibition you see is the new mural at the VFW Hall. There's a lot to you, a lot inside you, Dani."

"Dad ..."

One of those long silences that so rarely happen in real life and that third-rate fictionists throw in when they are trying to contrive poignancy.

"I'm not arguing, okay? I am asking. Does it have to be Chicago?"

"Yes."

His voice is tight but there is nothing small or grudging in the words he finds hard to speak. "You have real talent, Dani, and me, well I do not pretend to understand talent. I am a plodder, and I realize it, and it's worked for me, so I'm not unhappy. But I know you cannot ignore talent and if that means Chicago, then that's what it means."

It meant Chicago.

☙ • ☙

after hours voices
absent friends I

scott talks
to me over
telephone lines
comic edge and marlboro
rasp subdued now

says he's
just out
of a methadone clinic
says he's
all right
now

MORT CASTLE

thinks
he is

says he's
just a goddamned
junky
is what
he is

laughs

a goddamned
junky

says he will go
to california
has to go
to california
now

a quest
sort of

something
like that
see the ocean
something about
healing waters and power
get it all
worked out

says he will
get settled
see the ocean
call me

that was 1975

directory assistance
cannot assist

i
have not

heard from him since

❧ • ❧

**after hours voices
absent friends II**

It was the catcher in the rye, Holden Caulfield, who told us you
can get to missing everybody, even the people you never knew.

I miss Groucho Marx. Josh White. Jack Benny. Blind Louie.
Aunt Kate and Ozzie. Harry Truman. Thelonius Monk. Joe
Louis. Franklin Delano Roosevelt. Gold Tooth Liboro. Delmore
Schwartz. John Bubbles. Janis Joplin. John Coltrane. Uncle Nate.
Martin Luther King. Miss Kitty. Jack Kennedy. Bobby Kennedy.
Jackie Kennedy. Fats Waller.

You can get to feeling that everyone who was anyone is dead.

"Ain't it a gasser?"
—*The Late Lord Buckley*

… the 27th of Sept., and I can't say I've wrapped the
story for your last ish.

But I am, however, hearing many muttering of The
After Hours Voices, and they ain't doing no meditative
Gregorian chants!

Know what, Will-yum, ain't impossible Mort has himself
a kick-ass mid-life crisis. But hey, I can handle it, and
if you listen to any of the talk shows, you know you do
get through it, put it all together into a viable philosophy without resorting to Shirley MacLaine religions or
Everything-You-Need-to-Know-You-Learned-in-

Reform-School books.

And then, when you have GOT IT, Satori! Big Bingo!

Then you DIE!

Hit that one Sam Kinnison style.
The late Sam Kinnison!
THEN YOU FUCKING DIE!

"The only guarantee you get with life is your inability to survive it."
—*H. L. Mencken*

Now, isn't he one cheery motherfucker, though?

∾ • ∾

"So, you want me to go ahead with it now, Dani?"

"Yes. You've fooled around long enough, haven't you? Story time, beginning, middle, end. It's you. You don't want to write it, do you?"

"I'll write it. I told you I would. Don't you worry about that." I will write it and what I want has nothing to do with it.

What I want has never
stopped a single tidal wave or a teenage suicide
or an IRA bomb or a two-year-old's AIDS death
What I want?
I am not God.
And judging by what I see, God isn't, either.

> *Let's hold a sec with the*
> *self-pity and the grandiosity, okay?*

All right! We have another After Hours Voice.

I've been here before, but you weren't listening.
You weren't willing to listen.

Okay, I am listening. Tuned in. Going to
impart some wisdom or what?

NEW MOON ON THE WATER

Just the truth

Vincent Van Gogh
looks through
mad eyes
of horror

and sees
sunflowers

Now, get back to Dani. Her story needs telling. And let's state the obvious,
Mort. It's not just for Dani you're telling it

ᴇↃ • ᴇↃ

She is going to The Hard Rock Café where she will meet her friends,
Cathy One and Cathy Two. She is waiting for the elevator.

The orange-pink light over the bronze sliding doors. Down. The
sound is Bink! It is exactly Bink! Later, she will hear that precision of
sound in her head.

Dani steps into the elevator. She is the only passenger.

(That's right! You just caught it yesterday on the Geraldo-Oprah-
Leeza-Sleeza-Sally-Jerry Jibber-Jabber Show! The guy—and it's ALWAYS a
guy—who tells you ladies how NOT to be a VICTIM! NEVER get on an
elevator alone! Never get on an elevator that has fewer than 1,232 people
on it! Never get on an elevator if you can help it 'cause the fucking thing
can faw down! If you absolutely MUST get on an elevator by yourself,
have your WWII-surplus bazooka in easy reach, strap a 55-gallon drum of
MACE to your back, carry a starving weasel in your purse ...)

Descending
BINK!
The Ninth Floor.
Stop.
Doors slide open.
He enters.

Horror
not just yet
I need to take a breath
okay

here we go

What is it with you? Why does it always have to be horror?

They used to ask my friend—my now absent friend—Bill Wantling, why he wrote so many poems about prison. Bill's final book was called SAN QUENTIN'S STRANGER.

Bill did seven years in San Quentin and they used to ask him that.

I write horror because that is what we've got. Please, no platitudinous re-bop about, "It's all in how you look at it," and don't give me that "You decide if the glass is half-full or half-empty," when the glass contains Jonestown Special Kool-Aid, and don't quote me that putz with ears, Wayne Dyer, or the putzette, Joyce Brothers, and don't give me any *Reader's Digest* inspirational tripe, "If life hands you a lemon …"

"…it was probably picked by a one-armed, hare-lipped, illegal alien who was the product of incest between his syphilitic sister and his hydrocephalic brother, and one day, Mr. Lemon Plucker will go wacky-wacky-WACK-oooooOOOOOO!!!! Fully transmogrified and living up to his fullest potential behind the meanest Mexican brown and crack and animal tranq and four gallons of Liquid Plumber, and he will climb on top of a building and play rock 'n' roll Uzi on a bunch of preschoolers on their field trip to the zoo to see the newborn giraffe.

"The horror. The horror." Good old Kurtz looked right into the Heart of Darkness and he had a take on it.

Yo, Mort, you like quotes. Here's one for you:

Upon this awkward ball
of mud
I see
All
All
is ecstasy

You know who wrote that?
Yes.
Bill Wantling.

NEW MOON ON THE WATER

Who wrote *San Quentin's Stranger*.
Who was San Quentin's Stranger.
Who knew Caryl Chessman
and Van Gogh's sunflowers.

☙ • ☙

All right. Dani. I guess we're both ready now.

Dani. In the elevator.

He has just stepped in.

Average height. Weight: 145-165, who can tell. Late 20s, early 30s, young 40s, who can tell. Dark blond hair. Maybe light red hair. Can't recall. Cannot summon or create a visual for the police.

Bland face. That's all. Dressed all right. Sports coat. Swirling tie, a touch too much on the polyester, too shiny, meaning he is not quite with it. Think of all the so-so/okay actors on the one or maybe two season television shows you "watch sometimes" instead of "really liked" or "really hated." You'll realize that you cannot recall any of their faces because they're just blah-ho-hum, they are people whose looks you can say are "average ..."

But there is the smile. It's loose, teeth very TV-commercial (Caps? Bonded?), and then, his breath, and she understands: he has been juicing. He is perhaps a jigger or so from utterly ossified. She sees it in his eyes that want to operate independently of one another. His voice, words too cleanly separated and enunciated. "You are very cute. I would like very much to go to bed with you. I would like to touch you and make love to you."

He is pathetic.

Barney Fife.

Frightening.

Lee Harvey Oswald.

She is confused and outraged.

His loose smile hangs here. It is all she sees.

She slaps him.

A slap in the face sounds like nothing else but a slap in the face. Smile twists like cartoony rubber. Solidity of cheekbone beneath oily skin.

God! She has not struck another human being in anger since second grade when Marsha Voerner called her a "pig poop."

Slapped him. Hates him. Hates herself.

God! Wants to kill him or to apologize wants
wants to get away because
now she sees

250

she is in trouble.

Hand to his face. Amazed. Sorrowful. "You hit me," he says. "You don't. You hurt me. You can't do that. You just don't hit people. That isn't right. You just don't."

And he moves and touches the magic button on the panel and the elevator stops and she is trapped.

She tries

Tries nothing.

Because she cannot scream. He has her throat with his left hand and he is strong. He has her slammed against the wall.

Rape her. Beat her. Kill her.

She must cooperate. Submit.

Whatever he says. Wants.

No!

Go along with him until you have a chance … Fight.

Pinned to the wall. Tries to kick him in the balls. Cannot. Cannot breathe.

Women of Power, All Ye Mighty Amazons, the fact is most men are stronger than most women. Men typically have a height and weight advantage. And even when there's a question, well, what kind of odds do you think we'd have for Roseanne Barr versus Roberto Duran?

He says, "You just stop right now." Orders.

Cannot breathe.

Is going to die.

Be killed.

And KILLED is worse than dying.

(And this is not the horror. This is bad, this is BAD, but this is NOT the horror!)

"You hit me in the face. I am going to hit you in the face. I'm going to hit you only once, but I am going to hit you hard. I want you to remember, don't you ever, ever, ever hit anyone. What is the matter with you, anyway?"

He draws back his right hand, a fist now. She is kind of zoned, like overmuch nitrous oxide at the dentist's, so, some things are all foggy, but she can concentrate intensely on others.

Like the sound of *KRACKSHK!* and the crackling and squishing, an impossible, pulping, slow-motion sound, that fills her whole head when he punches her right on the nose.

This is no television punch on the nose. An honest-to-God punch on the nose is probably not as painful as having your appendix removed without anesthetic, but it's not exactly eating M & Ms, either.

Dani is gulping blood and snot and a little air, trying not to pass out.

When he lets her loose.

She slides to the floor.

He starts the elevator.

Gets off at the next floor.

The elevator going down.

You know, Dani thinks, Wow! That hurt!

Stand up. Okay. A little shaky but some of that is just the elevator itself, right? Sure. Don't throw up. Try to be objective, and you know, the pain is really quite amazing. Really.

So, what we've got, I'd imagine, is assault and battery. A guy hit me.

Assault and battery. I hit a guy.

Got a punch in the nose. Bop in the beezus. Sock in the snoot. Snarfed your snufflupagus, girly, and smashed your schnozzola and slammed your Cyranose ...

That is not horror, is it?

ↄ • ↄ

Gee, way back when, I thought you said something about your writing a horror story. Got any plans to get around to that during this incarnation? Come on, damn it! Just write it already!

Right. Nothing to it. After all, I write fiction. I just make up all this stuff. Why don't I just do it already? Why don't I just do it already? Nothing to it, a little imagination and throw in a vampire, and there you go!

ↄ • ↄ

Uh, Suffering Artist, lighten up a tad, okay?

Hey, there! It's Mr. After Hours
Voice, not quite as well known to
us Baby Boomers as Mr. Tooth Decay,
but, nonetheless, a real player in my life.

What's to say? Do we
get...philosophical?

MORT CASTLE

AFTER HOURS VOICE: Soitainly! Nyuck, nyuck, nyuck! (A halfway-decent impression of the immortal Curley.)

MORT CASTLE (Struggling Writer Who Sometimes takes Himself Too Seriously and has a tendency toward Self-Indulgence): So, lay down your spiel, yuh ole sidewinder, and let me hear the wisdom of the ages.

AFTER HOURS VOICE: Uh, let's check on what you are listening to as you work on this story for William R. Sounds like the Bill Evans Trio.
Sounds like currently dead Bill Evans when he used to be alive. Sounds quite beautiful, you know.
Sounds like Scotty LeFaro on bass. Scotty was killed in a horror movie of a car accident some months after this recording.

And later, you will listen, I'll bet, to Lady Day and Chet Baker, and no one understood sorrow like they did, and they lived tragedies and insanities, and they are gone now, but what they left behind, well, there is some of the horror there, has to be, goes with the territory, but there is more, isn't there?

They took it all in, and what they created is this lastingness, this music that is as close as you're going to get to the holy.

Yes, pain has its place in the creation of this man-made sacrament.

But so does EVERYTHING else!

❧ • ❧

Dani, it is very late.
I will finish your story now.

❧ • ❧

Main floor.
Every broken-noser out! Dani has arrived.
Staggers. "Uh-hmmm ..." A bubbling throat sound she makes again and again, her *Bridge on the River Kwai* song to keep her moving.
A step.
A step.
Has to keep moving. Must. "Uh-hmmm ..." "Uh-hmmm ..." "Uh-

hmmm ..."

This is not the horror.

This is bad.

But this is not the horror.

The doorman is there. Just appears like he's following a script. Hands on her shoulders. She flinches.

"All right," he says. "Okay." Broad, dark brown face. Coat with epaulets. His good eyes narrowing. Concern. "All right."

Funny, you know. For a second, she thinks he is her father and everything is all right.

Click, and she's tracking right once more. The doorman is named Kelly Green. When she first heard it, she thought that was a funny name, especially for a black man; she wondered later if it was wrong to think that.

"Uh-hmmm ..."

"Looks like something happened, didn't it? We get you fixed up real soon. First, let's just sit you on down ..."

"Doan go ..."

"No, no. It's all right. I'm here. Right here, okay? Just get my phone here and get you some help. Everything be fine. You see ..."

She is sitting down. He has made a call. He is holding her hand. "Uh-hmmm...."

He is a nice man.

He says, "It's all right. Okay, now. It's all right. It's all right."

ભ • ભ

Dear William,

It happens weird sometimes, you know?

Here's what I thought was the ending of this story:

ભ • ભ

Okay, Horror Reader, you've been patient as hell, so now, at last (right?) this is—

THE HORROR!

Dani is unable to identify her assailant for the police. She will always be afraid of him. If she lives 100 years, she will be waiting for him to explode out of her dreams and into her life.

Okay, no question the rhino repair surgeon will do a superb job, and not to sweat the financial, she has a fine medical package from the ad agency, so, really, you won't be able to tell she had a broken nose.

But the horror is that never again will Dani accept as a given that this old world is a good old world in which to be.

Think of: A butterfly torn apart simply because it was there for the tearing.

Think of: Your favorite uncle, the one who took you fishing and made jokes about the fish you caught, giving them Biblical names like Hezekiah, Jeremiah, and Nehemiah ... How did it feel when you learned he was a suicide?

Think of: Yourself old and lonely and nobody calls.

Think this way, and you will feel something of the loss Dani has suffered. A unique dimension of her selfness is gone, can never be restored. Trust replaced by cynicism. She is smarter and she is bitter. The edge is there. She has that sharpened awareness that becomes city paranoia to enable her to survive.

It is no exaggeration to say Dani is gone. The Dani who *was* has been destroyed. She is lost to us and to herself.

And that is the horror, the horror conclusion of this horror story.

But William, that is not it, at all.

The story does not end that way.

Dani won't let it.

ᘒ • ᘒ

"No," Dani says. "because it not true. It's not that way."

She tells me I have written the ending of my story.

Not her story.

"See, the ending of my story is Kelly Green. You know, sometimes when it's real late, and I wake up frightened, I can hear him. What he's saying is, 'It's all right, it's all right.' And then after he says it for a while, I can get back to sleep."

I ask, "So, then, how does your story end?"

"The way it should end. It ends with

ᘒ • ᘒ

sometimes I think us horror guys, William, can deal with everything—except hope!

255

NEW MOON ON THE WATER

What happens, I guess, is we write a few horror stories, then more of them, and we get caught up in it, become darkness junkies, and we put on these glasses that let us see the horror, and by the time we hit our 40s, we are wearing horror bi-focals, good for seeing the up-close horror and the distant horror, and because we have picked up some shakiness along the way, had our disasters and disappointments, had too much that should have gone right go dead wrong or just go away forever, because we have known too many losses, after a while, all we see is the horror of it all.

Horror. It gets so it's the only thing. That is, it gets so we make it the only thing. And William, if I sound like I'm either preaching or teaching, hell, after all, I was your fiction writing teacher some time back there, and, damn it, I am older than you—as well as four-fifths of the semi-civilized world—so there!

So, you've got my story here. Not heavy on plot this round, but there is some fiction. Into each life that comes my way, some fiction may fall!

That is, you have my story—Dani's story—once we wrap it. We can wrap it with the words that are a prayer, a prayer of one person to another person, a prayer of one person for another person, a prayer without God getting in the way, a prayer to speak mercy and touch you and know your tears, a prayer to speak kindness and ease and rest and know your pain, a prayer of hope a prayer of hope a prayer of hope

It's all right. It's all right.

ALTENMOOR, WHERE THE DOGS DANCE

One day in spring, when the boy came home from school, he did not find Rusty in the backyard, on the screened-in porch, or anywhere downstairs in the house. He knew Rusty could not be up with Grandpa. Last winter, when the weather had gone so cold, Rusty's back legs had gone cold, too, so cold he could no longer climb stairs.

The boy's mother took him into the kitchen and tried to explain, though he hadn't asked her. "Rusty's gone, Marky."

He hated being called "Marky," but she was his mom, so what could he do? Dad called him "Mark," and sometimes "Son," and that was better but it still wasn't right.

Grandpa knew and always called him "Boy." He felt like a "boy," not "Mark," or "Son," or (phoo!) "Marky!" Once in a while he wondered if that would change when he got older.

Mom said Rusty was very old. In a dog way, Rusty was more than a hundred. She said Rusty had had a very good life because everyone loved him a lot, and now Rusty's life was over.

The way Mom talked made the boy think she was trying not to frighten him. Then she hugged him so hard all his air rushed out and he thought Mom was trying not to be frightened, too.

But the boy didn't understand, so he said, "I'll go see Grandpa." Grandpa knew how to talk about things so the boy understood because Grandpa was very smart. He was so smart that long ago, when he could still see, Grandpa even used to write books.

"He'll like that," Mom said. "Go see him."

Upstairs at the end of the hall, across from his own room, the boy knocked on Grandpa's door. He waited one-two-three, then heard Grandpa say, "Enter." Grandpa always made him wait *one-two-three*, never *one*, or *one-two*, or *one-two-three-four*.

Grandpa sat in a straight-backed chair by the window. Grandpa didn't have a rocking chair and the boy knew why because once Grandpa had told him. "Old people are supposed to sit in rockers. Seldom in my life have I done the 'supposed to's.'"

Through the window, the sun shone a square of light at Grandpa's feet. The boy stood with his sneakers at the edge of the square. If he stepped inside, it might break, the yellow oozing out like the yolk of a poached egg.

The boy said, "Grandpa, Mom says Rusty is gone."

"Your mother is truthful enough," Grandpa said, "though so sadly lacking in imagination it's often difficult for me to acknowledge her as my daughter."

"Oh," the boy said. Sometimes Grandpa talked funny, except he never did when he was talking about important things—like Altenmoor.

"Mom says Rusty was very old," the boy said.

"Indeed," Grandpa said.

"You're very old."

"Once more, indeed."

The boy remembered when Grandpa had been old, but not very old. Grandpa got very old when the cloudy-looking white film covered his eyes. After that, Grandpa couldn't read anymore, not even the Altenmoor books Grandpa had written himself.

"I'll miss Rusty," the boy said. "You know, like how he used to sleep with his head between his paws. He had big paws."

"I will miss that too, Boy," Grandpa said. "The picture of Rusty asleep and the sound of his adenoidal snore are preserved and treasured in my memory."

Grandpa tipped his head. For a second the boy thought Grandpa wasn't blind at all because the boy could almost feel himself being seen. "Do say on, Boy," Grandpa said.

"Is Rusty dead?" the boy said.

Grandpa said, "There are some who would say and some who would believe it as well. And you? What do you say? What do you believe?"

The boy thought. Then he said, "No."

"No?"

"Rusty went to Altenmoor," the boy said and he hoped he believed what he was saying. "He went once through the Rubber Tree Woods and he jig-jogged left past the Marmalade Mound. Then he followed the winding Happy-To-You River to Altenmoor."

"Continue, Boy." Grandpa leaned forward, elbows on his knees, hands folded under his chin. "Speak to me of Altenmoor. So long since I've written of the noble realm and longer still since I've gone a-journeying there."

"In Altenmoor, every morning is a Sunrise Surprise and the buttercups thunder like twelve tubas."

"Only louder," Grandpa said.

"Much louder! And the winds are all hot winds and happy winds and wild winds!"

"And the animals?"

"Oh," the boy said, remembering the animals. "The pigs whistle 'Dixie' in four-part harmony and the cats play silver cymbals in three-quarter time."

"And the dogs?"

"The dogs dance!" the boy said. "The dogs do dance all the day!"

"You see," Grandpa said, "it was time for Rusty to be where the dogs dance. Yes. Rusty has gone to Altenmoor."

The boy smiled but the smile didn't feel all the way right because it pinched at the corners of his mouth, and so he had to ask. "Really?"

"'Really?' The modern rephrasing of the ageless 'What is Truth?' The metaphysicians ponder as they will, all we truly know, we know only here." Grandpa patted himself on the chest.

The boy said, "There is a real Altenmoor?"

"Were there not, could I have written the seventeen books that comprise the complete Altenmoor chronicles? If there were no Oz, could Mr. L. Frank Baum have related the adventures of Dorothy and Tin Woodsman and Scarecrow? What of Treasure Island and Never-Never-land, or savage Pellucidar and Wonderland? If they did not exist, how could people tell of them?"

Again Grandpa patted himself on the chest. "Books, Boy, are from the heart and of the heart. That makes them not merely true, but truer than true. Do you understand?"

"Some," the boy said. "Not everything."

"Some is more than most people," Grandpa said. "It will suffice."

The boy had something else to ask. "But how could Rusty get to Altenmoor, Grandpa? It's a long, long way and his legs were no good."

"Excellent point, Boy," Grandpa said, "and logic demands an answer."

Grandpa stretched out his arm and spread his fingers. In the sunlight the veins of his hand were ripply blue and strong. "I touched Rusty's head, you see. I patted that bony knob at the back of his skull and tickled between his ears. I touched him, and all the strength I could give, I gave to Rusty so he could make the trek to Altenmoor."

"And then he went?"

"He did," Grandpa said. "He went once through the Rubber Tree Woods and he jig-jogged left past the Marmalade Mound."

"Then he followed the winding Happy-To-You River to Altenmoor!"

the boy and Grandpa said together.

"Yes," Grandpa nodded, "and now Rusty is dancing, he is dancing where the dogs dance. I believe that."

"I do too," the boy said.

ℰℐ • ℰℐ

On a winter night so cold that the house could not keep out all the winter chill, the boy awoke. He thought at first that a dream had frightened him awake, but he realized he was not frightened.

Then he knew it was a thought that had pulled him from his sleep.

He got out of bed. Even through the carpet the floor was shivery, so he slid his feet along instead of lifting them. He did not need a light.

He stepped across the hall and quietly knocked on the door. It would have been wrong to wake Mom and Dad. They did not mind getting up if he had a stomachache or a bad dream, but his stomach felt fine and he was not dreaming.

The boy waited *one-two-three*.

Then he waited *four* and *five* and *six* and *seven* before he gently turned the knob and went in.

Winter moonlight seeped through the window. Grandpa was in bed, lying on his back, the blankets drawn halfway up his chest. His hands were outside the blankets, fingers of the right over those of the left.

"Grandpa?" The boy stood beside the bed, thinking *one-two-three-four-five-six*.

Then the boy thought about what he would miss about Grandpa, things he wanted to keep in his memory. There were a lot of things, and once he was sure he had them all, the boy touched the back of Grandpa's hand, then took hold of three of Grandpa's fingers and squeezed.

Grandpa's eyes opened. Beneath the milky glaze his eyes looked right at the boy, and this time the boy was almost certain Grandpa could see him.

"Yes? What is it, Boy?"

"Are you going to Altenmoor now?" the boy said. Slowly Grandpa sat up. "Yes, I believe I am."

"Then I have to help you."

"Yes." Grandpa nodded. "Keep hold of my hand, Boy."

The boy did. It took a long time, but he could feel himself giving all the strength he could give to Grandpa. He knew it was happening because he started to feel as though he were going to sleep, the way he did in the back of the car after a long day at the beach.

260

Then Grandpa said, "Thank you," and took away his hand.

"Grandpa, will you go now?"

"Shortly." Grandpa said. "No longer than it takes a pig to whistle 'Dixie.' Now you must return to bed. There is still much of a winter's night to sleep away."

"Okay," the boy said. He went to the door, then stopped and looked back. "Grandpa, you know. The Rubber Tree Woods and the Marmalade Mound and the winding Happy-To-You River."

"Of course, Boy," Grandpa said. "Where else?"

The boy said, "Goodbye, Grandpa."

The next morning the boy was up early because his mother and father came to his room and woke him and told him he wouldn't be going to school. Dad stood by the door. He had the same look on his face he'd had when someone stole the car last year.

Mom held the boy close to her. She was crying.

She said, "Grandpa is gone, Marky."

"Yes," the boy said. He wished he could explain but he knew she would never understand.

NEW MOON ON THE WATER

I DON'T KNOW, IS WHAT I SAY

What do you think of this? he wants to know.

This is his concept for a horror novel and he is enthusiastic.

Because I have written horror stories, have led workshops on writing horror, have edited a book dealing with horror, he has come to me.

And then, he shares this with me.

೧ • ೧

Earlier, on the morning of this same snowy day, I turned on my radio to learn which tollways were icy and if commuter trains would be running late.

Tollways were normal and trains were on time and there was news about what had happened in Tinley Park, a suburb some 20 minutes from mine. Five women had been found shot to death in the back room of a clothing store. Police announced they had died in a botched robbery attempt.

೧ • ೧

Vampires, he says. More vampires than any one book has ever had. A greater variety of vampires. Some will drink only the blood of children. Others have forsworn drinking blood. Some are devout Christians. Others see themselves in a God-abandoned universe ...

೧ • ೧

The clothing store specialized in plus-sized apparel. This was mentioned so often that it was as though it were something of great importance or even a clue or a code.

Mentioned almost as often was the fact that the victims had been bound with duct tape. It was not thought to be duct tape that had been in

263

the store. The killer had brought his own.

ᴇᴏ • ᴇᴏ

You see what we can have here? It's a totally claustrophobic atmosphere, with walls of blood and rivers of blood and showers of blood. The poor human beings who are caught up in this world, well, what chance do they have? It's like Lovecraft meets the Naturalists ...

ᴇᴏ • ᴇᴏ

The women who died ranged in age from 22 to 42. They had not known each other prior to their becoming the women who were bound with duct tape and shot during a botched robbery attempt.

ᴇᴏ • ᴇᴏ

Okay, I ask, what about the people?

They're, you know, just people, like people you could meet every day. But now, they have to be more than just people, okay, because they are encountering the Greatest Horror anyone could ever know. There is no safety.

So they can hide or they can fight.

And as they confront the horror, they have to reach deep within themselves.

ᴇᴏ • ᴇᴏ

One woman was the store manager. One woman was a nurse. One woman was a recent college graduate. One woman was a social worker at a high school. One woman was a stay-at-home mom.

ᴇᴏ • ᴇᴏ

You see, there's not just gimmick! There's humanity here.

ᴇᴏ • ᴇᴏ

Something quite strange happens. It is late in the day when we have the news that there was a sixth woman. She was shot, but the bullet just grazed her neck. She is alive and in protective custody.

We do not learn if she was shot first or fourth or last. Somehow, the news teams are held at bay and not permitted to ask if she was praying or crying or if she now feels there is a special grace in the universe reserved for her.

The survivor is able to provide police a description. There is a reward offered.

The survivor says, My deepest sympathies and condolences go out to their families and friends. Please know that during the unfathomable events of that day, their thoughts were focused on you and coming home. My heart aches that they were unable to do so.

⁂ • ⁂

So, what do you think, he asks. Do I have horror or do I have horror?

Vampires hunting people

I don't know, is what I say.

Because right now, I don't think he knows anything about horror.

And neither do I.

NEW MOON ON THE WATER

About the Author

A former stage hypnotist, folksinger, and high school teacher, Mort Castle has been a publishing writer since 1967. He's been deemed a "horror doyen" by *Publishers Weekly*, "El Maestro del Terror" by South America's *Galaxia Cthulhu*, and "the master of contemporary horror" by Poland's *Nowa Fantastyka* magazine. Castle has published about 600 "shorter things," mostly articles and short stories, in a variety of magazines, including *Penthouse*, *Twilight Zone*, *Cavalier*, *Bombay Gin*, *Writer's Digest*, and books, among them *Still Dead*, *Lovecraft's Legacy*, *Poe's Lighthouse*, and *Masques* (he is the only living author to have stories in all five of the *Masques* volumes edited by the late J. N. Williamson). His novels include *Cursed Be the Child* and *The Strangers*, optioned for the screen by Whitewater Films, and cited on the list of "Ten Best Horror-Thriller Novels" published in Poland in 2008 by Newsweek.pl. Castle edited the essential reference work *Writing Horror* and the expanded and revised later edition *On Writing Horror* for the Horror Writers Association (Writer's Digest Books). In 2012, William Morrow published *Shadow Show: All New Stories in Celebration of Ray Bradbury*, the anthology he co-edited with Sam Weller; the book's contributors include Neil Gaiman, Dave Eggers, Margaret Atwood, Joe Hill, and Alice Hoffman, garnering a starred review in *PW* and *Booklist*, and such praise as "... a Who's Who of the absolutely best in modern literature ... may be the greatest collection of short stories ever compiled." (*Art Attack*). *Shadow Show* was a Book of the Month Club Alternate and was produced for audio with readings by Neil Gaiman, F. Murray Abraham, Kate Mulgrew, George Takei, and Sam Weller and Mort Castle. Castle's forthcoming or recent publications include: (editor) *All American Horror of the 21st Century*, Wicker Park Press; (as co-editor with David Campiti) J.N. Williamson's illustrated *Masques*, IDW; and *Writing Historical Fiction*, Self-Counsel Press. Castle has twice won the Black Quill award for editing, has been a Bram Stoker award finalist seven times, and has had four Pushcart Prize nominations. He teaches in the fiction writing program at Columbia College Chicago and at writing conferences and seminars throughout the country. Castle and Jane, his wife of forty-one years, live in Crete, Illinois, known for both its bandstand and bubbling fountain.